ONE SUMMER NIGHT

ISBN 9798879378511

ONE SUMMER NIGHT

by

SAUNDRA JO HAYMAN

Dedicated to the memory of

Ruth Ann Stevens DeFord

CHAPTER ONE

Good girls don't. Don't what? Dance on Sundays? Use curse words? Pick their nose? Anna Ruth Scott wasn't sure what it was that good girls don't do, but she had been hearing these words for years from her parents, their church, and some of the girls at school. The word sex never came up at any point. That was a dirty word in her home, as in most homes in the mid-fifties. Living on a farm, sex and birth were happening with their animals seasonally, but Anna didn't understand the connection. It was never explained to her. Her father, Ernie Scott, didn't want his daughters at the barn when the cows were inseminated, but surprisingly, he was delighted when the girls could witness the miracle of birth as the calves arrived. It was a fascinating event, but they really didn't understand how the calf got inside the cow in the first place. In fact, when their mother, Dottie Scott, gave birth at home to little Eddie four years ago, all four daughters were sent to the barn as soon as the doctor arrived. They spent their time in the hay loft conspiring on how to get rid of this new arrival.

"What if this baby is a boy? Did you ever think about that?" Anna questioned her sisters as they all sat on bales of straw with hands on their chins and elbows on their knees, frowns of disappointment on each of their faces. Sitting in a row according to age, with their hair in braids and dressed in matching yellow calico dresses, were Anna, 13, Janet, 12, Patricia, 9, and Susan, 7.

"I don't understand why nobody told us," wondered Janet.

"Yeah. We don't hear anything until it's too late. It is too late, right?" asked Patricia.

"Yeah, I'm sure it is," Anna responded with dismay.

"I thought storks brought babies to their families. If the doctor is bringing it to us now, where was it before?" asked Susan of her older sisters.

"Well, the doctor's no stork. I don't know how our mother could hide this from us," added a frustrated Janet. "I just don't understand."

"If it's a boy, I think we need to give it away," said Patricia after some deep thought about the predicament. "It's just us girls. We don't need no boys in the house."

"You're right on that! One of us will need to give up a bedroom for the baby. And I think I know who that person will be," Anna added, looking at Janet.

"Not me. Oh, no you don't! I think it should be you, Anna!"

"I think you will both have to share a room. Susan and I have to. Why shouldn't you two?" Patricia asked.

"I say we just get rid of it!" pouted Susan. "We can simply tell mommy and daddy to give it to somebody else."

Just then Ernie Scott appeared at the top of the ladder to the loft to give the girls the good news.

"It's a boy! You all have a baby brother! We are going to call him Edward, or Eddie for a nickname. Come on down, girls! Come meet your little brother!" And with a shout of excitement, he descended with a jump and ran back to the house to be with his wife and newborn son.

"Oh, no!" The girls said to each other after their father left.

"I'm not happy about this, but we better go see it. A boy! That's rotten!" Anna protested to the others as they all made their way back to the house.

Dottie Scott was a short, stout woman who had hidden her pregnancy well wearing her roomy, homemade dresses and long aprons. She and Ernie didn't even tell the girls that a baby was coming until that day as she started to feel discomfort and the contractions began. The subject of pregnancy was not discussed within the family by anyone. The adults figured out that she was carrying a child at some point, but very little was mentioned of her condition. Prenatal care being minimal or not at all in those days, especially for rural families, there was always a possibility of losing a child before or even after childbirth. Friends and family waited until after the announcement of a healthy baby's arrival before visiting and delivering gifts. Hospitals were considered an unnecessary expense and meant for those who were sick. Having a baby was a natural part of their lives on the farm.

* * *

Four years later, by the spring of 1954, Anna Ruth Scott, had spent all of her seventeen years of life on her family farm located on Maryland's Eastern Shore. Their county consisted mainly of family farms and small rural villages filled with two-story houses with large front porches, a Methodist church with community building and a well-stocked country store. The Scott farm was located on a dirt road about one and one-half miles outside of Greenville, a village not far from Edentown, where the children attended school. Stevens Store was the mercantile for the locals and the place where farmers could buy overalls, work boots, straw hats and grey work gloves, their standard uniform. Their wives purchased everything from flour and sugar, bobby pins, frying pans, thread and needles to brooms and bag balm. The Scott children enjoyed going there for the penny candy and cold bottled sodas from the Coke-a-Cola cooler. Anna and Janet Scott also enjoyed the movie and fashion magazines they sold. Stevens Store, as it was called since it was built at the turn of the century, was the gathering place for farmers to discuss the price of crops, local politics and area news. It was also where their wives would run into each other to gossip about their neighbors or spread good news about an upcoming wedding or birth of a child. Their lives were intertwined by their faith and reliance upon each other's help to work their land and survive.

Life was difficult for the farm families. Managing their herds of milking cows along with raising hogs and chickens was not just a full-time job, it was work that required attention seven days a week and every week of the year. There were no days off. Milking was done twice a day; once in the morning and again in the late afternoon or early evening. The fields also required full days for planting and harvesting depending on the season. Most families had several children to help with this work. Ernie and Dottie Scott had four daughters and a young son. So, although they had hired help on the farm, the girls still needed to pitch in for some of the less strenuous chores.

Since Anna Ruth was the oldest daughter, more was expected of her. When she finished her chores at the barn and in the house, she spent most of her free time reading books about innocent adolescent adventures or mysteries. She and her sisters also enjoyed board games or playing cards. Like most farm homes in her area, there was no television in the living room. Although a few neighbors had recently purchased their first set. At night, the whole family gathered in the parlor to read magazines and the local newspaper and listen to radio shows for entertainment.

"I don't know why we can't have our own television," Anna stated for her parents to hear. "Do you know that Betty's parents bought one last weekend? They aren't any richer than we are!"

"My friends have a television, too," added Janet. "Can't we have one, Daddy?"

"You know you would love to watch Uncle Miltie or Lucy!" pushed Anna.

"I don't know what you are talking about. He's not my uncle. Those televisions are too expensive."

"Girls, that is a luxury we simply don't need now. Maybe one day, but not now. You have your radio shows. They're fun, aren't they?" Dottie asked.

"I read that in the future we won't have radios anymore, only television. If we don't get one, we won't have any shows," said Janet.

"And, how will you know about news and weather?" added Anna. "We're so old-fashioned! You never let us have anything fun!"

"I'm tired of hearing this nonsense over a television. Why don't the pair of you go to your rooms. You can do without the radio tonight! Go on! Both of you!" Ernie Scott shot Dottie a look, so she knew not to defend the girls. His mind was made up.

* * *

Even though Ernie and Dottie Scott were considered strict parents, by their daughters and their friends, they were more lenient than their own parents had been. They really didn't mind their girls going out with friends to see movies or to a dance. They wanted them to have fun and experience new things, but when boys joined in on those activities, they were more rigid.

Anna Ruth had started dating the son of family friends during her junior year. They knew Jimmy Baker was from a decent family and had a good reputation. They approved of him and felt they could trust him to be the gentleman his parents had raised him to be. They made a nice-looking couple. Jimmy was tall and muscular with dark brown hair and a large single curl on top. He had a beautiful, warm smile that could melt a girl's heart and a sense of humor that often made him the center of attention.

Anna was shapely and of average height, coming to Jimmy's shoulder when she stood next to him. Her round eyes squinted cutely when she laughed. She had naturally wavy, shoulder-length brown hair and she often held her bangs back with a barrette. Anna loved wearing full-skirted dresses that her mother made for her, but also wore stylish pencil skirts and button-down blouses that she made herself. She and Jimmy were not the most popular kids in their class. They had several close friends they hung out with, most of them from farm families like their own.

As the school year was winding down, plans and preparations for the school prom were being made by the junior students after classes ended for the day. The theme chosen was "Moonlight Serenade," so many hands were needed to cut out the large full moon backdrop and many sparkling stars. Anna's best friends, Betty Andrews and Kay Monroe, were helping on the planning committee. When they finished what they could accomplish that day, Jimmy suggested that they go to Murph's for a burger.

"Hey, kids! I'm starving! Who wants a burger and shake?" asked Jimmy climbing down from a ladder after measuring the space for the paper ropes of stars.

"Well, it looks like we have done all we can for today! I'm ready for a shake!" responded Betty. "How about it, girls?"

"This looks good for now. Let's go!" added Kay.

"Are you driving, Jimmy?" Anna asked. "I'm ready!"

"I'll take whoever I find in my car in the next two minutes! Let's go!"

The four friends piled into Jimmy's black Bel Aire. He was one of a few boys in their class who had his own car. Jimmy's grandfather gave him the well-maintained car when he bought a new model in the fall. Several other kids from school met them at Murph's Snack Shop to grab a bite to eat, listen to the jukebox and dance in the back of the restaurant. It was the usual fun-loving gang of friends out to blow off a little steam and clown around.

Murph's became the local hangout for the teenagers in Edentown since opening at the corner of Main Street and Third. The grey block building with a bright red door was just around the corner from the movie theater, an excellent location to grab a burger and fries when the movie let out. It was also a favorite spot for classmates to gather after school was done for the day.

Lately, there was a daily battle over which music to play. Several regular customers were beginning to like the colored singers, such as, Johnny Mathis, the Four Tops, and B.B. King, while others believed the music to be immoral and didn't hesitate to voice their opinion on that. The owner had threatened to remove the jukebox if the ongoing argument didn't stop. No one wanted that!

One of the kids from school dropped a few coins in the jukebox and chose some dance tunes. He called for everyone to get up and dance to 'I've Got A Woman'. It was a favorite for most of the kids who hung out in the shop after class. The next song was a tune by Nat King Cole, so those on the floor began slow dancing. Jimmy grabbed Anna's hand and pulled her onto the dance floor. They were swaying with the beat when a couple of townies came in.

"Stop playing that colored music! What do you think you're doing? We don't want to hear that shit!" One of them yelled out as he strutted into the place and sat down on a swivel counter seat.

"Yeah, we don't want to dance to that shit!" shouted the other thug joining him at the counter.

"Oh, my gosh, what's their problem? I really like that song, don't you?" Anna asked Jimmy as they walked off the dance floor and slid back into their booth where Kay and Betty were sitting. They really didn't want to be on the floor if any trouble started.

"I like it alright, but I'm not going to allow those jerks to take out their anger on us for dancing to a colored singer. No matter how much I like it, I don't want anyone to get hurt over it!"

Tensions ran high for some people in town ever since Brown vs. Board of Education had been sent to the Supreme Court, and a decision was expected to come soon. The older citizens of the town were mostly against desegregation; however, there were also plenty of other residents who were fearful of the outcome, especially what it would mean for their children.

Edentown High School teachers were known for high standards and were well respected in the community. Now that the war in Korea had ended, the county expected to graduate 94% of the senior class. Some boys ran off to join the war during those years, while others dropped out to help on the farms or move away to work in city factories. The school had returned to normal this year and the fine citizens of Edentown didn't want any disturbances to their educational system.

"I have to finish writing my paper on 'The Dangers of Communism' tonight," said Betty. "Did you guys finish yours?"

"Not me!" said Jimmy pulling out a cigarette from his pocket and lighting it. Kay slid an ashtray in front of him.

"You always wait until the last minute for these things, don't you?" asked Anna. "I finished mine last week."

"Goody two shoes, Anna!" teased Kay.

"Are you just trying to show me up? I've had ball practice or a game almost every night for a week," Jimmy explained.

"Tell me about it! I've barely seen you lately!" Anna said as she stuck out her lower lip in a pretend pout.

"You better watch out, Jimmy, the football players are looking for dates to the prom. I know one who has been eyeing Anna," said Betty, trying to get Jimmy riled up.

"That's not true, Betty! Stop that!" Anna responded. "Don't believe what she says!"

"You know there is no one but you for Anna, right Jimmy?" said Kay coming to Anna's defense.

"She knows she's got it good," said Jimmy as they all laughed.

Jimmy was a good boyfriend. He and Anna had been going steady since last October. Jimmy and Anna's parents had been friends for many years and as kids, their families had visited back and forth playing cards and having dinner parties together. It was only last Fall that Jimmy noticed how much Anna had filled out and was no longer a child. He and some of the other boys in the junior class thought she was very attractive.

Anna also knew that Jimmy was one of the most desirable boys in her school and any one of the girls there would love the chance to go out with him. He was also a good student, very athletic, and the teachers loved him. They all knew he was probably college bound and would likely take over one of the family businesses. Yes, he certainly was a good catch!

"We have to get you home, Anna!" Jimmy said suddenly. "I don't want your father yelling at me for not bringing you home in time for chores. Finish your soda and come on. Let's get going."

"Can you drop me off on your way?" asked Betty. She lived just a couple of farms down the road from Anna.

"Come on, troublemaker. We'll drop you off!" Jimmy messed up Betty's hair as she slid out of the booth and followed behind the two to his car.

"See you later, Kay!" Anna said as she gave her friend a quick hug.

* * *

"Have you asked your parents yet about what we discussed last week?" Betty inquired from the backseat of the car as they neared her home.

"About working at Rehoboth Beach this summer? No, not yet. I have to catch my dad in a good mood. I have been hinting a little to my mom and I think she will say yes. My dad is always the difficult one."

"Okay, but don't wait too long. The owner of the restaurant will want an answer soon or he will give the jobs to someone else. Kay and I both got the okay from our parents. Kay's dad is looking into a boardinghouse near the boardwalk for us since he is familiar with Rehoboth. There are only a couple of 'women only' houses that will allow us to rent, especially for our age. We need proof of a summer job and permission from our parents to stay. Kay said her dad will sign the lease for us."

"I understand. I'm really excited, too. I just hope I can go with you. I definitely don't want to hang around here all summer working in the cannery and picking vegetables in the blazing hot sun."

"That's no way to get a suntan, girl!" Betty laughed as she climbed out of the car as Jimmy pulled up to her home.

"Are you going to leave me here all summer long, babe?" Jimmy said after Betty left them.

"You said you would be working at the lumberyard anyway. I don't think there will be much time for either of us to go out. I want a better chance to make some money."

"I'd still find time for some fun. How do I know that I can trust you at the beach with all those lifeguards and beach bums?"

"Are you kidding me? I'm going with my girlfriends. Other guys are not on my mind."

"Little Miss Innocence! I forgot. You don't think about anyone but me, do you."

"Not funny. Now take me home," she said suppressing a laugh.

* * *

"Now, Anna, get Emmitt's table set for his dinner. He and your father will be finished milking soon. He'll need a glass of iced tea, too."

Dottie Scott was scurrying around her kitchen pulling pans off the stove, mashing potatoes and rolling fresh dough in her hands to make biscuits for dinner. Anna had just walked in the door. She knew it was her turn to help her mother put dinner on the tables.

Dottie prided herself on being able to provide a tasty hot meal for the family. She knew her husband looked forward to her home cooking and often commented to her about what a fine cook she was.

"Children! Come on to the table now. Your daddy just turned out the barn light, so he and Emmitt are on their way to the house."

Sure enough, as soon as the children took their places, Ernie Scott and his hired hand, Emmitt Leatherberry, came in the back door and washed up at the sink in the enclosed porch. Ernie came on into the kitchen, but Emmitt took his seat at a separate table set up especially for him on the porch. Anna took his plate full of food and set it in front of him.

"Thank ya kindly," Emmitt said with a yellow-toothed grin.

He was a World War II Veteran who had suffered from shell shock and had to be hospitalized for a period of time after the war ended. His family had lost the sharecropping farm they had been tilling when he left for Europe. They moved west to find other work but didn't leave word where they were going for Emmitt. When he was finally able to return home, he discovered they were no longer there, and no one knew where they had settled. Not a word had been communicated to anyone.

Apparently, they left owing for some groceries and supplies at the local grocery store. Emmitt gave the store owner what he could to pay off the debt and then went in search of work and a place to stay.

He walked up the Scott's lane one day while Dottie was pregnant with Eddie. Ecstatic that Emmitt had come his way, Ernie hired him that very day and began fixing up an old storage shed with two windows for him to have as a place to sleep. Dottie found a used bed and washstand at an auction house. She also painted a dresser and a wooden dining chair that had been in the attic since they moved to the farm and took that to him. Then she bought him a new table lamp and shade. With his last few dollars, Emmitt bought a radio so he could listen to the boxing fights at night. It was the best home he had ever had, he said.

Ernie was very pleased with Emmitt's work. He was a great help, and he knew a lot about farming and caring for animals. However, Dottie didn't want him at the family table. She found his eating habits atrocious! He spit food out of his mouth while talking. And he was always talking! He wouldn't shut up! Ernie and Dottie couldn't get a word in edgewise and the children thought he was disgusting. He ate a large fork full at a time and chewed with his mouth open. A few times, Dottie had to leave the table afraid that she might throw up. Finally, she put her foot down and moved him to his own table in the next room. It had to be done!

All of the children had scattered from the dining table, except Anna, and her sister, Janet. As Ernie read the daily evening news, Dottie and the girls finished their desserts and then Anna gathered the courage to ask about the summer job at the beach.

"Mom, do you think I can work at Rehoboth Beach this summer? I can make good money. Betty and Kay are getting jobs there this year. We can get a room together at an all-girls' boarding house with your permission," Anna pleaded hopefully. If she could just get her mother on her side, maybe she would help convince her father what a great opportunity it was for her.

"You are only 17!" Ernie Scott protested looking up from his paper. "The beach is like a carnival and there are some unsavory people who work in those places. I don't want you to be around that."

"This beach is more for families. I'll work for a Greek restaurant there serving food to families, not hoodlums."

"I hear that they pay well for that work. Better than she can make around here," Dottie chimed in trying to help the argument. She thought it would be a good experience for their daughter. Since she would be with friends, they could all help each other out. Three in a room would be safer and cheaper for them.

"Are you saying that you approve of her going to the beach, Dottie? Don't you need Anna Ruth to help with the vegetable crop this year?" Ernie asked not understanding how they could manage planting and harvesting the tomatoes, cucumbers, and peppers that they raised every summer without the help of their eldest daughter.

"I'll still be here for planting, daddy," Anna explained. "And I should be home at the end of the summer to help get out the last of the peppers. I won't leave for the beach until the day after school lets out."

"Do you know how to behave yourself? We don't want you running wild while you and your girlfriends are away from home," Dottie said.

"Yes, of course. We know how to behave. We are going to be busy, day and night. They give lots of hours of work there. I could make enough money to help pay for school clothes for the girls. You know how much it costs for all the dresses and shoes we kids need," Anna stated as she made her final case to her parents. "I just want to make some money and swim in the saltwater with my friends."

Ernie hesitated just a bit longer, not convinced that Anna would make much to help out.

"Do you know how much you will make at this restaurant? They probably don't pay very well."

"Betty says that the pay is better at the beach because the customers leave good tips and the employers give long hours."

Ernie pondered what Anna could contribute to the family account, and then finally gave in with a simple "Okay."

Anna hugged her father and mother and then hurried over to the telephone to call Betty and Kay with the good news. She was so excited while making her plans with them that she didn't notice how upset Janet looked.

"Maybe you can go next year, Janet," Dottie told her next oldest child when she saw the disappointment on her face. Janet realized that if Anna was away, she would have to take on more responsibility for work during the summer months. Anna was so lucky! She was getting out of farm work to have a good time at the beach.

"We are going to have such fun, Anna! I really didn't think your parents would allow you to go," Betty said.

"Actually, I'm very surprised they said I can go, too!" Anna chuckled.

"Do you have a suitcase? If not, I have an extra."

"Yes, I have the one my granddaddy gave me for Christmas last year. I only have one bathing suit, though. Maybe I can buy a new one with my earnings. They are probably cheaper there than at Carpenter's in town."

"Have you told Jimmy yet?" Betty questioned.

"Not for certain, but he knows about the plan. I can tell him that I'm going for sure when we meet after school tomorrow. He's going to be working at his father's lumberyard all summer anyway. And he will be needed on the farm some, too. I would hardly see him, you know. Besides, I want to get away from here for a while. I'm usually stuck at home all summer with no fun. Just planting and picking vegetables, helping mom with the canning, or working with Emmitt at the barn. You know what fun he is! God, I hate it here."

* * *

"I knew you would go! If your parents said yes, you would not hesitate," said Jimmy after Anna told him she had permission to spend the summer at Rehoboth Beach. "What am I supposed to do? My girlfriend is gone for the summer, and I have all these things I want to do!"

"Maybe you and I can get a day off and you can come for a visit. We can spend the whole day on the beach relaxing and cooling off in the ocean. Wouldn't that be fun?"

"I suppose. I'll have to see what I can do." He realized that it might be attractive after all. "The whole day to ourselves does sound like fun. And the night, too?"

"I don't know about that, Jimmy." Anna wondered if he thought he could stay in their tiny one-bedroom apartment. "You know that we can't put you up for the night, right? We are renting a room at 'Mermaid House'. It's a 'girls only' building. We can't have any boys there at any time – not even for a visit."

"Damn! Can't you sneak me in?"

"No, do you want to get us thrown out?" she questioned whether he was serious or not.

"I'm just kidding, Anna. Don't worry," he reassured her. "I am coming to see you though. I'll figure it out."

Jimmy looked around to make sure Anna's parents weren't looking and then he gave her a quick kiss before she climbed out of his Bel Aire.

* * *

The dust had settled after Jimmy drove down the lane and a new puff of dirt trailed as Anna's granddaddy, Wilbur Daffin, pulled up next to the house in his black Plymouth Cranbrook. He lived just a mile down the same dirt road and often stopped by to spend short visits with his only daughter and her family. He couldn't be away from home too long as his wife was an invalid. Margaret Daffin had suffered a stroke in 1948 rendering her legs useless and paralyzing her right side. He needed help to care for her so he could run his painting business. Anna and Janet took turns helping out and sometimes slept over for the weekend. Their mom often prepared meals for them and Granddaddy Daffin would bring money to cover the costs. He also had a neighbor come in to assist while he was working. Ethel Walbert lived next door with her husband, Roy, and they had been friends since moving there 16 years ago. They used to play pinochle on Saturday nights, but after Margaret's stroke, the visits stopped. Now, Ethel came over, as needed, to care for her friend. Having no children, it gave her a way to be out of the house and make some money of her own while her husband, who was a milk truck driver, was on his delivery job.

Ethel and Wilbur had become close friends and confidants over the years. They had discussed Margaret's inability to be affectionate, as she was in constant discomfort and depression due to her circumstances. She no longer wanted Wilbur to kiss her and turned her head whenever he tried. The rejection was disheartening for he was still a healthy man who craved a woman's touch.

Concurrently, Ethel confided that she and Roy wanted children very much but were never able to conceive. After a while, Roy had just stopped trying. He no longer had any interest in her, so she rarely tried to fix her hair or make herself feel pretty. It seemed pointless. Roy didn't even notice her. He only noticed whether there was a plate of food on the dinner table for him. It was a lonely, sad existence for them both.

The power of human nature can be great. To love and be loved did not outweigh the consequences of committing adultery, however. They were both God-fearing, church-going people, so they were not willing to risk going to Hell for human affection. They could not bear the hurt they would cause their spouses if they're feelings were ever exposed. There were no other choices for them. They had to be cautious with every minute they could steal for themselves and the affection that was developing.

* * *

Anna walked through the side porch door with her grandfather and heard her siblings running from all over the house. "Granddaddy! Granddaddy's here!" they all shouted. Wilbur Daffin was a tall muscular man with neatly groomed graying hair. He usually showed up in dress pants and a clean shirt, but occasionally he came by in his white painter's coveralls with specks of various colored paint. He always smelled of Old Spice cologne to cover up the turpentine he used to scrub the paint off his hands when he finished a painting job.

Eddie took his grandfather's freshly cleaned rough hands as he climbed into his lap when he sat in a kitchen chair. The other children gathered around waiting for a treat or silly joke from him. They all adored him!

"Who wants a stick of chewing gum?"

"Me!" they all chimed in.

"This is all you get today," he said passing the gum around to each one. "Any hugs for your old granddaddy?"

"Thank you, granddaddy!" they each said as they wrapped their arms around his thick chest and then ran back to what they had been doing.

Dottie Scott came over and hugged her father too. "How's mama today? Ethel told me she slid out of bed while she was there one day last week. I don't know how she was able to get her back in. I wish she had called me."

"She used the sheet. I guess she has some strong muscles for a woman!" he chuckled. "Your mama has been sleeping a lot lately. She seems fine though. I'm thinking about getting a television. Maybe that will be more entertaining for her. What do you think?"

"That might work. I know she doesn't read the magazines I take her."

"What are you up to, Anna?" Wilbur Daffin asked his eldest granddaughter. "Are you still seeing Fred and Hazel Baker's boy? What's his name again?"

"It's Jimmy. You know his name granddaddy. Stop teasing!" said Anna. "I do have big news though. I'm going to work at Rehoboth Beach in a Greek restaurant for the summer! Isn't that wild? Kay and Betty and I will be sharing a room in a boarding house for girls that is only one block from the beach and close to our work."

"What? When did you grow up? I think that will be a great experience for you girls."

"We are really looking forward to making money and having a good time hanging out in the sun and sand."

"When do you leave? I want to come by and give you a little something to buy some food until you get your first paycheck."

"We have to be there the Thursday before Memorial Day weekend for training. They open for business the next day and I understand we will be really busy!"

"Are you still having a big Easter dinner here next weekend, Dottie? Am I invited? I didn't get my invitation yet, I guess."

"Now Daddy, stop that! You know there is an open invitation for you on any occasion. You are such a teaser!" Dottie said ruffling her father's hair as she walked by to take a pitcher of iced tea out of the refrigerator and pour them both a glass. He would need to go back home soon. Margaret couldn't be left alone for very long.

CHAPTER TWO

The Scott farm was 162 acres of tillable land, some of which they kept for grazing their herd of Holsteins. This was the average size of the farms around Greenville. The flat countryside was dotted with scattered farmhouses and barns each with a long dirt lane at the end of which sat a mailbox with the family name. Besides the dark red milking barn, the Scott farm also had a granary, milk house, and hog house, and there were several other outbuildings to store equipment and tools. The white two-story, L-shaped house with black shutters was centered at the end of their lane. It had an attractive front porch with yellow metal chairs, a black porch swing, a couple of black rockers, and green flower boxes of petunias nestled at each window. Bright yellow marigolds lined both sides of the walkway to the front steps. Ernie and his father-in-law made sure a fresh coat of paint was applied to the porch furniture every couple of years. Wilbur Daffin always had leftover paint available from his business. Dottie was never sure what color would be used next!

The Scott girls filed out of the side porch door slamming it behind them as they exited the house on the warm Easter Sunday morning in April 1954. They each wore a light blue gingham dress with a blue satin sash and matching ribbon in their wavy brown hair. Their shoes were freshly polished white Mary Jane's, and they carried white purses in their white-gloved hands. Feeling they were much too old for Easter bonnets; they refused that purchase this year. Anna and Janet, however, asked for stockings instead of socks and their mother reluctantly agreed they could have them.

Ernie Scott leaned against his Buick with his camera and asked his four lovely daughters to stand in front of the bed of purple irises in his wife's backyard flower garden, so he could take a picture of them in the matching dresses. As soon as they heard the click of the camera, they ran toward the car and climbed into the backseat, each vying for a window position. What a lucky man he was! Four daughters and a son! His son, Eddie, stormed out next with a loud crash as the door slammed against the white clapboard siding, followed by his frazzled wife, who was busy trying to button the obstinate tyke's shirt and comb his hair. The four-year-old was a handful, and being the youngest and only son, he was very spoiled by the other members of the family.

Eddie sat on his mother's lap on the front seat of the Buick as she continued to button his matching light blue shirt and properly position his gingham bow tie. They all must look perfect today since Louis and Mabel Scott would be attending the church service with them. They often came on special holidays such as this to attend with their son's family and have a celebration dinner afterward. The Scott girls had been asked to perform a song for the Easter service. Their grandparents loved to hear their granddaughters sing and looked forward to visiting their son and having the whole Scott family together later that day.

The Scotts took up more than an entire pew in the sanctuary, so Anna sat in front with Betty Andrews and some of the other young people. She and Betty whispered back and forth about their ideas for the beach apartment until her father shot her an angry glance and silenced her. He did not like any nonsense from his children while in church.

Soon the Scott girls were introduced, and they moved in front of the pulpit forming a line, oldest to youngest, as always. While the girls sang to the congregation, Ernie and Louis Scott, held their heads high as the members of the church turned and smiled to them in approval of their beautiful girls and their lovely harmonizing voices. It was a proud moment for the men.

After church, everyone filed out the front door expressing what a nice service it had been that day, wishing Happy Easter, and shaking hands along their descent of the walkway. A light breeze filled the yard with the scent of forsythia bushes in full bloom. Several parishioners remarked on the vibrancy of the yellow flowers, knowing that they could all be gone by this time next week. Like many events in life, one must enjoy the moment.

After all proper introductions and acknowledgments had been performed, the Scott family headed back to their farm for their annual Easter dinner with grandparents and other members of the Scott family. Unlike Dottie's family, Ernie's relatives only gathered for special occasions with the expectation of being served a proper meal on their best dinnerware.

Dottie planned and prepared for several days prior to each of these events. It was a great amount of stress on her to make sure the meal was acceptable to Ernie's family, especially his father, and that there were no mishaps to occur during their visit. There always seemed to be something for Louis Scott to complain about whenever he was around.

Dottie and her daughters, who still wore their Easter dresses, placed the hot bowls of mashed potatoes with gravy, buttered peas and carrots, succotash, pickled beets, and deviled eggs on the table alongside the large platter of sliced country ham and a basket full of hot Maryland Beaten Biscuits. The adults ate at the large dining room table, covered with Dottie's best white tablecloth and the blue oriental dishes she had inherited from a maternal great-aunt. The children all gathered around the kitchen table for their meal using the plain white everyday dishes.

"I thought your father was coming for dinner today, Dottie," said Ernie to his wife. "I hope everything is alright."

"He said he could come by. I don't know why he isn't here."

"Everything is delicious, Dottie. Is this one of your hams from last fall?" asked Mabel Scott.

"Yes, Mama. We butchered two hogs this past year. Seven of us and Emmit too. We needed both in the smokehouse for the year," explained Ernie to his mother.

"You don't plan on having any more mouths to feed, I hope," Louis Scott said, embarrassing everyone at the table. Ernie and Dottie looked at each other, waiting for the other to respond.

"Oh, father, don't you want to watch the children look for eggs in a while?" offered Ernie's sister, Carrie, to change the subject.

"No, I don't want to go outside. I have my Sunday best on. You don't expect me to go out in the yard with these good clothes on, do you?"

"We could watch them for just a bit, Louis," said Mabel who was interested in seeing the children run around the yard.

"Not doing it, Mabel. We can stay right in here and have some conversation. We haven't seen our children in months. You wanted to visit with them, so here we are." Mabel nodded her head.

"Your mother can be difficult sometimes," he added, speaking to Ernie and his sisters.

Once they all had finished eating, Dottie told the young children to run outside to search for the eggs that had been hidden earlier that morning by Emmitt. The eight cousins charged for the door with brown paper bags in hand. Susan was permitted to help Eddie search for eggs, but the other three girls had to sit in the living room with the adults.

Grandfather Louis took the best chair, and as always, was the center of attention. He led the conversation, and no one spoke unless he asked for a response. At one point he asked Janet if she was wearing lipstick.

"What's that red mess on your lips, Janet? What do you have on?" he questioned.

"Nothing, Grandfather Scott. My lips are chapped. I've been biting my lip," Janet responded shyly.

"You better not wear that nasty stuff. That's for cheap girls," he said and then turned his attention to another granddaughter.

"Anna Ruth! You don't wear any powder on your face, do you? You girls think that makes you pretty, but it doesn't. Harlots wear that nastiness. You don't want to look like a harlot, do you?"

"No, Grandfather Scott. I only use Noxzema on my face," Anna responded.

"What's that? Do you paint your lips with it?"

"No, I wash my face with it," Anna said hoping he would leave her alone.

"Oh," he grunted back. "I've never heard of that. I'm telling you girls you have to be respectable if you want to marry a good man. Anna Ruth, you are almost 18 and should be getting married soon."

"I'm only 17, grandfather. I still need to finish my senior year before I think about marriage."

"You know what I mean! Don't be sassy. Family is important. You children need to understand what it means to be a Scott. We are a fine family with good standing, and you don't ever want to do anything to bring shame on this family. You hear me?"

"Yes, grandfather," all three girls responded.

"Patricia, come here! Take my pipe and empty it outside. Bring me my pouch on the bench when you come back."

The Scott girls were used to running errands for their grandfather. It gave their grandmother a break because at home she was the one waiting on him constantly. He barked his orders from a throne wherever he was.

"Old stinky pipe!" Patricia exclaimed to her mother as she passed through the kitchen, pinching her nose between her fingers and holding the pipe in front of her. Wanting to escape any further questioning from her grandfather, Anna stepped into the kitchen too, on the pretense that she should help her mother slice the pound cake and top it with strawberry preserves.

"Put extra preserves on your grandfathers. He always says my cake is too dry," Dottie fretted.

"Why is he always so difficult to please?" Anna inquired. "Whenever Grandfather and Grandmother come over, we have to sit still, and we aren't allowed to change out of our good clothes, play games or say anything unless they ask us. We can't play our records or the radio. We can't go outside. I hate it when they are here!" Anna whispered afraid she might be overheard. "I wish Granddaddy Wilbur had been able to come today. I wonder what happened. Maybe he didn't want to be around Grandfather Scott," Anna and Dottie both chuckled softly.

"Ahhhhh! Come quick!" yelled Patricia as she ran into the house slamming the back door. "That dog is back! He has one of the chickens!" she continued.

"Ernie! Get your gun! The Anderson's dog is back chasing our chickens!" Dottie called to her husband.

Ernie grabbed his shotgun that hung over the door in the kitchen, checked it for shot, and stormed out the back porch door yelling for everyone to stay in the house.

"Blame dog! I've told them to keep that dog chained up," Ernie muttered as he walked around the corner of the house and saw the scrawny, mixed-breed dog shaking his head back and forth with the head of one of their laying hens in its mouth. Ernie aimed and shot at the dog, hitting him in the rear end and hind legs. He dropped the hen and took off with a yelp. Ernie saw that the hen was badly hurt and bleeding from her neck. She had to be killed, for there was no way to save her.

"Anna Ruth!" Ernie saw her peering out the porch window and called out to her. "Run over to Emmitt's shack and tell him that I need him to take care of this chicken. He can bring it up to the house when it's clean," he ordered. "Looks like chicken for supper tomorrow. Right, Dottie?" He laughed and his wife agreed with a smile.

Everyone sat at the tables again enjoying their cake and strawberries with cream on top. There was some small talk from the adults, but the children remained silent while they ate their treat. The phone rang, breaking the silence. Anna started toward the phone to answer it when her Grandfather Scott called out to her from the dining room table. "Where are you going, young lady?"

Anna responded, "To answer the phone. That might be a call from Granddaddy Wilbur."

"It can wait!" He snapped at her in disgust. "Ernie, do you let your girls jump up from the table during the meal like this? Where are their manners? They should know better! Especially Anna Ruth at her age!"

Dottie came to her defense. "She knows that we don't answer the phone during supper. Right, Anna Ruth? I think she is just concerned about my dad."

"I didn't mean to be rude," Anna said with tears coming into her eyes. She hung her head and trembled with frustration and embarrassment. *How could her grandfather be so mean,* she thought to herself!

"Really, Ernie, all these girls in your house! I don't know how you stand it. Better get them under control now or you will have a problem with them one day. I'm telling you. Mark my words, these girls are going to give you trouble!"

* * *

As soon as they all finished waving goodbye and watched Louis Scott's dark blue Cadillac pull out of the lane and onto the road, all four girls ran upstairs to take off their dresses and put on everyday dungarees.

"He was in a good mood today, wasn't he?" Janet asked sarcastically.

"I think he is worse every time he comes over. I don't know how Grandmother Scott stands him," Patricia added.

"I can't believe that she has a very happy life," said Anna.

"That's sad. Why doesn't she just leave him?" asked Susan.

"Are you kidding? Scott women don't get divorces," Anna informed her sisters. "Grandfather Scott won't allow it!" With that the four girls broke out in laughter. Falling on the bed, they continued laughing, determined to have a little fun while it was still daylight.

Dottie was concerned that her father hadn't come to Easter dinner. "I better give dad a call, Ernie. It's not like him to miss dinner."

Wilbur picked up the phone after the first ring.

"Daddy? Are you and mother alright?"

"We're fine. Sorry I didn't make it over for dinner. I called, but no one answered."

"Oh, I guess we missed it," said Dottie realizing that it was her father who was calling when Anna tried to answer the phone. *Old buzzard*! She thought of her father-in-law.

"Actually, your mother was not having a good day. She only ate four spoonsful of oatmeal for breakfast, and she wouldn't eat any dinner at all."

"I wonder if she didn't want you to leave her."

"I ended up calling Evelyn and she was able to get her to eat a little. It was so late then that I just decided to stay home. That's when I telephoned you."

"Miss Evelyn is such a wonderful person! I hope she knows how much we all appreciate her."

"I tell her, sugar. I tell her quite often."

CHAPTER THREE

Finally, the last day of school arrived for 1954! Some of the boys at Edentown High ran through the hallways throwing balls of paper at each other, ducking behind locker doors and using the groups of students gathered alongside the halls as shields. Girls exchanged phone numbers and addresses with their friends and promised to be in touch over the summer months. Those relieved to have the school year behind them dumped their folders off in a trashcan by the exit door. Anna and Jimmy walked out the large front doors and found their close friends gathered around one of the cement benches.

"Hey, guys, ready to celebrate?" Jimmy called out to them.

"What do you think? Want to head over to Murph's?" asked Kay.

"Sure! Who wants to ride with me?" Jimmy asked.

"You and Anna go ahead. Meet us there. We all have our own rides," answered Betty.

"See you there!" Anna called out as they turned to leave.

* * *

"Order me a burger and some fries, Anna, will ya? I need to see some guys in the back. Get whatever you want too, babe!"

Anna placed the order with the waitress. Betty and Kay sat down with her as their boyfriends went to the counter to pick up milkshakes.

"Hey, do you think we'll have neat uniforms like hers?" Kay asked pointing to the pink and white dress the waitress was wearing.

"I bet so. But I hope we have a better cap than hers," said Betty.

"She has tennis shoes on. They're probably better on the feet when you have to run around all day serving food," added Kay.

"I am so excited. I can't wait to get there tomorrow morning. What time is your father picking me up, Kay?" asked Anna.

Kay's father was driving the girls to Rehoboth Beach early Thursday morning so they could begin their training at the restaurant and check into their room at the boarding house.

"Five o'clock, he said. And don't be late!"

"Yeah, like I wouldn't be ready for the biggest adventure of my life! I may not be able to sleep tonight," Anna said. "A whole summer with my best friends! This will be a time in our lives that we will never forget! Bring your camera, Betty!"

* * *

Betty, Anna, and Kay sat on the back seat of Mr. Monroe's car chattering the whole way to Rehoboth Beach. All conversation stopped though as soon as he turned onto the Rehoboth Avenue, a wide street lined with cars parked on both sides leading to the ocean. There was a U-turn at the park that connected with the wood planked boardwalk and the two-sided parking continued back towards the canal bridge at the entrance to town. An American flag waved proudly in the center of the park. The girls were wide-eyed as they drove past the white and brown shingled cottages with wide front porches, colorful striped awnings and neatly tended flowerbeds of blue hydrangeas. The main boulevard was dotted with shops selling colorful beach balls and towels, and snack bars of greasy burgers, fries and hot dogs. Vacationers walked about in sandals and tennis shoes carrying blankets, umbrellas, and metal picnic baskets and thermoses. Kay and Betty rolled their windows down all the way so they could take in the sounds and sights more fully.

"Breathe. It's true! You can actually smell the salt in the air!" Kay exclaimed to her friends as the car rounded the horseshoe top of the street.

"The beach is right there. Can you see it?" Mr. Monroe asked slowing down for a longer look.

"Oh, look! It's so very blue! This is it!" Betty yelled as she pulled herself closer to the open window to get a better view.

"I see it too! The waves are incredible, aren't they? I love them!" Anna declared as she caught a glimpse out the side window.

"Yeah, look at all the umbrellas! The beach is covered with people," Betty added.

"How about that bathing suit over there? A bikini, right?" Anna asked although she was certain that was the style she saw in Ladies Home Journal recently.

"Make sure you girls cover up when you are off the beach! Don't go traipsing around like you're in your underwear on the boardwalk. Alright?" Mr. Monroe warned with concern. "And don't talk to strangers. There may be some disreputable people around town. You don't want to get hooked up with any of them. Just be careful!"

Within a couple of minutes, they arrived at the all-female boarding home located just one block from the ocean where the girls would stay while working for the summer. The home was filled with young women who were employed by various businesses in Rehoboth. All expected to work hard and hoped to make plenty of money during the 1954 summer season.

The girls checked in with the manager as Kay's father delivered the last of the three girls' bags to the lobby of the newly painted pale-yellow clapboard boarding house. The girls were required to carry their bags the rest of the way to their room on the third floor. There was no elevator in the three-story building.

"Did you request the room furthest from the front door or did management choose this place in Siberia for us?" Anna asked with a laugh.

"They didn't ask me which floor we wanted. I would have told them the first floor for certain. That's where the television and the telephone are located. The only ones in the building too," explained Kay.

"I don't care!" exclaimed Betty reaching the top step, setting down her bags. "We are on our own for three months. I don't need anything but a bed to sleep in and a place to get some French fries!"

They all nodded in agreement and laughed until they found their door.

Room 304 was laid out just as the owner had described. Each girl had a twin bed with clean white sheets and pillowcases. Each bed was covered with a light blue cotton chenille bedspread with a swirl and diamond pattern in the middle. They each had dresser space to store their clothes, but there was no closet, only hooks on the wall next to the bathroom where they could hang their dresses and work uniforms. The wooden oak floors were smooth with age and covered by blue scattered rugs. A food cupboard, dishes, a couple of pans, and a hot plate in one corner completed the room. A refrigerator to be used by everyone staying on the third floor sat in the hallway. They had their own bathroom with a bathtub and fresh clean white towels. The landlord explained that they were responsible for washing the items in the room using the washing machine in the laundry found on the first floor.

Kay read aloud from the notice on the back of the door. "It says here that all sheets, pillowcases, towels and kitchen equipment must be cleaned and put in place as we found them when we leave. We will be charged for any items missing or destroyed."

"No problem there. Did you see the signs all over the front lobby with the restrictions of the building?" asked Betty. "No men are allowed, period. All visitors have to wait in the lobby for a resident to meet with them and are not permitted to go beyond the manned front desk of the lobby. Oh, and violators will be expelled from the building and lose any deposits or money paid."

"Well, at least it should be safe here," said Anna.

"Yeah, but I didn't know we were staying in a jail."

"Oh, stop, Kay! It's not so bad. At least we don't have our parents around," Betty added.

"So true! Hey, I have some canned food and bread to put away. My granddaddy gave me some money to buy a few things to start us off until payday. We can have bean soup and jelly sandwiches for supper one night," Anna said.

"Oh, my gosh! Girls, it's almost 11:00. We need to get going. Training is about to start!"

Although the girls had some difficulty understanding Mr. Kokkinos' accent, they still learned how to properly address and serve customers at the tables and boardwalk counter. They would not be cooking any food since Mr. Kokkinos and some of his family would oversee all food preparation. He was most particular about the manner of presentation of his food and didn't trust anyone who was not Greek to prepare it properly. There were six girls working every shift and he had hired 20 for the season. They each had either one or two days off per week depending on how busy they were on the weekends. Each girl was given two red and white uniforms for the season that must be washed and ironed after each shift. They also had red and white checkered hats and aprons to accent the uniform and were asked to buy their own white tennis shoes to wear daily.

The new hires tried on uniforms to pick the correct fit. They were all impressed at how sharp they looked. Mr. Kokkinos, whose name means 'red', told the girls that those who stayed on for the whole summer would enjoy a bonus at the end and have their picture taken for his restaurant wall. He showed them the pictures of years past hanging on the entrance wall. None of the uniforms were faded and still showed bright red and white colors through use after Labor Day weekend and the girls displayed huge smiles.

"We're going to be on this wall in a few months," Anna professed. "We can make it through!"

The Kokkinos family then served up dishes for everyone to taste and share, explaining to the servers how each was prepared and the cost. They were also learning the names of their employees and rating their personalities. When they finished the meal, each girl was given a schedule for the week. Anna and Kay started the next morning, and Betty had the Friday evening shift. They gathered their uniforms, said good night and walked back toward their room.

The sun had just descended, and several people were out walking the boardwalk, eating ice cream and snacks. The smells of hamburgers, French fries, caramel popcorn, and steamed crabs wafted along the boardwalk. Such a pleasant combination of smells, and unlike anything the girls had ever experienced.

"I'm so full, but I would love to have some ice cream to take back with us. Want to? I'll buy," asked Betty. "We can eat it later."

"We have all summer to eat ice cream, but if you insist . . . " Kay responded not sure how Betty could think of food now.

"Look how beautiful the ocean is tonight. I wonder if it will be like this every night," said Anna admiring the reflection of the moon on the water. "This is such a gorgeous place. No wonder so many people want to come here on vacation. I think I could live here."

* * *

Over the next couple of weeks, the girls worked every day except one. They decided to spend that day together to work on their summer tans and enjoy the ocean water.

The mail arrived before they left the boarding house and to the girls' surprise they each had a letter from home. Kay and Betty decided to wait until they were settled on their blanket in the sand before opening theirs. Anna, however, saw that her letter was from her Grandfather Daffin so she wanted to be sure nothing had happened to her grandmother before spending time on the beach having fun. As she opened the letter, a dollar bill fell out onto the floor.

"Money! You got some money!" Betty exclaimed.

"How nice!" Added Kay.

"Yeah," Anna stated as she read the few lines from her grandfather. "He says a friend told him about some really good saltwater taffy he had while staying in Rehoboth last year. He is sending the dollar so we can get some and enjoy it together one day. Says he's treating us to Dolle's Saltwater Taffy and wants to know if it is as good as his friend said. How about that! Just like my Granddaddy Daffin to do something like this.

"But not your Grandfather Scott?" asked Betty knowing how Anna would respond.

Giggling, Anna said, "Are you kidding? He's so tight, he squeaks!"

Laughing, the three friends walked out into the hot, bright, sunny day in the direction of the beach covered with sunbathers on towels shaded by brightly colored umbrellas. Children squealed with delight as ocean water and sand flowed over their toes. The roar of the ocean drowned out the surrounding conversations and laughter. The three girls were amazed at how loud the ocean could be. It was unexpected. The friends laid their towels side by side facing the ocean and removed the covers over their bathing suits. They wore bathing caps, each with a different pastel color. The waves tumbled forward and disappeared into the glistening wet sand. A heavy scent of suntan lotion, salty water, and perspiration hung in the air.

"Remember that this water can pull you in if you are not careful. How well do you two swim?" asked Betty.

"Not well," said Kay.

"Me either," added Anna.

"Then you better not go out too far."

"Oh, come on! It's too hot to sit here all afternoon. I want to get my suit wet!" said Kay as she ran off toward the water. Anna and Betty watched Kay throw her body against a wave that nearly knocked her down and then tried to swim with the waves.

"I better show her how to swim in this water. I'm going in! Coming?" asked Betty.

"In a bit," responded Anna. "I'm not quite ready."

She watched her friends struggle with the high waves. She saw how the water rose further out and then rolled toward land, spreading a foamy finish over the sand before pulling out and under the next wave to arrive. The sound of tumbling water was much like the sound of gentle wind causing a clatter of leaves on the forest trees in fall. Anna wanted to feel the power of the waves. Building up her nerve, she finally stood up and ran to join in. The water felt cold on her feet, but she inched her way in further until a larger wave saturated every inch of her black bathing suit. Anna's body stiffened at the sudden chill. She squealed with the others along the water's edge who had just been hit by the same wave.

Anna decided to go in further and submerge her head under the water. She was starting to acclimate to the temperature and felt refreshed after each time she plunged under. The girls gathered around talking and laughing, bobbing up and down with the waves as they rolled in time and time again. Suddenly, a large wave came barreling forward and took the girls with it. Anna tumbled under, rolling and swirling, unable to breathe, and feeling panic. Then she fell forward onto the sand, landing on her side. The girls ran over to her to see if she was hurt. Anna coughed up water and her throat burned. The girls helped her up and they walked back together to the towels as a couple of bystanders asked if she was alright.

"Anna, have you ever been in the ocean in your life?" asked Betty with concern.

"Yes, my family has been to Tolchester Beach a few times. The water there is not strong like this. I haven't felt water so forceful before."

"That's because Tolchester is on the bay side of the peninsula. This is the Atlantic Ocean!" exclaimed Betty.

"Like I said, I had no idea it would be so strong!" Anna replied.

"You could have drowned! Don't scare us like that anymore!" Kay reprimanded her friend.

"You? I had a pretty good scare myself!" Anna said as she wrapped her towel tighter around herself.

* * *

The girls' work schedules were staggered, so they only had a few more opportunities to spend time on the beach together. This was not exactly what they expected. They all met some new girls from work who were on the same shifts and spent time hanging out with them. Making new friends was fine with them, but they had expected to see more of each other than they did. The money was great! And they didn't mind hard work at all.

"We farm girls are running circles around those city girls!" joked Anna late one night when all three were in the room together getting ready for bed.

"Yeah, but some of them meet up with guys in the evenings when we are already asleep. Their nights don't end after work. They move on to more exciting activities," Kay said laughing.

"Kay, you're terrible. How do you know what they are doing after work?"

"Anna! Don't tell me you haven't heard some of those girls from Pennsylvania talk about their dates. They are going out with different guys every week."

"I guess I haven't been paying attention," said Anna disappointed that she was missing out on some juicy conversations. "I'll have to stick around longer when I finish work."

"I saw a couple of the girls with some guys one night. They looked like greaseballs. I wouldn't want to go out with them. No way!" Betty added.

"Actually, I think that tall blonde-haired dishwasher at the restaurant is cute. I'd love it if he asked me out!" said Kay.

"A dishwasher? I wouldn't waste my time!" responded Anna.

"Is that so? Well, that dishwasher is here earning enough money to help out when he goes to the University of Delaware in the fall. He's studying to be a lawyer."

"That's different! Maybe he has potential then," Anna changed her tone.

"At least Kay and I are free to date anyone we want, Anna. You've tied yourself down to Jimmy. You could be having such a good time if you weren't so stuck on him!" Betty teased.

"You're loyal," added Kay.

"True blue, too!" Betty continued.

"I wouldn't be unfaithful to Jimmy. We're going steady, for gosh sake! He'd never do that to me either. I know him!"

* * *

Anna and Kay had the following day off. They decided to share the job of washing their uniforms and cleaning up the sand on the floor of their room. Once they finished, they would treat themselves to lunch and an afternoon movie at the theatre in town.

"Anna Ruth Scott! There is a phone call for you in the lobby," called out someone from the hallway.

"Who could be calling me? I hope it's not Mr. Kokkinos asking me to come into work," Anna said hurrying out the door and down three flights of stairs.

"Hello. This is Anna Ruth," she said picking up the heavy black receiver.

"Well, hi there, babe! Are you missing me yet?" asked Jimmy.

"Jimmy! Oh, Jimmy! I can't believe it's you!" Anna practically screamed his name. The attendant at the front desk turned and gave her a dirty look.

"Did you get my letters? I've sent two, one each week."

"I got one. Sounds like you are working all the time. I tried calling three times earlier, but whoever picked up the phone said you were at work."

"It's true. All three of us work long shifts and only get one day off each week. Never a weekend. We're too busy."

"That's why I am calling. I want to come and see you one day. Which day do you have off next week?"

"Next week? I'm off on Wednesday. Can you make it then?"

"I believe so. I'll try to make it there around 1:00."

"Ok. That will be good. I'll have time to do my laundry that morning."

"Are you being good for me? You aren't misbehaving or going out with some other guy, are you, Anna?"

"No, Jimmy! I wouldn't do that. I'm just working and going to the beach."

"Make sure you put your bathing suit on for me. I'll meet you in front of your building around 1:00. See you Wednesday, babe!"

* * *

The next six days passed slowly for Anna. She was anxious to see Jimmy. They had been apart for almost three weeks! She took some of her earnings and bought a new bathing suit. Her plain black one was too hot to wear, not to mention dull and unattractive. After seeing the colorful bathing suits other girls were wearing, Anna knew she couldn't be seen on the beach with Jimmy in the old black suit.

There he was! Anna waved as she stood up from the white bench in front of her building.

Jimmy gave her a big hug, picking her up off her feet and swinging her around. "God, you look good, Anna! You have a tan!"

"A little one, but not like some girls. I don't spend that much time in the sun."

"I have really missed you! I had to make a trip! I needed to see you and spend some time together!"

"I know what you mean. I've been counting the hours!"

"We've never had a date at the beach. Hell, we've never had a date out of the county and away from prying eyes! It's great to visit you here, Anna!"

"Great! What do you want to do today?"

"Kiss you again!"

"And after that?" Anna quickly asked another question before he could respond. "How about going for a swim?"

"Sure! Let's hang out on the beach for a while."

"I have my new bathing suit on!"

"This I need to see!"

Anna and Jimmy stepped onto the hot sand. "You have to take your shoes off or they will fill up with sand. I learned the hard way. It's best if you go barefoot."

"Ahhh! It's hot!" Jimmy yelled as his feet burned on the sand.

"Come on! Let's find a place to sit closer to the water. It's cooler there."

They held hands and ran toward the ocean settling on a spot several feet away from three large blue rental umbrellas. Anna spread an old handmade blanket on the sand and placed her bag and sandals on it to hold the corners down. Jimmy took his shirt off. He wore his swimming trunks under his pants, so he was ready to take a dip.

"Be careful that you don't get sunburn, Jimmy. You may want to cover yourself from time to time."

"I'll just get in the water and cool down. Are you ready to go in?"

Anna stood up and turned her back pulling the cover she wore over her head. She tossed it on the blanket as she turned around and said "Let's go! Come on!"

"Wow! You look amazing in that suit!" he said as they trotted off towards the water.

They spent the afternoon in and out of the ocean, cooling their bodies each time the heat became too much to bear. Anna had learned how far she could venture out safely and stayed within that limit. A few times though, she trusted Jimmy to hold her hand or wrap his arm around her to keep her safe as they rode the waves. Later, as they rested on the blanket, Jimmy caught Anna up on all the local gossip.

"Remember that new girl whose father owns the clothing store in town? Rhonda Carpenter? Blonde hair?"

"Yeah! I had Home Economics with her. She always had on pretty store-bought dresses. She was nice when I first met her, but later in the year she seemed to be stuck up."

"I don't think she wanted to move to a hick place like Edentown. She was in Murph's with a guy named, Gus, who graduated four years ago."

"Her parents let her go out with a boy that old? Crazy!"

"Maybe they didn't know. He didn't drive her to Murph's, I'm sure. Anyway, she got mad at him for something he said and stood up on the booth seat with a full milkshake in her hand and poured it all over his head."

"What? He must have said something pretty bad!"

"That's not all. Gus, then grabbed her around the waist, pulled her down and out of the booth, and pushed her into a table full of people eating ice cream sundaes. She fell into the food, the table flipped up and it was all over her, the floor, and everyone who had been sitting at that table."

"You're kidding. Didn't someone call the town police?"

"Hell, yeah! They came, but it was too late. Gus left and no one has seen him since. Rhonda was not cut or anything, but I heard she was really bruised and sore the next few days. See babe, you are missing all the excitement in town!"

"Sounds like it. I must be missing it here too. I haven't seen anything like that happen in our restaurant. But I'm sure the manager would not stand for any nonsense like that either."

Early that evening, Jimmy bought them hot dogs, fries, and sodas at a snack bar on the boardwalk where they watched the people walking by – all kinds of people. As the sun slowly set, Jimmy and Anna held hands and strolled along the boardwalk lined with benches filled with vacationers.

"I'll need to go home soon," Jimmy said. "It takes almost two hours to get back, and I have to get up early."

"I need to get out of this bathing suit and take a bath. My morning will come early too."

They had reached a single bench near the end of the planked boardwalk. "Just a little more time, Anna. I need to be with you." He pulled her toward his chest and lowered his lips to meet hers. He felt her tense up and pulled her in even tighter. They kissed for a couple of minutes and Anna started to pull back.

"Not yet, Anna!" Jimmy wrapped his arms around her whole body and his tongue parted her lips for a longer more vigorous kiss. Anna felt weak in his arms. He kissed her neck as his hands fell to her butt.

"Jimmy! Jimmy, that's enough."

"Not yet. Come on, Anna."

"We can't. That's enough."

"Hey, didn't you hear the lady. She said that's enough. Now, you two better get on home," said a police officer who patrolled the beach at night. He walked up to them just as he heard Anna tell Jimmy to stop.

"Sorry, officer. We didn't see you there," said Jimmy with surprise.

"Get on out of this area! No need for you two to hang out here!"

Jimmy grabbed Anna's hand and they took off on a jog back to the congested part of the boardwalk and then walked on to the front of Anna's building.

“What an asshole! Who does that cop think he is? We weren’t doing anything wrong!”

“I didn’t know there were places that are off limits here.”

“They’re not. He’s just trying to hassle us! Look, I’ve got to go. I’ll call you in a few days. Maybe I can come for another visit before the Fourth of July. Okay?”

“That’s sounds good to me. I had a good time today, Jimmy! I’ll see you again soon!” Jimmy gave her another kiss on the lips. “Goodnight, babe. Be good.”

CHAPTER FOUR

Two more busy weeks passed. Anna thought about Jimmy every day. She wondered why he had been so pushy with her. He wasn't like that back home, but then they never had time alone there. Here it was different. She had seen some young people making out in dark places on her way home late at night and she heard that after dark, the beach was full of lovers. *It must be the bathing suits that make the boys go crazy*, Anna thought. *Next time Jimmy visits I'll wear a dress for our date instead.*

Anna agreed to another visit from Jimmy on June 23, her only day off that week. He couldn't get there until 4:00, so they decided to go out for dinner. Anna dressed in a sleeveless, blue seersucker dress dotted with little white row boats and finished with a plain white collar. There was a white belt cinched around her waist and a full skirt with crinoline slip. She wore imitation pearl earrings and a necklace with three small imitation pearls. Anna spent some of her last paycheck on the outfit, a little more than she expected to pay, but she loved the look of the nautical theme. She wanted a special dress for her date with Jimmy. She expected he would take her to one of the nice restaurants on the boardwalk.

"Do you realize that we have been out of school for almost a month? Time is really flying," she said with a sigh as she and Jimmy walked hand in hand near the park at the main entrance to the beach. Children darted in and out of the crowds of people gathered in groups and older people sat on benches lining both sides of the boardwalk in that area to be entertained by the sights and activities around them.

"It feels like you have been away longer than that, Anna."

"Have you missed me that much?"

"You know it! I couldn't wait to get here today!" Jimmy exclaimed, pulling Anna into an open-air restaurant with an available table for two facing the ocean.

"This is perfect, Jimmy! Good eye! It's not easy to find one of these tables."

A waitress came to them quickly and they ordered crab cake platters, a specialty of the house. Anna had been wanting to try the highly acclaimed delicacy since she overheard the girls at work talking about their boyfriends taking them to this place for the best crab cakes in town. Even though Anna came from Maryland's Eastern Shore, she had never eaten steamed crabs or any dish prepared with the crustacean. Her area was better known for its farms of beef, pork, and chicken, gardens of canning vegetables, and fields of corn, wheat, and soybeans. Tonight's meal was going to be a rare treat!

"Any more good gossip from home? How is Rhonda doing?"

"She must be recuperated. I saw her with a new guy over the weekend. They didn't go into Murph's though. I'm not sure she can go back there."

"Where did you see her?" inquired Anna.

"Just on Main Street walking arm-in-arm with some older man. She had on a dress that was cut low in the front and high heels. They may have gone into the pool hall. They were in the area."

"Sounds like you were really looking her over!"

"Not really. Besides, you know I only have eyes for you, sweetheart."

* * *

The food was delicious. Her coworkers were correct in their recommendation. Anna was enjoying her evening out with Jimmy. It was a very grown-up experience for them. He pulled her chair out for her when they arrived, stood up when she went to the ladies' room and took her hand in his while they waited for their main course to arrive. He expressed how happy he was to spend this time with her and how beautiful she was in her new dress. Anna was thrilled!

"Dessert?" asked their waitress.

"I can't eat another bite. No, thank you," said Anna.

As the waitress went to retrieve the check, Jimmy said "I have some dessert for us. Want to take it out on the beach later?"

"Sure! Later sounds good!"

"How about a few rounds on the bumper cars? You won't mess up your pretty dress, will you?"

"Oh, no, that shouldn't be a problem. I'd love that! There's a Ferris wheel, too. Let's go on that!"

"Anything you want, darling! I've got the money to treat my special girl tonight!"

After spending two hours in the amusements of Playland, the couple was exhausted and thirsty. They stopped for a lemonade at one of the stands. Strolling along sipping the ice cold, sugary drink, they stopped occasionally to watch players at the arcades along the boardwalk as they made their way to Jimmy's car.

"I need to get something," Jimmy said as he and Anna turned down a side street where he had parked.

Jimmy entered his vehicle and picked up a blanket and a small paper bag containing a bottle. Then he grabbed Anna's hand as he carried these items back up the street to the boardwalk steps leading out onto the beach. Anna saw the blanket and thought how nice it would be to share that beautiful view of the full moonlight reflecting on the ocean with Jimmy. She knew he would enjoy it as much as she did.

"Do you know that this is one of the longest nights of the year?" Jimmy asked as he helped Anna step off into the sand. "We better take our shoes off, right?"

"Yes, I don't want to ruin my sandals." Anna took them off and carried them in her hand as she strolled hand-in-hand with Jimmy along the edge of the beach. The further they walked, the fewer people they saw out for the evening.

"I love to feel this wet sand on my feet. Don't you think it's cool, Jimmy?"

"Yeah! It feels great until you walk onto the dry sand, and it clumps to your feet. Let's put the blanket down over here. I hope it doesn't smell like mothballs. I grabbed it out of my mom's big blanket chest."

Anna laughed. "Ewww! Mothballs have a terrible smell. Maybe it will air out on the beach."

Jimmy was satisfied that they had walked far enough to be totally to themselves. He spread out the old patch quilt blanket. Anna was impressed with the attention Jimmy was giving her tonight. The moonlit shimmer on the water was an intoxicating sight, and the melodic lapping of the waves was soothing enough to lull a person to sleep. She sat down on the blanket and spread her dress out around her. Jimmy pulled the bottle out of the paper bag he had carried and opened it.

"Here, try this. Dessert," Jimmy said with a sly smile.

"What is it?" Anna asked as she cautiously took a taste from the amber-colored bottle.

"Apple brandy. Good stuff."

"Yuck! It tastes terrible! Burns my mouth," Anna pushed the bottle back to Jimmy as she wiped the back of her hand across her lips.

"You barely drank it. You have to have more than that," He handed it to her again. "It tastes better the more you drink. Here."

Anna took a larger swig and struggled to swallow. "Aggggh!"

"Have another one. Isn't it tasty?"

Anna tried to take three more large swigs wanting to please Jimmy. *I don't understand how he can drink this stuff,* she thought, swallowing a mouthful. "It's too sweet and it burns. I can't drink anymore."

The couple sat on the blanket taking in the beauty of their surroundings. The beach felt dark even with the brightly lit sky. The boardwalk lights didn't extend to this area of Rehoboth. There were no businesses or flashing neon signs. Jimmy drank another swig of apple brandy and then capped it. He felt a little buzz and hoped that Anna had had enough to feel the same. He knew she didn't drink, so the alcohol should affect her quickly.

"Are you okay, Anna?"

"Yeah, I'm fine," Anna said as she began to feel a warmth move through her body and up to her face. She was relaxed and enjoying the moment. *It is such a wonderful night!*

Jimmy leaned over and kissed Anna gently on her lips. She kissed him back as a sense of euphoria ran through her body. He continued to kiss her, moving down her neck as he scooted closer to her. He landed on top of her dress that was still spread out on the blanket. Anna felt blissful as she enjoyed Jimmy's kisses and the closeness she felt with him that night. It was all so perfect. She wrapped her arms around Jimmy's neck, and they kissed more passionately.

"You feel so good tonight, Anna," he whispered moving his hand to cup her left breast feeling the soft fullness as he circled and explored her. She didn't resist. He sought more, moving his hand down her back as he lowered her onto the blanket. Jimmy kissed Anna again and again, touching and rubbing his hands all over her in a frenzy of desire. Anna felt her head swirling and waves of tickles raced through her stomach making her giggle out loud.

"You like that, don't you?" Jimmy asked thinking he was causing her to be so giddy.

"Hmmmm! Yeah, I feel funny inside."

"I'm going to make you feel real good tonight, babe. You want that don't you?"

"You always make me feel good, Jimmy. Really, I'm feeling so strange inside," she laughed out loud again. "Is this how it feels to be drunk? I think I had too much of that apple stuff."

"You'll be fine. Don't worry about that. You'll feel much better soon," said Jimmy taking that cue and moving on top of Anna. He lifted her dress, searching for the prize he sought and when he found it decided to take it for himself. Anna felt his fingers probing her. It was a strange, wonderful sensation, yet suddenly felt wrong. She tried to get up, but his weight on top of her and his knee on her full dress made it impossible. She tried to pull his hand away, but he was too strong for her. Jimmy continued to satisfy his need for her, sliding her satin underwear down her legs as she squirmed to prevent him. She couldn't roll to either side. Although Jimmy had pulled her dress up to her waist, his weight continued to pin her down. Anna's thoughts were fuzzy.

What's going on, she asked herself. *I don't feel so good. What's happening to me?*

"You have to stop. Jimmy, please. Don't." He paid no attention. Her pleading fed his desire for more of her. He was in a frenzy as he unbuckled his belt while spreading her legs with his knees. Anna felt panic as he held her arms over her head and kissed her harder. She moved her head to one side. He grabbed her jaw and turned her back to him. He held her as he parted her lips and jabbed his tongue into her mouth. Anna could taste and smell the apple brandy on him. It disgusted her. He disgusted her. She tried once again to break free of his grip, but there was no stopping him now.

"Jimmy! Sto . . . Stop!" she said as a sharp pain struck from inside her. She thought she felt a thousand pointy needles sticking her from inside her body. Pleasure turned to pain as Jimmy thrust himself inside her.

"Nooooo!"

Anna pushed against Jimmy's shoulders as he continued to take her. Anna was powerless. She felt defeated. Finally, he rose up and then collapsed on top of her. His breath was quick and heavy against her neck. Anna lay bewildered and hurt on the Baker family quilt as the smell of mothballs rose to her nostrils.

How could he do this to me? I loved him. This isn't how I heard it should be! Anna thought as she tried to make sense of what had happened.

When Jimmy finally stood to zip his pants, Anna sat up and smoothed her wrinkled dress. Neither one spoke. There was an uncomfortable feeling between them as if they were strangers. Anna looked at Jimmy as she wondered who he had become. She no longer felt she could trust him. Feeling terribly awkward now, Jimmy was anxious to leave the beach and avoid any further conversation with Anna.

"I better be heading back to Edentown soon. It must be almost eleven o'clock by now." Anna couldn't look at him. She grabbed her sandals and shook the sand off.

"Hey, aren't you speaking to me?"

"You hurt me."

"Sorry. I didn't know."

"We were having a good day together."

"Yeah! It's been swell, hasn't it?"

"No! You ruined it. How could you?"

"Come on, Anna! You know it was time. We've been messing around long enough. Do you expect us to go on forever just kissing good night?"

"I certainly didn't expect you to do this!" Anna yelled as she took a swipe at Jimmy with her sandals. He ducked out of the way, and she missed her target.

"What was that for?" Jimmy chuckled. "Are you mad at me or something?"

"What do you think?" Anna asked as she stopped walking and folded her arms in defiance. "And you are laughing about it?"

"You are making a big deal out of everything! It's not!" Jimmy stepped closer to Anna pulling her arms down and holding them to her sides. He moved in to kiss her on the cheek. Anna froze.

"Everybody is doing it, Anna. It's time you grew up," Jimmy whispered in her ear as he continued to hold her arms in his grip.

Anna couldn't move and didn't know how to respond. *Was he right? I have always believed in being a good girl.*

"I feel dirty," Anna spouted back at him in anger.

"Come on. Let's get out of here. You're fine," Jimmy replied dismissing Anna's feelings entirely.

Disappointed with the turn of events and unsure how to handle Anna, Jimmy decided he better call it a night. He walked her back to the boarding house in uncomfortable silence.

"I'll call you later, okay?" he said kissing Anna on top of her head. With tears in her eyes, she simply nodded her head and walked inside the building.

I hope he doesn't call me! I don't know what to say to him anymore! I feel so strange. Am I wrong? No one can know what we did tonight. I can't even tell Betty or Kay about this. I won't say anything about it. That's what I'll do. Just forget it ever happened! And I will never drink another drop of alcohol again!

CHAPTER FIVE

Jimmy didn't call again until the middle of July. Anna was actually relieved that she hadn't heard from him. She didn't know what she would say if he called her. She didn't know what to say to anyone for a while. Kay and Betty knew something was bothering her but gathered that Anna had fought with Jimmy during his last visit. They asked questions but she simply said she didn't want to talk about him.

Anna had been sore for a few days after their night together. She had also tried to understand why he had been so insensitive and aggressive. She felt grungy. *Did I ask for his behavior by drinking the apple brandy*, she wondered. *Was his reaction somehow my fault?* She pondered over and over. Anna felt guilty, but she didn't know of what. She spent time alone on the beach listening to the waves, the same calming sound she had heard that night, searching for understanding. Alone in her thoughts, she heard her Grandfather Scott telling her that she had acted shamefully and her parents yelling at her for misbehaving while on her own and that she could no longer be trusted. After several days of indecisiveness, Anna concluded that she would forget about the incident, and she would make sure that Jimmy never had an opportunity to treat her that way again.

"Hey, babe, I'll bet you thought I forgot about you," Jimmy said when he finally called Anna. "I've been really busy at the lumberyard. We had a big order come in for some new houses being built outside of town and we have been running the mill night and day to fill it."

"Sounds like it was a big job."

"Yeah, but we are finished now and have a couple of days off. I was thinking about coming to see you tomorrow if you are off. You are usually off on Wednesday, aren't you?"

"I'm off. I suppose that would be fine. It's my turn to clean the room tomorrow, but I should be finished by the time you get here."

"Good! Then I'll see you around noon. We can get some crab cakes again. How about that?"

Jimmy showed up at Rehoboth the next day around 1:30. Anna thought he must be ready for lunch since he arrived later than expected. She was starving! Passing on breakfast in order to get the cleaning and laundry completed, Anna had been looking forward to crab cakes since getting up that morning.

"Hey, Babe!" Jimmy picked Anna up at the waist and swung her around. "Did you miss me?"

"Yeah, what took you so long? I thought you would be here sooner."

"I slept late this morning, so I didn't get off as soon as I thought I would. Sorry, Sugar! I came here as soon as I could."

"It's okay. Ready for a crab cake? I'm so hungry! I waited for you to arrive."

"Oh, no! I had a big breakfast before leaving home. Our new maid makes the best buttermilk pancakes and scrapple I've ever had. I couldn't refuse her after she went to the trouble of making it. You know? I'm just not hungry right now." Anna was hurt but held her tongue. *Did he forget that he was taking me for lunch? Had I known he had already eaten, I would have made a sandwich before he arrived.*

Jimmy kissed her and gave her a big hug instead of apologizing. He gave the big smile that she loved. He appeared to be making an effort to return their relationship to the way it had been previously. For Anna, things had not returned to normal. Although she decided not to speak of their last date, she had not forgotten what occurred or how Jimmy had treated her. Chalking his behavior up to the effects of too much apple brandy that night, she was willing to give him another chance. However, she would be more alert as they spent time alone on the beach today to make sure that never happened again.

"What do you want to do?"

"I want some Thrasher's fries! I need to eat," Anna said.

"Let's get some then and you can eat them on the beach. Do you have a blanket?"

"No, but I have two beach towels we can use this time," Anna told him, hoping he would understand the message.

The afternoon heat was unbearable. Jimmy and Anna went into the water to cool down and within a few minutes of sitting on their towels felt the need to go back in. Anna had gotten better at bobbing along with the waves, so she didn't need Jimmy's help any longer. They mostly talked about the news from home since Anna had nothing but work happening in her life.

"The state fair is coming up in a couple of weeks," Jimmy said struggling to make conversation. "Dad wants me and my little brother to take a couple of Holsteins to show. It will be his first time. I guess I'll be training him for the competitions.

"I didn't know you've ever shown cows. Did you win any ribbons?" Anna responded trying to sound interested.

"Yeah, a few. I really wasn't into it though. I think that is why my dad is pushing this on my brother. He wants one of his boys to carry on the tradition."

"You're probably right. It's important to him."

"I can't stand spending the night in the barn with the animals. The smell, heat and flies are too much for me! Everybody sleeps in their clothes on bales of straw, or they bring cots. That's fun when you're thirteen, but not now."

"I'll miss the fair this year. I don't know if my dad will take any hogs this time. He has in past years," Anna said.

"I could find out for you."

"It doesn't matter. Besides, I'm sure I'll hear all about it in the next letter my mom sends me. Her letter last week told me all about what my sisters are entering in the 4-H competitions. Good luck though! I hope your brother wins a ribbon or two."

By five o'clock, they were exhausted from the heat and really thirsty. They decided to grab a sandwich and drink from a snack bar near the boarding house. While there, they continued to struggle in their conversation.

"I'm so tired from the water today," Anna exclaimed. "I feel like I could just take a nap."

"I know what you mean. We could go to a place under the boardwalk and nap there for a while. Since I'm not allowed in your room…"

"I don't think so. Not after last time"

"What about it? Didn't you have a good time? Didn't I treat you good? I took you out to eat and …"

"You hurt me. I was hurting for days after you left that night."

"I don't think that's my fault. You must have done something wrong."

"We both did, Jimmy! And what if you knocked me up? Did you ever think about that?"

"You can't get knocked up on the first time! Don't you know that?" Jimmy shook his head in disbelief. "There are more kids in school who are doing it than you can imagine."

"My friends aren't! I'm sure of it!"

"How can you be so sure?"

"They would have told me!" she answered.

"Did you tell Betty and Kay that you did it?" He laughed as Anna shook her head. "I didn't think so. Girls don't talk about it."

"Who have you told? Oh, God, Jimmy, please say you didn't tell anyone! It'll be all over school when we go back."

"No one you know. Don't worry about it."

But she was worried.

Jimmy grew impatient with Anna as he realized that she was not willing to go under the boardwalk with him. After finishing their meal, he decided it was time to go home. She walked with him to his car wanting some sign from him that he still cared for her, that he respected her even now. He took her hand and brought her fingers to his lips. "I'll miss you, babe." He said without much feeling.

"When will I see you again?" she asked not ready for him to leave, still hoping he would say a few words to make her feel better. She wanted desperately to stop the tension between them and return to the carefree, playful relationship they once enjoyed.

"Not until after the fair is finished. I'll give you a call when I get back home. I can tell you all about the prizes we've won," he chuckled nervously as he pulled Anna in toward his chest and hugged her. He then kissed her lips three times rather quickly and one last time on her forehead.

"I'll call you," he said as he got in his car. As he backed his car out of the parking space, Jimmy threw his hand up in a good-bye wave and then drove away.

Anna stood on the sidewalk watching Jimmy speed off. She gave a wave back to him but wasn't sure he actually saw it. Something had changed. She didn't feel comfortable around him anymore. Anna wanted to rid herself of the terrible feelings she was having concerning Jimmy but didn't know how to achieve it. *Is it my fault? Oh, God, I really don't want to lose him!*

Jimmy didn't call. Anna spent the rest of her time at the beach with Kay and Betty and a few other girls they met in their building or at work. There was always someone to hang out with on the beach, or to eat dinner out, or go to the dances that were held on the boardwalk on weekends. Sometimes boys working at the beach would join them for a casual evening of fun. Nothing was serious between any of them. They were simply a bunch of hard-working kids out for some fun!

By the first week of August, Anna realized that she hadn't had a period since June. She knew that this could be an indication that she was pregnant. She had overheard some of the girls at the restaurant talking about a friend who missed her period and thought she was expecting.

"Oh, my God, well if you did it there is a good chance that you are knocked up. Well, did you two do it?" one of the waitresses asked of her friend.

"Yes, but he used a rubber, I think," the friend replied.

"You think? You mean you don't know?" Anna heard the girl question her friend. "Oh, you are knocked up for sure! How many periods have you missed?"

"Two."

"Oh, my God, you've got to tell him. He is going to flip out! You've missed your period for two months; you are definitely knocked up!" said the friend as the women took the rest of their conversation outside the business.

Anna also left the building as she wondered if it was possible that Jimmy was wrong. He told her that she couldn't get pregnant the first time. She didn't feel like she was. *Maybe there is another reason to miss a period,* she thought. She gave little more thought to it for the rest of their stay at the beach, and she never said a word about it to her best friends.

Just two more weeks of freedom and then they would go back home to start their senior year of school. Betty and Kay were looking at the new fall Sears catalog picking out clothes they wanted to buy with their summer earnings. It was a rare night in for the three friends and they were catching up with each other.

"Anna, did you see the letter that arrived for you today? I left it on your dresser," asked Kay.

Anna found the white envelope with a return address from home and opened it to find a two-page letter from her sister, Janet. She started out complaining about the heat and long hard days of hauling tomatoes from the fields on their farm. She told Anna that she wanted to go to the beach with her next year. Then she wrote about going out to the movies with some friends the previous weekend. She said that they had seen Jimmy at the movie theater with Rhonda Carpenter holding hands like they were on a date. And as they left the theater that night, she saw the two of them kissing in the back row. Janet wanted her sister to know.

"No wonder I haven't heard from Jimmy lately! Damn him!" Anna exclaimed throwing the letter across the room. Kay and Betty were shocked by her sudden outburst. It was not like Anna to curse.

"What's wrong?" asked Betty.

"What has Jimmy done?" questioned Kay at the same time. "I've been wondering why he hasn't been back lately."

"Is he two-timing you, Anna? You look terrible. What a jerk!" asked Betty concerned for her friend.

"Janet saw him out with Rhonda and they were kissing during a movie," Anna explained.

"Rhonda Carpenter? You've got to be kidding!"

"I can't believe he would be seen with Rhonda. She's trouble. I heard she's not allowed to go in Murph's anymore," added Kay.

"Well, I guess it's over then. I don't know why he hasn't told me. Don't you think he should say we are broken up? After all, we were supposed to be going steady!" A frustrated and confused Anna began to cry as her two best friends ran to her side to comfort her. They sat beside her while tears rolled down her face. Betty went into the hallway and came back with a soda for her, and they continued to talk about what a creep Jimmy turned out to be. The girls wouldn't be going home until they finished their work for Mr. Kokkinos, so Anna would have to wait a bit longer before confronting him about dating Rhonda. She didn't want to send him a letter or call him on the phone about it. This called for a face-to-face confrontation!

After sleeping in until 9:00 the next morning, a rare luxury for Anna, she woke up feeling an upset stomach. Splashing cold water on her face, she caught a glimpse of the worry lines wrinkling her forehead. She made a cup of tea on the hot plate, sipping it slowly, but her stomach didn't settle down. Thankfully, Kay and Betty were working the morning shift that day, because she suddenly ran to the bathroom with urgency and threw up. Clinging to the toilet from her seat on the floor, Anna thought about what she had eaten the day before. She had cried for quite a while last night and the anger she felt towards Jimmy probably resulted in her sick feeling. When the nausea passed, she splashed more water on her face and got dressed in blue shorts and a red and white polka-dotted blouse. Then, she heard the landlord calling out.

"Anna Scott! There's a phone call for you!"

It's Jimmy, I'll bet! He must be calling to apologize or explain why he was out with Rhonda. Anna went flying down the three flights of stairs and grabbed the phone. Out of breath, she said "Hello."

"Anna Ruth? It's your mother. How are you dear? I'm calling with some bad news. Your Grandfather Scott passed away in his sleep last night. He must have had a heart attack."

"Oh, that's terrible! Is grandmother alright?"

"She's fine, but of course, very upset. She found him in his room like that this morning. I wanted you to know. I'm not sure you can come to the funeral. What do you think?"

"I don't see how I can, mom. I know Daddy will be mad at me for not showing up, but I am scheduled to work every day until we finish the season. I don't have a way to go home and back again. Do you know the arrangements yet?"

"Oh, dear, not yet. I'm sure we'll know something later today."

"Besides, mom, Grandfather Scott didn't like me very much. I don't think he liked any of us girls, honestly," Anna said to further explain why she would be absent.

"He only had a rough way of showing his love for you. Some men are like that, Anna Ruth. We'll miss having you at the funeral, you know. I can explain to your father. He really hoped you could be home to be with us. See you after Labor Day then, Anna Ruth," Dottie said, hanging up the phone as she hoped the long-distance call wouldn't cost too much. She would have written a letter had she known Anna couldn't make it to the funeral.

* * *

Mr. Kokkinos lined up all his employees in front of his restaurant just as he had done for eleven years as a professional photographer took the picture of everyone smiling in their red and white uniforms and checkered caps. When they were finished, Mr. Kokkinos thanked them all for a good season and handed out a $25.00 bonus check to each one of the employees who finished out the summer. Anna, Kay, and Betty were among them. Feeling quite satisfied, the three girls packed up their belongings, said their goodbyes to all the friends they had made for the summer, and waited in front of the boarding house for Kay's father to pick them up.

They had learned a lot over the last three months. Their hard work had paid off as each girl made more than they had expected. There had been time for fun, new experiences, and exposure to different types of people than those from Edentown. The girls knew they wouldn't look at anyone or anything the same way they had before going to the beach. They had matured and felt their expectations for the future were greater now. They would enter their senior year of high school with the hope of forging a new path.

Although Anna also believed she had learned about other possibilities for her life, she was more uncertain of what lay ahead for her. The incident occurring that summer night on the beach haunted her. Something wasn't right. She would need to figure it all out when she arrived home.

CHAPTER SIX

Anna was the first one to be dropped off. Along the drive home, they passed familiar fields of green corn and the last of the truck crops being worked. The local cannery was in full operation. The families and migrant workers on every farm seemed to be racing to get their crops out. The Scott family was no different. As soon as Mr. Monroe pulled up to Anna's house, her sister Susan came running to greet her.

"Mom and Daddy said for you to change your clothes and come to the back field and help. They told me to tell you," Susan blurted to Anna as she tried to catch her breath.

"Well, I guess that's my welcome home!" Anna said to her friends with annoyed sarcasm. "Back to the fields! Well, it was fun while it lasted, girls."

"We'll see you at school tomorrow! We can wear one of our new dresses! Okay, Anna? You'll look gorgeous!" Betty said trying to cheer up her friend.

"See you in the morning, Anna! It was great fun this summer!" Kay yelled out the car window as her father pulled around the driveway.

After changing into dungarees, an old plaid shirt, and a straw hat, Anna grabbed a peanut butter sandwich as she ran out the door and joined the rest of the family picking the last rows of peppers.

"I wish you could have gotten here earlier today. We thought you would be home this morning," Ernie Scott said as he walked by with a full basket and placed it on the back of the farm truck. "Head down to those rows over there and bring back the baskets that have been filled. I'll get them loaded on the truck. We need to finish up this field today."

Anna did as she was told while letting her mind wander back to the fun times she had spent in Rehoboth. Thinking of happier days made it easier to handle the job. The afternoon heat beat on their shoulders and faces, but they each continued on, picking the large green peppers and placing them in baskets to be carried to the back of the truck. Ernie stopped loading baskets around 5:00 to help Emmitt with the milking, so Anna then took his place. Around 7:30, they finally loaded the last basket on the truck and Ernie drove it into the shed for the night. He would deliver to the market in the morning and collect a check.

Exhausted and dusty, the women in the family walked back to the house and washed up in the big sink on the back porch. Dottie and the girls were too tired to make dinner and almost too tired to eat it. She pulled a package of cold hotdogs out of the refrigerator, some leftover potato salad, and a pitcher of cold milk and set them on the table. They didn't want to dirty up the dishes so they each grabbed a spoon and ate from the bowl as they munched on a cold hotdog from the other hand. After washing it down with a glass of cold milk, the children slipped off to bed. Tomorrow was the first day of school and they all needed to catch the school bus by 7:35.

Anna changed out her clothes, thinking she would get up earlier than rest in the morning so she could wash her hair and clean up. She wanted to look nice in case she ran into Jimmy. Maybe she would have some classes with him again this year.

As she removed her underwear, she noticed a few spots of blood. *Wonderful!* She thought. *I must be getting my period after all!* She felt truly relieved and in no time fell into a deep sleep.

* * *

All four Scott girls wore new dresses and saddle shoes on the first day of school like so many other students heading back to class that day. There was a smell of new satchels, binders with paper, and notebooks on the thoroughly cleaned and polished school bus. The kids were happy to see each other after the summer break and spoke incessantly about adventures or misadventures of those days off.

Anna met up with Betty and Kay as soon as she descended the bus steps. They had been waiting for her arrival.

"Look over there!" Betty pointed to a tree near the school parking lot where students could park. Rhonda Carpenter was leaning against the tree as if she were waiting for someone.

"So, what? I don't care," said Anna as she started to walk away. She felt better today than she had for a couple of weeks. "I'll catch up with him sometime today and see where we stand. Come on, girls! This is our senior year! We are top dogs now! Let's live it up a little this year!"

"I like the way you think, Anna! You surprise me sometimes!" said Kay with shock on her face. Betty shook her head in agreement.

As it turned out, Anna had a third-period World History class with Jimmy, but he sat in the back of the room while she was closer to the front. She caught up with him when they left to go to lunch.

"Hey, babe, where have you been? I looked for you when I arrived this morning," Jimmy said with that Cheshire cat smile of his. It was no longer a sweet smile to Anna. Jimmy had a smugness about him. He was concealing something and behaved as if Anna was too ignorant to understand.

Anna didn't want to get into an argument in the hallway. "Can we meet up after school?" she asked. "Do you want to drive me home?"

"Sure, I do. Anna, you know you are still my girl, don't you?"

"That's not what I've been hearing, Jimmy. We'll talk about it later."

When school let out for the day, Anna met up with her sister, Janet, and told her she was catching a ride home with Jimmy. She found him in the parking lot leaning against his car, and he told her to get in to take a ride.

"What's this nonsense you have in your head? Why do you think you aren't my girl anymore?"

"When was the last time you called me? Why didn't you come back to see me at the beach?"

"Honey, I tried. I didn't think you wanted me to come back. You were always working."

"I also heard that you have been going out with Rhonda Carpenter. Is it true?"

"What? Where did you hear that? She may have been at the same place as me a couple of times, but she wasn't on a date with me."

"Then you weren't making out with her in the movie theater a few weeks ago?" Anna pushed for answers.

"It wasn't me! If someone told you that, they are lying!"

Anna was confused. She wanted to believe him. *Maybe the rumors were wrong,* she thought. She pressed for more. "Are you taking me to the back-to-school dance? I saw an announcement today for September 25."

"Of course, sugar! I don't want to go with anyone else but you. Count on me!"

Anna let the subject of Rhonda Carpenter drop for then. She didn't want to be a jealous girlfriend, and she knew what a tease Rhonda could be around all the boys. She just couldn't imagine Jimmy going out with someone like her. *It must not be true! Then, why did Janet write to her about them,* she asked herself.

* * *

The next morning before school, Anna had a wave of nausea so bad that she couldn't eat breakfast. She didn't throw up, but she thought she may have been wrong in thinking she wasn't pregnant. She didn't feel well, at all.

The old gang got together again, whenever they could. Jimmy seemed a little distant, but still hung out with everyone and sat next to Anna when they ended up at Murph's. Betty had a new boyfriend within the first week of school. He was a friend of Jimmy's. Whenever they were together there seemed to be constant playful arguments and lively conversations. Anna and Jimmy were rarely alone as dating occurred with their group of friends.

The Friday before the dance, Anna woke up early feeling like she would be sick. She ran downstairs to the only bathroom in the house and threw up. Shaky and afraid it would happen again, she ate a couple of saltines and readied herself for school. Luckily, her father was at the barn and her mother was busy with Eddie and her sisters upstairs, so no one in the family saw what had happened. She later threw up during her first-period English class. Fortunately, no one else was in the ladies' room at that time. She wondered how long it would be before she was caught getting sick since it seemed that the waves of nausea were getting worse.

Jimmy told her he would come by to pick her up around 7:15 on Saturday night. She ate very little dinner, so she could fit into her new navy blue short-sleeved dress accented by a yellow belt and collar. It looked very smart on her, but she noticed that it was more snug on her than when she tried it on at the store. It was an end-of-season sale dress she bought before leaving Rehoboth Beach. Quite a deal!

As Jimmy saw Anna descend the stairs into the living room, he commented on how nice she looked that night. Ernie and Dottie thought the couple looked handsome too. Jimmy wore a navy blue suit that matched perfectly with Anna's dress, and he also wore a plain white shirt with a blue and yellow tie that accented well.

"You two have a good time tonight. See that Anna is brought straight home after the dance, Jimmy. We'll see you a little after 11:00, Anna," said Ernie to the pair.

"I'll have her home right after. Don't you worry. I'll take good care of Anna, Mr. Scott," Jimmy reassured him.

"Good night, Jimmy! See you a little later, Anna!" called out Dottie as the couple walked out the door.

Everyone who attended the first dance of the year appeared to be having a fabulous time. A local group played the music for the evening and the guys knew a lot of the current dance tunes. Anna couldn't dance as much as Jimmy wanted; her stomach began bothering her again about halfway through the night. She sat out while he danced with others in their gang and then he took a turn with Rhonda when she cut in on a slow dance. As Jimmy came back to his seat, Anna stood up and told him that she was ready to leave.

"Why? There's still a half-hour more and this band is cool."

"I feel sick, Jimmy. I need to go home. Please."

"Well, alright then. Guess we have to go guys. Anna says so," Jimmy rolled his eyes and sniggered.

The pair headed back to Anna's home with the passenger window down a little so air would blow in her face.

"I know you don't believe me, Jimmy, but I really don't feel well. I feel like I'm going..." And then it came up. She pulled her dress up and bent her head down, so she threw up on the carpeted floor of the Bel Aire. She didn't want to get her dress messy. Jimmy stopped the car suddenly and she banged her head on the car pocket but continued to throw up again. Jimmy jumped out of his car yelling and cursing Anna for the disgusting mess she made on the floor of his car.

"Shit! How am I ever going to clean that up? What's wrong with you? You could have told me to pull over so you could get out. Damn it! It smells awful!"

"I told you I was sick. I'm so sorry. I didn't mean to do it in your car. I couldn't stop it," Anna said as she began to cry. She felt horrible.

Jimmy pounded his fists against the hood of his car in anger. "What a dumbass! How could you not know you were going to throw up? Why didn't you put it in your dress? No, you had to spread that shit all over my carpeted floor!" Then he remembered that he had some rags in the trunk of his car to check his oil stick and retrieved them.

"Here, clean that shit up! I can't stand to look at it." Anna did as she was told, as best as she could. It didn't all clean up and she was sure there would be an awful smell and stain if it didn't get scrubbed soon.

As she wiped the floor, Anna looked at Jimmy and told him what she suspected.

"Jimmy, we need to talk."

"About what?"

"I think, I mean, I might be, but I'm not sure, but I think I'm pregnant," Anna dropped her head waiting for Jimmy to respond. He stared at her in disbelief. He came nearer to her, and she felt him breathing hard into her face.

"What did you say? Are you kidding me?"

"I'm sorry," she said, afraid to look at his face.

"You're sorry? Damn it! Damn it! No! You can't be! Maybe you aren't really. How do you even know?" he exclaimed in disbelief. "You're really disgusting right now, you know that? Look at you! I don't know how I could ever have kissed that face. You're repulsive!"

Anna tried to take Jimmy's hand and put it to her cheek that was now streaming with tears, he pulled away and wiped his hand on his pants.

"This is not how this night was supposed to go. I'm taking you home. Now! And you better find out for sure if you're knocked up. Don't go telling shit like that unless you really know."

"I can see my doctor, I suppose. I don't know what to do. I was hoping you could help me figure this out."

"Go to your doctor. Ask him! How would I know? I'm no doctor!"

* * *

Dr. Isaac gave Anna's urine sample to his nurse for testing. Then he made the usual check of her vitals.

"Hmmm. Your blood pressure is up a little. Any reason for that?"

"If I am expecting a baby, could that cause my blood pressure to be higher?"

"Well, a baby can make a whole lot more changes than that. High blood pressure is not something you want to have then. Do you think you are pregnant?"

"I think I may be," Anna said looking down at the floor.

"Do you have a reason to think this? I mean, have you been with a boy?" he questioned Anna noticing that she seemed embarrassed and shy. He wondered if she understood what he meant. "Did you have sex with a boy?"

"Yes," she replied quietly.

"Then we better see what is going on here. You know that I will need to tell your parents if you don't."

"I know. I will tell them, but you won't let anyone else know, will you? I will just die if people in town find out. I couldn't face..."

"Not a word of it will leave this office. Don't you worry. You have enough to think about already!"

Dr. Isaac felt around Anna's abdomen and with her other symptoms came to the conclusion that she probably had a baby growing inside her. "We'll get back to you with the test result by Friday. Do you want to stop by after school again to get it? I'm sure you don't want me to call your home, right?"

Anna nodded her head confirming that she would stop by. Then, she walked back to school to catch her bus home just before it pulled out. What luck! She left class early to go to the appointment. She hoped she didn't need to ask Jimmy for a ride home. She couldn't face him today.

Over the next couple of days, Anna devised another plan so she could pick up her test results without anyone finding out. She passed Jimmy in the hallway on Thursday and asked if they could meet up at Murph's after school Friday.

"Sure, you feeling better now? Maybe we can go for a ride or something," he asked as if the incident in his car had never happened. "I'm not mad at you anymore. I had my car cleaned up at work and it's good as new."

"You seemed to be avoiding me."

"Nah. Football practice this week, you know. I'll see you tomorrow."

Fortunately, her parents had no issue with her staying after school when she told them Jimmy was taking her out for dinner. A little lie, but maybe not. He usually bought her something to eat whenever they went to Murph's. She had a very healthy appetite lately, so she would probably want to eat there.

* * *

Dr. Isaac called Anna into his office before he saw his next patient, an older man she didn't know, thankfully. He handed her a form showing the words 'positive' in red ink. "Just as we expected, right Anna? You are going to have a baby. Now, we need you to inform the father and your parents. How old are you? Not quite 18. Do you think the father will marry you?"

"I'm not sure."

"Is he still in school, too?"

"Yes. He's my age."

"I've found that boys in high school are not reliable or responsible as fathers. I feel bad for your situation, Anna. I wish there was something more I could do. I see more and more young girls with your problem lately and there are no easy answers. Behavior among young people has changed since the war, both wars. You kids have more free time, fewer overseers of your actions, and access to automobiles to spend time alone in, than when I was your age. Most of the girls I see have gotten in that state from sex in the backseat of a car."

"You sound a lot like my Grandfather Scott. He was always telling my father that girls are nothing but trouble."

"There is some truth in that statement, but if girls, or young women, had a means of protecting themselves from these situations, I wouldn't be dealing with so many sad cases of unwanted babies. Your grandfather may have been a wise man who saw the changes that have occurred in our society since his boyhood. He's gone now, isn't he?"

"Yes, he passed away last month."

"I thought I read his obituary in the paper. Yes, well, you need to find out quickly what your young man has to say about your circumstances. Your parents need to know too, Anna. Please tell them soon."

Anna tried not to cry. A lump developed in her throat that stayed with her as she walked the streets of town. She refused to cry. *I'll work this out,* she thought. *I need to talk it over with Jimmy. We can work this out together.* "I know it," she said out loud hoping that would make it so.

* * *

Late Friday afternoon and Murph's was crowded. The joint would be hopping tonight! The jukebox was already blaring 'Shake, Rattle and Roll' just released by Bill Haley and the Comets, and the dance floor was packed. Anna took a deep breath and walked over to the booth where Jimmy and a couple of the other football players were smoking cigarettes and trying to impress each other.

"Hey, sugar, come here!" he yelled motioning for Anna to sit with him. He planted a kiss on her lips and swiped his finger down the bridge of her nose.

"Did you miss me?" Jimmy didn't wait for her answer but turned to see the reaction from his buddies instead. Anna was an attractive girl, and he knew that they were impressed that he was seeing her. He wanted to make sure they knew that they were still a couple.

"Jimmy, are you ordering something to eat?" Anna asked, but he ignored her. "Jimmy! Are you going to order us burgers?" She tried again. Jimmy was too busy showing off with the boys that he didn't hear her.

Then the tears came! She had held them in and now the floodgates were opened over a burger and some fries? *What's wrong with me,* she asked herself.

"What's the matter?" asked Jimmy finally noticing her. His buddies were suddenly uncomfortable around the couple, so they moved to another booth.

"I'm hungry. I thought you were going to buy me a burger."

"Tell you what. Let's get you out of here and I'll buy you a burger down the road at the ice cream place. What's it called? Oh, yeah, The Big Dipper. They have good burgers there. Okay? Let's go!" He squashed out his cigarette and took her arm leading her out of the building, hoping no one they knew saw how upset she was. He didn't want to be hounded with questions as to what was going on between them.

Anna got her burger, fries, and a chocolate milkshake too. Jimmy drove to the picnic area on the state road and pulled in. They sat in silence eating their food for a while and finally, Jimmy had to ask.

"What was that all about at Murph's? I've never seen you behave like that, Anna!"

"I need to be alone with you," she answered wiping her mouth clean.

"Why didn't you say so! Here I am," Jimmy whispered as he slid over on the bench seat and took her head in his hands pulling her to him. He kissed her with force as he worked his tongue into her mouth. Anna grabbed his hands and pushed him backward against his car door.

"I need to talk to you, Jimmy!" She said trying to catch her breath. "Seriously, I have to tell you something."

He was rubbing his head where he bumped it on the car window. Not really paying attention to her, Jimmy moved in once again and tried to kiss her more gently on the second try.

"Jimmy! I'm being serious!"

"Come on, baby! What's wrong?"

"I'm pregnant!" She shouted at him. "I received the test results from Dr. Isaac today." She pulled the paper from her purse and handed it to him.

"He said I need to let you know. I also have to tell my parents, Jimmy! My father will be furious. If I don't tell them, Dr. Isaac will do it. I'm not sure which way will be worse for me."

Jimmy held the paper in his hands while staring at Anna. She could feel him breathing rapidly.

"Are you shittin' me?" He said tossing the paper back to her.

"I told you last weekend that I thought I might be."

"I didn't believe you."

"Didn't believe me? Do you think I would lie about something like that? Really?"

"Some girls do."

"Well, I don't. I would never lie about getting pregnant!"

"I don't know how this could happen, unless that wasn't your first time. You can't get preggers the first time you do it. Damn it, Anna! How could you!"

"I'm sorry," she said back, afraid to look at his face.

"You're sorry? Damn it! Damn it, Anna! What are you going to do?"

"Dr. Isaac said I should see if you want to marry me."

"Marry you? Hell, I'm still playing football. I'm not ready to get married," Jimmy responded. He was repulsed by the thought of marrying her. In fact, he felt totally disgusted with her. Anna saw his answer written on his face.

"I guess I will have to figure this out on my own. You have no intention of marrying me, do you?"

"I don't know, Anna. Marriage, now?"

"Well, now would be the time to do it. You know, before the baby arrives!"

"I don't know what to do! Stop pushing me!"

"So, you just used me. How stupid could I have been to think that you cared for me? Take me home, Jimmy. Just take me home."

CHAPTER SEVEN

The chickens ran out of their bins, leaving freshly laid eggs in their nests, raising a fuss and flapping their wings as the dirt and straw swirled around inside the chicken house where Anna and Dottie gathered eggs. They could barely see each other as the fog of dust held thick inside the building while a heavy rain fell outside. Rain hit hard against the tin roof in a soothing and musical, yet deafening sound. The two women gathered eggs in silence, as the disturbed hens pecked at their hands, breaking the skin and causing them to bleed.

Dottie reached into the last nest and retrieved one more pure white, oval treasure. The hens had been laying more eggs than usual lately, which pleased Dottie greatly. She sold eggs to neighbors and a local country store to make a little money for extra expenses and gifts. Any money made from the chickens was hers to keep and spend as she wanted. Ernie never asked how much she had put away, but he knew where she kept her special round, blue-flowered tin in the kitchen cabinet and could have checked it at any time.

With baskets filled, Anna and Dottie ran quickly through the pouring rain to the back porch of the house, where they wiped down and cleaned each egg, checking for cracks, and then placing them carefully in egg cartons. Dottie was very satisfied as she counted the number collected that day.

"I almost have enough saved up to buy a new car coat for Eddie. He's growing so fast. I know he won't fit into last year's. It's going to turn cold one of these mornings."

"That's great, mom. I'm sure he needs it."

"Here, put these cracked eggs in the trash. Oh, look! This one had a double yolk! Too bad it broke!"

Anna threw the eggs out and walked back into the porch. As she finished helping with the eggs, Anna thought about seizing this moment, when her mother was in a good mood, to open up to her. She had always been close to her mother, but certain things were off-limits in their conversations. Boys and dating were never really discussed.

"We're done here, Anna! You can go on now. I'll need you to help with supper in a little bit."

Anna still hesitated. She wasn't sure how to begin. Her mother always remarked how proud she was of Anna and her accomplishments in school, 4-H, and the church youth group. *She will be so disappointed in me,* Anna thought to herself. *I really hate telling her. It's terribly embarrassing!*

"Anna? What's wrong? Is something the matter with you?"

Anna took a deep breath, placed her hand on her mother's arm, hanging her head as she softly let her words flow out of her mouth.

"Mom, I need to tell you something."

Dottie's smile faded as she lifted her daughter's face with her hand and saw the seriousness written on it. She was suddenly afraid to hear what her daughter would say next.

"Alright. Let's hear it. What do you need to tell me, Anna?"

Since Anna returned from her summer at the beach, Dottie had an intuition that her daughter had been hiding a secret, especially after she had had several upset stomach episodes and seemed to be gaining weight. At first, she believed it was because it was her senior year with a lot more pressure and work to complete. Dottie sighed and waited for Anna to continue.

"I'm not sure how to say this," Anna said, lowering her head again to avoid her mother's eyes.

"Did you let a boy have his way with you? Did you take things too far?" Dottie asked hoping for a negative response.

"I didn't mean to. I'm so sorry, mom. I told him I didn't want to, but it happened."

"Did he force himself on you?" She asked angrily. "Did he make you? Did he hold you down? Tell me what happened, Anna!"

Anna began to cry as she remembered back to that night. "I couldn't get away. He was on top of my dress. I didn't understand what was happening."

"What does that mean?" her mother quizzed. "You certainly knew it was wrong, Anna!" Dottie became angry by her daughter's answer. "How could you not understand? Your father is going to have a fit!"

"Please don't tell him! Mommy, please! I can't bear to think what he will say," Anna dropped to the floor begging her mother not to tell her father. She began sobbing as the fear of his wrath coming down on her welled up inside. Dottie dropped down beside her. She saw the fear in her eyes as she also understood how her husband would feel about this tragedy that had befallen them. He would not be easy on Anna, or her, for that matter. He would probably feel she had blame in this too since she was usually in charge of their daughters.

"You and I both know what he will say. He will say that you have shamed us. That is what he will say!" Dottie narrowed her eyes as she spoke the words that cut into the heart of her daughter. "How could you let this happen? You could have stopped him, couldn't you? Why, Anna Ruth? We won't be able to face our family or friends!"

"I know it was wrong, mom. I wish it didn't happen, believe me. It was not a pleasant experience, at all."

"I should hope not. Don't talk like that! Good girls don't behave this way! You know that!"

Dottie took off her apron and hung it on the hook inside the kitchen. "You haven't said who you were with. Was it some boy you met at the beach? Did you even know the boy?"

"All the boys we met at the beach were nice. We were just friends."

"So, which 'friend' did this to you?"

"None of them! It wasn't any of those nice boys, mom! It was Jimmy! My boyfriend, Jimmy! The one you think so highly of, and trust with your darling daughter. He's the one I couldn't get off of me one night when he came to visit. He's the one!" Anna shouted as she covered her face with her hands to hide her shame.

"Oh, my Lord! I can't believe he would do such a thing. I'm stunned."

"Imagine how I felt. I trusted him," Anna said wiping tears from her eyes.

"Wait! You went out on the beach alone with him? Weren't any other people around?"

"Yes, but they weren't very close to us."

"You should have been more careful. You needed to tell him not to take you to a secluded spot. The woman is always in charge, Anna. You should have said no to him!"

"I did," Anna began to cry again. "Really, I did! Please, believe me, mom!"

"Well, I'm afraid we have to talk to your father after supper tonight about this," Dottie stated as she walked away from her broken daughter bent over on the floor holding her hands to her face as her tears continued to flow. Her other children, who were in the living room playing had heard the raised voices and crying but didn't understand what had happened. They only knew to stay away and not say anything. They listened to their older sister as her deep cries subsided to a whimper. They also heard their mother whaling in her bedroom upstairs. They sensed something really bad had happened.

* * *

Ernie pulled away from the supper table and went into the living room to search for the "Progressive Farmer" magazine that arrived the previous day. He settled into his favorite chair and turned on the bright table lamp so he could enjoy reading the agricultural articles, personal stories, and jokes. He relaxed there with a full belly of Dottie's good cooking, his children playing board games on the floor of the room, the sound of soft country music playing on the radio, and his favorite magazine to entertain him; Ernie Scott was feeling quite good about his life that night.

In the kitchen, Dottie and Anna cleaned the dishes and put them away. The last of the day's work was finished. Dottie gave Anna a nod indicating that it was time to speak with her father. Anna took a seat at the kitchen table and waited.

"Girls!" Dottie called into the living room where they were playing. "Take Eddie upstairs with you and play your games in your rooms for a while." The young girls promptly gathered the pieces of their games, grabbed the hand of their brother and scurried up the stairs to their rooms. But, still curious as to what was going on, they didn't close the doors. Something was happening with Anna.

“Ernie, I need you to come in here for a bit. Do you want a cup of coffee?” Dottie asked as she poured them both a large cup of steamy black coffee from the tin coffee pot that sat warming on top of the stove. Ernie walked into the kitchen and sat down at the table across from Anna. Dottie set the hot coffee and a spoon on the table in front of him. There was silence as they both added a teaspoon of sugar and stirred. The clinking of the spoons against the cups unnerved Anna and she began to tremble. She looked at her mother and waited for her to speak.

Ernie looked back and forth at both of them and finally spoke up. “What’s going on here?” he asked.

“There’s no easy way to say this. Anna Ruth is in trouble. Not with the law or anything like that. Anna Ruth is carrying a baby,” Dottie blurted the words out quickly and then sat staring at the swirling coffee in her cup. Ernie paused to take in the words looking at Anna to determine if this could be true. She could not look back at him, however. He knew it must be true!

In his mind, he heard the words that his father had told him so many times “Too many girls! You have too many girls in this family! They will give you trouble! That’s what they do. Mark my words! One day you are going to have trouble with these girls!”

Ernie turned to his wife and said very matter-of-factly, “My father was right! I’m glad he is no longer alive to know about this.” He paused to think. He had to ponder what to do. “Who is the father?”

“Anna Ruth says that it’s Jimmy’s,” Dottie jumped in before her daughter could respond. Ernie turned to his wife with a frown.

"There's no question about that, is there? Has she bedded down with more than just Jimmy?" He asked in anger.

"No, just Jimmy! While they were at the beach,"

Dottie again spoke for her daughter as Anna sat silently with her eyes staring at the pattern of little blue and yellow pansies on the oil cloth covering the kitchen table. *Oh, how I wish I were back at the beach right now! I would step off the boardwalk, slide my feet to the edge of the water and keep on walking!* Anna thought as she tried to escape from the moment at hand.

"I knew that was a bad idea. Letting a 17-year-old go to the beach with her friends was not smart. We shouldn't have trusted her to behave away from home. We never should have let her go!" Ernie shook his head in disbelief.

"I see that you were right about that. I don't know why Jimmy was at the beach with her. Only bad things can happen when cheap girls invite boys to places where they aren't chaperoned, Anna Ruth!" Her mother chimed in taking her husband's side. "Just like that Copper girl who got herself in trouble. Remember her, Ernie? When we were kids? Alice Copper, that was her name. She was running around with several boys. Her parents had to leave our church and they haven't been back since. That was almost twenty years ago."

"Stop your blabbering, Dottie! Who cares about the Copper girl now! We have our own mess to deal with!"

Ernie looked directly at his daughter. "Damn! How could you bring this on our family? Damn it! We need to speak with that boy. Dottie, call Fred and Hazel to see if we can go over after church tomorrow to speak with them and have them make sure Jimmy is there too!"

Anna finally spoke. "Oh, Daddy, do we have to go?"

"Of course, we do. You think this is something that I want to bring up with our friends? Do you know how we are going to handle this? Obviously, you don't think, Anna Ruth! So, now I will have to make the decisions. Jimmy needs to marry you and make this right. It's the only way to avoid shame on you and our family," he said believing with certainty in his decision.

"Oh, my, the gossip! There will still be gossip, but it will go away eventually after you are married," Dottie added.

"What about school?" Anna questioned. "I need to finish school. It's my senior year."

"That's not happening. You can't finish. You won't be allowed to go while carrying a baby. Besides, once you are married, you will need to be at home, keeping house and caring for the child. You'll need to drop out soon. Once you start to show, the school board will not permit you to attend classes anyway."

Dottie's words were a smack of reality to Anna. Although Dottie knew this was upsetting to her daughter, she needed to tell her the truth of the matter. Anna Ruth would need to leave school by the end of October, even if she wore big sweaters and loose dresses.

"I'll miss out on all the games and dances, too? Oh, my gosh, what about my Senior Prom? I can't go back for any of it?" Anna asked as the reality of what dropping out of school would mean. "I'm really not going to graduate, am I?"

"No, you are not," Dottie confirmed. "You can't go back. You'll have missed too much time. Anna, you must drop out of school. There is no other way for you to finish."

"My life is over then! Nothing will ever be the same," Anna said while covering her face with her hands.

"Well, you only brought it on yourself!" Ernie barked at his daughter.

"I never meant for this to happen. I want to graduate and maybe go to secretarial school. There are lots of jobs available to girls who can type and take shorthand, or even dictation…"

"Be reasonable, Anna! That is not possible now. Don't you understand what you have done to yourself?" Dottie questioned in disbelief.

"Come here, girl!" Ernie yelled across the table to Anna. "I want you over here! Now!"

"Why, Daddy?"

"You know why! How could you do this to us?"

Anna got up and sheepishly walked toward her father on the other side of the table as Ernie scooted his chair back. When he could reach for her, he grabbed her by the arm and threw her across his lap.

"Do you think you are too old to spank? Well, you're not!" He took his right hand and came down hard on her buttocks. She began to cry out from the humiliation. That wasn't enough to satisfy his fury. He pulled his belt from his pants, just as Anna stood up, thinking he was finished. Through her blurry eyes, she saw her father stand up with the belt in his right hand and reach for her again. He let the belt fall across her backside, and then twice against her legs. Anna pulled back and turned from side to side trying to avoid the leather strap as it smacked against the upper part of her legs and her shoulders.

"No, Daddy, please! Daddy, don't! Daddy! It hurts so bad!"

"Ernie, stop! You're hurting her!" Dottie called out to her husband. She was horrified. She had never seen him so angry before. "Ernie, do you hear me? Stop it!"

"Ahhhhhhgg!" Anna screamed as she pulled away from her father's grip momentarily. This was not the first time her father had spanked her. They were common in her family, but Anna had never seen her father use a belt on any of the children up to this time. He grabbed at her again, but she escaped his grip and fell into the corner next to the large black stove and covered her face with her arms.

"Mom! Help me, Mom!" she screamed out.

Just then, Granddaddy Daffin ran through the door with Emmitt close behind him. He had come by to bring some sticky buns that Ethel made them and heard the screams coming from the house. Emmitt had been sitting on a stump outside his shack when he heard the commotion. He thought someone must be terribly hurt and also ran toward the house. The two met up in the driveway.

"Lordy, Mr. Daffin! Something bad is happening in the house."

"I hear it, Emmitt! Let's go see! I may need your help."

Granddaddy didn't like what he saw when he came through the door! Anna was huddled in the corner of the kitchen with Ernie standing over her, a black leather belt in his raised hand. Dottie had grabbed his arm and was trying to pull him back towards the kitchen chair. Both women were hysterical. Ernie was beet red in the face and out of breath.

"What's going on here? Ernie, give me that belt! What's wrong with you!" Granddaddy yelled.

"Are you alright, Dottie?" Then he saw Anna cowering in the corner. "Oh, my God! Anna! Oh, my Anna! Are you hurt?" He knelt down beside her and wiped her hair back. Then taking her by the shoulders he slowly brought her to his chest and held her close for several seconds while she continued to sob deeply. Dottie came closer and knelt down beside her father and started rubbing Anna's back. No words were spoken. Dottie was alarmed and terrified by her husband's reaction to the news. She hoped he had not hurt the baby that Anna carried.

Ernie sat down on a kitchen chair, with the belt still in his right hand, and hung his head in exhaustion.

"Emmitt, take Ernie's belt and put it in my car," Wilbur Daffin ordered. "You'll get that back when you know how to treat the women in your family," he said in anger to his son-in-law. Emmitt stepped over to Ernie and waited. He didn't take orders from Mr. Daffin but knew this was best for his employer and hoped he handed it over. Ernie did. Emmitt then walked out the back door dropping the belt off in Mr. Daffin's car as he headed home to his shack.

"You don't know what has happened! Anna needs to be taught a lesson," Ernie defended himself. "She got herself knocked up. How am I supposed to react? You would do the same!"

"Dad. Anna is carrying Jimmy Baker's child."

"Is that reason enough to beat her so viciously? She is a child! Doesn't Jimmy have any culpability in this?" Granddaddy asked coming to Anna's defense. "My God, Ernie! How could you?"

"What's done is done, I suppose. Now we have to figure out how to handle this mess. I'll give the Bakers a call now and see if we can talk to them tomorrow afternoon," Dottie walked over to the phone only to discover that someone from their party line was on it. "I'll have to wait a bit," she said.

"Anna, come here and sit at the table with me. Let me look at your injuries," Wilbur took Anna by her hands and pulled her up and out from the corner.

"Don't coddle the girl! She deserves a good whipping!"

"For what, Ernie? She hasn't done anything that you didn't do before you married Dottie. You think I don't know about that?"

"Dad! What are you saying? Stop it!"

"Don't act flustered now, Dottie! We were all young and seemingly in love once! We know what that means. Anna, unfortunately, through ignorance or heated untimeliness, didn't beat the odds."

"I have to get out of here. I can't handle any more of this!" Ernie rushed out of the house to his pickup truck. He sat in there for a few minutes and then took off down the lane, with a large trail of dust following him.

"Should I take Anna home with me tonight?"

"Thank you, Granddaddy, but I'll stay here. Daddy won't hurt me again, will he, Mom?" Anna turned to her mom for reassurance.

"No, certainly not. It's over. I'll make sure that he doesn't touch her again. We're fine, Dad," Dottie told her father. "I'll tuck Anna into bed. She'll be fine."

"You'll need to tuck in those creatures, too," said Granddaddy as he saw the other children on the stairway peeping around to look into the kitchen. "Come here, you snoopers!" They ran over and received a hug from their grandfather. "Miss Ethel made some sticky buns for you. Here! Have one before you go to bed," he encouraged them as he slid the plate of buns across the table.

Dottie pulled Anna's dress up to her buttocks to look at the marks left by the belt. There were a couple of spots with broken skin and several stripes of red that were certain to become bruises. Her right arm also suffered some abrasions when Anna covered her head as she cowered in the corner of the kitchen. Fortunately, there were no cuts to her face.

"Oh, I need to put some salve on these. Let me wash off the blood first," Dottie told Anna as she swallowed hard at the sight of the cuts. She tried not to show her shock as she grabbed a clean washcloth from the laundry basket.

"You will need to look at her back, too. I'll take off then. I'll stop back in the morning. You give me a call if you need me to come back over. Ya hear?"

"Thank you, Granddaddy," Anna wrapped her arm around his neck hugging him tightly.

"I'll take care of her, daddy. Thank you for being here. I don't know what I would have done without you here tonight," Dottie said feeling repulsed by her husband's behavior. She did not fear him, since she felt he believed he was justified in his punishment of their child. Dottie truly believed that discipline was given out of love and as a means of correcting bad behavior. It was what they had both been taught. Dottie struggled now to understand how the severe manner of punishment could correct behavior that could not be rescinded. It was too late.

Wilbur kissed both women on their cheeks and then walked out the door.

* * *

Later that evening, Dottie tried the phone again and was able to speak with Hazel Baker after the first ring. Her hands were shaking as she heard the familiar voice of her friend.

"Hello."

"Hazel? It's Dottie. Dottie Scott. How are you, dear?"

"I'm doing well, Dottie. My, it's been a while since I have talked with you! Is everything alright?"

"That's why I'm calling you. Ernie and I are hoping to stop by tomorrow afternoon and talk to you about the kids. Is that good for you?"

"Sure, we'll be home tomorrow. What's going on?"

"I would rather discuss this when we are all together. Can you make sure that Jimmy is there, too? Anna will come with us. I suppose we should come by around 2:00. We don't want to interfere with Sunday dinner."

"Okay, but I'm concerned, Dottie. Can't we talk now?"

"Ernie wants me to wait. We'll see you tomorrow, Hazel. Thanks!"

With the meeting confirmed and bag balm applied to her scrapes and cuts, Anna went to her bedroom for much-needed rest. She stood in front of her mirror, as she changed into her nightgown, looking at the medicine glistening on the marks on her body. At least her face was not bruised, though the same could not be said for her spirit. There was no medicine for that!

CHAPTER EIGHT

"Why are the Scotts coming over tomorrow?" Fred Baker asked his wife.

"Not sure, but Dottie said they want to talk with Jimmy, too."

"What for? That's strange. Jimmy!" Fred yelled upstairs for his son. "Get down here!"

Jimmy knew that tone in his father's voice and came on the double. He hurried down the steps meeting up with both parents when he reached the bottom.

"Do you mind telling us why the Scotts need to speak with us? What have you done?"

"Gee, what do you mean? How would I know?" he lied.

"Well, they want to talk with us about something that involves you and Anna. They said to make sure you would be available. It sounds serious."

"Is Anna in trouble, Jimmy?" Hazel came straight to the point. She knew her son was interested in sexual material and had had a curiosity about girls ever since she found girlie magazines hidden in the back of one of his dresser drawers. She felt that he could be sexually active if the girl he was with let him. *Wouldn't any man jump at the chance, especially at his age?*

"I don't know. I guess she might be," he said turning his head as he lied again.

"Have you talked to her about this? Has she told you anything? Come on, Jimmy! You're not telling me the truth!" his mother suspected.

"Jimmy! Stop being a little shit and tell us the truth! Did you knock up this girl, or not?"

"Okay! Anna said she is."

"And the baby is yours? Is that possible?"

"Sure. That's possible. She says it's my kid and I believe her."

Fred and Hazel, stunned by his words, now dreaded meeting with the Scotts who had once been their good friends. That was before Fred Baker went to work in the family lumber yard and started making the big bucks building new homes for the returning veterans. Jimmy's grandfather had owned the local lumber mill for years. After the war, there was a demand for more lumber and builders for developments springing up as GIs returned home. The business flourished during those years. The Bakers no longer had time to visit their friends, the Scotts, and before long, Fred and Hazel moved their family to a larger house on a riverfront farm. They also started to associate with a different group of friends, many being members of the country club who were employed as bankers, accountants, and lawyers with whom they had business.

In their younger days, the Bakers and the Scotts had played 'Rook' on many Saturday nights while their children played games in the living room. The game nights stopped after Fred bought the Wright Farm. He managed the 323-acre property, as well as the lumberyard. His hope was that one of his three sons would one day take over the farm operation. He doubted it would be Jimmy.

Fred Baker took Jimmy into his study so they could speak man to man. He wanted him to know that he had options for this situation. There were other families in town whose sons had gotten girls in trouble. Most of them were girls from the north side of town and could be handled with a payment of a few dollars. This was a different situation. Anna is the daughter of friends and comes from a good family. The gossip would be brutal.

"Jimmy, I want you to know that your mother and I will help you handle this little problem you've gotten yourself into. Now, Anna is a nice girl. You know we like her and her family, but you don't want to marry her. Do you, son?"

"Marry her? Hell, no!"

"Since we have an understanding of that, and it's a good thing, you need to realize that you have a bright future with the family business. You don't want to ruin that opportunity. You need to be smart now. I'm sure Ernie Scott will not accept a payment from me. That'll be insulting to him."

"Payment for what?" Jimmy questioned.

"To get rid of the baby, son. Don't you know anything about what's going on here?"

"Yeah, I've heard of girls doing that. I just don't think Anna would do it."

"You're probably right. I need to run it by Ernie though. I don't know how desperate they are to fix this. Any idea how many months she is?"

"I didn't ask her."

"Don't you remember when you were with her? How many times were you there, for God's sake? Boy, are you really that stupid?"

"Only one time with Anna. She wouldn't let me touch her any more after that."

"Figures. Look, when they arrive today, I think it's best if your mother and I handle this mess with the Scotts. We'll do the talking. I know how to manage Ernie. You just keep silent unless we speak to you, understand?"

* * *

Ernie and Dottie Scott sat together on the large, blue-flowered sofa in the Baker's living room. A white crocheted afghan hung over the back and matching white doilies covered the arms of the sofa protecting them from wear. Dottie noted that the Baker's farmhouse was filled with much nicer furniture and rugs than in the previous home they owned when the children were younger. They even had a television!

Anna sat in a chair next to the fireplace, not wanting to be near her father today. She was feeling sore and stiff from the beating the night before. The bag balm helped to soothe the broken skin and areas scraped by the belt, but she was still hurting both physically and mentally. Luckily the full skirt she had on last night softened some of the blow, but her legs had several marks that she hid with knee-high stockings that day. She was not speaking to her father and didn't dare to appear belligerent to him. She didn't want to give cause for him to light into her again. She believed the feelings would pass eventually. They always did.

"Afternoon, Ernie! Man, it's been a while since we've had you over. Good to see you both!" gushed Fred as he walked into the living room. Hazel followed him in carrying a tray with glasses full of lemonade.

"I don't think we've ever been to this house, Fred," Ernie stated.

"Here, everybody. Help yourselves to a nice cold glass of this lemonade. I just made it."

"Sorry to hear about your father's passing, Ernie. How is your mom doing? She is such a sweet lady," Fred asked Ernie.

"She's decided to move to North Carolina with my sister and her family. They have plenty of room for her. She wants to sell her house, so I don't know if she'll ever move back."

They all took a sip of lemonade feeling a moment of awkward silence and unsure how to broach the subject at hand.

"I believe Hazel and I understand why you wanted to meet with us," Fred began.

Ernie nodded. "Good. Then we all understand the terrible position we're in."

"Jimmy says Anna believes the child is his," Hazel added.

"Of course, it is! Jimmy, you know it is! What are you saying?" Anna jumped up, taking offense at the innuendo.

"Anna, sit down! Let the adults speak," her mother reprimanded her, and then, turning to Hazel, stated, "Yes, Anna says it happened while she was at Rehoboth Beach."

"How could that be? Maybe it was another boy? Jimmy wasn't there. Jimmy, you never went to Rehoboth, did you?" his mother asked.

"Yeah, I went a couple of times," he responded. Looking at Anna give him the evil eye, he corrected himself. "Three times, actually."

"You know what they say - boys will be boys! Well, Anna must have asked him to come see her at the beach. Jimmy didn't have any reason to go if Anna didn't want him to visit her. Is that what you did, Anna?"

Anna hesitated to answer him in the hope that Jimmy would respond instead. He didn't. "We both talked about spending time at the beach before I left."

"If you encouraged him to come, any boy would jump at that chance! No doubt about it!" Fred sniggered. "I think we know who was making plans. Not that Jimmy didn't go along with it, as I said."

"I'd say he was more of the driving force, Fred. He's the one with a car to go to her," Dottie jumped in.

"Oh, Dottie, you know how young girls can be. Teenagers today are not like when we were kids! Some girls are so forward!"

"Hazel, you know our Anna is not like that!"

"There are several girls in this senior class that would like to trap Jimmy. We have warned him about that. Anna, is that what you thought?" Hazel questioned an embarrassed Anna. "A lot of girls think that way."

"What? No, I, I never…" Anna stuttered.

"Dear, you know that Jimmy has a bright future. He will be taking over the family business one day. But it will be quite a while before he is ready for a family," Hazel admonished Anna.

"We think the kids should get married as soon as possible. That is the best way to prevent a scandal," Dottie jumped into the conversation to avoid further chastisement of her daughter. "Anna is not solely responsible for this situation."

"They both have responsibility for what has happened. Certainly, Fred, you agree that they are equally at fault here!" added Ernie.

"We disagree," said Fred sternly. "They are just kids – too immature to take on the responsibility of marriage."

"How old were you and Hazel when you got married, Fred? You two were barely 18. It seems, looking around here, that you have done okay for yourselves," asked Ernie, upset with Fred's response.

"Things were different for us back then. We were stronger and learned to scrape by. We had the depression going on. Kids today are not as mature as we were."

"I want to join the Army next year," Jimmy interjected.

"What? Jimmy?" Anna shot him a quizzical look. *When did he decide to go into the service*, she wondered. *He told me he wouldn't like all the rules and regulations of the service, especially having to get up early.*

"I told you all that I was thinking about joining after graduation. Remember?"

"No, this is news to me! You should finish school first, but if there is any gossip, Jimmy could go into the Army, if he wants. Right, Jimmy?" Hazel asked her son.

"I know you are concerned for Jimmy's future, but what about Anna? What about this baby?" Dottie filled with tears. "She can't finish school now."

"You know, there are homes for girls like Anna. I can find out where there might be one to take her in. I'd be willing to help out on the cost of that, Ernie." Fred said. "I'm not sure how much these places cost but there must be some charge. Let me look into that for you."

"Fred knows one of the fathers at Rotary who had a daughter get in trouble. He said that she went to a place in Delaware. Fred can get more information from him. A lot of wayward girls go there apparently," Hazel stated as she turned to address Anna.

A wayward girl! Is that what I am? This was not just my fault! Doesn't anyone understand that? Anna sat silently listening to the decisions being made for her life. She felt that feeling of wanting to run away again. *Where can I hide away? I have nothing. I am totally dependent upon my father. There is no way out on my own,* she thought.

"Let me talk to this guy for you, Ernie. I can help you pay for it, too."

"No, Fred." Ernie replied. "We are clearly on our own with this mess. I don't need your money."

"I didn't mean to insult you, Ernie."

"Yeah, I think you did. As a matter of fact, I feel that you and Hazel have tried to make us feel inferior to you since we arrived. I think we better leave before I say something I may not regret."

Ernie took Dottie's hand and pulled her up. He motioned for Anna to walk out ahead of them.

Anna passed in front of Jimmy as she left the room. Not a look or word passed between them. *What a jerk!* Anna thought. *How could I have ever loved him?* No one walked Ernie and Dottie to the door, so they let themselves out without further conversation. The Bakers were stunned by their behavior towards them, believing they had done more than what was appropriate under these circumstances. *What did they really expect them to do about their promiscuous daughter's problem*, thought Hazel to herself.

All the while it was perfectly obvious to Ernie and Dottie that their former friends felt their son bore no responsibility. They realized that they were on their own in handling the situation. Anna understood that she was to allow her parents to make the decisions that were appropriate for her life and try to salvage her reputation.

* * *

The following Tuesday, Dottie stared out the window of their Pontiac, watching the rows of raggedly clipped stalks go by in the freshly picked cornfields as her husband drove into town. It was their marketing day. They had stops at their bank, insurance company and the A & P for a few groceries.

Noticeably, there was no traffic coming from the opposite direction and then traffic on the main road came to a complete halt.

"What's going on?" Dottie asked sitting up on the bench seat trying to look at the side of the road ahead. There were about a dozen cars and pickup trucks in front of them. An ambulance and a police car arrived almost at the same time.

"This is not good. I'm going to see if I can help," Ernie said as he stepped out of the car and looked down the road. "It appears that a milk truck has overturned. Someone may be trapped."

"And look, there is milk flowing into the ditch!" Dottie observed. "What a loss! All that milk! He must have been loaded."

"I see it's all over the road too!" Ernie added. "I hope it's not our milk truck driver."

Dottie watched as Ernie and a few other men carried a person covered by a bloody, white sheet in a makeshift gurney across the road to an awaiting ambulance. A deputy arrived to direct traffic after the ambulance crew left and a wrecker pulled up. It would still be a while to clean up the mess and get the milk truck loaded onto the wrecker. Ernie trotted back to his car before the traffic started to move.

"You look upset. Is the driver dead?"

"Oh, my Lord, Dottie, it's Roy Walbert! I don't believe it," Ernie said shaking his head. "Looks like he tried to avoid a deer crossing the road, maybe more than one, and he swerved to avoid it. He hit the deer. It's stuck in his windshield! Almost came completely through! I've never seen anything like it!"

Dottie drew a deep breath thinking of the horror.

"The front end of the truck ran into the ditch and turned over. He was all cut up. Slammed his head against the side window. There's glass everywhere. God, what a horrible sight. I'm sorry I went up there."

"Oh, goodness, have mercy! Poor Ethel! What will Ethel do without Roy?"

Their lane of traffic began to move. They sat in silence the rest of the way contemplating what they could possibly do to help their friend and neighbor, Ethel Walbert. Her life would never be the same.

CHAPTER NINE

"I took Ethel some chicken salad and biscuits last week. She said she hadn't had much of an appetite. I hope she doesn't waste away," Dottie told her father as they sipped coffee and ate a slice of fresh apple cake she had made that morning.

"I think she will be alright eventually. It's only natural that she should need time to mourn the loss of her husband."

"Well, I hope you have been looking in on her. Is she back to help with Mother yet?"

"She needs a few days to deal with legal matters concerning his estate and the farm. I was hoping that since Anna will be leaving school this week maybe she could sit with your mother for the days that I have painting jobs lined up."

"I'm sure she can. That will give her something to do away from here. She and Ernie are still not speaking. The time away will do her good."

"I am also looking into a place in Wilmington for her. Your Aunt Victoria knows a house there that takes in girls in Anna's situation. Let me get more information on it and we'll talk. Okay?"

"Yes, that's wonderful, daddy. Thank you!" Dottie responded with appreciation.

She was grateful that her father had taken on the responsibility of discretely managing Anna's delicate situation. Ernie had all but abandoned any obligation where Anna was concerned. He and Dottie had not discussed anything further in regard to their oldest daughter since the night he lost his temper. Dottie knew decisions must be made quickly, as each day inched closer to exposure of her pregnancy. Yet, she feared upsetting her husband further. Their marriage had already become strained by Dottie's failure to support Ernie's actions that night. Feeling torn, she turned to her lifesaver and confidant – her father.

* * *

"It's called Bassett House. It's run by a charitable organization. They help the girls through the pregnancy and delivery, and then place the babies with a good home. They have been a huge success here," Victoria informed her brother.

"Thanks, Victoria! Now one more favor. Anna and Ernie are not getting along. Do you think she could stay with you for a couple of months until the home has a space for her?"

"Absolutely! Oh, I'd love that! I can look in on her while she is at Bassett House, too."

Victoria was Wilbur Daffin's youngest sister. She had left home after school and pursued a career in fashion merchandising. Never married, never interested. Victoria had done well on her own and achieved a reputation for not only being dedicated to the fashion industry but also for having an intuition on styles that would sell in the next season.

Victoria owned her own apartment in Wilmington, Delaware which she had furnished and decorated herself. This activity was foreign to her family, but a familiar topic of conversation among her circle of friends and colleagues. She owned a car that she drove when out alone, having obtained a driver's license a few years back, while most women did neither. She was pleased with her savings account. She ate out often, with or without friends. Her brother was her closest relative and the one who seemed to understand her best. Her sisters were scornful of her lack of interest in having her own husband and children. She knew she could not have everything, so she chose to do what made her happiest.

* * *

So, it was decided. Anna would stay with her grandparents and care for her grandmother until she left for Wilmington in November, and then she would stay at Victoria's home until she could get into Bassett House.

Anna didn't tell anyone that she had left school for good. Her friends hadn't seen much of her lately and knew she had been sick. Betty and Kay called the house asking for her but were only told that Anna had to help out with her sick aunt for a while and no one knew when she would be back to school. Both girls had new boyfriends and were active in the student council as they began their senior year. They felt bad that their friend was missing out on the fun and hoped she could return soon to join them.

The days dragged on and Anna's belly started to show. Anna was told not to go outside while she attended her grandmother for fear that a neighbor or one of her friends would see her and ask questions. She had cared for her grandmother many times over the years, but not for this length of time, nor as a shut-in herself. Anna fed, bathed, and dressed Margaret Daffin daily. She cleaned the house and made supper for her granddaddy. Most of her time was spent watching the television in her grandmother's bedroom or reading to her. There wasn't much communication between them, but Anna had learned to read her expressions. Margaret had a close relationship with her granddaughter before the stroke, spending many days together while Dottie dealt with her other daughters as they were born.

Anna missed those days. She missed the silly laughter and the warm hugs. Oh, how she would love one of those hugs now!

An oil delivery truck pulled into the oyster shell driveway and a tall, thin young man dressed in white coveralls and cap descended from the cab, as he put on leather work gloves. Anna watched him pump oil into a large, silver tank behind the kitchen wondering if he would expect payment. Once finished pumping, the man returned the hose and walked towards the side door screened porch of the house. He knocked on the door and Anna panicked when she heard the sound. *What should I do*, she thought hiding in the dining room but seeing him through the lace-curtained window. He knocked again a little harder this time. Anna opened the kitchen door slowly and then took a couple of steps onto the porch, careful not to get too close to the screened door.

"Hi, I delivered the oil Mr. Daffin ordered. Do you want to pay now?" He asked smiling. Newly trained in the business, he had been told that a friendly face was good customer service.

"I'm sorry, but my grandfather didn't leave me a check for you."

"Actually, I am here a day early. He probably wasn't expecting me to deliver this soon."

"Can he send you payment?"

"Sure. May I come in for a minute? I'll write it up and leave the bill."

Anna hesitated.

"I need a hard surface to write on. It won't take long," He explained.

Anna stepped forward and opened the door slightly. The young man felt her hesitation, taking the handle of the door, but not stepping inside.

"Is it alright if I come in? I won't take long, I promise."

Anna opened the door wider and let him in.

"You can use the kitchen table if you want."

"Thank you. Route 3, Box 160, right?" He confirmed.

"Yes. That's it."

"Do you live here?"

"No, I'm taking care of my grandmother for a while. I actually live down the road a bit."

"Okay. I'm just learning who my customers are. I've only been doing this job a couple of weeks. You didn't go to Greenville High, did you? I don't remember you."

"No, I go, I mean went, to Edentown High."

"Our rivals!" He chuckled. "Just kidding. I don't consider you an enemy or anything!"

Anna enjoyed his company. He was the first friendly face she had seen in a few weeks. No judgment from him!

"What's your name? I like to know my customers' names."

"Anna. My family calls me Anna Ruth. And yours?" She asked, starting to feel more comfortable around him.

"Buddy. Buddy Merchant."

"That's a nickname, right?"

"Yep! Here you go," he said handing her the invoice. "I'll just leave this for Mr. Daffin. He can mail a check or stop by the office to pay. I'd like to talk a while longer, but I have other deliveries today. Maybe I'll see you next time I have a delivery on this road."

"Maybe. I don't know how much longer I will be staying here."

"Okay." He said feeling she may be brushing him off.

"I'll bet you'll have a delivery at our farm one day though. You might see me then. It's the white house with black shutters and whitewashed fencing along the lane, just down this road about a mile or so."

"I'll make sure that I handle your delivery. It's been good to meet you, Anna Ruth!"

"My friends just call me Anna."

"In that case, it's been very nice to meet you, Anna!" He gave her a big grin as he walked out the door back to his truck. For a brief time period, she felt alive and normal again. Her loneliness and depression were lifted as she felt someone was interested in her.

Anna's relationship with her parents had been strained since the night her father had used his belt on her. She hadn't spoken but a few words to either of them for several days and was relieved when Granddaddy asked her to stay with him after Roy Walbert's death. Feeling demoralized and fearful of invoking another incident of rage from her father, a downtrodden Anna escaped the hostilities in her home by caring for her grandmother. She felt that her parents would never trust her again. They were ashamed of Anna. It would be devastating to the family if her predicament was discovered. Since it was impossible to change her situation, every effort was made to hide it.

* * *

By the 12th of November, Ethel returned to the Daffin home to care for Margaret. Anna was no longer needed so she returned home that morning and began packing a bag for her trip to her Aunt Victoria's home. All the children were in school, except for Eddie. Wilbur Daffin waited in the kitchen with

Dottie as Eddie sat on his knee holding onto his favorite toy, a stuffed, gray sock monkey named Zippy.

"Isn't Ernie going to see her off? He knows she's leaving now, doesn't he?" Wilbur asked his daughter with disappointment in his voice. He respected his son-in-law's right to discipline his children but felt he had taken it too far by using his heavy, leather belt on Anna. Ernie was a good man, decent and kind, but the anger and disappointment of his oldest daughter overwhelmed him. He reacted irrationally. Wilbur knew Dottie was grateful to her father for intervening in protecting Anna. She didn't have the strength, and her words fell on Ernie's deaf ears that night.

"Here she comes. All packed? Do you have everything you need?" Dottie asked. Anna carried the same suitcase she had taken to Rehoboth a few months ago. She only had four outfits and a couple of nightgowns that she felt she could continue to wear for a while. Dottie gave her a couple of well-worn maternity tops and skirts she found in the attic; not that they would fit Anna, but maybe she could cut them down to her size.

"Alright, then, we better get going. I have your ticket for the 12:45 bus, and we still have a half-hour drive," Wilbur said, grabbing Anna's suitcase to carry to his car.

Anna gave her mother a hug and Dottie kissed her cheek. She choked up so badly that she could barely squeak out the words 'take care' to her daughter.

Anna then hugged Eddie and Zippy as he protested and walked out the side door to her granddaddy's car. Just as she opened the car door, she saw Emmitt wave to her from the open barn door, and she waved back. Turning to get in, her eye caught movement in the backyard as her father came walking at a brisk pace, so fast that Anna was startled and a little afraid.

"Here is some money for your bus ticket or if you need a little cash."

"I still have my summer money, daddy. I can buy my own ticket," Anna replied.

"Then, you might need it for something else while you're up north," Ernie replied feeling awkward and useless. He gave Anna's right arm a tight squeeze, turned his head toward his father-in-law giving a nod of appreciation, and then walked on toward the barn without looking back.

Anna stood still for a few seconds watching her father's back. She had wanted him to hold her as he once had. She needed him to tell her everything would be alright, and she would be welcome to come home, but instead, she felt empty. Her father's behavior indicated that her life would never be the same. How could it be? He was unable to forgive her.

CHAPTER TEN

Wilbur stayed with Anna at the bus station in Delaware until she boarded the silver and blue coach and he saw her seated. It wasn't her first time on a travel bus to Wilmington, but it was her first time alone. Two hours away, Anna thought she could take a nap or get lost in her thoughts for a while, but a heavyset woman with a bad smell and terrible teeth sat next to her making sure that didn't happen. The fifty-something woman with long, graying hair, partially held back with two large black barrettes, was spilling out her life story to everyone around her, causing great discomfort to the passengers. She wore a faded blue dress with yellow daisies that was stained down the front by coffee, gravy, or some other dark matter. The stench that exuded from the woman's body was unbearable. Anna kept her face close to the corner of the bus window. Although she hadn't had morning sickness in a while, she started to feel sick. *How can anyone talk that much*, Anna wondered, and continued to count the minutes until arrival in Wilmington.

Aunt Victoria was waiting for her just as she said she would. Her bubbly personality was in full display that day.

"I'm so excited to have you visit me, Anna! It's been too long. I know how we always get too busy. We say we are going to visit and then something comes up and we don't get around to it."

She helped Anna to her car and deposited her suitcase in the trunk.

"Is this your car, Aunt Victoria? Do you drive it?" Anna didn't know many women who drove cars. She could probably name all of them on one hand.

"Sure, I do! I have to get around, you know. How am I going to do that when I don't have a husband? Can't wait for one either!" She laughed. "Sometimes we girls just have to figure it out for ourselves!" Anna loved her aunt's uniqueness. No wonder she moved away from Edentown!

"Are you up for dinner out tonight? If you are too tired, I can make something for us, but you may not like it. I'm no cook. I'll admit it."

"I'm not too tired," replied Anna, who was anxious to go out and be with people after sheltering out of sight the last few weeks. "I don't know if I have the right clothes though. You see, most of my skirts are getting too tight in the waist."

"I thought about that, and I have a few sample dresses that I kept just for you. They are full in the waistline. A style that returned last year called a jumper. It used to be popular in the 1920s, too. I hope you like them."

"You think of everything! Thank you! And thank you for being so nice to me," She said almost in a whisper. "You act like you don't know that I'm carrying a baby. You do know that, right?"

"Anna, of course I do. But why should I treat you any differently? I am happy to have you here no matter what."

Once Anna settled her belongings into the spare room at the apartment, Victoria took Anna's hand and told her to have a seat next to her on her large burgundy velvet sofa. Anna ran her hand over the soft, rolled arms and down to the wooden scrolls admiring the intricate work. She looked around the room at original artwork, a crystal vase filled with an artificial flower arrangement, an oak curio cabinet filled with figurines collected during her travels, and a television with the largest screen she had ever seen. The apartment reminded Anna of the kind of place seen in movies. She loved it but felt uncomfortable at the same time.

"Your home is amazing, Aunt Victoria!"

"Why thank you, Anna! I hope you will make yourself at home while you are here."

"Everything is so beautiful and well-organized. It seems that all your things have a certain place. I would be afraid to touch any of it."

"I have accumulated a lot of pretty trinkets, dust collectors, all of it! Sure doesn't beat having a family to come home to at night, you know."

"But you are so successful. I always thought you liked your job."

"Oh, honey, I do. I love it very much! I have been able to travel and experience so much of this world. It's been truly wonderful most of the time. It is the life that I never expected to have, but fortune has been kind."

"It's a divine life. Simply marvelous. I can only dream of being so successful as you!"

"Look. I'm going to tell you something about me. You'll see that my life is not so perfect. Things happen to all of us that can't be helped."

"What do you mean?"

"My parents, your great grandfather and great grandmother, who both died when you were young, had eight of us children. Did you know that?"

"I think I have heard that from granddaddy," Anna looked pensive, remembering back.

"Well, yes, they had eight children and then decided that they couldn't get along. My father was Catholic, and my mother was Methodist, so divorce was out of the question. They decided to live apart. My mother stayed on the farm and lived with all of us children, while my father moved into a boarding house in town. He didn't work the farm daily and needed to get a day job to support himself and us. I don't think he was a very good farmer anyway. My mother couldn't handle it by herself, so they hired a man who knew how to run things. I was fifteen at the time. The man was in his late forties, I believe. Anyway, one day I was cleaning some buckets we had scraps in for the hogs, and this man tells me he needs my help. I didn't know any better, so I did as I was told and followed him into the loft of the barn. My mother had gone to visit a neighbor for a couple of hours and the other children had gone with her. It was just me and this hired man on the farm that day. Once I climbed the ladder and looked around in the hay loft, I wondered what he could possibly need me to help him do. Nothing was obvious. And he had moved around to block me from going back down the ladder. He stood there with a smirk on his face, and I still didn't understand what he wanted. I was so naïve! He came at me so quickly, Anna, and he tried to kiss me. He was pulling at my shirt, trying to unbutton me, and holding my wrists. I was so startled by him, and he was strong. I tried to fight back, but he had huge muscles that pinned me down and I couldn't do anything to protect myself. I screamed out, but he knew there was no one to hear me from the loft. He raped me, Anna! He was rough and forceful. I was bruised and sore from…from his handling of me. And then he left me. I lay there on top of the straw, in pain, in the hot loft with no one to help me."

"Oh, my gosh! I understand. Were you okay?"

"No. No, I wasn't," She hesitated a moment and then asked, "Were you, Anna?"

Victoria suspected that Anna had not been honest about what happened to her and that even now it was difficult for her to admit the circumstances. She was sure that Anna didn't feel that anyone would believe her. Lowering her head, Anna remained silent. Victoria continued her story hoping it would help Anna finally open up.

"I didn't tell anyone. But I made sure that the hired man never had an opportunity to get me alone again. He stole some money from my mother a month later and she sent him packing. It was a relief for me, until I discovered that I must be carrying his child. I knew a few things about pregnancy from hearing some older girls discussing it. I was afraid and determined that I wasn't going to have that man's child. I wasn't going to let him ruin me. I had heard about a girl who used a knitting needle to get rid of a baby. She died from an infection. I was too afraid to try that. So, I started throwing myself against the bags of cow feed that were piled up in the granary. I was bruised so badly that I could barely walk. My mother was busy canning and didn't notice that I was limping. I was afraid she would say something, and I didn't know how I would explain it to her. After trying that for a couple of weeks, I decided to try steaming hot baths in water as hot as I could possibly stand."

"It must have been so horrible for you! Couldn't you ask someone for help?"

"Who could I ask, Anna? This was something I had to figure out on my own! And I was getting desperate. Late on a Friday afternoon, I took one of the geldings out for a ride; astride, not side saddle. I let him canter for a while and then took him to a full gallop through our back field near a large ditch. As I came closer to the side of the widest part of the ditch, I closed my eyes, pulled the reins back while my horse reared up on his hind legs throwing me off at the edge. I hit on my side and tumbled down into the ravine. I came to a stop in about a foot of water and lay there. The horse stayed and eventually I worked my way up the side and got back on. As before, I expected instant satisfaction. That is not how it happened though."

"Did that make you lose the baby? You're lucky you weren't killed in the fall!"

"At that point, I really didn't care. Later that night I woke up to serious pains in my lower stomach. Not wanting my mother to know anything, I went to a shed where we stored tools, milk cans, and some old horse blankets. I laid the filthy blankets on the dirt floor. And then the pains became worse, and I got on my knees… Oh, Anna! It was terrible! I can't tell you how I cried when it was over. I never want to suffer through that pain again or lose a precious human being in such a way. I caused that baby to die, Anna. I have to live with that for the rest of my life. I still ask myself what kind of person I am to do that."

"Aunt Victoria! It must have been dreadful! I can't imagine the horror of it all!"

"It was just unbelievably gruesome! It made me sick. I literally vomited at the sight! I can't think about it anymore just now."

"You don't have to say anymore. No need to explain. I think I understand. You didn't feel like you had a choice, I suppose," Anna responded. "Did you ever tell anyone what happened?"

"No, you have to remember that this happened forty years ago, Anna. Our family was already looked down on because my father didn't live with us. Some parents wouldn't let their children come over to visit or play at our house. Can you imagine what would happen if gossip got around about an unwed daughter in the house with a child?"

"That type of gossip hasn't changed in the last forty years! My father is very fearful of rumors over the scandal I have caused. It has devastated him! And I feel terrible. I haven't had anyone to talk to about it either. I understand what you mean. I think I know how difficult that was for you."

"Now, back then, Wilbur, your grandfather, may have known something, but he has never spoken to me about it."

"What makes you think that?"

"I went back to the shed the day after I lost the baby. There was a lot of blood and vomit on the rolled-up horse blankets, and I needed to get rid of them before someone found them and questioned what had happened. Wilbur came in the shed as I finished stuffing the blankets up in an old burlap feed bag. He didn't say anything, at first. He never even asked what I was doing with the blankets. Wilbur just stood in the doorway watching me finish filling that bag. When I had it tied off, he said that he needed to burn some trash and he could take the bag and burn it in the oil drum trash can with the other garbage. I handed it to him and that was the last we spoke of it."

"To this day?"

"Yes, to this day. Never once. But I've always sensed that he suspected what happened. I felt that if I didn't talk about it, it didn't actually happen. Does that sound strange?"

"No, I see what you mean. Am I the first person you've told?"

"Oh, no! I had a close friend a number of years ago who confided in me that she had been raped by a neighbor boy when she was young. She didn't get pregnant, but she suffered many of the same fears I had. Her confidence in telling me her story gave me the strength to tell her mine. We are still close and talk on the phone often. She married a widowed veterinarian about eleven years ago and moved with him to Indiana."

"You must miss her. How nice that she found love after all those years," Anna said softly feeling sorry that her aunt had not been so fortunate.

"Of course, I wish she lived closer, but I am so very happy for her. I also grew up wanting a husband and children, a nice home in town to raise a family, but that afternoon in the loft changed everything for me. I found out years later from my doctor that I couldn't have children. I figured then that no man wants a wife who can't give him children." Victoria said sadly. "So, I became a working woman who can do whatever she wants with no man to tell her what to do! Everything I have, I've earned by myself."

"Aunt Victoria, I know I said I wanted to go out tonight for dinner, but can we do that tomorrow night? I think I would like to stay in, after all."

"Of course. We can eat out tomorrow night when everyone is out on the town. How about a grilled cheese sandwich, then? I know how to make that."

"I do too. Let's make them together."

* * *

The following week, Victoria took Anna to the well-known and highly regarded Winkler's Restaurant, located in downtown Wilmington, to celebrate Thanksgiving. They served up a traditional meal of turkey with oyster stuffing along with spectacular desserts. After filling themselves, they decided it best to take a stroll through a small local park to walk off a few pounds.

"Thank you so much for taking me to such a fine restaurant, Aunt Victoria. I've never been to a place that nice. Actually, I don't even know where to find a good restaurant where we live!"

"But certainly your mother is serving up a huge meal today, right?"

"Oh, of course. Turkey and ham, for sure. She always makes a lot of side dishes, too. No one ever leaves hungry from my mom's table!"

"I remember! I have always admired her ability to cook so well. She knows just what she is doing, never needs a recipe, and times it all perfectly. She's great!"

"Yeah, I never really thought about it. She makes it seem so easy."

"I can barely boil water, Anna! You should learn what you can from her."

Shortly after returning to the apartment, Victoria heard the doorbell ring. She opened the door to see a tall young man in a gray overcoat.

"Hello, ma'am. I am looking for Anna Scott. I heard she is staying with you. I'm Jimmy Baker, her boyfriend."

"Oh, my! Please come in," Victoria said opening the door wider for him as he removed his hat.

Anna walked into the living room at that time stopping to be sure she wasn't hallucinating. *Why is he here, she wondered.* She froze in place not sure what to do next.

"Jimmy? What are you doing here? How did you find me?"

"Janet told me you were up here. She gave me your aunt's name and I found her in the phone book. I have to see you, Anna."

"Do you two want to sit down in the living room? I can get some sodas for you if you'd like," Victoria offered.

"I don't think Jimmy will be here very long, Aunt Victoria. Please don't go to the bother. It's better if we go downstairs and sit on the bench in front of the building."

"You don't have to leave," Victoria said with suspicion.

"I don't want us to interfere with your plans. It will be fine downstairs."

"Alright then. Take your coat and hat. You know, it is getting colder out," Victoria said, helping Anna slip her arms into her coat sleeves. Anna darted out the door as Jimmy trailed behind her.

Once they settled on the large wooden seat, Jimmy tried to hold Anna's hand. She pulled back in anger. He didn't think she would be disinterested in him touching her.

"What? You won't let me hold your hand now? After I came all this way to see you."

"And just what are you doing here, Jimmy? I know you didn't come to propose to me. You and your family have made it very clear that we will never be married. Why are you here?"

"I needed to see you. I've missed you."

"You haven't called or written to me since that humiliating day at your house. You and your parents made me feel like trash! You didn't stick up for me at all. You just let them put the blame on me for my condition. Why? Why did you do that, Jimmy?"

"You saw how my parents are. They wouldn't let me talk. They wanted to handle everything."

"Right. I'm sure they did. They need to protect their precious reputations."

"Believe me, they feel really bad about all of this. They've been pressuring me to leave the area for a while. I think they are afraid I will let the cat out of the bag or something. They know a lot of the kids are asking questions about you. A lot of them want to know if I have heard from you. Honestly, I'm tired of lying to our friends about where you are."

"You didn't say anything about me to anyone, did you?"

"No, I said you left to help out your aunt. That's it," he confirmed. Anna gave a soft sigh of relief.

"I hope they believe you." She waited to see if there was more, but Jimmy changed the subject.

"So, I have decided to go into the Army. I think it's time to do something different with my life."

"The Army? Really? I never figured you would go into the service. When do you leave?"

"Well, I'm not eighteen until January 8, but they are going to take me a little early. I'm leaving for boot camp next week. I wanted to let you know."

"Why me? Do you think that will make some difference?" Anna asked still not understanding the reason for his visit. "Are you here to ask me something, Jimmy? I don't understand."

"It's just that I've been thinking about things. About us, and you carrying my baby and all. You are wrong, you know. I wanted to ask you to marry me, but my dad said I shouldn't. He told me I would ruin my life if I got married now. I'm so confused. I don't think I can do it." He said, not making sense. "I never said I loved you. I've never told any girl that I love her."

"What can't you do? Are you talking about marriage or going into the Army? That's a pretty big step in your life, too!"

"I don't know. I can't think straight. I'm not sure what to do. I don't think I'm in love though, Anna. I can't see being tied down to you and a kid forever."

"I'm so stupid! I thought that you did love me, Jimmy. Even though you never said it, I truly believed that you cared for me, for a time."

"A guy should love the girl he is going to marry, right? You understand that don't you?"

"Jimmy, have you been drinking?"

"Nope," he lied, and she knew it.

"This is pointless. You have no idea how bad it has been for me. My dad beat me with his belt. He can't even look me in the eye, he's so ashamed of me."

"That's why I'm gettin' out of town, man. Everyone judges you and I'm not goin' to be talked about behind my back. I want to get away from everything and see the world and do something besides farming and working at the lumberyard. That's why I enlisted. I'm getting away from it all. And once little Jimmy is given up for adoption, you should too."

"Where will I go? I have no money. At least you have a car."

"Not for long. Because of all of this, my grandfather is giving the car to my brother now. But that's alright. I'll get another one before too long." He reached into his coat pocket and pulled out an envelope. "I almost forgot. My dad wants you to have this. Don't open it now."

"I don't need anything from your family. You can take it back to him.

"Awww. Come on, Anna! Please just take it, so I don't have to put up with his bullshit over this, too!" Jimmy said pushing the envelope into her hand.

Although apprehensive, she kept it.

"So, you leave next week? Should I let you know when the baby arrives?"

"No, don't bother. I don't want to know anything. Besides, I'm sure I'll be really busy with training. I hear they are pretty tough on us."

"I understand. Then, I wish you good luck," Anna stood up to let Jimmy know that she was finished talking with him.

"May I have a kiss to send me off?" Jimmy asked, as he rose up next to her.

"You had your kiss!" Anna blurted out as she turned and walked back into the apartment building. The large wooden door in the lobby closed behind her. Pressing her back against the carved panels, she waited just a bit to make sure he did not follow her inside. She was done with him! Satisfied with herself that she no longer needed him in her life, Anna went upstairs into the apartment and locked the door shutting Jimmy out of her life for good.

CHAPTER ELEVEN

The call came on December 6. The admissions director from Bassett House advised that they had a room available for Anna and she was expected the following morning. Anna spent one last night in Victoria's apartment. The two women washed and packed all of Anna's belongings in her suitcase which was now brimming over with the additional clothes that her aunt had given her.

"How about taking these fashion magazines so you have something to do at night? And feel free to borrow any of my books from the living room shelf."

"I don't know how much free time I will have, but I'll take the magazines just in case I'm bored. Thank you, Aunt Victoria. And not just for the magazines, you know. I thank you for everything - the clothes, eating out, entertaining me, and most of all, thank you for understanding my situation. You have been wonderful to me, and I am so happy that I spent this time with you instead of back home. I'm ready to face tomorrow now. I can do this!"

"Of course, you can! You are going to be fine. You are young and strong enough to pull through and then put all of this behind you. And I will always be here to help or listen when you need me."

The next morning, Anna sat at her aunt's kitchen table trying to sip a cup of coffee and eat a slice of buttered toast. Her stomach was so upset that she felt like throwing up. She had bathed and dressed for the day in a navy blue jumper and white blouse that Victoria had given her. It was one of three outfits she brought back for Anna from a recent buying trip in New York.

"Oh, Anna! That jumper is just adorable on you! How does it feel? Roomy enough?" Victoria asked as she stepped into the kitchen and saw Anna scrape half of the toast off her plate.

"Not hungry?"

"My stomach is in knots. I'm really nervous about going today."

"Understandable. Fear of the unknown. I wish I had some words to soothe your nerves. A lot of girls have had babies at Bassett House. The nuns must run a good facility. So many other girls have been in your position and made out fine. I've never heard anything bad about the place. As a matter of fact, it seems that nothing is ever reported or advertised about it."

"I'll be alright," Anna responded walking into the living room to gather up her possessions. Grabbing her suitcase and coat, Anna looked around the living room of the apartment, taking in the beauty of the décor, the pieces of original art, and cute knick-knacks from Victoria's travels. It had been a nice escape, but the reality of her purpose for being in Wilmington must now be faced. Her life, she supposed, was about to take a drastic turn.

The two women walked in silence to Victoria's car. They placed Anna's belongings on the back seat and then entered the large, dark green Buick for the drive to Bassett House.

"Ready?"

"As much as I am ever going to be."

Driving through the streets of Wilmington, Victoria remarked on the inhabitants of certain homes along the way. Anna realized that her aunt knew many of the prominent residents of the city. *Yet*, she thought, *Aunt Victoria does not appear to be ashamed to be seen with me. What a fine lady she is! I wish it was as easy to talk with my mother as it is to have conversations with Aunt Victoria.*

Victoria was especially well-dressed this morning, Anna noticed. She had chosen to wear a stylish brown tweed suit with a matching hat. The jacket was scalloped around the large lapels and at the skirting that flared surrounding her hips. She wore a gold broach of the Eiffel Tower and had matching brown leather shoes, purse, and gloves. She exuded wealth and status, and Anna hoped the nuns would believe that she also came from a prominent background. She feared being looked down on or accused of being a promiscuous girl. That she couldn't handle!

Finally, Victoria turned her Buick onto a street where a prominent Catholic church made of large gray rectangular stones, several building additions, and a steeple that towered over the block spread out over a neatly groomed lawn. Although the grass had turned brown with the change of seasons, the flower beds still contained green plants and some flowering bushes. Behind the church stood another large gray stone building, three stories tall with a basement. It did not project the same distinction as the church but was rather obviously void of signage or address. The U-shaped structure, although meticulously groomed, appeared empty and lifeless. Anna wasn't sure that any other girls would be inside. Victoria came to a stop in front of the gloomy building, put her car in park, and breathed a heavy sigh. "This is the place," she said. "Are you ready to face this, Anna?"

"Do I have a choice?" Anna looked at her aunt through bleary eyes. "If I could run away and never go home, I would do it now. But you and I know that isn't possible," Anna hesitated. "I also can't do what you did. I wouldn't want to. I..."

"It's okay, Anna," Victoria hugged her grand-niece and gave her a peck on her cheek. "You will survive this. I know you will. I'll pick you up in a few months and life will begin anew. You'll see. You won't end up like me, Anna. Don't worry. You can have other children and a home and a husband and whatever else you want!" Victoria said tearing up and removing her glasses to wipe her eyes. "Let's go then."

Anna nodded and then grabbed the car door handle and stepped out onto the sidewalk. She stared up at the old dark building. Something about its appearance gave her the shivers. It was not what she had expected. The three-story, granite structure had a large black front door with a gold lionhead knocker on it. Over the door, an arched transom with etched glass containing a picture of Jesus, cradling a lamb in one arm and a staff in the other, welcomed all wayward girls. The main building had three double sets of windows on both sides of the front door and the third floor had dormers. Perpendicular wings extended towards the street at each end. A plain single door was centered on the front of each wing.

Victoria lifted the large knocker and let it drop two times. She and Anna heard the approaching footsteps and the turn of a key in the locked door. An elderly, small-framed nun in a clean white habit struggled to open the heavy door to let them in.

"Hello. May I help you? Oh! Will you be staying with us?" She asked in a soft voice.

"Yes, this my grand-niece, Anna Ruth Scott, and she received a call stating that her room is ready."

"Come on in. Yes, we have a bed for you. I know you're expected today. I'll take you to our admissions director. She'll tell you which room you are in. Most of them are on the second floor." They listened as they followed behind the little woman shuffling down the main central corridor to an office with high ceilings, red tapestry rugs, and brown leather furniture. Behind a neatly organized large, wooden desk stood a tall, thin nun in a brown and white habit. She wore round glasses that were continuously slipping down her pointy nose. Her starched, firmly pressed clothing stood out in contrast to the many wrinkles on her face and hands. Anna knew by the stance of this stern woman that she was a force to be reckoned with in this place.

"You must be our new arrival. Please have a seat. So glad to meet you, and your mother, I assume?" she said.

"Actually, I'm Anna Ruth's great-aunt, Victoria Daffin. Anna's parents have a farm to operate on the Eastern Shore of Maryland. It's a busy time of year for them, so I offered to deliver her," Victoria explained.

"I see," she responded with hesitation. "Well now, let's get to it. I am Sister Mary Agnes, the admissions director. I'm going to get you registered and take you to your room. Is that alright?" Anna nodded her head in agreement. "Good. You will have the rest of the afternoon to settle in. Mass is at 4:00 for you girls and dinner at 5:30 in our dining hall. Lights out at 10:30. Our rules are laid out in this folder." She spoke slowly in a monotone voice indicating she gave the same directions several times a week. "Oh, we need to choose a new name for you."

"What do you mean by a new name?" Victoria questioned.

"Why can't I use my own name?" Anna chimed in.

"When you girls enter our home, we have you assume a new name to use for privacy reasons. No one will know who you used to be. When you leave and take your old life back, you may use your own name again."

"Just a first name?" Victoria asked.

"Yes, we don't use last names outside this office. I am the only person who knows your full real name."

"What do you think, Anna? Do you have a name you like?" Victoria asked turning to Anna for a response. She didn't know how she would respond to such an odd request. Then it came to her!

"How about Grace? Like Grace Kelly. I can remember that one."

"Alright. We don't have anyone using that name just now. You will be called Grace." Sister Mary Agnes wrote the name in red ink on a folder and pulled out a handful of forms to be signed. "May I have your signature on these documents, Miss Daffin, since you are the responsible party today? And, Grace, I'll need you to sign these forms to allow us to care for you and handle the adoption of your baby when it arrives," Sister Mary Agnes requested, placing the two stacks of paperwork along with black fountain pens at the edge of her desk.

Anna didn't take the time to read every word. Some of the wording didn't make sense to her and she was too nervous to concentrate, so she simply signed everything and handed it back to the sister. She wished her aunt could read it over for her, but she was busy completing the forms given to her. When they were both finished, the Sister called for the counselor in the next room.

"This is Sister Catherine, a counselor for the girls here at our facility." Sister Mary Agnes introduced the rather tall and yet stocky, round-faced nun who sported a noticeable growth of black upper lip hair. "She is going to take Grace on a tour around the building. Miss Daffin, I'm afraid you will need to leave now. You may have a few minutes to say goodbye. It was a pleasure to meet you." With that she turned on her heel and abruptly left the office leaving them alone with Sister Catherine.

"I'll give you a few minutes. Excuse me," said the Sister as she went back into her office.

Anna faced her aunt. Victoria recognized how profoundly troubled her niece was at that moment of separation, by the tension and bewilderment in her expression. She searched for the right words to comfort her but came up empty. There were no words to help her through this.

"Thank you so much for everything, Aunt Victoria! You have been so kind and generous to me. I really appreciate it," Anna said, giving her aunt a tight hug.

"I think you will be just fine here, don't you?"

"Yes, if I can remember my name," They both chuckled. "At least you know who to ask for if you call me. Do you mind telling my parents? I don't know if they will call or write me while I'm here, but just in case."

"Certainly, I'll give them a call tonight and let them know you are here and doing fine."

"Oh, I forgot one thing," she said pulling an envelope from her purse. "Jimmy gave me this money when he stopped by the other day. I want you to have it for keeping me and feeding me these past few weeks. I don't know what I would have done without your help."

"How about if I just hold it for you until you leave? You may need it. I enjoyed our time together, Anna. I feel we have gotten to know each other so well these past weeks. You are like a daughter to me. I'll truly miss not having your company."

"Thank you. I enjoyed it, too. I appreciate our talks. You have helped me cope with all of this."

They stood together and hugged one more time, both with tears in their eyes in the knowledge that they shared the memory of a visit that neither would ever forget.

* * *

Sister Catherine led Anna around Bassett House for about an hour explaining the various activities in each of the rooms of the large building. Even so, it appeared to Anna that there were still areas of the building that were not included in the tour. Then, the Sister explained all the rules of Bassett House and let Anna know that she was expected to work for her keep during her stay there.

"That will be good for me. I want to stay busy," Anna said softly, keeping her head focused away from the sister.

This was her first encounter with a nun. Anna's impression of the bleakly covered woman was of a cold, somber, no-nonsense workaholic. There was no warmth or kindness on her face, and she carried her body through the halls of the home in a stiff manner.

"What type of work experience or schooling have you had?" Sister Catherine continued to interrogate Anna.

"Well, I worked in a restaurant at the beach over the summer. I know how to serve food and clean tables. I have also picked vegetables in our fields, milked our cows, fed our animals, and hauled straw."

"Those skills are of no use here, of course. Did you work in the prep kitchen of the restaurant?"

"No, the owner only allowed his Greek family to handle the food."

"Hmm. Did you help your mother in the home?" the Sister questioned further.

"Some. Since I am the oldest, my father needed me at the barn to help. But I know how to sew my own clothes, mostly. I made practically all of my school clothes last year."

"That is wonderful! We need help in our sewing room, so maybe I can put you to work in there."

"I'd like that!" Anna felt satisfied that she could spend her time doing something she liked. She hoped it would help occupy her mind and make the time pass quickly. She had been feeling uncomfortable since she walked through the front door, but this news gave her some hope that she might be able to endure this strange environment.

Finally, Anna was shown to her room located near the end of the north wing on the second floor. As she and Sister Catherine entered, a strong odor of ammonia-based cleaning solution smacked her in the face and she started to sneeze.

"Wow! That is really strong stuff!" Anna said before sneezing again.

"Yes, the room was cleaned before your arrival. Two beds were emptied yesterday. The girls in here had their babies. We always clean the rooms between new arrivals. There are some girls who simply do not keep themselves clean. We have standards!"

"Is there a bathtub?"

"Certainly! It's through that green door," she said, pointing to the door on the far-right corner. "Four girls share that bathroom and all four are expected to keep it clean. You are expected to do your part around here until your child arrives."

"I will. I don't mind cleaning toilets."

"Good thing."

Anna looked around as Sister Catherine checked for clean towels. There were four black wrought iron beds in the bedroom, two on each side. Quilts of scrap material covered the beds that were made by girls who had resided at Bassett House over the years, products of their sewing classes. Clean starched white sheets and pillowcases also covered each bed. The walls were stark white, and the tiled floor was also white with black speckles. Anna wondered why everything was so plain in this room, while all the rooms she visited on the first floor seemed so rich and opulent. She also noticed that since there were no rugs on the floor, it was cold to walk on, especially with bare feet. She wished she had brought some slippers.

"Why don't you choose a bed and dresser. You can put your clothes and belongings away before the call to mass. I'll come back to take you over to church when it's time."

"Okay. Does it matter which bed I take?"

"Well, these two are already taken. You'll need to pick between the two against this wall by the bathroom. Another girl will be coming in one day soon, I believe. There is always a steady flow. There are just three of you in here for tonight."

* * *

Just as she said, Sister Catherine returned a few hours later to escort Anna over to the church with the other residents for mass. Not being Catholic, she was unfamiliar with the practices of the religion, but she was pretty certain it did not require her to miss lunch. No one had called her to eat all day and she was too afraid to ask, so she suffered in silence. Not an uncommon practice for Anna. She would rather be uncomfortable than inconvenience anyone to assist in meeting her needs.

Anna fumbled through the readings and prayers and was always five seconds behind the rest of the congregation as they performed what is known as Catholic calisthenics. It was all foreign to her. Those around her could tell that she was new, and she felt embarrassed.

Anna was relieved when mass was over and dinner time finally arrived. Not having had anything to eat since breakfast made her feel faint and definitely famished. She ate chicken noodle soup and biscuits in the dining hall with the other girls. She looked around the room wondering which of these girls were her roommates. She didn't have long to wait. They were waiting to meet her, too, when she entered their shared bedroom.

The two other girls assigned to the room seemed shy and initially ignored her while they took care of their daily hygiene. They both took baths and made up their beds with fresh linen that had been dropped off earlier in the day. After they were all settled and dressed in their nightgowns, Anna spoke to the girl in the bed across from hers in an effort to get to know her.

"How long have you been here?"

"A week. It feels longer." The girl responded quickly. Anna felt she wanted to continue the conversation.

"I checked in this afternoon. I spent the day alone. Well, until now, of course. Everyone has been nice so far."

"Did they give you another name?"

"Yeah, that was odd. I guess you are supposed to call me Grace. What name did you choose?"

"Call me Leah! It was close to my real name. And her new name is Penny," Leah said, pointing to the younger girl on the other side of the room.

“It’s the name of a dog I once had,” Penny stated as they all laughed. “I’m afraid I won’t know who I am when they call my name unless they say ‘Here, girl, Here, girl!’ So ridiculous, don’t you think?”

That was all it took for the three girls to begin opening up to each other. Leah and Anna were the same age, from the same county in Maryland, but lived in different towns. Penny was only fourteen and she came from the southern part of Delaware. They had similar interests in styles, movies, and activities, but their home backgrounds were very different. Anna was the only one from a farm.

Penny was a short, thin wisp of a girl with a sizable baby bump. The immature teenager was not particularly bright, but she had fair skin, blue eyes, and delicate features along with blonde hair indicating that she could be a real beauty in the near future. She had a sweet personality and was generous to others, but terribly naïve. So much so that she ended up in her predicament.

Leah was a medium-sized young woman with black horned-rimmed glasses, pearly white teeth, and mousy brown shoulder-length hair who lived in a rental home in a small town located in the northern part of the county with her widowed mother and two younger brothers. Her father died in France during the war, in February 1944, just days after Leah turned seven years old. Life has been difficult for her mother and her siblings since then. Leah understands how hard her mother works to keep enough food on the table for the four of them. She also has a lot of responsibility on her as she helps to watch over her twin brothers, help them with their homework, prepare dinner, and clean up around the house. Her mother is always tired when she comes home from work since she stands on her feet most of the day in a factory.

"I wish I still had my dad. I know my mother wouldn't have to work so hard if he were still alive," Leah lamented. "I wouldn't be here if my dad were alive."

"What do you mean, Leah?"

"My mother wouldn't have so many boyfriends if she still had my father."

Not wanting to push her new friend too far this first night together, Anna changed the subject. *Everyone in this place must have a story,* she thought.

The next morning, a new routine began. Her roommates had jobs helping in the kitchen for breakfast and lunch. Anna was given the chore of mopping the hallway downstairs and cleaning the toilets in the administration area. She had a scheduled private meeting in the afternoon with her counselor, Sister Catherine. Anna scurried down the hall to her office once she had finished putting the mop and bucket away for the day.

"Come in. Grace, isn't it? You go by Grace?"

"Yes, ma'am. That's my name now, I guess."

"Have a seat in that comfy chair. Let's get to know one another. How does that sound?"

Anna sat down in one of the dark green wingback chairs in front of the sister's big mahogany desk awaiting further instruction. She felt nervous and unsure of what she was supposed to do. She had never had counseling in her life.

"So, Grace, you are now almost six months pregnant. Does that sound right?"

"I suppose so," Anna responded.

"Don't you know when this happened?" Sister Catherine questioned her. "You do remember, don't you?"

"Yes, I was on the beach with my boyfriend. I didn't mean for this to happen though. I didn't know and he said I couldn't…"

"Boys tell girls all kinds of lies. You should know that by now, right? You are responsible for your situation. You have committed a sin, but we are going to help you. That is why you are here. Your parents sent you to us to handle your situation. Do you understand what you have done to yourself?"

"Not, really," said Anna sheepishly. "I suppose I've messed up my life."

"Who do you think will marry you if you have a baby? No man wants some other man's baby to raise. It is a sin to have carnal relations before you marry. You're not Catholic, are you?"

"No ma'am. My family is Methodist."

"Still, they taught you that only whores give themselves to men before marriage, didn't they?" questioned the Sister, snapping back in disgust as she robustly flipped to the next page in her file.

"Are you saying that I am a whore?" Anna asked as tears welled up, and her head practically fell on her chest.

"You need to cleanse yourself. We will find a good Catholic home for your baby. One with two respectable parents who will be able to give your child everything it needs and more. They will be able to provide more than you ever could. You know that, right? We will handle everything."

"My mother told me that my father would never let me keep the baby," Anna muttered folding her arms around her waist.

"Do you know why? You have shamed yourself! Your parents are good people and look what you have done to them.

Do you want them to walk the streets of town with everyone talking about their promiscuous daughter? Is that what you want to happen?" Sister Catherine licked her finger and quickly flipped another page over in the folder.

Anna shook her head as she looked down at the gold fringe on the edge of the red Persian rug that covered the office floor. She felt horrible! She was extremely embarrassed. The Sister continued to berate her several times during their hour together. Anna felt she must endure this relentless debasement of her character as part of her punishment. She couldn't walk out, so she continued to stare at the fringe, concentrating on how many pieces of them lay between the wide planks of the wooden floor.

One, two, three . . . That's fifteen sitting on the first plank. Anna tried to concentrate on the fringe as she grew restless, squirming in the chair, and crossing and uncrossing her ankles.

She could hear the words coming from the Sister's mouth, but her mind had gone numb. All that mattered was passing the minutes without a hysterical outburst or passing out onto the floor. The heat that had risen from deep inside Anna and moved to her face caused her to fear that one or both could certainly happen if this torture didn't end soon. Finally, Sister Catherine rested.

"That will be all for today, Grace. We have more work to do though," Sister Catherine stood up and waved to her patient to leave. Anna was freed for the moment but scheduled to return the following week and every Wednesday afternoon from there on.

These counseling sessions are hell! I can't stand that hateful woman! She makes feel like garbage.

Anna pondered the sessions with the sister, for each one created a lower opinion of herself. Every meeting was meant to undermine her ability to care for or provide for her child. Each time reinforced her unworthiness to raise a child. She was forced to acknowledge her sinfulness and to accept that such behavior has led to her pitifully, shameful circumstances. The only way to regain acceptance in her family and redeem herself with society, in general, is to give her baby to parents who will be able to raise it in a good Catholic home. Anna believed this to be true even before Sister Catherine started drilling the thought into her brain.

Granddaddy Daffin and Aunt Victoria told me I could obtain a clean slate staying at Bassett House. I wonder if they know how a girl achieves this. I can't believe they know how the nuns speak to us! What if they do?

Anna returned to her room after one particularly difficult session and flopped on her bed to rest and think about the Sister's words. Suddenly, she began to feel hot. The heat welled up from her stomach to her face and she felt an immediate need to bathe herself. She ran warm water in the tub of their bathroom, removed her clothes, and settled into the water. She took one of the white washcloths from a stand next to the tub and dipped it into the water, rubbing the pure white bar of Ivory soap over the cloth working up a full hand of lather. She squeezed the soapy water out of the washcloth as she held it over her head letting it trickle down her face, her breasts, her stomach, and to her…. She started to hyperventilate. She couldn't stop. She took the soapy cloth and stuck it in between her teeth and let out a muffled scream. The soap tasted terrible! Anna began using the washcloth on her arms and then her face. Vigorously she worked her way to other parts of her body, rubbing hard, trying to remove the invisible filth that covered her - until she was exhausted. She sank down into the water and came up crying. Not wanting anyone to hear her, she held the cloth over her face, covered with both hands. She felt loathsome.

A knock came on the bathroom door.

"Grace? Are you alright? Do you need help?" Leah called out to her.

"I guess I'm just a little homesick. I'll be okay."

"It's almost time for mass. You better get dressed soon. The sisters don't like us to be late."

"I'll be right out. Thanks, Leah!" Anna called out still feeling shaky. Soon the heat subsided, and she put on fresh clothes before facing her friends in the other room.

The three roommates attended mass and had dinner together. Anna felt better outside the bedroom that night, so they all hung out in the common area with some of the other girls on their floor. It reminded Anna of the days at the boarding house in Rehoboth Beach. The girls chatted about the last movie they saw or what they would do about finishing school. They helped each other put curlers in and style their hair and read letters from home aloud. Some of the girls simply zoned out watching television in the far corner of the room. The lights flashed at 10:25 and the girls made their way back to their rooms before the lights went out. Mother Claudette made her rounds to check on everyone promptly at 11:00. No one wanted to get her riled up!

"Grace?"

"Yeah?"

"What happened to you? I mean, how did you get knocked up?" asked Leah curiously.

Anna liked Leah and started to trust her as a friend and confidant, so she was comfortable to answer her.

"It happened one night at the beach. With my boyfriend. At least, I thought he was my boyfriend. He didn't want to get married. Not to me."

"He used you?"

"Yeah, I guess he did."

"My boyfriend used me too," said Penny from the other side of the room. "He is older than me. He's 25."

"And you're 14? He can't be your boyfriend!" exclaimed Leah.

"Can too," said Penny as she laid back down in her bed to pout.

"Did your parents allow you to date a 25-year-old man?" asked Leah, seeing how immature Penny was. "You are just a child. You probably got knocked up when you were only 13, didn't you?"

"He said I was his girlfriend, but we couldn't tell my parents. He said they probably wouldn't like him on account he's been in jail. Just for a few months though. Nothing bad."

"How do you know for sure about that?" quizzed Anna.

"He told me. He's really a good guy, but he stole some parts for his car from the filling station where he was working. He was going to pay them back when he got his paycheck, but they called the cops and had him arrested. I mean, how was he supposed to get to work if his car isn't running. I don't think that was fair!"

"Where did the two of you go when you dated? Didn't people say anything about your age?" Leah wondered. People would surely talk!

"He said people might get the wrong idea and start blabbering, so we avoided being seen. I would meet him behind the library in town and he picked me up in his car. I made sure I always had books to carry so no one would be suspicious."

"Oh, that was smart! You two had it all planned out, didn't you?" Leah spoke sarcastically shaking her head. Anna suppressed a chuckle and then asked, "Penny, where did he take you in his car? Weren't you afraid to be alone with that man?"

"No, like I said, he was nice to me. He talked to me and told me that I was the prettiest girl he ever knew. He gave me things, too, like a necklace one time and chocolates for Valentine's Day. I've never had anyone give me chocolates before."

"Where is he now?" Anna wondered.

"When my parents found out, they threatened to have him sent back to jail. He left town after that, and I haven't heard from him. My parents said I wasn't supposed to have anything more to do with him and then when they found out I was going to have a baby, they sent me here. But you know what, he's going to pick me up one of these days. I'm sure of it. Once he finds out that I'm here, he'll come to get me."

"Yeah, he definitely will. That man is so far gone," Leah said rolling her eyes. "At least you both know the guys! I don't even know who my baby's father is," said Leah sounding angry.

"What do you mean, Leah? What happened?" Anna asked.

"It's not easy to talk about, Grace," Leah said as she paused to wonder if she could trust her secret to her new friends. "Okay. On Fourth of July weekend, my mom and us kids had been invited to go to a big family reunion picnic. We were really looking forward to it. All the cousins, aunts, uncles and grandparents were going to my Aunt Phyllis's house. Around 11:00, mom took her baked beans casserole out of the oven and wanted to run it over to her sister's house and drop my brothers off early to play with their cousins. I had invited my friend from school, Arnie Hoffman, to go with me, and he was supposed to pick me up around noon. I was supposed to take my mom's homemade peach pie when it cooled down. A man who said he worked with my mom came by with a couple of cantaloupes for us. I'd never seen him before, but we don't turn away food, so I let him in the house to put them in our refrigerator. He seemed nice enough to me. I didn't feel uncomfortable letting him in the house. Anyway, when I walked over to the kitchen table to see if the pie was cooled, my back was turned away from him, and I thought he was leaving. Instead, I suddenly felt his arm around my waist. He began pulling me into my mother's bedroom. I couldn't grab onto anything because his arms were holding my arms to my side. He threw me on the bed and landed on top forcing himself on me. I tried to hit him, kick him, anything I could to make him get off. I screamed, and he put his hand over my mouth and laughed at me. Like it was a joke to him. Anyway, no one heard me."

"Oh, how horrible for you!" Anna said understanding her trauma.

"So scary!" added Penny.

"When he finished with me, he ran out of my house. I didn't know his name, but I won't forget his face."

"Where did he go? Did you see his car?"

"I don't think he had a car. I don't know where he came from, and I didn't look to see where he ran off. I honestly believe he knew I was alone in the house. I felt like he must have been watching to find me alone, you know. Soon after, my friend found me huddled in the corner of my mother's bedroom, with half my clothes off and crying. He didn't know what to do, so he drove to my aunt's house and told my mom to come help me."

"It was good that he showed up."

"Yes, but I wish he had been there a little sooner."

"Yeah, if the guy was watching you, he wouldn't come by when someone else was in the house; especially, another guy," Anna thought aloud.

"The worst part, believe it or not, was that my mom blamed me. How do you like that? She thought I did something to make this man attack me. Apparently, the asshole really worked with her. He told her he would stop by sometime to bring her the melons, but she didn't know it would be that day. She knew his name but never told me. She didn't want to get him in trouble. I hate her. It wasn't my fault! My own mother accusing me of something like that!"

"Why would she say that?" asked Grace.

"Yeah, I don't understand why your mother is upset with you!" added Penny. "Makes no sense!"

"I have asked myself a thousand times. I figured that she liked the guy. She didn't want to believe that he would do that on his own. Maybe that is what he told her, and she believed him. She believed him over her own flesh and blood. I don't ever want to see her again!"

"So, she knew the guy? I'm so sorry this happened to you," Anna said sincerely, but not knowing what she could do to soothe her new friend.

"And when she found out I was going to have a baby, she didn't believe it could be his. How crazy is that? We were arguing every day. When she was fed up and couldn't stand to look at me anymore, she packed me up and sent me here. I'll give my baby up just like the rest of you. It's okay. I don't feel anything. I don't know who's inside me."

"I am so sorry."

"Me, too!" Penny got the last word in before the girls became quiet. There was nothing more to say that night. Silence surrounded them and soon they fell asleep.

* * *

The next day there was another suitcase sitting on top of the remaining bed in their room. When Anna, Leah, and Penny returned from handling their chores for the day, they saw the large dark green suitcase and matching round overnight case. They were anxious to meet their new roommate, each believing she must come from a wealthy family to have such nice travel baggage.

"I was in and out of the offices emptying trash cans and dusting today, but I didn't see anyone I didn't recognize," Anna stated. "Maybe she just arrived."

It wasn't long before Sister Mary Agnes opened the bedroom door and introduced a tall girl with long black shiny hair pulled into a ponytail as their fourth roommate. Her chosen name was 'Rose', her favorite flower, and she was from Philadelphia. She had beautiful smooth, light olive colored skin with high cheekbones that she highlighted with makeup. Her lips were bright red, and she wore several pieces of jewelry around her neck, wrists, and ears. She was almost seven months pregnant and wore a red flowered maternity top with two buttons left undone and a gray skirt.

"I want you to help Rose get settled before dinner. And you can also show her where the dining hall is. She arrived late today, so I haven't had time to take her around." With that directive, Sister Mary Agnes left them.

Anna felt intimidated by Rose, and she could tell by the expression on Leah's face that she also felt uncomfortable around her. Penny picked up a book and pretended she was reading as Rose opened her suitcase and began removing her clothes and personal items. Penny peered up over the book for a quick glance.

"What cha' lookin' at kid?" Rose asked, bugging her eyes out at the young girl and laughing.

"How far is Philadelphia from here? Did you have a long drive?" asked Anna, quickly trying to deflect attention from poor Penny, who was about to cry.

"I dun't know ex'atly. My brothers drove me here. Mario and Vinny. The rest of my family thinks I'm livin' wit my sister in New York. And look, here I am in this place!"

"Is she your only sister?" asked Leah.

"Yeah. She's older wit two kids. I'm the baby girl. I got five brothers, and they're all older than me. I dun't get any breaks wit them either. They're always on my back."

Anna enjoyed listening to Rose talk, but she really struggled to understand certain words. She had never heard that accent before. Although Anna was curious about Rose's hometown, she didn't feel she should bring attention by asking. She didn't know how Rose would take it. No need to start something ugly. Besides, maybe Rose thought Anna had an accent too!

All four girls ate supper together in the dining hall. As they got to know Rose better, the less intimidating she seemed. She had a sunny-side-up disposition, even finding humor in her own predicament. In a place where humor was in short supply, the girls discovered that Rose's witty comments could be entertaining and a welcome relief to their monotonous days.

"It ain't the Rittenhouse, but it'll have ta do fa now. I espose I been in worser places!"

Rose's boisterous voice caught the attention of everyone in the dining hall. They all turned to listen as she continued to gain attention.

"Aww, shit, I've lost a nudder button! I mean . . . Sorry, sistas!" Rose cried out as she looked down at the gap caused by the missing button on the front of her blouse. "My tits are jus' too big! Youse guys havin' that problem?" She asked the stunned and speechless group that stared back at her. A few girls were sniggering. Rose seemed unaware of the stir she had caused. Even if she had been aware, it wouldn't have stopped her comments. She obviously liked being the center of attention.

CHAPTER TWELVE

Two weeks before Christmas, Sister Gertrude organized decorating parties for the girls to prepare the facility for the holidays. She and some helpers pulled down dusty boxes of ornaments, tinsel ropes, and a large white and gold angel topper. A member of the parish donated an impressive well-shaped, nine-foot fir tree for the front entrance. Select girls were chosen to hang the old glass ornaments and tinsel that were used on the large tree. When they finished decorating, the Sisters gathered the girls to sing Christmas carols around the tree with them. The harmony of voices resounded against the tall ceiling amplifying the sounds of the familiar music.

For the common room upstairs, a local farmer delivered a small cedar tree from his woods that the girls placed in a red, three-legged stand with a rusty bottom. The girls decorated it with their own handmade ornaments designed from paper, ribbon, buttons, popsicle sticks, and freshly made popcorn. Sister Margaret, who managed the kitchen, delivered the large bowl of popcorn and set up the only two records of Christmas music they had on the hi-fi. The Andrews Sisters and Bing Crosby could be heard all over the second floor as the girls sang along with the familiar tunes. It was a carefree, lighthearted day for them. Sister Margaret tossed a piece of popcorn at one of the girls who had complained that they didn't have any Frank Sinatra records.

"Nobody gets to complain while we decorate our tree," she chuckled after seeing the surprised look on the girl's face. The momentary tension passed, and everyone began to laugh and feel more at ease.

For a few minutes, the popcorn flew back and forth around the room, with boisterous laughter, until someone mentioned not having enough to string for the tree. The joyous holiday mood continued throughout the day until time for Saturday mass.

"I had such fun today. It was the best day I have had in this place so far. Even the Sisters were pleasant," said Anna to her roommates as she brushed her wavy hair back from her face.

"Did you see that fancy tree downstairs? That's where they have our families meet us for Christmas, I heard. It all looks very nice, doesn't it? Won't they all be so impressed?" asked Leah sarcastically.

"Will your family come for Christmas? Or yours, Penny?" Anna asked.

"I'm not speaking to my mother, so I doubt it," Leah responded.

"I don't know about my parents yet, but my boyfriend might come for a visit. I'm sure he has a present for me," Penny told them.

"And you, Grace?"

"I don't think so. My parents don't even know that I exist for now. They have no interest in visiting me here. Besides, they have my little brother and my younger sisters at home to celebrate the holidays. I'm just their dirty secret and no one can mention my name. My father doesn't want my sisters to even ask about me," Anna lamented as a wave of homesickness came over her. "Maybe my Aunt Victoria will come by."

* * *

Excitement grew among the residents of the home as Christmas drew closer. An open house for family and friends was planned for the afternoon of Christmas Eve with punch, finger sandwiches, and cookies with sprinkles laid out on the welcoming tables. Some of the visitors were members of the church who provided simple gifts for the residents in order to satisfy their need to give to those less fortunate. It allowed them to have a good long look at the lost women and feel pleased with their own advantageous lifestyles.

Aunt Victoria arrived late in the afternoon after rushing around for last-minute gifts for a party she was throwing with friends on Christmas Day. She stayed for about half an hour, and after finding Anna looking quite healthy, gave her a store-wrapped box with pink slippers, and a matching soft flannel nightgown and bed jacket.

"Thank you so much, Aunt Victoria! I love it! I need these slippers on the cold tile floors of our room."

"I'm glad you like them. Now here is a small box of chocolate-covered peanuts I bought in New York that you can share with your roommates or keep just for yourself. I hope you are eating well. You certainly look healthy. And here is a Christmas card that arrived for you at my address – from your granddad. I'll bring you more when they arrive, but this is the only one for now. Hopefully, it will alleviate some homesickness. I'm sure you must have some during the Christmas season. Look, I have to run. There are still a couple more stops to make. I am so happy to see you, Anna!" She put her finger to her lips. "Sorry, I mean Grace."

"Here is an ornament that I made for your Christmas tree. It's not much, I know. It's strips of birch wood woven into a star. We made them in a weaving class here."

"I'll be sure to hang it as soon as I get home. Thank you! What a dear you are!" she said rising from her chair. "Merry Christmas to you. Take care of yourself."

"Thank you again, Aunt Victoria!" Anna said giving her a big hug before her aunt walked out the big front doors and into the cold windy evening.

Such a short visit. Oh, well, at least she showed up.

* * *

Later on Christmas Day, the girls were called for midnight mass. At 11:00, everyone filed through the large double doors laden with large green pine wreaths decorated with bright interwoven red ribbon and fresh holly berries. The nuns' voices beautifully harmonized the old traditional carols as flickering candles spread light throughout the massive church. Anna missed her family. She would have attended the annual Christmas pageant in her own church, probably contributing or participating in some fashion. Every year has been celebrated in the same manner, until now. *This doesn't really feel like Christmas. I feel disconnected from everything around me in this place. It will be a relief to be finished with the holidays.*

* * *

Ernie and Dottie masked their eldest daughter's absence for the sake of their other children. Other than the anxiety of being questioned about Anna's absence, they managed to pull off the appearance of a joyful holiday. Dottie missed having Anna to help with the baking of cookies and breads they gave as gifts to neighbors and friends, and all the decorating she enjoyed in preparing their Christmas tree. Her laughter was always infectious joy as the other children gathered to assist in placing the ornaments.

Little Eddie looked for Anna in her room everyday thinking she was hiding from him as she sometimes did. Their other daughters didn't understand why Anna had not come home for Christmas. There were gifts for her under the tree. They remained there until the tree was taken down, and Dottie then placed them on top of the dresser in Anna's bedroom.

When Granddaddy came by with his gifts, he asked if anyone had spoken with Anna.

"We decided to send a card to Anna instead of calling. It costs so much to phone long distance to Wilmington. Besides, she can read a card again and again," Dottie said. "That Sister Mary Agnes doesn't want us to phone Anna for now or make any visits to see her. She said it is better for the girls to not have contact with family and friends or other influencers during this time. They need to work with them alone."

"The Sister said some girls try to convince their parents to let them come home. We certainly didn't want to go through that!" Ernie explained.

"No, I'm sure you didn't, Ernie!" Wilbur Daffin responded to his son-in-law.

"We didn't want to upset her either. You know, make her homesick," Dottie added.

"True. No, you don't. I'm sure things are difficult enough for her. Victoria called last night to wish us a Merry Christmas. She visited Anna yesterday for a while and she said she looks well. She appears to be eating enough and staying busy there."

Ernie and Wilbur were trying to get along better since Anna left. Dottie had enough worry and they agreed not to add to her angst. Tension was still felt by everyone in the family. Janet was suspicious of Anna's quiet departure to care for Aunt Victoria, and she also wondered why Jimmy Baker had dropped out of school to join the Army so suddenly. Anna's friends kept asking about her and wanted to know when she would be back to school. Patricia and Susan sensed that something was wrong, and their parents appeared to be keeping secrets from them. They discussed it late at night and came to an agreement not to speak to anyone about their sister or Jimmy. They didn't know when she would be home!

"What's this I see?" Wilbur looked into the living room and saw all four children sitting on the floor in front of a new television. "Ohhhh! No wonder I didn't get any hugs from my grandchildren today! How do you like that thing?"

"Amazing, just amazing!" Dottie exclaimed.

"Good! Well, I guess in that case no one wants any of my old presents!"

"We do! We do!" And with that all the children ran over to give their grandfather a hug and to see what he had for them. As always, he treated them well.

* * *

The Christmas card from her parents was delivered to Anna on the twenty-sixth of December, already opened. It was clear that someone read the contents before giving it to her. She was happy to know that her parents still cared about her and missed having her home. Just being acknowledged raised her spirits. Seeing the trees in the common room and the entrance dismantled, and all the decorations about the home packed away for another year squelched some of Anna's holiday blues. The lowest point for her was on the Wednesday after Christmas when she had another counseling session with Sister Catherine.

"As you may know, Anna, we have begun our search for the right family to raise your child. Several good, respectable Catholic couples have sent in applications. Many want blonde-haired baby girls. I see that dark hair must run in your family. Now, did the baby's father have blonde hair, per chance?"

Anna wasn't sure she heard her correctly. "You want to know the color of my boyfriend's hair?" She asked. "Will that make a difference whether my baby gets adopted?"

"No, it's not that. We will still be able to place your baby with a fine family. Sometimes parents want specific traits for their baby so it will look more like them."

"What if I decide not to give up my baby?" Anna asked the question Sister Catherine had been anticipating. The girls always asked this question at some point in the counseling period. She had the answers and was ready to strike. She stood up and bent over her desk with her eyes staring straight into Anna's.

"What a selfish, egocentric, stupid girl you are! You are thinking only about your life! What about the life of the innocent child you are carrying? What can you give this child? A life as an outcast, a bastard child, that will be made fun of and called names by other children? A child that will not have a decent home or food to eat or clothes to wear because you are not able to provide the things it needs to survive? You don't want what is best for your baby! You have proven already that you make bad choices and here you are ready to make another one! How ignorant can you be!"

Anna stiffened in the leather chair, rising up, and turning her head away from Sister Catherine who scurried around her large desk and came within a few inches of Anna's face. As the Sister bore down on her, Anna felt droplets of spit as it flew out of her mouth. The heat of her garlic-scented breath seared her face and burned her eyes as Sister Catherine stayed uncomfortably close to Anna. For a moment, she thought the nun might smack her.

"I'll do whatever I have to do. I'm not saying I won't give the baby up. Believe me. I'm not saying that. I was curious, that's all."

Sister Catherine slowly returned to her desk and flopped down in her office chair, exhausted from her tirade. She took her time responding, as Anna continued to squirm uncomfortably in her chair. Her hands noticeably shook and her stomach tightened.

"You really are incapable of handling this situation you have put yourself in, Anna. You must see that. You are too young. The baby's father doesn't want you. Your parents are ashamed of you. You have no money, no job, no home. Think, Anna! Think about what you would be doing to yourself and your child. Don't be stupid!"

"I do want the best for my baby. I really do," said a shocked Anna.

"Don't contradict me. You wouldn't have such crazy ideas if you wanted to do right for this child. We are here to help you out of the mess you created and allow you to resume your life where you left off. You are being given an opportunity to rid yourself of this burden. Let us help you and your baby. We are only trying to help you!"

"Okay," Anna squeaked. She felt a choking sensation in her throat. She couldn't wait to get out of the office. "Okay. I'll do it. I'll sign the papers to give my baby to a good family.

You'll make sure that they will be good to my baby, right? Is that a guarantee?"

"We review all of our candidates. We even check out their bank accounts and homes. You needn't worry about that!"

"May I go now?"

"Yes, that's all for today. I'll let Sister Mary Agnes know that she can start your paperwork."

Anna rushed back to the bedroom. The other three girls were down the hall in the common area, so she was able to have a good cry before they returned. She threw herself onto her bed and let out a wail in her pillow. She sobbed for several minutes feeling the release of anger and frustration with every rise and fall of her chest. Finally, she exhausted herself.

Leah came back to their room first because she was scheduled to help with dinner that night. She noticed Anna's face was red and blotchy.

"Bad day?"

Anna nodded her head.

"We each take our turn. I'm here if you need to talk about it," Leah sat on Anna's bed next to her and gave her a strong hug. "I need to get down to the kitchen now. Let's hang out after supper, how about that? We can play some cards or something."

Anna wasn't very hungry, but sloppy joes were on the menu that night and she loved them. Rose sat by herself at one of the white linen-covered tables in the far corner of the dining hall. Anna thought she might want some company and asked if it was alright to sit with her.

"Shu-ore. I dun't mind," Rose said in her thick South Philly accent. Anna had become fascinated with her speech. It all seemed foreign to her and she loved hearing Rose talk.

"Did you have a sloppy Joe? They look delicious," Anna asked as she took a seat.

"Yeah, but I could kill for a hoagie 'bout now."

"What's a hoagie?"

"Only the best sandwich evah made! Vito's down the street from my house makes the very best."

"Sounds like you are having cravings or maybe you are a little homesick."

"Nah, I wanna move out on my own anyway. I figure when I git back on my feet, I'll make it happen. I'm not goin' back watressin', I know that. My brothers wun't hear of it!"

"Your brothers won't let you be a waitress? Why not? I was one over the summer and I liked it. The money wasn't bad either," Anna said taking a bite of her sandwich.

"They don't want me hangin' round none of them guys that come in. One of them is the papa of this baby," Rose said pointing to her belly.

"You don't know which one?"

"One of the three of 'em," Rose waited for a reaction. "You shocked?" Anna didn't answer as she tried to understand Rose's story. *Did I hear her correctly,* she thought.

Rose wasn't sure if she had astounded her new friend with this remark or if she was actually cool with it. So, she continued to find out.

"Look. My brothers run around town wit this girl and that, every night. Nobody says nothin' bout it. When they found out I'm doing like 'em, they pulled me out of the damn car and called me a slut. Told me to stop whorin'. I didn't want my family to know. My papa has a business to run. Reputation is important where I come from. It would just kill him to know what I had dun wit those boys. Mario and Vinny drove me to and from work every day, keepin' an eye on me, see."

"Your parents don't know about the baby?"

"Nutin'! My brothers are making sh'ure of it."

"That's amazing. How are you hiding the baby from your parents? Don't they suspect something?" Anna asked curiously.

"Easy. I have a married sista with three kids livin' in New York. She and my brothas told my parents that she needs my help up there. My parents are always tendin' the store. They never know where I am anyway. My brothas are in charge of me," Rose explained.

"So, they think you are living in New York City now? I could never get away with that."

"Like I said, my brothas will handle everything. Whateva' Mario and Vinny tell my Mama and Papa, they'll believe."

"I don't have any older brothers. My only brother is just four. I don't think my sisters know anything. At least, they didn't know when I left home. I don't know if my parents have said anything to them or not."

"Look, it's good an' all havin' brothas, but they can be a pain in tha ass, too."

* * *

Anna and Rose scraped off leftovers and placed their dirty supper dishes in the collection bins sitting on a cart. All of the girls were responsible for cleaning up their own plates once they finished their meals.

"I'm supposed to help with cleanup, so I betta get my ass and this cart to the big sink. I'll see you lata!" Rose said taking the handle to steer the cart.

"Ahhh! What's this?" yelled a very pregnant girl at the next table as she stood up with water running onto her chair and the floor around her. She looked frightened and bewildered.

"You're peeing yourself! Oh, my gosh!"

"What are you doing?"

"Look out! It's everywhere."

"Somebody get a mop!" said the girls around her who were also in shock.

Sister Margaret came running out of the kitchen to help and explain to the young women that this girl's water had broken, and she was going into labor. Sister Mary Agnes heard the commotion and with one glance went back to her office to call for a car to carry the girl to the hospital.

Anna watched the activity surrounding the girl in labor intently. She had never seen a woman go into labor before. *I wonder if this happens the same for everyone. Will I wet myself too when the time comes?* She thought to herself. *How mortifying!*

Some girls were trying to help the Sisters, but most had gathered to see what was happening. Finally, a car appeared at the front door and the Sisters helped the young patient into the back seat that was covered with a rubber topper. Her friends walked to the side of the car standing in the cold gray evening, as a light, freezing rain fell, giving well-wishes and waving goodbye.

As soon as the car raced to the hospital, Sister Mary Agnes started shooing the girls back inside the building. "That's enough now. Go about your business! Head on inside! Your turns will come soon enough!"

Later that evening, after the roommates had slipped into their nightgowns and gathered to talk about the day's events, Anna and Rose told the others what had happened in the dining hall.

"What a mess! Did you have to clean it up, Rose?"

"Not me! I had dishes to wash."

"Yeah, when they called for the mop, Rose high-tailed it out of there!" laughed Anna.

"Not my job! No sir. Not me!"

"That's disgusting! I hope I don't pee myself when my baby comes out," Penny said scrunching her nose.

"It's not pee. Sister Margaret said that it's fluid from our bellies. It happens sometimes, but not always. They don't know why some girls do that and others don't. I just hope I'm not one of them!" Explained Anna.

"She wasn't too concerned about it, was she?" Asked Leah.

"I heard the doctor has to cut you to get the baby out, if that happens," Penny spoke up.

"They dun't cut you! It just comes out down there, just slides out real natural like," Rose explained to her young friend. The truth was, they were all ignorant of the process. All four girls were just weeks away from giving birth with little knowledge of how they became pregnant and almost no information about what would happen at their parturition.

"Does the baby come out with poop all over it?" asked Penny, innocently curious.

"Really? Oh, my gosh! I hope they give me medicine to knock me out. I don't want to see that!" said Leah trying to understand.

"The doctor gives you medicine and you probably won't remember a thin'. I heard that my cousin got somethin' that made her sleep the whole way through," added Rose.

"That's what I want!" Anna chimed in.

"It was for the pain. I think they knocked her out cuz she couldn't stand the pain."

"I thought you have to be in pain to get the baby out. Sometimes when women get together and start talking about having their babies, they describe how much pain they were in before the baby arrives. It's as if it's some kind of competition with them." Anna said.

"I know what you mean! I've heard the women in my neighborhood talkin' like that wit each uder," Rose said as she laughed. "They also say they'd ne'va let their husband touch 'um again! Then they turn around and have another baby the next year!" The girls broke out in laughter. It felt good to laugh. They hadn't felt free to be silly in a long time. They continued their silliness until it was time for lights out.

* * *

Bassett House celebrated New Years the same as all other special occasions, with a mass and confession. The Sisters made sure that each Catholic girl took a turn in the confessional, for certainly, they all had committed sins. The non-Catholics sat quietly to the side and waited for the others to finish. No one was permitted to leave until every girl had made confession.

There was cake and punch for them back in the dining hall when they returned. Sister Margaret made her special vanilla cake with buttercream icing decorated with tiny pink flowers and the words 'Happy New Year' in the middle.

"I hope you girls have a better year in 1955! Wishing you happiness and good fortune! Come celebrate with a piece of my good cake!" the jolly nun called out in sincerity. She often felt empathy for the young women and tried her best to offer up some comfort. Her special treats and baked goods seemed to bring a little pleasure most of the time.

"Sister Margaret! One's happiness and good fortune come from obedience to the commandments. Unless there are serious changes made, the new year will be much like the old year. Think about that, young ladies," Mother Claudette reprimanded after following the girls over from mass. She was totally surprised to see such merriment occurring so late at night. She was against allowing these girls to have much pleasure. This was not a holiday for them! There should not be any parties, either. The Mother Superior believed that suffering would make more of an impression and prevent these girls from committing such sinful acts in the future. She stood firm as the girls placed the slices of cake and cups of milk back on the table. They walked silently up the stairs to their rooms. Mother Claudette's intrusion had not only destroyed the party, it also destroyed their spirits.

Sister Margaret grabbed the remaining cake and quickly cleaned off the table. She should have known better. It was her nature to supply some enjoyment and comfort into the lives of the suffering. She believed these girls had each experienced agony in varying degrees or they wouldn't be at Bassett House. They needed relief, if only for a while. They were just schoolgirls. If they hadn't been sent away, and ostracized for their predicaments, they would have been celebrating with friends and family that evening. She felt bad for them.

"I'll speak with you further in the morning, Sister Margaret. It's too late now and I need some rest. Make sure all the lights are turned off."

* * *

Anna tried to fall asleep, but the sound of the voices on third floor annoyed her. She believed someone was upset. There was crying. She could hear low, muffled cries and then there was a scream. *Someone must be upset or in pain,* she thought.

"Did you hear that?" Leah whispered to Anna. "Listen. Footsteps coming up the stairs."

"Yeah. I wonder what's going on."

More footsteps hurried about over their heads and then stopped. They heard voices on the main staircase and went to their door to open slightly and peer out. They saw two men and two Sisters carrying a girl writhing in pain on a gurney down the large staircase. Mother Claudette was leading the way giving instructions on how to manage the steps. Once the patient was out the door, all fell quiet again.

"That girl was really hurting. Did you see?" Leah whispered as she and Anna continued to spy out their bedroom door.

"Yeah. I guess she couldn't even walk."

"Another one gone. The same men took her away. They must be hired to drive us to the hospital," Leah said.

"I suppose. I wonder if the Sisters go to the hospital with us?" Anna pondered.

"I don't think so. No one went with that last girl in labor. I'd like to know what happens to us after we leave the hospital. Did you notice that the girl never came back to get her clothes?"

Anna continued to have trouble falling asleep as she wondered about Leah's question. She too was curious. What happens to the girls once they leave Bassett House to have their babies? She decided they needed to find out soon.

CHAPTER THIRTEEN

Anna and her roommates fell into a routine over the first few weeks of the new year. Every day they had specific chores to complete; some days there were classes or activities. Every evening, they all enjoyed a little free time socializing in the common room. Very few visitors came to the home. Most of the girls never had a single visitor during their stay.

Aunt Victoria stopped by one Sunday afternoon in the third week of January to bring Anna a couple more jumpers in a larger size. She realized that Anna's belly was growing larger when she saw her at Christmas. They visited for a while, catching up on family news. She also delivered another letter from her Grandfather Daffin. There wasn't much to say. He mainly described the Christmas meal her mother had prepared and advised of the progression of her grandmother's illness. Before leaving, Victoria felt the baby move as she laid her hand on Anna's belly.

"That must be the strangest sensation! To have your body touched from the inside!"

"Oh, it truly is an odd feeling, but a nice one. I know my baby is real. I really have a human being inside me. That's just an amazing thought!"

"I'm feeling envious. I will never know what that feels like. Ever!" said Victoria as she rose to leave. "I'll stop back to see you in a few days. Take care of yourself!"

Rose also had a visitor that same day. Her oldest brother, Mario, came by with a bag of things she had asked him to bring her. He said something that upset her and then there was a shouting match between the two siblings. A couple of the Sisters heard the commotion and had to tell Mario to leave. It didn't seem to be a big deal, since Rose made sure to give her brother a hug before he ran out the entrance door. She carried her bag of loot up to her room with a satisfied smile.

"Hey, look what Mario just brought me! A radio! Now we can have our own music."

"I thought we couldn't have one," Anna stated.

"Nobody told me. Look! I can put it next to my bed so youse guys can hear, too."

"That's great, Rose! If you think it won't cause trouble. Thanks!" said Leah, as Penny came running through the door.

"Well, another one is leaving! I just saw her going out the front door downstairs. She could hardly walk."

"Penny, are you going to go out skipping, you think?" Anna teased.

"Maybe."

"You aren't very big yet. How many months are you now?"

"Seven, or almost seven, I guess," Penny said, counting on her fingers.

"I think all of us are goin' to have the babies at the same time!" Rose laughed. "Let's listen to some music, okay?"

"Fine by me but keep it low. We don't want any of the sisters coming in."

"I wish we could get American Bandstand here. I haven't seen it for so long," Rose said out loud as she listened to the dance tunes.

"What's that?" asked Leah.

"Never heard of it," added Anna.

"It's a television show in Philly where the kids dance to the latest songs. They get to pick the best ones for the week. It's really neat. I used to watch it all the time."

"That sounds like fun!" Leah said.

"We don't even have television yet, but I guess I couldn't get it in Maryland anyway," said Anna.

"When I am out of here, I am going to get a ticket for the show and youse can see me dancing with a bunch of guys," Rose laughed again. "I'll have one for each arm."

"Rose, you are wild!"

"You can't dance with two boys at one time, Rose. That's silly," Penny added.

"Oh, no?" Rose grinned over her shoulder. "Just watch me!"

* * *

For the next two weeks, the girls managed to keep the radio low enough that the Sisters did not hear it. They loved having a secret and especially getting something past Sister Mary Agnes. Rose showed the girls some of the dances she had seen on American Bandstand. She not only had all the moves, but she also knew the names and which tunes were best for dancing.

Rose also opened up to the others telling her roommates more about her tight-knit Italian family in Philadelphia and her close relationship with her brothers. Clearly, she was proud of her heritage and enjoyed talking about their uniqueness.

"So, I got five brothers and an older married sister. Mario and Vinnie are my older brothers, and they look after me a lot. Always have. My parents run a market on the corner two blocks down from our house and are always working. I worked there. We all did, but it wasn't what I wanted to do with my life. My mama is always trying to find a husband for me. Papa, not so much. He has other worries," she hesitated as she felt a twinge of homesickness. Anna, Penny, and Leah listened intently with curiosity.

"Ya know, my brothers go out wit three, four different girls every week and nobody says notin'. Good for youse guys! But, when I do it, I get read the riot act. Especially by my brothers! They tell me good girls don't run around like that. They say it makes me a slut and word gets out 'bout me. Why is it that a girl is a slut, but boys get a pass and even brag about it? Sometin' wrong wit that thinkin'!" Her words caused the girls to ponder for a moment.

"Jimmy, my old boyfriend, and his parents, never thought he was responsible, but I know different. I never asked for this to happen, but here I am, and he has joined the Army. He is free to go on with his life," Anna exclaimed in anger. "He probably has another girl by now. Who will want me when I go back home? I won't get to finish school or enjoy my senior year. All my friends are having a good time now planning for graduation. I can never get those days back."

"Same here. I won't get my diploma either," lamented Leah. "We can never say anything about what has happened to us. We have to go home and act like it never happened. Isn't that what the Sisters keep telling us?"

"Yeah, we get a fresh start as long as we never say nutin' about this place," Rose added.

"I'm going back to school next fall. I want to graduate," interjected Penny.

"Now you will be a year behind and won't graduate with your classmates."

"Oh, I didn't think about that."

"Will you go back to your parents' home when you leave, Rose?" asked Leah, already knowing that the others would return to their homes.

"I don't think so. I'll probably go to New York and stay wit my sister. I'm sure Mario or Vinnie will pick me up and take me where they want me to stay," Rose replied. "Ever since they found out I was preggers, they take care of things for me. They told me I brought 'vergogna' to our family. They called me a whore and tramp, and Mario slapped me on my face. It was an ugly scene. I wasn't goin' to take no shit off them boys, but they got to me," said Rose, anguishing over the memory. The other girls suddenly saw fear in Rose and decided to end their conversation for this night.

* * *

One snowy Saturday evening at the end of January, Penny was taking her bath while the other roommates put clean sheets on their beds and listened to some music. There was a sudden tumbling sound followed by a loud thud in the bathroom. They all heard Penny moaning and ran to the door. It was locked from the inside. Anna called to her. No response came.

"Leah, get one of the sisters to bring a key for this door. They must have one."

"Let me get rid of this radio. We don't need that to come up now," Rose said as Leah hurried off.

Anna and Rose both called to Penny. There was a faint indecipherable sound.

"Sounds like she is on the floor. She must have fallen," Anna deducted.

Mother Claudette and Sister Mary Catherine flew into the room with their brown habits fluttering with each brisk step.

Mother Claudette had keys and quickly selected the one that fit the bathroom door. As she threw open the door, those closest could see little Penny lying in a pool of blood that was still flowing out of her. She had a cut on her head from a fall she took miss-stepping out of the tub. It appeared that she hit the corner of the sink on her way down. However, there was more blood than that coming from her head wound.

"Call for the car. Quick. She has miscarried in here. We need to get her to the hospital fast."

"Hemorrhaging?" asked Sister Mary Catherine.

"Yes, I believe so. She is also unconscious. Someone get me some towels."

It seemed too long for the men with the gurney to arrive. Penny started to come around as they picked her up and loaded her along with several rolled bloody towels that Mother Claudette placed on the gurney with her. She appeared so small and frail as she was taken out of the room and on to the hospital. All of the girls stood by solemnly as she passed by.

"Go about your business everyone. Everything will be just fine," Sister Catherine ordered.

"Poor little Penny. What will happen to her now?" Anna asked aloud. No one had an answer.

The remaining roommates slept in the room that night. The bathroom door had been locked, so they used the one in the adjoining room. It was an awful, bloody mess that no one wanted to see. The next morning the three girls were dressed for the day and ready for breakfast when Mother Claudette and Sister Catherine showed up at their door with buckets, rags, and mops to disinfect the whole area. They unlocked the bathroom door to reveal the dry and sticky horror on the floor, walls, and in the tub. Mother Claudette insisted that it be spotless when she came back to inspect it.

"You want that we should clean this up? Is that what you're espectin' us to do?" Rose asked the Mother Superior, cocking her head to one side signaling defiance.

"This is your room. If you ever expect to use this bathroom again, or any bathroom for that matter, I do expect you to clean it, disinfect it, and sanitize it to my standards. Now, I want no further lip from any of you. I will come back to inspect this room before breakfast is served to you today."

The three stunned girls remained speechless with eyes glued to the floor for a few minutes. Finally, Leah broke the silence.

"Well, I have a small bladder and it is getting smaller every day. I can't hold my water for too long, so I say we get to it!" That was enough to motivate Anna and Rose, while giving them a chuckle at the same time.

It was a terrible sight, but the girls dealt with it by singing some of the new songs they had heard on the radio lately. Anything to take their minds off the bloody chore. It actually took less time to complete with all three girls scrubbing, wiping, and mopping to meet perfection.

Once Mother Superior approved of their clean-up job, the girls set out once again for breakfast, but not until they scrubbed their hands and arms clean of the bloody residue.

* * *

"Sister Margaret, have you heard anything about Penny?" Anna asked as she sat at the dining table that the Sister was cleaning off. She felt comfortable enough to approach the friendly Sister about her roommate's condition. Of all the sisters at the home, she was the least intimidating.

"I probably don't know any more than you. She lost her baby. Poor thing. A baby girl. Also, Penny may have had a seizure, but the doctors weren't sure last night. We may never know."

"I thought you might know what happened. We cleaned up a lot of blood. It must have been frightening for her."

"That is what I heard from Mother Claudette. She was quite upset and hardly slept last night. She is fearful of having another incident like the one at her previous home in Quebec. That's where she was before she was relocated here in Wilmington." Then realizing she had said too much, Sister Margaret quickly turned and started to walk back toward the kitchen. Anna sensed that she had said something she shouldn't mention but wanted to know more about Penny.

"Is she still in the hospital? Will she come back here?" asked Anna before Sister exited the dining hall.

"Oh, they never come back here," she said on her way out of the room. Sister Margaret must have been right on that because someone cleared out all of Penny's clothes and belongings that afternoon. Every trace of her was gone.

The girls filed over to the church later that morning as the winds howled around them and an icy snow stung their faces. Most of the girls in the third trimester did not have coats that buttoned properly, so they hugged their garments as close to them as they could. They also tied scarves around their heads to keep their ears warm.

"I'm freezing!" Leah said.

"Me, too!" Anna exclaimed. There wasn't much conversation among the girls that day. A sense of melancholy had befallen them as they wondered about Penny. The scene in the bathroom had shaken them up, and it seemed that none of the other Sisters would tell them how she was doing. Sister Annemarie stood at the doorway making sure all the girls had head coverings. Those that didn't were given white tissues to pin down in their hair.

Anna sat in the middle of a pew of six Catholic girls on her right and four non-Catholics on her left. Father O'Connor was long-winded that morning. His homily seemed longer than usual to Anna. The Catholic girls were standing and kneeling constantly throughout the service while the rest of the girls sat frozen in their seats trying to comprehend the Latin spoken during the mass. Father O'Connor spoke briefly of the loss of Penny's child and had a special prayer for the child's soul.

Anna couldn't wait to go back to her room. She felt detached from everyone and everything around her. Something didn't feel right with her. The stained-glass window to her left depicted Christ hanging on the cross, and she imagined blood dripping from his hands as Father spoke of the blood of the lamb being slaughtered for our sins. Anna felt strange inside as her temples began to throb. The room began to spin slightly, and her heart felt as if it would come out of her chest. She put her finger next to the side of her neck to feel the increased pulse. Father O'Connor continued to speak words she didn't understand, and the stained-glass window glared back at her as she thought she saw the blood trickle down the picture. Her heart pounded and she was breathing harder. She put her head down between her legs as best she as could. Her belly prevented her from bending too far. Breathing became worse and she felt she might pass out. She wanted to leave, had to leave, but she was in the middle of the pew. Where could she go? She turned to her right. The Catholic girls were on their knees. She turned to her left the Non-Catholics were sitting in the pew. Her heartbeats continued to pound in her chest. *I have to leave*, she thought. *Get out now*! She stood up. Turning to her left, she scooted past everyone seated on the pew and headed to the bathroom in the back hallway. Once inside, she splashed water on her face and began washing herself with lots of green soap from a dispenser. She didn't feel clean, couldn't get clean. It still felt like she was covered in Penny's blood, and it wouldn't come off. She continued to throw cool water on her face and try to slow her breathing. After several minutes, her pulse came down and her breathing was normal again. She felt exhausted.

"Grace? Are you in there? You okay?" asked Leah.

"Yeah, I'm alright now. I felt a little sick. I must have had too much bacon for breakfast this morning."

"I saw you leave in a hurry. I was afraid something was wrong. Want me to wait for you? Mass is over now."

"No, you go ahead. I'll be along in a bit. I just need to settle my stomach," Anna said, not knowing how to face her friend about what had just happened to her, and also feeling quite embarrassed by it. *What was that?* She wondered. *It felt like I was having a heart attack. But, at my age?*

* * *

All three girls hung out in their room that evening, after suffering through a long, somber, and dismal day.

"I've had enough of this shit! Let's listen to some music!" exclaimed Rose suddenly as she plugged in her radio and tuned in to a Perry Como song.

"'Papa Loves Mambo'! I love this song!" Rose began dancing to the music and singing the words. "Come on, youse guys! Let's have some fun!"

Leah and Anna slid off their beds and began dancing and then twirling each other. Feeling very carefree, they continued on dancing and laughing through the next song. Rose showed Anna and Leah how to do the Cha Cha. They roared with laughter at the sight of their big bellies rocking back and forth. They looked so awkward and silly. The next song that came on was also good for dancing.

"I can't wait to go on American Bandstand when I'm home," Rose said walking over to turn the radio up. The three of them were dancing around the room singing along and having a fun time when the bedroom door slammed open suddenly. In the doorway stood Sister Mary Agnes with a face as red as the tomato sauce they had for dinner. They knew instantly that she was angry about the music coming from the radio.

"How dare you girls behave in this manner! Dancing on Sunday! I won't have it! Proper young ladies do not behave like this. It's the type of sinfulness that has brought you to us in the first place and you should know better than this."

Their gay hearts sank to a new low. Immediate depression set in. *What have we done wrong,* Anna wondered.

"Give me that radio. Is that yours, Rose? You know you are not permitted to have a radio in your room."

"Sista, I thought we could," tested Rose.

"Don't lie to me. Get yourselves ready for bed. I don't want to hear a peep out of any of you again tonight." With that she yanked the cord from the socket, tucked the radio under her arm, stomped across the floor, and slammed the door behind her.

They needed the release that laughter brought. This had been a terrible weekend for them. They just wanted to feel alive again. Instead, they were shamed once more.

After the lights went out, Anna cried into her pillow and prayed that this nightmare would soon be over.

CHAPTER FOURTEEN

As new girls came into Bassett House, they took over the cleaning jobs and Anna was moved to a room on the third floor that had sewing machines and equipment to make blankets, sheets, and other items for the home. Mother Claudette found out that Anna and Leah were experienced in sewing, so she gave them the task of making several baby nightgowns and caps. After grabbing straight pins, measuring tape, and scissors from the storage boxes on a counter, the girls set about cutting pieces off a soft white ream of cotton material.

"Hey, Grace, do you think these nightgowns are for the babies? You know, our babies?"

"I'm wondering where they are going, too," pondered Anna. "Mostly, I am just glad that I don't have to clean toilets again! I would much rather be sewing!"

"Me, too! I want to know if my baby will have some of these nightgowns, though. I don't have any clothes for it. They must provide something to put on them when they are born, don't you think?"

"Sounds reasonable. Wouldn't it be great to know that we are making the clothes that our babies will wear?"

Leah nodded. "At least it's something we can give them. I don't have anything else."

They worked for several hours each day. By Valentine's Day, they had made one hundred forty-four gowns and fifty-one caps. They felt very proud of their work as they placed the folded gowns into boxes that Sister Annemarie brought them.

"You two have done an excellent job. These look very nice. You are quite skilled, and your mothers have taught you well."

"Thank you, Sister," Anna and Leah responded in unison.

"As a reward for such good work, how would you both like to have a banana split or ice cream sundae?"

"That's nice," Anna responded, although feeling this was a childish gift.

"Oh, not here," Sister Annemarie said, understanding the glib response. "I'll give you some money for a snack bar three blocks down on Third Avenue. You can get whatever you want. You are probably craving some French fries or something like that."

"That's great! We'd love that!" Leah said enthusiastically.

"Do you want to go this afternoon? It's only 2:30 now. You will have plenty of time to go and get back before dark."

"Sounds wonderful, sister! May I also stop at the drugstore for another pair of socks? I really need some heavier ones," asked Anna.

"Of course. Let's go downstairs to notify Sister Mary Agnes and get you some wedding bands."

"Some what?" Leah asked.

"When you go outside the building, you need to wear wedding bands so people will not talk about you. It's for your protection. You won't get the stares, or at least not as many."

"I've never given that a thought," Anna said.

* * *

Sister Mary Agnes opened a drawer in her credenza and took out a jewelry box that contained plain gold wedding bands of all sizes. Anna and Leah tried them on until they found ones that fit. They signed out on a ledger with the time they were leaving.

"Back before dark, you understand?" Sister Mary Agnes reminded them. The girls nodded in response and off they went.

It was a pleasant afternoon for the middle of February. The recent snow had melted away and the sun glared down on the sidewalk as Anna and Leah found their way to the local drugstore. They stayed together as they searched the store for socks that Anna needed. She had hoped for wool, but they were sold out. She could only buy a two-pack of thick white cotton socks.

"These will do. At least I will have some without holes now," she laughed.

The store was full of shoppers looking for last minute cards and chocolates for their sweethearts. The girls passed down the aisle containing specialty items for Valentine's Day wondering who would be receiving the pretty red and pink boxes topped with bows and plastic flowers.

"Look at the size of that one. Ten pounds of chocolates and nuts! Must be for a heavy-weight girlfriend!" Leah and Anna laughed. It felt so good to be out among regular people, shopping, laughing, and feeling free of scrutiny. None of the shoppers paid attention to them but went about their business. It wasn't at all like sister said it would be. Tiny boxes of chocolate-covered cherries sat next to the cash register. With a sudden impulse, Anna chose one and included it with the purchase of her socks.

"I'll take the chocolates back to the room for us to share with Rose tonight. We can have two each."

"If she hangs out with us. Since that new girl from Philly arrived, she has been spending more time with her than us. They speak Italian sometimes so no one can understand what they are talking about."

"Clever! Well, if she isn't with us tonight, we get to have three pieces."

Nothing could bother Anna this day. *I am so happy to be outside and feel the sun on my face. I don't care how cold it is! I'm away from that gloomy place for a while!*

The girls continued on down the street to the snack shop gazing into the store windows along the way. Anna felt like it had been a very long time since she had been shopping. She enjoyed looking at the new styles and products displayed. *I love the gray pencil skirt with that white sweater! I wonder if I will ever be able to fit into an outfit like that now! Oh, my, look at that price! I can't afford anything like that anyway.*

The snack shop had an old-time soda fountain area in the front of the store with red swivel stools lined up at the spotless white Formica countertop. Silver napkin dispensers, glossy menus, and bottles of ketchup and mustard stood together in evenly spaced metal racks. At this time of day, only a couple of patrons lingered over their newspaper, a cup of coffee, and a cigarette. Anna and Leah chose seats near the front window, away from the smokers. A middle-aged waitress in a neatly pressed white uniform and cap with red trim came over to take their orders.

"Know what you want? Or do you want to look at the menu first?" she asked sounding disinterested.

"No, we're ready to order. We know what we want," said Leah, anxious for her treat.

"We'd like a chocolate sundae and a soda, Coke-a-cola if you have it."

"You both want the same thing?"

"Yes, please," Anna confirmed.

While the waitress prepared their sundaes, they looked at the menu for all the items they hadn't had in months and made plans to order them all when they got back home.

"I think we need to get jobs when we are home, so we don't have to depend on a boyfriend to treat us to ice cream or burgers, don't you?" asked Leah.

"Definitely!"

"Grace, do you mind if I ask you what your real name is? I was thinking that since we live so close back home that maybe we could visit each other. I won't know how to find you if I don't know your name. I'll tell you mine, too."

"Sure. I'd like to meet up once we are out of here. We should be friends for life after this experience. My name is Anna Ruth Scott. And yours?"

"Marilee Potter." They smiled at the revelation. They could be themselves with each other, not a make-believe person who had to hide from the world. Miraculously, they felt whole again and comfortable in their own skin.

"May I call you Anna?"

"As long as the sisters don't hear us, we can call each other by our real names whenever we feel like it!" she declared.

They continued chatting without reservation about hopes for the future and upcoming changes, for as long as they could. When they noticed the outside starting to turn to dusk, they paid the check and hurried back to Bassett House to check back in and return their wedding bands. They made it just in time! No reprimands from Sister today!

* * *

The sewing projects continued on into March. Anna and Leah were pleased because they had been given another opportunity for a trip to the snack bar after they finished the next work order request – 210 cloth diapers. Having an incentive boosted their mental health.

Rose was due to deliver any day and she looked it. She didn't have any specific chores this close to her time. Her days were spent in the common room or wandering around visiting with others in the building. On a couple of nice afternoons, the first week of March, she asked to sit in a garden off the kitchen at the rear of the building. Rose liked to sit on the bench among the raised beds which would soon contain herbs, tomatoes, cucumbers, peas, corn and other vegetables for consumption over the summer months. She would have enjoyed working in the garden but knew she would be long gone when planting began. When Rose stood up to go back inside, she felt a stabbing pain in the lower part of her belly.

"What the hell!" She took a couple of steps and felt another one. She hurried into the back door to the kitchen and called out for Sister Margaret.

"Oh, dear, you must be going into labor. Let's get you to the car."

With that, she ran off for help that set the standard wheels in motion. "It's Rose's time!" she called out. "Somebody call for the car!"

The new girl from Philly burst into the sewing room and yelled out "Rose is having her baby. They are getting ready to take her to the hospital. She wants to see you two before she leaves. Better come now."

Anna and Leah ran down the stairs as fast as they could and caught up with Rose before she was out the door. They saw the usual black car parked at the end of the walkway.

"Oh, good. I hoped to see you. I guess I won't be back. Looks like this is it. I'll be back on the dance floor before youse know it. Will ya pack up my stuff for me? One of my brothas is comin' by to pick it up. I dun't want nobody else to touch my stuff, ya hear? Youse are the best! Thanks!"

"Send us a message if you can, will you Rose?" Anna whispered to her.

"Yeah, sure. I'll try to do that. And it's Dolores," she whispered back. "Dolores Costello."

Anna, Leah, and a few other girls watched as Dolores was helped into the back seat of the awaiting car. They saw her grimace with a contraction just as the car pulled away from the front of the building. She missed seeing all the girls standing on the sidewalk waving goodbye to their friend. Dolores had been fun, entertaining, and a joy to have around in the somber environment they had all been placed. She would be missed.

"There she goes! Now, which one of us is next?"

Anna and Leah packed up Dolores's belongings and left them on top of her bed. Hours passed and there was no word. None of the sisters told them anything about her, not even Sister Margaret. Four days later, Vinnie showed up to get Dolores's things and left a note from her on Anna's bed.

"Hey preggos! I had a baby boy! I feel great. Almost ready to dance the Cha Cha with you. The baby is the cutest. He has dark eyes and lots of black hair. He weighed 7 pounds and 10 ounces. A nice size! He really is beautiful. I didn't expect to love him so much. It's going to be hard to say goodbye. Sister thinks she has a family that wants him. You won't believe

this, but we are both out of the hospital already. They took us to the south wing of Bassett House. That is where they keep the babies until they are adopted. My brothers paid off what is due for my stay so I will be going home soon. Maybe I will see you before I leave. I don't know. I think I know who his father is too. Looks just like him. Hang in there! Rose

* * *

"She's in this building? The mothers and babies come back here?" Anna was stunned.

"How did we not know that?" added an equally stunned Leah.

Anna and Leah sat on their beds pondering the new revelation. No one had ever said anything about what happens after the baby arrives. They were in the dark about everything after that point. Sister Mary Agnes told them that she was in charge of finding a good home for their babies and Sister Catherine would draft the paperwork, but the rest was a mystery.

"Sister Catherine, what will happen to me after I have my baby?" Anna asked in her next counseling session.

"Let's see. You are only three weeks from your due date, aren't you? I would expect you to be asking questions now."

Sister flipped through a folder and pulled out a white paper to hand to Anna. "This is the invoice for room and board for your stay here at Bassett House. You will need to stay and work off the remainder due. You were fortunate enough to work off some in advance by sewing the outfits and diapers, but that does not take care of the whole bill."

"I don't understand. No one told me that I had to pay anything," Anna said trying to think back on previous conversations.

"I thought once the family takes my baby, I could go home. Don't they pay money? Isn't it enough to pay off my bill?" Anna asked, becoming upset.

"Here. We'll let you know more after you have your baby. You shouldn't stress yourself so much, Grace. Soon you will be able to forget all about this mistake. You can go on and resume a normal life," Sister Catherine said in a peculiar consolation. "Oh, yes, I may have a fine family for you. I'll interview them tomorrow. The husband works for DuPont."

Anna left in a huff. She felt lost. Imprisoned inside the gloomy, gray building under complete control of the women in charge, Anna felt helpless and vulnerable. She was utterly bewildered by the procedures for the adoption of her baby. And the truth was, the reality that she had a small human growing inside became genuinely apparent with each movement and kick. She was no longer certain that she could so easily surrender her child to strangers. *Even if they are a wealthy DuPont family, can they love my baby as much as I do,* Anna questioned.

* * *

The following day, a new girl was assigned to the room and took Penny's old bed. Anna and Leah stayed mostly to themselves those days in March, but they discovered that their new roommate came from New Jersey.

The lights went out at 10:30, as usual, and there was dead silence, except for the wind blowing outside and an occasional rattling of the old window casings. Anna had trouble falling asleep again. She just couldn't find a position that was comfortable for her belly. Just as she began to doze off, she heard someone crying in the distance. *Where is that coming from,* she wondered. She heard it again. She could see that Leah was asleep and didn't want to disturb her. The sound continued.

Anna got out of her bed and walked over to the window. The sound appeared to be coming from outside. On the back lawn was a bench between two statues meant for a place of meditation and prayer. Tonight, there sat a woman in a white nightgown sobbing uncontrollably. Her arms were around her waist, and she rocked back and forth. After a while, two sisters and the men who drive the car to the hospital arrived and tried to coax her to leave with them. She fought back and ran from their grips.

Anna recognized the woman by the long black hair that flowed around her nightgown. It was Delores! She saw her fall on the ground and the men caught up to her. They picked her up and carried her limp body towards the street where they had parked the black car. She had surrendered to them. There was no more fight left in her. Anna was shocked by what she saw, but she didn't tell Leah about it. She struggled to sleep and when she finally achieved rest, she heard Leah call out to her.

"Anna? Anna are you awake?" She said in a loud whisper. "Anna, please wake up."

"What? What's wrong?"

"My bed is wet. I don't think I peed myself. Do you think my water can break in my sleep?"

"Oh, no! I have no idea. We better find out."

"Not now. I don't feel any pain." She looked at the clock. "Besides, it's not even 3:30. I don't want to wake the sisters yet. I'd rather stay here with you until I have to go."

"Alright, but if you start having pains, you need to get to the hospital. Deal?"

"Of course," Leah responded. "Anna, I don't mind telling you that I am a little scared."

"You are going to be fine. I know you will get through this. Then when we both get back home, we can go out for a good time."

"I have your number memorized. That's in case I never see my suitcase and things again."

"Smart idea."

"Hunter 2-8594, right?" Anna repeated.

"Yep. You got it."

"And if my mother won't let me come home with her, I'll probably be at my aunt's house in Greenville, so that will be close to your place."

"Don't worry. We will be in contact."

By the time everyone was called for breakfast, Leah had cleaned up, removed her wet sheets and dressed for the day. She still hadn't felt any pains. She ate a piece of buttered toast and drank some hot tea before heading back upstairs. With one foot on the first step, she felt a strong contraction come on that made her bend over in pain.

Sister Margaret heard her cry out. She and Anna ran over to see Leah sitting on the floor.

"It happened all of a sudden. It really hurts," she grimaced.

Sister Margaret could see that she was in a great deal of pain and believed she needed to get Leah to the hospital quickly. Everyone scrambled to assist. The black car came, and the men loaded Leah onto the gurney. Anna held her hand and walked with her until she reached the car door.

"You are going to be fine. I'll see you soon," she said releasing her hand.

The men lifted the gurney into the back seat of the car as Leah was calling out for someone to help make the pain stop. She didn't notice that Anna was still standing on the sidewalk telling her to stay strong. She felt so alone at that moment.

Anna would miss Leah's company in this depressing place.

"I certainly hope she doesn't need a cesarean," Sister Margaret said as Anna walked back into the building.

What the heck is she talking about? It can't be good! Anna decided, shaking her head but unwilling to ask for an explanation from the sister.

CHAPTER FIFTEEN

The hospital called Marilee's mother to let her know that her daughter was in labor and having a difficult time. She drove up to Wilmington within hours to be by her side. Marilee had to be sedated due to the amount of pain and because she needed to stay strapped to a gurney in the hallway until a bed was available for her. When a doctor finally looked at her, he realized that there was a problem. Further observation revealed that the baby was not fully in position.

Marilee was rushed into the delivery room and attempts were made to turn the baby. Between the two doctors who worked on her, they were able to achieve success before there was too much stress on either the baby or mom. Late that afternoon, Marilee gave birth to a red-headed baby boy weighing in at eight pounds and three ounces.

The next morning, Marilee's mother came by Bassett House to retrieve her belongings. Anna had made sure that all of her friend's possessions were packed and ready to go. She asked Sister Mary Agnes if she could deliver the suitcase to Marilee's mother, and to her surprise was granted permission.

"Hello. Mrs. Potter?" Anna asked as she carried the suitcase with two hands down the staircase. At the bottom stood an attractive woman in a belted pink gingham dress looking clearly stressed and anxious.

"Yes, oh my, let me help you. You shouldn't have carried this down by yourself."

"I'm fine. How is Marilee doing? Did she have her baby?" Anna gushed.

"She and the baby are fine. She had a rough time for a while, but it all turned out fine."

"I was worried about her. We have become good friends and I saw how much pain she had yesterday.... Well, I just didn't have a way to find out anything."

"I appreciate your help. I need to return home today. I slept in a chair in her room last night, you see. After the baby is adopted, Marilee will be coming home with me. As you probably know, we didn't part on good terms. I was pretty upset with her, but I understand now. I don't blame her for what happened. That jerk was not the person I thought he was. I never should have doubted my daughter."

"That is so wonderful to hear, Mrs. Potter. I'm sure Marilee is happy that you have been here to support her now. Please tell her I was asking for her."

"I will. I'm taking this suitcase to her before I leave. Thank you, again." With that, she took the suitcase in hand and quickly left out the front door.

Anna was pleased for her friend. She wished her mother could be with her when she went into labor, but she was sure her father would never allow it. The last couple of letters she received from her mother said as much. She was surprised at how much she longed for her mother to be with her. As her time drew near, her anxiety level increased.

The next couple of weeks were terribly lonely. Another girl arrived, but Anna didn't make any effort to become friends. She stayed to herself. She thought about her former roommates every day, wondering where they were and if they were in good health. At the same time, she worried about her future. What was in store for her in this process? She felt affection for the child she carried, spending time each day to tell her unborn stories of her family and personal thoughts. Believing that the baby understood her helped to build a connection. How could she ever give up this part of her? She had loved Jimmy once. Even if she didn't now, it just didn't seem right to turn their child over to strangers. She didn't know anything about the people. How would she know if they would protect and care for their baby; no, make that her baby! From now on, this was her baby only.

It was March 30, 1955. Anna had been a resident of Bassett House for almost four months. She had seen her roommates leave with barely a word afterward. She had a feeling that something peculiar was happening. This was a mysterious place. Nothing was familiar or normal to her. With the first pang of a contraction, she realized that today was her turn to cross over. She not only had anxiety over the birth process but also for what lay ahead of her after the baby arrived.

Anna didn't say anything about the contractions immediately. She stayed in the common room looking at a Sears catalog from last fall and periodically watching a program on the television. She walked the hallway a few times as the pains grew stronger.

Sister Annemarie came into the common room to organize a painting class. As she set up the items needed on the activities table, she noticed that Anna was behaving oddly.

"Grace are you feeling okay?" she asked walking over to Anna.

"I believe I'm in labor. Or I have food poisoning," she chuckled.

"How bad are the contractions? How long have you had them?" Sister asked with concern.

"Long enough that I should probably go to the hospital soon," replied Anna as another one overcame her.

"Let me call for the car. We'll get you there right away," Sister Annemarie told her as she ran off to advise Sister Mary Agnes.

Within a few minutes, the black car arrived, and the driver and his helper hurried through the front door looking for someone to direct them. The tall man carried a folded canvas gurney. Sister Mary Agnes called to the men from the top of the stairs and pointed in the direction of the common room on the second floor.

They had made the trip together up the stairs many times, weekly at least, finding the old army-style gurney the easiest way to get the young women out of the building and into their car. The sisters didn't like the girls in labor to linger around for too long, fearful that it may be too late to get them to a hospital, and also because it made the other girls upset and restless. It was one more ordeal to be dealt with in the facility and they simply didn't want to take it on.

The men approached Anna who was relaxing on the sofa trying to breathe slowly.

"I don't need that," Anna told the men. "I want to walk down the stairs by myself."

"Nothing doin', miss. You need to git yourself on this gurney now! We ain't going to be responsible for you hurting yourself and that baby."

Anna frowned but stood up and complied. They took their time cautiously carrying her down the steps and out the front door. Luckily, there wasn't any of the chaotic fanfare that she had seen with her roommates. Anna and the gurney were slid into the back of the car where the seat was missing to accommodate her. The car had been modified to haul the girls specifically to the emergency room just like an ambulance.

Upon arrival, Anna was placed on another gurney, with wheels this time, and then moved into the maternity ward hallway. The attendant that delivered her there explained nothing, simply walking away and leaving her there totally alone for a couple of hours. No one checked on her the entire time. Her contractions intensified. A janitor came into the hallway pushing a large dust mop. Anna noticed the old man advancing towards her in his dark green coveralls. He had greasy, slicked back hair and dirty long fingernails. His eyes kept glancing up at her and then around behind him, making Anna more uncomfortable by the second. As he pushed his broom by Anna, he stopped, looked her over from belly to her face, and then laughed at her with total contempt.

"Got yourself in a pickle, don't you, missy?" He uttered in a low voice with a partially toothless sneer.

Anna was now very afraid. "Get away from me!" She yelled at him. "Someone please help me!" There was no one to hear her. No one came to assist her.

And although he knew help would not arrive, like a filthy rat, he went away, hunched over and slinking around the corner of the hall with his mop.

Finally, Anna saw a nurse heading in her direction.

"Can you call my mother?" Anna pleaded as a nurse walked by. "I want to speak with my mother. I don't know what to do."

"Sorry, but I can't call your mother, honey."

"But there was a janitor here and he was looking at me in a strange way and I am afraid he'll come back. He was creep..."

"Why don't you just settle down. There is nothing to worry about," said the nurse without empathy as she kept on walking.

Contractions came harder and closer together. Anna went into a trancelike state. She blocked out everything around her and thought back to her stay at Rehoboth. Remembering the smells of the beach; the fries and burgers, suntan lotion, and salty sea air. She pictured Betty and Kay bobbing with the waves and laughing at silly jokes late at night. Her thoughts also turned to waiting on the customers at Mr. Kokkinos's restaurant; the sand that covered the floor and seats, the children with ketchup on their faces, and the couples who shared the large portions of French fries and vinegar. Then she remembered that night, that hot summer night in June when she and Jimmy had such fun and ended up on a blanket on the beach where he kissed her and rubbed his hands over her body as she had never been touched before. When he took her…

"Has anyone checked this girl yet?" asked a doctor walking by. "I think she is ready to go in. Better let me examine her immediately."

"I need some water. I'm so thirsty. May I have a drink?" Anna requested.

"Nurse, get this girl a glass of shaved ice. How long has she been in the hallway?" The doctor questioned. No one had an answer.

"What's wrong here? Why wasn't this patient taken into a room a long time ago? I don't ever want to see another woman left in a hallway while in labor. She is ready to deliver! Who is responsible for this?" Again, there was no response. Attendants rushed up the hall to take Anna in the operating room immediately. Her doctor went in to scrub down and join her.

An examination revealed that she was almost fully dilated. Relieved that he had discovered this patient when he did, he didn't want to think of the consequences had she been left much longer.

Shortly before 9:00 that night, Anna gave birth to a beautiful blonde-haired baby girl. She weighed 7 pounds and 6 ounces, and she was the most precious sight Anna had ever seen. She immediately fell in love with her. The baby was cleaned off and swaddled in a flannel receiving blanket with pink teddy bears covering it. The nurse who was wrapping the baby girl put a little pink cap on her head and turned to put the babe in her mother's arms. An older nurse standing next to her grabbed her arm stopping her from the delivery. She simply shook her head, signaling that the child was not to stay with its mother. They didn't want any bonding to begin.

"She needs to go into the nursery now," said the baby's nurse. "We'll take you to your room shortly. Please try to get some rest. We'll take good care of her. Don't you worry."

Anna shared a room with a mother having her third child. Their babies were born a few hours apart, having the same birth date. Although the curtain between the beds was pulled, she could hear the woman's visitors come and go – her husband, both sets of grandparents, her sister, her best friend and a neighbor, all came in to bring flowers and gifts and gush over the newborn. No one came to see Anna. She wasn't even sure her parents had been told that she was in the hospital. Anna was able to feed and change her baby throughout the day, but the nurses had orders not to let her have too much time alone. The baby needed a temporary name to use until the adoption was final. Anna chose the name, Suzanne, so she could include a part of her name. The adoptive parents probably wouldn't keep the name, but at least it would appear on her hospital records.

One minute Anna was elated about being a mom, holding her sweet little Suzanne, touching her soft chubby cheeks, and counting her tiny toes and fingers. Then the realization of how temporary the precious moments would be hit her like a brick wall and she fell into a depression. She felt completely unworthy of loving her. She had nothing to give.

After three days in the hospital, Anna and Suzanne were delivered to the South Wing of Bassett House. The sisters in charge took Suzanne into the nursery on the second floor and placed her in one of the cribs among several other babies. A couple dressed in business attire stood in front of the large window overlooking the crib area making remarks about each one's characteristics. They were obviously shopping.

Anna was escorted to a room on the third floor that was smaller than the room she previously had at Bassett House. There was only space for one roommate and there was a shared bathroom in the hallway. The common area was at the top of the stairs with the usual television, games, books, and magazines. The residents of this wing were not allowed on the second floor without permission. This was the area that housed the nursery which was locked for the security of the babies. In the past, there had been some mothers who tried to steal their babies and leave with them. The sisters in charge took every precaution to keep that from happening again.

Anna found that her suitcase had been delivered to her new room. She looked forward to putting on some of her own clothes and rid herself of the backless nightgowns. As she was changing into one of her jumpers and blouse, in walked her friend, Marilee Potter.

"Leah! Do I still need to call you that?" Marilee stepped over to give her friend a hug.

"Yeah, we are still stuck with those names a while longer here."

"Are you in this room, too?" Asked Anna.

"Yep, they are keeping us together. They must trust us to not cause a ruckus!" Marilee responded.

"It's so truly good to see you! Any of the others here too?"

"Penny was here but left soon after I arrived. She is having difficulty speaking and will need additional care at a hospital for quite some time. She didn't look well when I saw her. Mind you, it was only for a few brief minutes."

"So sorry to hear that the kid isn't doing so well. She will pull through though, I'm sure of it!"

"Her boyfriend never did make contact with her, she said. I hope he never does. That creep has probably moved on to another young girl by now!"

"For certain, but we all knew that snake wasn't going to show up. He's long gone!" Anna said. "What about Rose? Have you seen her? It's a weird thing – I thought I saw her one night on a bench in the back of the building. She was crying."

"I'm not surprised. She is in a room by herself on the second floor. She needs medication all the time. I heard that she tried to run away twice. She saw her baby, named him Eduardo, and cared for him while at the hospital. Then, when she arrived here the nurses took over and wouldn't let her have him so much. That's what they do. You're not needed anymore."

"Did they do that to you, too?" Questioned Anna.

"Of course! You'll see."

"I thought I would still see Suzanne later today. You know, feed her and hold her for a while."

"Don't count on it. Some of the babies leave here before we do. That's what happened to Rose. That little boy was so cute that an Italian couple came in and wanted to take him home as soon as they saw him."

"It happens that quickly?"

"It did for him. Rose couldn't handle it. You could hear screaming down the hall. She was cussing the nurses and the nuns like you wouldn't believe. They couldn't do anything but sedate her. Now, she just sleeps and looks terrible with dark circles under her eyes. She also lost weight and without her makeup, she doesn't look like herself."

"I'd like to see her. Maybe I can talk to her. She was the strongest of all of us. How did this happen to her?"

"They broke her."

* * *

The dining hall on the first floor was for residents of the south wing. Anna and Marilee ate supper together that night. Looking around at the few girls in the room, Anna recognized that they had all once stayed with her on the other side of the building. They all looked weary and sad. A few were leaving tomorrow after fulfilling their obligations to Bassett House. Family members would pick them up at the side door and off they would go to resume their lives, just as if this episode had never occurred.

Anna and Marilee still had an obligation to repay Bassett House so they would be there a while longer. Anna was given a work order. She would be handling laundry with Marilee in the mornings and a few sewing projects in the afternoon during the week. Weekends were her own, but she was not allowed outside the building without permission. She was able to occasionally catch a glimpse of Suzanne throughout the day when she entered the nursery to gather dirty diapers and soiled blankets. The nurses who cared for her refused to let her hold her daughter and she was told to keep her distance, so they didn't get germs from the nasty laundry. At night she cried herself to sleep as her arms ached, her heart felt pain, and her mind couldn't comprehend how to live without the tiny life that was a part of her.

Marilee was also dealing with the loss but didn't feel the same connection. She felt she should have a stronger sense of love for the babe she had borne, but since she didn't, there was an overwhelming feeling of guilt and self-loathing that ate at her soul. She couldn't kick it.

Luckily, the girls had each other for support. At this stage in the program at Bassett House, there was no therapy or grief counseling for the girls. The sisters believed suffering was penance and necessary for these young women to understand the sin they had committed. They believed their sorrow would prove to be so painful that the wayward girls would never allow a pregnancy to happen again. Most parents of the girls agreed with that belief, so there was no rescue from the agony by family.

After a week, Anna and Marilee fell into a new routine of working all day and talking about their dreams for the future late into the evening, until the call for lights out. Neither one could image suffering alone through the torment and distress of relinquishing their flesh and blood to strangers. To have your child so close and yet not be permitted to hold it was overwhelming torture. They poured their hearts out to each other. They held one another through the tears that they shed night after night. Only they cared about one another. Only they could ease some of the pain through their empathy and commiseration.

Anna and Marilee went to supper in the dining hall one Friday night and saw Rose sitting alone at one of the tables. It was a pleasant surprise to see her out of her room. They decided to approach her, but she didn't look up.

"Rose?" said Marilee.

"Dolores?" asked Anna.

She lifted her head slightly and looked at the girls through her bloodshot eyes. "Le'me alone."

"Talk to us, please. What happened? Please say something."

"Let us help you," Anna and Marilee pleaded.

"Youse can't help me. My baby is gone. They took him," Rose said in a whisper. "They stole him from me." She put her head down on the table and ignored any further questions. Anna and Marilee sat at a table next to hers in hope that she would speak to them further. She never did. After a while, a nun they did not recognize came over and led Rose back to her room.

The following day, Anna saw Mario escorting his sister out the front door to his car. Rose appeared dismal and weary as she scuffled along with him. Maybe it was the medication she had been given. Maybe she was suffering from the baby blues some of the girls had talked about. Anna knew something was terribly wrong with her once lively, boisterous, and opinionated friend. She appeared to be crushed and her spirit shattered by her experiences at Bassett House. Mario closed the door behind them. Anna wondered if she would ever encounter Rose again, or if they had simply crossed paths for this brief period in time. No matter what, she would never forget her. Not ever.

* * *

Easter came and went. Signs of Spring were popping up in the yard behind the home as daffodils and irises opened in the heat of the day. Thunderstorms came through at night flashing shadows on the wall of their room. Anna and Marilee often talked about family and school and friends from before this episode in their lives. They also discussed how they would make things different when they returned home. They made a pact to not let themselves fall into a depression like Rose. They knew hope for a better future was important. They were sure to have better lives after leaving Bassett House. They had to believe that was true!

On the fifteenth of April, Marilee received a notice from Sister Mary Agnes that her son would be leaving Bassett House on April 25 with his new family. She reported to the nursery at 9:00 that morning to feed, bathe and dress her son for his transition. Her job, the ultimate final punishment, was to hand him over to the adoptive couple. This was required of all birth mothers who remained at Bassett House. She would then be picked up at 12:00 by her mother for her journey home. Her debt to Bassett House ended at noon on the twenty-fifth.

"It's done," said Marilee. "I know he will have a good home. They have another child a couple of years older. I think I have done what's right."

"Oh, Leah!" Anna saw the sadness on her friend's face.

"Stop calling me that! From now on, I am Marilee!"

"Of course. What else can you do? What can any of us do?"

"It was the most difficult thing I have ever had to …". She started to cry.

"Marilee. You have to get past this somehow. I am so sorry."

"I'm going to be alright. I have to go now. My mother is picking me up in a few minutes. I just want to put this place behind me. I want to forget about all that has happened here. I hope you can understand that."

"Absolutely. Do you still want to write each other or meet up some time?"

"Not for a while, at least. Thank you for being my friend. You have made these weeks bearable for me. I appreciate it, but I also want to forget that I was ever here. You will only remind me that it was real."

The words stung. Anna was hurt that Marilee wanted to distance herself and forget about their friendship. Yet, at the same time, she also understood why she felt that way.

"Oh, Marilee, no matter where we go from here, I will never forget you. You have been a good friend. I pray that only good things happen to you once you leave here. Even if I never hear from you again, I will wonder about you sometimes and hope you are happy and well."

The girls hugged each other and cried. Marilee picked up her sweater and handbag off her bed and walked toward the door.

Turning one last time, she smiled back at Anna and said, "What an odd, horrendous time we have shared, Anna Ruth. But I know you're going to be fine."

All alone, Anna wondered how much more time she needed to stay. She walked by the nursery every day to pick up laundry hoping to see Suzanne in her crib. Instinctively, her eyes were drawn to the crib with the cutest chubby faced baby with curly blonde hair. She didn't know that there were several families interested in her daughter. Suzanne was in high demand.

A week after Marilee's notice, Anna received hers. She needed to report on May 5 to prepare her daughter for her new parents' arrival. It didn't seem real to her. Was she really bathing, dressing and feeding her daughter for the last time? Their eyes met. She soaked in the depths of her dark pools.

"Etch me into your memory, my little Suzanne. These precious few moments in time are ours. You will always be my baby girl. Please forgive me for what I have to do. Know that I do it only to give you a better life. I will love you, always and forever."

Anna carried Suzanne out in a white blanket monogrammed with an elaborate 'S' in each corner. She had made the special blanket while working in the sewing room. She swaddled her tightly in it and handed her over to the couple dressed in their Sunday finery. Anna kissed her daughter on the forehead and turned away. The couple, who appeared to be in their mid-thirties, immediately remarked on how beautiful the baby's fine blond hair was.

"Anna, your grandfather arrived a few minutes ago to take you home. You may get your things and be free to go home now," Sister Mary Agnes said, then turned back to the couple holding Suzanne. *Her child. They had her baby. How could she simply walk away and leave her here*? She grappled with the image until it overwhelmed her. Seeing Anna's reluctance to leave, the Sister quickly ushered the new parents out of the room and away from Anna. Never once did they speak to her or even look at her. She was no longer needed. Her job was done.

Their silence was a slap in her face. Not wanting to fall apart now, Anna quickly walked back to her room to retrieve her bag and leave for good.

* * *

"Thank you for coming all this way, Granddaddy. I could have taken the bus," Anna said as she gave her grandfather a hug and a peck on the cheek.

"I needed to see Victoria for a bit. It's been a long time since I've made a trip to Wilmington. I forgot how well she lives up here. She does just fine for herself."

"Yes, her home is beautiful. She has a wonderful wardrobe of clothes, too. She seems quite happy. Actually, I thought she was going to pick me up today."

"Your mom and I talked about that and decided that it is best to bring you home as soon as possible. Your parents have missed you, Anna. They want you back home with them."

"Even daddy?"

"Yes. You and your daddy need to mend your relationship. We're family and you have to find a way to get this worked out."

"He hates me for what happened. I don't know how to face him."

"We'll find a way."

Grandfather Daffin then told Anna that he and Ernie had made amends.

"Not that I have sided with him or anything, but Anna sometimes we have to do what's necessary to keep the family together. I didn't want your parents to be against each other. That wouldn't help you any."

"I understand, Granddaddy. This was all my doing. I am to blame."

"Well, now, you're not totally at fault here. That Baker boy bears responsibility. I hear the Army sent him to Texas or someplace out west. But I guess you don't want to know anything about him, do you?"

"No, not really. It's all over for us."

"Your mom and daddy are ready for a fresh start for you. I believe your mom has lined up a job for you in town at the shirt factory. Is that fine with you?"

"Yeah, it's very fine with me. I've learned to improve my sewing skills after using a modern type of sewing machine. It was definitely better than the one mom has."

"Good. You can start in a couple of weeks, I believe! The factory is in competition with some other companies for workers."

Anna was pleased. She had a plan for the immediate future. Just what she needed!

* * *

Anna slid out of her granddaddy's car, grabbed her suitcase from the backseat and turned to face her father. He took her suitcase from her hand and said "Anna Ruth, it's good to have you home! Everyone has missed you."

"Anna!" Eddie called running to jump up in Anna's arms.

"Eddie! Don't hurt Anna, now! Get down!" Their father called out to him.

Janet, Patricia, and Susan came out the door next, followed by their mother. The girls all gave Anna a hug and told her how happy they were to have her home.

"You made good time, I guess. Didn't you, daddy? I didn't expect you so soon," Dottie said.

"Well enough. Anna kept pushing my foot on the gas pedal, telling me to hurry up."

Everyone chuckled. "Oh, granddaddy!"

"Well now, I've made one of your favorites for supper tonight, Anna. Daddy, can you stay too? I made a big pot of spaghetti and homemade bread," said Dottie.

"That sounds delicious. I've missed your cooking, mom," Anna said.

"Didn't you like the food at Aunt Victoria's?" asked Janet.

"Oh," said Anna realizing her error. "She doesn't like to cook. We ate out a lot."

"Did she give you any clothes?" asked Patricia hoping their favorite aunt had sent some items for them as she usually did.

"She gave me some blouses to give you girls. I think a couple each," said granddaddy.

"Oh, let us see! Can we have them now?" The girls pressed.

"I'll bring them in for you. They're in my trunk," and then turning to Dottie he said "I want to talk to you about your Aunt Victoria for a bit. Do you have any iced tea for a thirsty old man?"

Once inside, the girls went upstairs to try on their new clothes, and the adults, along with Anna, sat down at the kitchen table for their cold drinks.

"Victoria asked me to visit with her these past couple of days, when she knew I was picking Anna up, because she found out that she needs an operation soon. She has cancer. On her left side," he said indicating the left breast.

"Oh, my Lord, no!" Dottie exclaimed.

"Certainly sorry to hear that. Anything we can do?" asked Ernie.

"We had some paperwork signed at her lawyer's office while I was there. She has no one to trust except for me. I'll go up and stay with her during the operation and to care for her when she returns home. I am her power of attorney and need to be there for her."

"Of course, you do!" said Ernie, understanding the seriousness of the illness.

"This is not something Anna can handle. But I am hoping that she can stay with Margaret while I'm away. I don't want Ethel to be obligated to stay around the clock. She has animals to care for."

"I can do that, granddaddy. I wish I could help you take care of Aunt Victoria, too, but I understand. I feel so bad for her."

"We've arranged for you to work at the shirt factory in town starting on May 16," Dottie told Anna. "That won't be a problem. Even if you are still in Wilmington with Aunt Victoria, Anna can work at the factory during the day and arrive in time to feed mother and stay overnight. It should work out fine."

"That's great! Granddaddy told me that you had a job lined up for me. I'm looking forward to it," said Anna as she stood up to take her glass to the sink and wash it. Something caught her eye in the living room. "Oh, my gosh! You bought a television!"

"We got that for Christmas. You happy?" asked Ernie wanting to rid the awkwardness he felt around his daughter.

"Yeah, that's great, Daddy," Anna responded still avoiding eye contact with her father. "Maybe we can watch something together one night."

"I'd like that. We like to watch *Lassie*. It comes on tonight, I think," Ernie said struggling with his words.

"Okay. I better take care of my unpacking. Thank you, granddaddy, for everything," Anna said as she hugged her grandfather one more time. Ernie looked on with envy for the close relationship his father-in-law had with his daughter.

Anna carried her suitcase upstairs, passing by Patricia's room where she saw her folding clothes. She called out to Anna as she walked by.

"Hey, Anna! Come here. I have something to tell you,"

Anna went into the room wondering what she had to say. "I was taking care of Grandmom Margaret a couple of months ago, and some guy came to deliver oil to their tank. I went out to pay him with a check Granddaddy left me and he started asking about you. He wanted to know where you were, because he saw you there last time he delivered. I told him you were working in another town for a while. I hope that was alright to say, because I don't know who he is."

"I think I know who you are talking about. If it is the same guy, he was there before I went to stay with Aunt Victoria. Did you say anything to mom or daddy about him?

"Nope. I'm no dope!"

"Please, don't. I can't deal with anything else just now," Anna pleaded, uncertain how much her sister knew about what had occurred.

"Are you alright, Anna? You seem down."

"I'm fine."

"Is Aunt Victoria doing better? Granddaddy stayed with you both the last couple of days, right? He said he was going to a doctor's appointment with her."

Anna seized the opportunity to continue the lie and decrease suspicion for her extended absence from home and school. She suddenly realized that for Aunt Victoria's part in perpetuating the deception, she was truly ill. *Could her aunt be punished for participating in Anna's deception and concealment of her secret.* "Oh, God!" Anna said aloud feeling guilt wash over.

"What? What's the matter? You can tell me! I won't say anything!" Patricia begged her sister.

"Aunt Victoria has cancer. It's in her breast."

"Oh, no! That can kill her, can't it?"

"I don't know. She needs an operation. Maybe they can take it out. I just don't know."

"No wonder you are upset! I love Aunt Victoria, too! She is my best aunt ever."

"Mine, too!" Anna was close to tears. The news was as fresh to her as it was to Patricia. It was difficult for her to comprehend why this was happening to someone as marvelous and kind as their aunt. However, selfishly, Anna was relieved that the focus was not on her at the return home.

At first, she was delighted to be home. The familiarity of the farm and surroundings were comforting. Outwardly she appeared to enjoy herself, but this was just a disguise. Beneath the façade, she felt she was sinking to a depth never before experienced. Looking at her face, one would never know the pain she was suffering. She couldn't wait for time alone, so she could release the pent-up anger and frustration she had building up inside her. *How could she have acquiesced and surrendered her own flesh and blood?*

CHAPTER SIXTEEN

It was torture. Anna struggled to listen to Janet describe the plans for the prom set for the Saturday night after she returned home. The theme the junior class had chosen was called 'Southern Plantation'. They selected a band that could play their favorite tunes and also knew how to play for a new dance called 'the stroll'. The kids had been practicing at Murph's for a couple of weeks. Janet had a date, a guy named Larry, she had recently started to see. He was two years older than her and had graduated from a different school in the county.

Dottie made Janet's gown in layers of white tulle over pink satin with a large pink satin sash and bow that hung off the back of the dress. The matching short sleeve pink top was cut in a modest V neck that Janet filled out completely. Dottie loaned Janet her mother's string of pearls. She knew Margaret would not mind since she had given them to Dottie to keep after she became too ill to go out in public. The necklace went perfectly with the lovely dress! Janet was elated as she posed in front of the sewing room mirror to admire her mother's handiwork.

Anna had been home for a little over a week, listening to Janet gush on about every aspect of the biggest school dance in a girl's life. A dance that Anna would no longer experience or have keepsakes to store in a drawer with other important memorabilia. She was happy for her sister and hoped that she had a great time. However, at the same time, she was saddened by her inability to participate in this rite of passage. She knew all her friends and former classmates would be out tonight. There would be parties after the dance, and they would hang out together for most of the night. Anna hadn't called her best friends, Betty or Kay, since coming home. She didn't want them to know she was back yet or face the questions they would ask. She wanted to wait until graduation was finished. For now, she needed to think about her next steps in life.

Anna stayed with her grandmother while her granddaddy traveled back to Wilmington to be with Victoria for her operation. Ethel still came by every day to make meals and help Anna bathe and dress Margaret who appeared to be getting weaker and unable to perform even simple tasks. It was difficult for one person to handle her alone.

Wilbur called Dottie on Wednesday to let her know that the operation had been a success and the doctors believed they had removed all of the cancer along with the left breast. He said he wanted to stay with her until Saturday. The family was delighted to get the good report.

The following weekend, Anna cleaned up the supper dishes after feeding her grandmother a finely diced vegetable beef soup. She looked up as she heard her granddaddy's car pull into the driveway. It was good to have him safely back home. Anna dried her hands on the apron she was wearing and met Wilbur Daffin as he opened the porch door with his arms full of strawberry cups.

"Hey, granddaddy! What do you have there? Let me take some," Anna asked as she took a couple of the brimming containers. "These look delicious!"

"I know! I stopped at a roadside stand on my way home when I saw the sign for fresh strawberries. Look how big they are! I've already eaten a few while I was driving."

"They look juicy!"

"Oh, they are! See, I dripped juice on my shirt!"

"Oh, no! I hope Ethel can get the stain out for you!"

"She is good at that. Some of these strawberries are for her, too. I'll bet she makes some shortcake for them this week. I'll buy more later this month so she can have some for canning jelly or preserves. There's nothing better with toast!"

"How's Aunt Victoria making out at home, granddaddy?" Anna asked while Wilbur put the strawberries in the sink to wash them off.

"She'll be just fine. She has good friends looking in on her. They all brought her enough food to last a month."

"That's good because we all know how she hates to cook!" They both laughed.

Wilbur looked in on Margaret and spent time with Anna while he ate leftover soup.

"I'll go home in the morning. Is that alright? I need to get ready to start work at the shirt factory on Monday."

"Certainly! Are you excited to go out in the working world? You'll start making your own money. Oh, that reminds me! Victoria told me to give you this envelope that she has been holding for you. She said it was yours."

Wilbur handed Anna the white envelope containing $200 that Jimmy gave her the last time she saw him.

"Thank you," she said simply. Aunt Victoria was right. She may need that money to get her life in order. One day it might be just what she needs.

* * *

Anna finished brushing her hair and tucked her pink blouse into her pink and burgundy rose printed skirt. She pulled the zipper up but had to leave the button undone since she still had not lost all the weight she had gained while carrying Suzanne.

She picked up the ham and cheese sandwich wrapped in wax paper that she had made the night before along with a handful of fresh strawberries from a bowl next to the sink. The Connolly sisters would arrive at the end of the farm lane to pick her up for work in a few minutes, so she scurried out the door to meet them. Anna had been catching a ride with them for the past three weeks when she joined them working at Ridgeway Shirt Factory.

A few days before Anna returned home to the family farm, Dora Connolly stopped by to purchase eggs from Dottie. She was a regular customer and a good neighborhood friend. As usual, the women were discussing the local news when Dora mentioned that her twin girls, both now thirty-eight years old and unmarried, were working at the shirt factory.

"Do they have any other openings? I think a job like that would be good for Anna," asked Dottie. "She does quite well on my machine and has made some of her own clothes for school."

"Of course. She needs a job so she can prepare to set up housekeeping. That's what my girls are doing," said Dora. "They still have openings as far as I know. And Anna can ride with the girls to work. They can pick her up at the end of your lane. Now, they may want Anna to chip in with some gas money from time to time."

"Certainly. I'm sure Anna would expect to help out."

"But, since they are driving by here on their way, it won't be much. The girls will enjoy her company."

"I'll call the factory. Thanks, Dora!"

Dottie called the shirt factory the following afternoon. The factory manager said he would hire Anna that very day if she had been available. He needed seamstresses. When Dottie explained that she was caring for her aunt, but would return one day soon, he agreed to hold the job until she arrived home. He said he was doing it as a favor and on recommendation from Dora. If the truth be known, he was desperate for good, knowledgeable workers.

* * *

Anna quickly entered the back seat of the car so the dust that trailed behind did not fly into her hair and fresh clothes. Marilyn and Carolyn Connolly spent most of the drive to work contradicting each other about trivial things as Anna ignored their pettiness as best as she could.

"Isn't that right, Anna?" asked Marilyn as she looked into the rear-view mirror at Anna.

"What? Sorry, I didn't hear you."

"She said that Sally Hall did not have blonde hair last week. She must have gotten it bleached."

"I guess I didn't notice."

"I say she was always a blonde," responded Carolyn. "I remember her distinctly when she started work there."

"I suppose I don't know her. I'm not sure," Anna said, trying to disengage from the meaningless conversation.

"Well, if she did, I must be thinking about someone else," continued Marilyn.

"It had to be another girl. You are always mixing people up."

"I am not! I have a good memory."

Anna was always relieved when they arrived at the factory. She couldn't stand to hear their constant bickering. Now, she could get lost in her work.

Although the job was monotonous and she had no friends, Anna was pleased to be making money. She was also doing inside work with a fan to cool her throughout the day. If she wasn't working at the factory, she would be spending her days in the fields with her parents and Emmitt planting and picking tomatoes, cucumbers, and peppers for the summer. Janet and Patricia would have to help again this year while Susan watched after Eddie. Not that Anna was off the hook completely. Her father had already told her that she would be expected to help after work on those evenings when the crops were ready pick. Anna hated it. She hated the farm and the daily struggle to care for animals and plants that put food on the table. *Why can't we just buy our food at the grocery store like other people*, she thought. *When I can get away from here for good, I will never live on another farm. I would never marry a farmer,* she said to herself.

Some days, to help pass the time, Anna's mind wandered back to the days in Wilmington at Bassett House. She would relive the events of her stay there and wonder about the girls she had met. She often thought about Marilee especially. The events of that time were still fresh in her mind. Her gaping wounds were invisible to those around her, but she could sense how frail she had become.

She couldn't stop thinking about Suzanne. Where was she? Who was feeding her? Holding her? Some days were worse than others. When it was bad, she would go into the bathroom, beat her fists against the cinder block wall behind the toilet and bite her arm muffling the sound of her scream. Her co-workers noticed the redness on the side of her hands and the teeth marks on her arm but did not ask her about it.

The women who worked in the factory all seemed to have a traumatic event or some drama currently happening in their lives. Anna heard some of them discussing their abusive husbands, who either resented their wives working or wanted them to work while they sat on their lazy asses doing nothing to contribute to the home. These women liked to broadcast their stories, each one trying to outdo the previous one. Nothing ever changed for them.

A couple of the girls who were Anna's age were preparing for marriage, putting their money away for a home of their own. Several were widows who needed the money from the job to survive. They were usually quiet and sat in the back corner doing their work, which was also Anna's favorite spot.

The women who worked boxing up the shirts for shipment were especially rowdy, often flirting and telling nasty jokes with the truck drivers who delivered to the stores. Some had been known to go off with the drivers for a few minutes of pleasure in the cab of a truck. Anna didn't believe this really happened until the day she caught a widowed woman she knew sliding out of a cab as she pulled her stockings up. The driver behind her was laughing and pulled the door closed after she walked away. It was shocking to Anna. From then on, she avoided the back lot and loading area whenever the trucks were parked there.

Keeping a low profile at home and at work was Anna's daily goal. Hell, she would have preferred to be invisible, but since that wasn't possible…

Her soul was in despair. There was no fun in her life, no hope, no plan, no future. She felt exhausted and lifeless most of the time. Her energy level was low and whenever she could, she slept. Her mother bought her vitamins to take, but they did not help. She could not concentrate enough to read a book and she had no interest in speaking with friends, especially now that school was ending, and they were all preparing for graduation. Her graduation! Only she would not be there. How depressing! That was it! She was depressed. Or was she? She didn't feel like killing herself, but she also didn't care if she didn't make it through another day.

"I think Anna needs to get out and have some fun with her friends," Dottie said to Ernie one evening as the two drank coffee after dinner. "She seems so sad and miserable. She never smiles anymore."

"I guess it should be expected. I know that she has been through a tough time, but she brought it on herself. She needs to figure out how to get over it," Ernie responded.

"I don't know if it is the baby blues or what is going on. I just don't like to see her like this. She doesn't even talk to me anymore."

"I noticed that she isn't saying much. I thought that was only around me."

"She doesn't seem angry with us. I can't tell really. She has no expression," Dottie said as she pondered the situation. "I wonder if she is upset that she didn't receive anything for Mother's Day? She arrived home from Bassett House just five days before the holiday."

"It's not a holiday, Dottie. That's ridiculous! Why would she think she would celebrate Mother's Day, too? She's not a mother. Just a kid. She is just a kid."

"Well, she will turn eighteen at the end of July. Remember?" Dottie asked.

"It takes more than a certain number of years for a girl to be adult enough to be on her own. For her to make her own decisions, good decisions," Ernie argued. "She still needs our help. We have to keep her out of trouble until she meets a decent man to marry her and bring into this family."

"I wish Jimmy had been better to her. This wouldn't be happening to her if he had just agreed to marry her."

"Well, he didn't. Good riddance! We did what we had to do for her, Dottie. I'm not second guessing this."

"I know. But Ernie, I'll admit that there are times that I wonder about that baby girl too."

"Stop it! Just stop it!" Ernie shouted as he got up from the table. Eddie came running into the kitchen calling for his mom to tie his shoes. "We have our hands full here, don't you think? Eddie and our younger girls need your attention, too. Just put this mistake of Anna's out of your mind. It didn't happen, right? We made sure that the slate was wiped clean for her. She should appreciate that. She'll come around one day. She'll see that we did what was best for her."

Dottie didn't respond. She knelt down in front of Eddie, tied his shoes and sent him off with Ernie as he went outside to check on a calf that was born that afternoon.

CHAPTER SEVENTEEN

By the middle of June, Anna finally decided to call her best friend, Betty, to let her know that she was home. It had been over a week since graduation, so all the parties and hoopla were over.

"I'm so happy that you are back, Anna! Oh, goodness, it's so good to hear your voice. I was truly worried about you! You didn't call or write while you were away. What was going on?"

"My aunt was very sick and needed my constant attention," Anna lied. "She has cancer."

"I know. Patricia told me."

"She wasn't supposed to tell anyone."

"It's no problem. I pushed her to tell me something. I couldn't believe you weren't going to graduate. You have missed too much!"

"Well, it couldn't be helped. Family comes first. Besides, it's no big deal. I'm working at the Ridgeway Shirt Factory making good money as a seamstress."

"That's great, Anna! That's what matters, right? Getting a job and making a few bucks!" Betty responded in her usual upbeat manner. "I need to catch you up on everybody. Did you hear that Kay is going to college in the Fall? She always was the smart one! I guess you know that Jimmy joined the service, right?"

"Yeah, I heard about him."

"He decided all of a sudden that he was quitting school after you left. I thought he had pretty good grades. But, he said he was sick of school and wanted to travel. I guess that's one way to do it! How is your aunt doing, anyway? I hope you don't have to go back to Wilmington again."

"No, I don't expect to. She had an operation, and it was a success."

"There is so much going on and now that we are graduated, the summer is full of things to do. Hey, the guys are playing ball now. Interested in going? They play at the ballpark in Greenville tomorrow evening."

"I'll need to check with my parents. Is it alright if Janet comes along? I think her boyfriend is playing on one of the teams."

"Sure! That'll be fun. I'll get my folk's car and we can have the night out. I can pick you both up around six o'clock, okay? See you then!"

* * *

The boys were already on the field practicing when Betty, Anna, and Janet arrived to watch the game. The sisters were both surprised that they were given permission to go out for the evening, but their parents liked Betty and her family, and trusted her not to get into any trouble. And Anna thought that with Janet along, she had a better chance of permission for an outing from their parents. Anna had been home for almost a month, and the local ball games had been in season for six weeks.

Janet's boyfriend played for the Edentown team that was playing against the girls' home team, Greenville. The air was filled with sounds of the balls smacking into leather mitts and the cracking sounds of players hitting balls off wooden bats. The spectators sipped sodas and ate peanuts, leaving small heaps of shells on the wooden stands. Children ran back and forth in front of and underneath the stands with dripping fruity ice pops, while the smell of grilling hot dogs blew into the spectators with every little puff of wind. What a great night to be at the ballpark!

"Now, which one is the guy you went to the prom with, Janet?" asked Betty curiously searching the field.

"He's on second base. The one with red hair and freckles. His name is Larry," Janet pointed in his direction.

"Oh, he's cute!" Betty exclaimed. "Are you going out with him again?"

"Well, I suppose so. He asked me if I would be able to come to this game tonight. And he hoped to see me here."

"That sounds promising. We'll stick around a little after the game, so you have time to speak with him."

"Who is that on third base?" Anna asked. "He looks familiar."

Janet jumped in. "Oh, that's Buddy Merchant. He and Larry are good friends. They graduated last year. I think Buddy works for an oil company in town. He also works on his father's dairy farm, I believe."

"I think I have seen him at the sale barn too," added Betty. "I believe he brought some calves to the auction one day. He seems shy, don't you think, Janet?"

"I have only met him one time, but yeah, he was quiet until Larry got him stirred up. They like to joke around."

"He delivered oil to granddaddy's house at the end of the fall. I paid him and we talked for a few minutes," Anna said thinking back. "He seemed likable."

"Oh, gracious, then he is also the guy who stopped by granddaddy's house one day while you were in… I mean, when you were away. Patricia said a man came by in an oil delivery truck asking about you. She said he was tall and thin, just like Buddy. Dark brown wavy hair, too."

"She told me some guy had asked for me."

"I don't know what she said to him. Maybe she told him you were helping Aunt Victoria." Janet didn't believe that was the real reason Anna had been away. She was suspicious of her parents' behavior towards her sister. It was curiously odd, and she knew there had been arguments and commotion in the house prior to Anna's departure. She also thought Anna's appearance and demeanor had changed since her return. Janet knew better than to ask questions. Whatever secret was being held by the family would not be revealed to her or anyone else. Maybe one day she would discover it, but not now.

A heavy-set boy from Greenville, who was in Janet's class, was at the plate in the ninth inning. Bases were loaded and their team had two outs. It was tense in the stand with a lot of chatter on the field. "Swing, batter, batter, swing!" the players called out. And the batter did, twice, missing the ball. On the third toss, he hit a line drive straight to second base and Larry caught the ball in his mitt with a loud "thwack". Most of the people in the crowd let out a raucous cry of excitement. No matter which team they were routing for, they admitted that it was a great catch and an exciting end to the game.

"Let's get down there. I want to congratulate Larry!" yelled Janet in between her cheering.

"Sure! Let's go to him before he is swarmed by everybody," Betty yelled back. "Come on, Anna!"

The girls descended the steps with the rest of the fans. Some stopped to congratulate the players while others beelined for their cars. Janet was finally able to approach Larry and boldly stepped up giving him a hug. He was obviously pleased.

This had been a banner night for him. They tried to talk but the cheering and victory songs continued so loudly that they had to step away and over to the dugout.

Betty and Anna were going to follow, but just as Betty turned to walk away, a stray ball that had been tossed from the outfield hit her on her right cheek, stinging her face and leaving a red mark. A couple of the players stepped up to find ice to put on her face and escorted her to a seat near the concession stand.

"That is going to give her a black eye, I bet," said a gentle voice behind Anna. She turned and saw Buddy Merchant holding a bag of equipment.

"I wish I had gotten that ball away from him before he threw it like that," he sounded sincere. "The ice should help for now, but it will be sore for a few days." Buddy continued, wondering why Anna did not speak to him. He started to walk away.

"Yes, you… I'm sure it will hurt. It's going to be sore. For days," she stuttered, and Buddy stopped in his tracks.

"Didn't I meet you once at your grandfather's house? I delivered his oil," Buddy smiled as he spoke this time.

"Yes, I believe so. I thought it was you," She returned the smile reluctantly. Not wanting him to leave, she piped in. "You played a good game tonight."

"Not as good as some of the others. Larry is really good. This was his night."

They both looked over toward the dugout where Larry and Janet were still talking and laughing.

"Janet is my sister," Anna stated. Buddy nodded his head.

"I should check on Betty to make sure she is okay. She is our ride home."

"It looks like the guys are making sure she keeps that ice on her face. Let's go over, though. I know you are concerned about her."

"Yes, I am," Anna said.

"How about a soda? I could use one."

The team players and several others had gathered to eat the last of the hot dogs and drink sodas before heading home. The sunset had already fallen, and the mosquitos were swarming.

"I swear, they are eating us alive," Janet called out as she and Larry joined the others. "Are you okay, Betty? Can you still drive?" Anna asked.

"I'll be fine," she said, quite happy to be surrounded by five of the players who had been attending to her since the accident, each one trying to outdo the other for her attention.

As the party broke up and everyone said goodnight, Buddy walked with Anna towards Betty's car.

"Do you mind if I call you sometime?" Buddy asked.

"I'd like that," she said, suddenly feeling like a young girl again. *Was it possible that a boy would find her fun and interesting? But he didn't know about her past. When he finds out, it will be different. Oh, God,* she thought, *he just can't find out. No one can.*

CHAPTER EIGHTEEN

"Anna Ruth, here's a letter for you from Wilmington. It came in the mail today."

Anna had just gotten home from work. She quickly ripped the envelope open and read the letter inside from Sister Mary Agnes stating that the adoption process would be completed for Suzanne on July 1, 1955, at 4:45 p.m. The three-month window would be closed at that time and the adoption would be final. *What window*? She wondered. She had to call Bassett House immediately! She didn't care that her father would complain about the cost of a long-distance phone call.

"Hello, Sister Mary Agnes? I received your letter. Does it mean that I can come back to get Suzanne?"

"It means that the process is nearly finalized. Anna! Don't get yourself worked up. You have moved on with your life. This is a form letter we send out. Suzanne has a good home, and she has settled in nicely with the family. She has a beautiful nursery, and her parents adore her. You made your choice. It is the right choice for both of you."

Anna understood the meaning now. She had until July 1 to get Suzanne and bring her back. *Then what? I have to speak with granddaddy. He'll know what to do.*

Anna rode the bicycle she shared with her sisters over to her grandparent's house. She was so excited when she walked in the house that Wilbur thought something had happened on the farm.

"Granddaddy, I need to go back to Wilmington on July 1, so I can get Suzanne. I have money. Will you take me to the bus station in Harrington?"

"What happens when you bring her back here? Have you thought this through?"

"I'm working now. I have a little money saved up. I'll get a room to live in."

"And who will care for her while you work? Caring for your grandmother is nothing compared to caring for a baby."

"I'll figure it out. I just know that I have to get my daughter. I need her!"

"Let me think about this. I'll see what I can do. I can take you to the bus station. Make sure you ask off from work. You haven't been there long. I'm not sure what your boss will say about you taking off a day so soon."

Anna received permission to be off without any questions. Her boss was pleased with her work and understood that women occasionally had female issues. When Anna had stated that she had 'a personal matter to attend to', he didn't question what it was about. He just didn't need to know!

Wilbur Daffin understood what a huge imposition he was asking of his friend and neighbor, Ethel Walbert. He also knew that she had wanted a child for many years. She was still young enough to raise one, especially with Anna's help. Maybe his plan could be advantageous to both women. He had a conversation with Ethel about taking Suzanne and raising her as her own. She was thrilled with the idea. They made plans for the lie they would tell family and friends to protect Anna and Suzanne. They worked it out, discussed the financial aspect and then filled Anna in on the plan. Although it was still a sacrifice to not have her child with her, she was willing to make it in order to be near her and watch her grow.

On the morning of Friday, July 1, Anna dressed as if going to work. She grabbed a peanut butter sandwich and a peach before heading down the lane. Her grandfather picked her up and they went to Harrington bus depot so she could catch a bus to Wilmington. Anna was nervously excited.

"One ticket for the 8:00 bus to Wilmington, please."

"That bus is full, and no one is getting off here. The next bus is at 12:15, do you want that one?"

"That puts me in Wilmington around 2:15. Alright. I'll take one ticket. What time is the return bus?"

"5:30, but you better get a ticket now. It fills up quickly, too."

"Do I need to pay for a three-month-old? I'll hold her in my lap."

"No, children under two ride free on their mother's lap."

"Then one round trip, please."

Once Anna had secured the tickets, she gave her grandfather a huge hug and Wilbur left her at the depot. He made a plan to cover for her lateness in getting home. Then he went to Ethel's house to finalize arrangements for Suzanne and Anna to stay with her later that night.

The hours slowly ticked by in the stuffy, hot waiting area of the station. Anna sipped a cold soda while passing the time. Other buses came and went as the ebb and flow of the waiting area saw people of all walks of life pass through. Finally, a silver-colored Greyhound bus turned into the parking lot. It was running six minutes early. Anna was anxious to board and be on her way.

Not having any baggage to deal with, Anna headed straight for the bus steps, showed her ticket to the driver and took a seat in the second row. She sat alone until the stop in Smyrna. A short man with a crew cut and pockmarked face boarded there and sat next to her. He immediately began talking incessantly.

His high-pitched voice irritated Anna. She tried to turn her attention to the passing scenery out the window, but the man kept pushing his finger into the side of her arm to get her attention. Feeling overwhelmed and wondering why she had attracted another horrible seat partner on a bus, Anna turned her face away and faked sleep. He continued to talk to others around him about his insurance business and the money he made. Anna and the other passengers were fed up. A couple across the aisle had turned their bodies toward the window and were whispering to each other about him, and the woman who was sitting in the seat in front of him moved to a seat in the back.

Suddenly, Anna noticed the bus seemed to be slowing down. The bus driver was pumping the gas pedal, and then using his brake, he coasted into a used car lot.

"Folks, looks like we have a problem with this bus. I need to call for a backup. I'll get you on your way as soon as I can."

Anna panicked. As soon as he could? She needed to be on the road now! *Sister Mary Agnes knows that I will be there. I told her earlier in the week that I was coming,* Anna thought. *Certainly, she will wait until I arrive. I have until 4:45.*

Anna and the other passengers descended from the bus to stand in the hot sun. At least, she was away from the smells of the inside. She heard their driver state that the backup bus was about an hour and fifteen minutes away. Anna sat on the edge of the sidewalk away from everyone. She put her face in her hands to hold back her tears. The time slipped away at a snail's pace. The passengers milled around anxiously looking at their watches and wiping perspiration off their faces.

Another bus arrived a little after three o'clock. Everyone entered the bus quickly, and soon they were back on the road to

Wilmington. Anna did the calculation in her head and realized that she could still make it. It would be close, but doable. She decided that she would need a taxi as soon as the bus arrived.

Since they were late arriving and off schedule, no taxis were around the depot at that time. The station manager called for several taxis, as she wasn't the only one who needed one. The first one to arrive was grabbed up by a businessman who was late for an appointment. He jumped in front of everyone and took off. Anna was able to take the second one.

"Bassett House, please. Third Street."

This was her first time in a taxi but having seen how to take one in the movies, Anna felt she knew what to do.

The driver pulled up to the front of Bassett House. Anna paid him 85 cents and stepped out of the car. She was shaking as she quickly walked up the steps to the big door once again and dropped the heavy door knocker three times to be sure she was heard.

"Grace!" Sister Margaret exclaimed. "So good to see you! Come in. What brings you here today?"

"I've come to pick up my daughter, Suzanne."

"Oh, my, I don't think any of the babies being adopted today are still here."

Anna looked at the clock in the dining hall. It read 4:52.

"That clock is wrong. It can't be that late. Where is Sister Mary Agnes?"

Anna ran down the hall to her office and opened the door without knocking. The Sister was sitting at her large desk completing paperwork.

"Grace? What are you doing here?"

"My bus broke down. But Sister, I was here before 4:45. Where is my baby?"

"The child has gone home with her parents, and you should too. You are too late. Even if you had gotten here earlier there was no way to complete the paperwork before the cut off time. You should have come yesterday."

"Nooooo! You can't do this! You are wrong! My letter said I could get her today."

"No, Grace, your letter said that the adoption was final at 4:45 today. You need to stop being so selfish and let your child have her life, a good life. You are only stirring up trouble for everyone. We have all done our best to help you and this is the way you repay our generosity. Please leave now. There is nothing more you can do."

Anna stood trembling, unable to scream, unable to cry, unable to move from the spot where it all ended for her. Sister Margaret, who had been listening outside the door, took her hand and led her back to the doorway.

"Goodbye, Grace," she said softly. "Take care of yourself."

She stood outside the door thinking about what to do next. She had fully expected to walk out with her daughter. She never gave a thought to going home alone. Home? Oh, my God! The bus will be leaving soon. I need to get home before anyone discovers where I have gone. There was no taxi in sight. In her rush to get to her daughter, she had failed to think about how to get back to the bus station. She ran to the end of the next block where there was heavier traffic. She saw a taxi pass in the opposite direction as she arrived at the corner. She flagged it down and the driver turned around in the street to come back to her.

She made it. Although it was right at the time to leave when Anna arrived, the bus driver was still talking to a pretty, young girl in shorts and a low-cut blouse. He seemed in no hurry to board everyone. A porter came along, finished taking baggage, and then collected tickets from those who were waiting to get on. The bus was packed. Anna chose a seat on the outside this time. She needed the two-hour drive back to settle her nerves. It all seemed like a bad dream. The stresses of the day left her drained and dumbfounded. Anna risked everything today. It was a tremendous chance she had taken, only to be made a fool. She knew now that it was never intended for her to retrieve her daughter. Whether the decision had come from the sisters of Bassett House or from her parents, there was no way possible that she would ever have Suzanne back. Her daughter was gone from her life, never to return. Somehow, she would need to accept that fact. Somehow, she had to go on. Her soul ached and her body was drained. She wasn't sure she could descend the steps of the bus. When Wilbur saw her standing with hesitation and empty arms at the open bus door, he went to his granddaughter as she practically fell into his arms.

"Anna! Anna! Come with me! Come on, now. Let's get you back home."

"No! I can't let them know where I've been! No, Granddaddy!"

"I won't, honey! That's not what I meant. I'll take you home with me tonight. You stay with me, okay? Your parents think you are with me anyway. I've already made arrangements."

Anna relaxed a bit and walked with her grandfather to his car. She stayed that night and the rest of the weekend at her grandparents' house. Ethel came by and made meals for everyone. Anna stayed in the spare room most of the weekend, sleeping and sporadically crying, and barely eating or talking.

Ethel took her a cup of chamomile tea, hoping she would feel like talking. She was also disappointed to not have the child in her home. It hurt that, once again, she was denied the pleasure of having an infant to raise. Ethel coped with her sorrow by taking care of others. It was her way. Although Ethel was sad, she knew Anna was reliving the pain of losing her child, a grief she could not imagine.

If her parents knew anything, they didn't bring it up with Anna. She didn't know what her grandfather had told her mother and father, but it seemed to satisfy them. She did not want to talk about what happened that weekend, ever. The anguish she suffered had overwhelmed her, and Anna decided to make a change in her life. She suppressed her tears. The agony was too great and in order to keep living, she had to quell the incessant feeling of sorrow. Anna's mind was deadened.

On the Wednesday after Independence Day, Anna walked through the kitchen door just as the phone was ringing. Janet charged through the dining room and rounded the corner into the kitchen to grab the phone before anyone else.

"Hello," said Janet as she picked up the receiver. "Hey, Larry! Good to hear from you."

Not surprised that the call hadn't been for her, Anna walked through the living room to go upstairs and change out of her clothes that were clinging to her from the July heat.

"Wait, let me ask her," Janet leaned into the living room just as her sister started to ascend the stairs. "Hey, Anna, how would you like to go to the movies on Friday night? You should be home from work to be able to catch the 7:30 show, right?"

Anna was startled by the request and unsure how to answer. "With who? Do you need to give an answer now?" she asked, walking back into the kitchen. "Will we even be allowed to go?" She whispered to her sister.

"Larry and his sister can pick us up. I don't think Mom and Daddy will object to that."

"Maybe not for you."

"I think Buddy Merchant is going to meet up with us when we get to the theater and some guy that Larry's sister is seeing. Let's try. Okay? We won't say anything about Buddy showing up."

Much to Anna's surprise, her mother said she and Janet could go out Friday night. Dottie knew Ernie had a Grange meeting that night, so she didn't bother to ask his opinion on the matter. Besides, it would be good for Anna and Janet to have some fun with friends.

* * *

Edentown on a Friday night was the bustling spot in the county. The ACME and other stores were open until eight or nine o'clock. The restaurants and burger shops were also open later for patrons. Many of the local residents received their paychecks on Friday and were eager for a fun night out. The streets of the town reflected the happy mood of the patrons.

The young people hung around the movie theater, the bowling alley, and Murph's Snack Shop for the best burgers, fries, and milkshakes, and the only juke box and dance floor in town.

Cars filled the streets making it difficult to find a parking spot anywhere close to the theater.

"We'll just have to walk a couple of blocks. I don't mind," said Janet to the others in the car.

"Fine by me."

"Me too."

Larry grabbed Janet's hand as the four weaved their way along the sidewalk. The movie was going to start in ten minutes, and they still needed to find Buddy.

"I'm skipping the movie. Catch up with me later at Murph's," said Larry's younger sister, Jeannie, as she darted off in the direction of a group of kids her age.

"Alright. But you better be there when I come by. If not, you're walking home! I mean it!"

"You wouldn't really leave her, would you, Larry? That was a joke, right?" asked Janet, hoping her new boyfriend was not serious.

"Of course not. I have to scare her a little to make her mind me. I don't want to run all over town looking for her when we are ready to leave."

"I understand. We don't want to be late getting home either. Our father won't let us out again until next summer if we miss our curfew!"

Anna was feeling very odd about tagging along with Larry and Janet, until they arrived at the ticket booth. There stood Buddy looking around the crowd. He held up four tickets and called out that they could go on in.

"What are we seeing?" asked Anna.

"Davy Crockett," Larry responded. "Thanks for picking up the tickets, Buddy, ol' boy."

Buddy took Anna's hand as Larry grabbed Janet's and they all went into the theater.

"I hope you are okay with meeting here," said Buddy. "I wasn't off work in time."

"That's fine. It worked out well this way," Anna was relieved that she had been able to go with them without incident from her mother. She supposed that her mom thought Janet would keep her out of trouble. But after seeing her sister flirting with Larry tonight, Anna felt that she was the one keeping Janet in control. It didn't take long before Larry and Janet started kissing in between the movie usher's trip with his flashlight to check on kids necking. They, along with a few other couples, were obviously not interested in this movie. It made Anna feel uncomfortable. She hoped Buddy would not try anything like that with her. She wasn't interested.

Janet rested her head on Larry's shoulder and then kept giggling every time he whispered something in her ear.

"That is really annoying," Anna said as she leaned over to reprimand Janet when she had enough of her behavior.

"What a killjoy! Just never you mind."

With a heavy sigh, Anna tried to continue watching the movie.

"Don't you like the movie?" Buddy asked as he noticed Anna's discomfort.

"Yeah, I like it fine. It's just that my sister can be a pain. I can't stand all that giggling when we are trying to watch the movie."

"I don't think they are interested in Davy. You know what I mean?"

"Got it. They have their blinders on! And Janet is just like an old mule we once had," Anna smiled as she whispered back to Buddy.

After the movie, the couples walked down the street to Murph's for milkshakes. Buddy had been a gentleman during the show and Anna felt no pressure from him. They had held hands off and on throughout the night, but just enough for her to feel comfortable with him.

Murph's was busy as usual on a Friday night. The place was the regular hangout for the kids in the area, and tonight it was packed with young people out for a little fun with their friends. Buddy found a table that had just been cleared. Calling Larry over with the girls, they took seats and ordered chocolate shakes. They sipped on their drinks as they watched some of the kids dance while the juke box pounded out tune after tune.

"They are playing all rock and roll tonight. I want to hear some Johnny Cash!" Buddy yelled out.

"You like Johnny? Really?" asked Janet.

"Johnny's okay, but I really like Marty Robbins," said Larry. "How about you, Anna?"

"I mostly like songs by Eddie Fisher or Tony Bennett. They have such smooth voices."

"Romantic songs, right, Anna?" Janet added, and then a new record came on.

"Well, this one is different. What do you call this?" questioned Janet as the song 'Papa loves Mambo' came on and everyone who had been dancing stepped off the floor. "Look you can't even dance to this song."

"I knew someone who could," said Anna and then suddenly realized what had slipped out of her mouth. She began to tremble inside, and her stomach did a flip. Janet shot her a look of bewilderment. "Who do you know that could dance to Mexican music?"

"It's not Mex… Don't you think we should probably get home soon? Larry, do we need to find your sister?" Anna asked as she began to feel panicked. Why had she said that? She didn't mean to bring up this connection to her past. She hoped the boys didn't think she was strange. She could see that Janet didn't know what was going on. Anna felt like they were all trying to figure out what had disturbed her.

"She's with her friends in a booth on the other side. Janet let's go find her. Back soon."

"Aren't you having a good time?" Buddy asked Anna. "I'm sorry if something upset you."

"Oh, not at all. I've had a fun evening. I've enjoyed being out with everyone tonight."

"Even me?"

"Of course, you. Especially, you," Anna turned to face Buddy. She saw the uncertainty in his face. "It's just that I haven't been out for a while."

"I hope you can go out more. With me, I mean. I would like to take you out sometime. Would that be ok with you?"

"Yes, but…" she hesitated. "My parents are very strict about dating. We may have to see each other in a group for a while longer."

"I'm fine with that too. I didn't realize. Your parents didn't seem to have a problem letting Janet go out alone with Larry a couple of times," he said, looking for an explanation. "It doesn't matter. I would just like to see you again. I don't care if your sister and Larry tag along."

* * *

The next weekend, they all went out again, Larry drove his car to pick up the girls. Buddy and Anna sat in the backseat and once they were out of the sight of their house, Janet slid over next to Larry.

"I would drive, but I have a '49 pickup truck and it would be a little tight for all of us," Buddy said. They laughed. Double dating was fun and safe for the girls. They all enjoyed each other's company and joked around about some of the silliest things. The dates continued this way throughout the month of July.

On Anna's birthday, however, Janet organized a weenie roast near the pond on one corner of the farm. Their father gave Janet permission and even had Emmitt help him haul some firewood and clear an area for a pit to burn it. She had sodas, marshmallows, hotdogs, and homemade potato chips for everyone. Betty brought her steady date, Doug Wheatman. Kay arrived with their friend and classmate, Walt Pearson, who always brought his guitar to gatherings to provide entertainment.

Before the others arrived, Kay took Anna aside. It had been a long time since they had talked, ever since Anna's last day at school.

"Anna, I'm so sorry to hear that you didn't graduate. When I heard you were away with your aunt, I assumed that you were finishing out school in Wilmington. I didn't know."

"It's alright, Kay."

"No, you worked very hard for your grades. I know that. You deserved to finish. I can't believe your family couldn't find someone else to stay with her."

"Well, they couldn't. Besides, you know how it is for farm families. The only thing important for girls is to find a good husband. It was never meant for me to have a profession or support myself. I just need to find a good man, according to them."

"I get what you are saying, but it doesn't have to be like that."

"Not for you, Kay. Your dad has his own business and works with men and women every day. He understands that you might want to be like those women. And, he has the money to send you to college. Not many of us in this county are so fortunate."

"I know how lucky I am."

"Don't misunderstand me. I am happy for you! I am very proud of you! You should take this opportunity to get away from here. Experience life out there as much as you can. I know you will do great!"

"That is wonderful to hear, Anna! I appreciate your encouragement. And you? What will you do? I thought you once said you would like to be a nurse?"

"That was quite a while ago. I don't think I would be comfortable working in a hospital. Too many sad things happen there. All the sickness and death are too depressing."

"You have helped take care of your grandmother and now your aunt; I think you have already had plenty of experience to become a candy striper. You could give it a try."

"Not now. It's no longer my dream job. I'm going to work in the shirt factory for the time being and save up some money. If the right guy comes along, I'll marry him. But I'll tell you, I am not marrying a farmer. I'm sure of that!"

Kay laughed with her friend at her bold statement. She heard many stories over the years from all her farm friends as to how much work goes into running the operation. She hoped, for her sake, that Anna would never fall in love with a poor farmer.

The four couples had a fun evening singing songs, telling stories, and roasting some hot dogs and marshmallows. The remaining marshmallows ended up in a battle between the boys as they chunked them back and forth at each other.

"Look out! Betty is known for taking one to the face every now and then!"

"Kay, you missed it! Betty was hit in the face with a baseball at one of the games. That is when she met Doug!" said Janet.

"So, that is how you get your dates?" asked Walt.

"Are you sure you want to go away to college? You'll miss all the fun here," asked Betty teasing her friend.

"I don't leave until the end of August. I'll be home for Thanksgiving and Christmas. We'll still have fun together," explained Kay to her friends.

"We always knew you would be the one to go on to college," said Anna.

"Yep! Kay has beauty and brains! Right, guys?" added Walt.

"Cut that out! Now I know you are making fun!" Kay said, laughing.

"Hey! We didn't sing happy birthday to our birthday girl yet! This is an important one for Anna! Number eighteen!" Betty exclaimed.

"Wait! Hey, kids, she's not eighteen yet! Her birthday isn't until tomorrow, July twenty-fifth!" Janet remarked before she started the gang off in song.

Kay cut the birthday cake afterwards and served it up to the group.

"Angel food cake is my absolute favorite!" Anna declared. "I have it for every birthday and my mom makes the best!"

"How about throwing another log on the fire, Buddy?" asked Larry since his friend was closest to the stack of firewood.

"I don't think we should burn any more. It's getting late. It's a work night, you know. Unlike some people, I have to be up at 5:00 tomorrow morning to milk cows before I go to work."

"I guess you're right. It's a workday for all of us. Anna, let us help you and Janet clean up before we head out."

The girls started putting the food away and covered the remaining cake with wax paper. Anna walked over to the edge of the field to toss out melted ice from a pitcher. When she turned to go back, Buddy stood before her. He came closer facing her directly. Without saying a word, he bent down to give her a kiss.

"Happy Birthday, Anna! I'm glad I was here to celebrate with you." Anna, though surprised, was not upset. It was a nice kiss, not pushy.

"It was nice of Janet to organize a party for you. It was fun. I like your friends, too."

"Honestly, I think it was just her scheme to have a night of necking with Larry."

"You might be right about that!" He laughed. "I saw those two off alone, too!"

"Yeah, I would have thrown some marshmallows at them, but the bag was empty by then." They both chuckled at the thought. "I'm really happy that you came tonight, Buddy. It's been a good birthday."

Seizing another opportunity, Buddy gave Anna an exhilarating kiss good night. One that left her speechless.

CHAPTER NINETEEN

"We're going pocketbooking, Anna!" Buddy exclaimed with excitement. "Walt's mother gave us one of her old purses and we are going to use it for some fun tonight!"

"What are you talking about? I don't understand."

"Haven't you ever heard of pocketbooking?"

"No, what's that?"

"Larry and I will pick you girls up around 7:30 and then we'll tell you all about it."

* * *

Ernie and Dottie sat in the rocking chairs on their front porch snapping green beans while Eddie played with his dump truck in the sandy area in front of the flower bed by the front steps. Dottie grabbed a couple more handfuls of beans as she noticed a black 1948 Ford Deluxe coming up the lane slowly.

"Looks like those boys the girls are seeing just turned up the lane," Dottie said matter-of-factly. "At least they don't come flying up the lane like some people."

"Good thing. I'd have to put a stop to that, right away. They could just head on back down the lane," Ernie stated with a frown.

The car circled around in the driveway and came to a stop alongside the porch. The two boys stepped out of the car as they smoothed their hair and adjusted their sports jackets, although wearing them on such a hot evening seemed ridiculous. The boys thought it would make a better impression on the girls' parents.

"Good evening, Mr. and Mrs. Scott! We've come to pick up Janet and Anna. We're taking them to a party at Walt Pearson's place. I think you know his family," said Larry.

"Yes, that's right. We know them. It's okay if the girls go out for a while, but you make sure to have them home by 11:00. You know we have church in the morning," Ernie called out to the boys.

"We do, too, sir," said Buddy.

The girls came out the front door wearing white buttoned-down blouses and full skirts Anna made from remnant pieces she bought on sale. Janet's was light purple with large pockets decorated with white brick-a-brack outlining them. Anna's was the same pattern, but she had a green skirt with yellow flowered buttons on the pockets. They also wore freshly polished saddle shoes.

Anna lost the remainder of her baby weight over the summer. Although she sat at a sewing machine all day, lately she had been helping the family pick tomatoes and carry baskets onto their father's truck for the cannery. Since she had been working so hard, her father allowed Anna to go out with friends as long as she and Janet went together, and if she was up and ready to help out the next day or go to church.

They still had very little to say to one another unless it had to do with the business of the farm. Anna didn't dare disrespect her father, so she always walked on eggshells around him. At the same time, he felt the need to continually monitor her behavior and check up on the friends she was hanging around. He still didn't trust Anna, believing that once a woman becomes promiscuous, they can't stop.

"You girls look real nice tonight. Behave yourselves! Hear me?" Dottie called out to them as they walked over to meet their dates and climbed into the back seat of the car. Once they were out of sight of the farmhouse, Larry pulled over and Buddy switched places with Janet. "Good idea!" Janet exclaimed sliding to the middle of the bench seat and slipping her arm through Larry's. The boys also ditched their sports jackets.

Betty Andrews had already arrived at Walt's house with her date, Doug. Once Larry and Buddy arrived, the guys immediately gathered in a huddle to make a plan for the evening. Establishing an agreement, Walt grabbed the large white purse his mother had given him, and the seven mischief-makers set out for some fun. Larry, Doug and Walt drove their cars to a wooded area along Route 320, which was a snow emergency route with a fair amount of traffic for such a rural area. They parked their cars up a small woods lane out of sight of the main road. They all walked along a path to a wooden fence at the edge of the highway. The girls were afraid of ripping their dresses on the briars but continued with great curiosity.

"What are they doing?" asked Betty untangling her skirt from a sticky bush.

"You'll see!" Larry called back to them. Then he tied a heavy black string around the handle of the old purse and tugged on it. "There. Good and secure."

Walt signaled for them to all kneel down below the fence, and when the road was free of cars, Buddy grabbed the purse and threw it onto the highway holding the end of the string in his left hand. The girls watched in amusement.

They waited in silence. A car drove by at high rate of speed. Another one from the other direction passed by. Buddy pulled the purse in a bit, so it was more toward the middle of the roadway. The next car came by and then slammed on the brakes. Buddy quickly reeled in the purse, and they all watched the car turn around in the road and drive back. The boys were suppressing laughs and had to cover their mouths to muffle the sound. The girls still didn't understand what was happening. The car drove back slowly with the driver's and passenger's windows down as they looked on both sides of the road for the bag.

"I know I saw it. That was a woman's pocketbook, for sure." They could be heard saying. Other cars drove by passing them and after ten minutes or so, they gave up and went on their way.

The boys were rolling in the grass with laughter. They had pulled off their trick with expertise.

"Seriously! That was funny!" said Anna.

"I get it now," said Janet.

"I don't believe you brought us out here for such silliness, you guys! But I'm glad you did! That's too crazy!" chimed in Betty.

The boys each took turns throwing the bag out on the road, and they all had a great time watching the cars stop and search the road. A couple of the drivers got out of the car, which was scary for them. What if they were discovered!

"Oh, my gosh! It's after 10:30!" Anna panicked. "Janet, we have to go!"

"Aw, come on! Are you kidding me? We're just getting started," said Walt with disappointment and disbelief that they had to end so early.

"No kidding, Walt! If we are ever to get out again, we need to be home by 11:00 and not a second after!" Anna informed him. Guys just didn't have the same curfews as girls, and they didn't understand how difficult it was for them.

"We promised their dad that we would have them home by 11:00 and I don't want to get in any trouble with him," Buddy said.

"Well, Buddy, you better get us back now if you ever hope to see Anna or me again in this century!" said Janet as everyone broke into laughter.

* * *

Anna and Janet gave the boys a quick kiss on the cheek and ran into the house with two minutes to spare. Their father was in bed, but their mother was still waiting up in the living room.

"I hope you both had a good time tonight. I'm going to bed now. Good night!" Dottie said as she climbed the stairs.

"Did you have a good time tonight, Anna?" Janet asked in a silly voice.

"Why of course, my dear! It was a splendid time! Quite an evening of jest!" The two sisters broke out in laughter.

* * *

The big Sunday meal had just finished, and the dishes were being cleared when the phone rang. Patricia answered and then called for Anna to come to the phone. "It's for you! It's a boy."

"Oh, stop!" Anna said annoyingly as she took the receiver from her with a jerk.

"Hello. Yes, this is Anna. Oh, hi, Walt!" Janet stepped into the room standing beside her to listen in. "What? A barbed wire fence? Where? Well, where is he now?" Only hearing one side of the conversation was making it difficult for Janet to make sense of anything. Then Anna hung up and turned to Janet with a worried look. With the rest of the family caught up in other activities, the two girls slipped out the door to the backyard and sat on a wooden yard swing.

"What's going on?" Janet asked as she sat next to Anna.

"The boys went back out to another spot on Route 320 last night after dropping us off. They were pocketbooking there and a car came along with a bunch of guys who knew about the game. They jumped out of the car and started searching for our guys."

"Was Betty with them?"

"No, she had Doug take her home after we left, and he didn't go back."

"Anyway, our boys took off running back to the car, but Buddy ran into an old, barbed wire fence in the woods and cut his belly pretty good."

"Oh, no! Poor Buddy!"

"I know! That had to hurt. They got away before that bunch of guys caught up with them. But they had to take Buddy to Doc Isaac and wake him to put a few stitches in. He had to get a tetanus shot, too."

"Wow! How many stitches?"

"Walt said just a few. He said Buddy was asking if I could visit him."

"Want to see if mom will let us take him some soup? That is what she always does for the neighbors?" Janet smiled slyly.

"Sure, that will be just what we can do. I'll call him later today to check on him."

Anna and Janet both tried calling Buddy, but no one answered the phone. They worried that the wound was more serious than Walt had said. They decided to try again later, but there was still no answer.

* * *

At the end of her workday, Anna went through the big wooden door of the shirt factory and took a deep breath. Stale air blew through her corner and the fans did not reach her area most of the time. It was pleasant to feel the sunshine of the late afternoon on her face as she waited, as usual, for the Connolly sisters to finish their work and make the drive home. She noticed a red pickup truck parked alongside the building with the driver's window rolled down. And then she saw that the man inside - it was Buddy! *What is he doing here,* she asked herself. Anna scurried down the steps of the building and ran over to greet him.

"This is a surprise! How is your cut?"

"Oh, I guess I'll live," Buddy responded with a laugh. "I only needed a few stitches. I've been able to work, so that's good."

"Let me see. It's not red or infected, right?"

"I don't think so," Buddy said as he unbuttoned his work shirt. "I haven't paid much attention to it."

"You have to clean it every day and keep a clean bandage cover… Buddy, did something happen to your chest? Why is it so deep?"

"Oh, I was born with that. My rib cage curves in toward my lungs, and it makes this concave place on my chest."

"Does it hurt you? You are able to play ball and the like though."

"Yeah, I can do what I want. It just kept me out of the Army. I went for a physical to join and they rejected me. I'd be in some foreign country now if I had been able to go. I didn't know they wouldn't take me for that reason."

"Wow, I've never heard of anyone having a concave chest. Your cut looks ok, but you should put another clean bandage on it soon. You don't want an infection."

Just then Anna heard the Connolly sisters chattering back and forth as they came out the double doors.

"We're ready to go now, Anna!"

"Yes, ready to go now!" They each shouted.

"Mother needs us home to prepare for her Homemaker's meeting tonight," yelled Carolyn.

"We're all members of the club, you know!" Marilyn added. "Come on, Anna! We need to go!"

"Yes, come on, Anna!"

Buddy and Anna watched as Marilyn stopped walking to motion with her hand for Anna to 'come on' just as Carolyn plowed into the rear end of her wide sister knocking her to the ground. The two women continued to fuss over who was not paying attention, as Buddy and Anna suppressed laughs.

"Stop. Don't let them see us laughing, Buddy. You know they are my ride home."

"I can't help it. They are hilarious. How can you stand being in the same car with them?"

"They are our neighbors, and their mother is good friends with my mother."

"I could take you home if you want," Buddy said hoping Anna would go with him.

"Not a good idea. Not yet anyway." She turned to leave and then called back over her shoulder. "Maybe another day."

A big smile broke out on Buddy's face as he watched Anna walk away. He really liked her. And he believed she might be starting to like him too.

CHAPTER TWENTY

Summer 1955 came to a sudden end. The yellow school bus returned to pick up three of the Scott girls. Eddie had to wait one more year to begin school. It was the start of Janet's senior year. Anna thought back to the start of school last year when she was excited to be a senior and looking forward to all the activities and privileges that come with being in one's final year. She had such hope then. She saw that same hope and excitement in Janet this morning as she prepared to catch the bus.

Anna also walked down the lane to catch her ride with the Connolly sisters. Another day of work in her monotonous life. If it weren't for the dates she had been having with Buddy, she would have nothing to look forward to in her week. The double dates had been great fun, but Buddy had been asking for an opportunity to take her out alone. Janet and Larry were also wishing that they would not tag along every time.

"Mom, can you ask daddy if Janet and I can start dating on our own? We have been double dating for months now and we don't always want to do the same thing," asked Anna.

"Larry always has to drive because Buddy doesn't have room for the four of us in his pickup," Janet added.

"Why don't you girls invite the boys over for dinner this weekend, so your father has a chance to spend some time with them and know them better. If he likes them and trusts them, then he may agree to separate dates."

"Mother, I'm eighteen, you know," reminded Anna, feeling her parents still treated her like a child. She was becoming more embarrassed by their dominance of her life.

"As long as you girls are under our roof, your father will set the rules and you will just have to live by them," Dottie admonished.

"We'll ask the boys to come for dinner and games this Saturday night. Anna, you are good with that, aren't you?" Asked Janet.

"Yes. Fine," Anna said and left the room before she said something to surely get her in trouble.

* * *

The boys arrived together in Buddy's red pickup truck wearing sports jackets and dress pants. Their hair was neatly trimmed with a little Vitalis hair tonic to hold it in place. Larry had shared his Old Spice cologne with Buddy being careful not to overpower each other with the scent. Buddy had borrowed a pair of pants from his brother, since none of his were clean, and they were a little too baggy on him. He hoped Mr. Scott didn't think he was wearing some new style or trying to emulate Elvis Presley. They were trying to make a good impression with Ernie Scott as they worked to win his approval.

"What do you boys do? You're both out of school I suppose," asked Ernie as he passed the peas.

"Yes, we graduated in '54. I'm working on our family farm full time for now, but I've had an application in at the DuPont factory in Delaware for a few months. I'm just waiting for them to call me. It's good money there, I hear," stated Larry.

"That's what I understand. Several boys have started working over there. They make nylon products, right?" Ernie asked.

"Yep, yes, I mean. They are expanding too. Once they finish building the new factory, I'm sure to hear from them."

"What do you do, Buddy? Is that your real name?"

"No, that is the name my daddy started calling me when I was born. My real name is William Charles Merchant."

"You have a dairy farm? I think I know your father from Farm Bureau."

"Yes, sir. We also have some pork that we raise. I help my dad, but I also have a job delivering oil. I'm trying to save my money for a school to learn milk testing. The Department of Agricultural is hiring for that position."

"Sounds like you boys have some good plans. Hope it works out for you," Ernie said, pleased with what he heard from them. *These are decent, respectable farm boys from good families! They should be just fine to date the girls!*

"Buddy, do you think I know your mother from Farm Bureau, or maybe Grange?" Dottie asked.

"I doubt it. My mom died in 1946. She was sick for a couple of years before she passed and couldn't get out much. Her name was Lydia."

"I'm so sorry. You were still young then."

"I'm the youngest. Two of my sisters, who were still living at home, helped raise me. There are eight of us, but some are married. I have one nephew who is a year younger than I am," Buddy said with a chuckle.

By the end of the meal, Ernie and Dottie felt comfortable with both the boys and their backgrounds. They were locals from solid farm families who all belonged to the same agricultural clubs of which they were members. Ernie believed the boys were well-behaved, churchgoing young men, and acceptable in his mind to date his daughters.

Larry and Janet sat in the swing on the front porch while Anna and Buddy took a pair of rocking chairs. They told stories and joked around until almost 11:00 when Buddy said they needed to hit the road. They said goodnight, careful to give the girls a kiss out of the sight of the Scott's bedroom windows. Ernie was aware of the time and remarked to Dottie that he felt it was time to allow Janet and Anna to date the boys alone. Dottie's plan had worked.

Anna couldn't believe it!

The months leading up to Thanksgiving were filled with the best Fall activities: bonfires at neighboring farms, a taffy pull at the church, a Halloween party at the community hall, and an impromptu baseball game at Larry's family farm. Anna and Janet attended every event with their steady dates. Even though they were permitted to date the boys alone, they usually ended up spending part of the evening in the same places.

"Anna! You'll never guess what! Larry asked me to his family Thanksgiving. Can you believe it?" Janet exclaimed.

"That's great! I don't think Buddy's family has a Thanksgiving meal. Without his mom, I suppose there isn't anyone to handle it. I'll ask him if he wants to come here."

"You should."

Buddy was pleased and readily accepted the invitation to Thanksgiving dinner. The Fall sun fought to warm the earth as a north wind blew over the bare fields of the Scott farm. Only broken stalks remained in the fields where corn had been harvested six weeks ago. Canning of vegetables and fruits was completed and neatly stored in the pantry with labels clearly marking their contents. Freshly butchered and packaged pork and beef were stacked in an orderly fashion in their chest freezer. But the Scott family had not raised a turkey for Thanksgiving. Dottie never wanted to care for turkeys, so she purchased one from a neighbor selling them for the holiday.

Since Dottie feared that the twenty-four-pound turkey would not be enough to feed everyone, she had also prepared one of their hams. It sat cooling on the counter while she fussed over the rest of the meal. The heat in her kitchen that day steamed the windows as a mixture of aromas tickled the noses of all who entered. Besides the herbed stuffed turkey, the sideboard overflowed with special dishes of candied yams, string beans, and potatoes cooked in fat back, collard greens, lima beans and dumplings, cornbread, and homemade hot cloverleaf rolls. Dottie made it all with the help of her girls.

As usual, Ernie's sisters and their spouses and children came for a big family holiday meal. Each one made a cake, and a neighbor brought over a mincemeat pie as a gift. There was plenty for everyone!

Although Buddy and his father had dinner plans, care of their animals came first, even on Thanksgiving. Both men cleaned up and took off in their pick-up trucks to enjoy turkey – Buddy to eat with the Scott family and his father to eat at his daughter and son-in-law's home in Edentown.

Dottie always invited her father to join them, as long as he could leave her mother for a couple of hours. Wilbur had to decline this year. Margaret Daffin was too sick to be left alone and he didn't feel right asking Ethel to stay with her while he attended his daughter's Thanksgiving meal. He bought a small turkey, Ethel roasted it, and the three celebrated quietly in Margaret's room. She appeared to enjoy the company.

Buddy was the last guest to arrive at the Scott farm for dinner. One of Anna's young cousins ran out the door just as Buddy reached for the screened door handle. Jumping back to let him pass before stepping inside to a kitchen full of busy, verbose women. Anna's aunts, uncles, and cousins made their rounds to greet everyone. There was quite a commotion with everyone talking at once, children squealing, and Dottie ordering her daughters on what needed to be poured, placed, or plated.

"Buddy!" Anna shouted across the room. "I'll be right there. I just need to put the butter on the table first."

Buddy walked over to Ernie, shook his hand and thanked him for the dinner invitation.

"We're glad you could come, Buddy. How's your daddy doing these days? Did he get all his corn out?"

"Yes, sir. Other than one breakdown with our old corn picker, everything was fine."

"Hey, Buddy, come over here and see this parade," Anna called. "My Aunt Victoria told me that she once saw it in person while she was in New York. I think it's amazing that we can watch it right here in our own living room, don't you? I'm so thankful to have a television now! I didn't think my father would ever give in and buy us one."

"Yeah, look, there's Danny Kaye. I like him. He's pretty funny!" said Buddy.

Everyone was called to take a place so Ernie could say grace. Buddy and Anna were allowed to sit with the adults in the dining room. It was a tasty meal topped off with delicious pumpkin, apple and sweet potato pie for everyone. Buddy, although somewhat shy, struck up a conversation with one the uncles about his pickup truck that made him feel right at home. Anna thought about how different this family gathering was compared to the ones where her Grandfather Scott had been present. Today, everyone was more relaxed. He had been such a nasty man that Anna was relieved that he could no longer torment the guests at their table. This was her first Scott family meal since he passed away last year.

It was a fine holiday meal. Ernie looked around the table at the abundance of food, his family, his lovely wife and thought, *I am truly thankful for all that I have.*

In the afternoon, Anna and Buddy took a walk to the barn and found a place to steal away for several kisses. The brisk wind made it difficult to carry on for too long. Emmitt was running around the barnyard putting fresh bedding down for the hogs and they were sure to be discovered. He was her father's watchdog. If any of the children misbehaved, he felt it was his obligation to report it to his boss.

As they walked towards Buddy's pickup, he said, "I have to get back home soon. I'm helping my dad with milking tonight. My older brothers and I take turns helping my dad. Tonight is my turn. Hey! Do you want to go to the movies Saturday night? Maybe catch the first show?"

"Sure. That sounds great."

Buddy took Anna by the hand and pulled her behind the tool shed and kissed her again. Anna responded with a hug. She loved the way he kissed her. They broke away laughing and continued the walk back. Buddy gave her a smile and a wink as he looked straight into her eyes.

"You're something else, Anna! See you Saturday night."

* * *

November 26, 1955, *Rebel Without A Cause* was playing at the theater in Edentown. Every show was packed with eager, excited teenagers from the moment it arrived. On this night of her date with Buddy, Anna was among the girls who practically swooned at the sight of James Dean. With a line stretching down the sidewalk for the 7:10 show, the couple was fortunate to make it in. Buddy found seats for them in the next to last row.

"I hope these seats are okay with you. I had no idea it would be so crowded tonight. Maybe I should have picked you up earlier."

"No, I can see the screen just fine. I guess James and Natalie bring out the crowds. I hear that Sal Mineo is pretty good too."

As lights came down and the movie began, Buddy wrapped his arm around Anna, and they spent part of the movie necking. They weren't the only ones that night. The theater manager sent the usher in to scan the crowd with his flashlight more than usual. Groans of protest could be heard periodically throughout the audience.

Anna and Buddy watched intently during the last 20 minutes or so as the movie came to a thrilling end. Then, the lights came up.

"Wow! That was great!" said Anna.

"Oh, you're talking about the movie," Buddy said joking.

Anna laughed. "The other part was great, too," she said demurely.

"Would you like to continue? The night isn't over yet."

"What do you have in mind?"

"Want to find a place to be alone for a while?"

Anna hesitated.

"Only if you want to," Buddy said, allowing the decision to be made by Anna.

"Sure. Let's go. I don't want to go home this early on a Saturday night."

Buddy obviously knew a good place to take Anna since he drove straight to an old woods road that was about fifteen minutes from her home. There was no traffic on the dirt road off the hidden lane either. There was only one large farm located there and it appeared that the elderly couple living in the farmhouse had already turned in for the evening.

"This is nice," Anna said.

"I hope you aren't too cold sitting here. I can run the truck a while longer, if you want."

"No, no need. My coat is warming me enough."

"Do you think kissing will help to warm you, too?"

"I'm sure it will," Anna responded with a giggle. She knew she was putting herself in a position for trouble. However, she had learned a few things from the conversations of the married women at the shirt factory. She found out how to prevent getting pregnant. It worked for them, so why not for her? She and Buddy had been going steady for almost five months and there had been some mention of long-term commitment, but Anna was not pushing for it since Buddy was a part time farmer with his father. She would not marry a farmer, period. Although Buddy had other plans in the works, too. He was going to take training to become certified as a state milk tester. If that came through for him, she might consider a marriage proposal one day.

"Did you hear anything more about the milk tester position?" asked Anna, as Buddy moved closer to her.

"Didn't I tell you? I leave after the new year for College Park. I'll stay on the campus for the 20-day course," Buddy explained and then gently planted several kisses on Anna's lips. She yielded instinctively wrapping her arms around his neck and running her fingers into his thick, dark, wavy hair.

"That's three weeks that you'll be away!" More kisses covered her mouth.

"But when I come back, I'll be able to quit the oil company job and start testing milk for a living. Better money!"

"Yeah, I know. But I'll miss you so much."

"You'll be working. I'll be studying. We can start planning for a future, don't you think?"

Anna didn't respond immediately. She had been through so much in the last year and Buddy came into her life during these most tumultuous times. She wanted a life of her own, a home and a chance to do something with her life. So far, she had been restricted by her parents' rules and stifled to a point of mental paralysis. She couldn't make any decisions of her own for her life. Even though she was of age, she would never be able to choose what she wanted as long as she was under their roof and the authority of her father.

Buddy continued to make love to Anna, saying what she longed to hear from him. He moved along her slender neck to whisper 'I love you' in her ear. She had never heard those words from anyone before. Anna didn't know how to respond at that moment. That didn't deter Buddy from continuing to pressure her into making love to him.

"Let me show my love for you, Anna. Will you?" Buddy said unbuttoning Anna's blouse. Even in the darkness, he could see the fullness of her firm, round breasts spilling over a bra that was too small for her. He touched her and she shivered with excitement. She unbuttoned his shirt to reveal his deformed chest. She ran her hand over the depth of the area, shocked at how far his chest sunk in.

"Does it bother you?" Buddy questioned.

"If it doesn't hurt you, it doesn't bother me."

"Good. Because I'm stuck with it. There's nothing that can be done about it."

"They can't operate?"

"Nope. Too dangerous."

Buddy finished unbuttoning Anna's blouse. She didn't resist. The movements were similar to the night with Jimmy but not as rough. She liked how Buddy made her feel. She wanted him to go on, but she knew where their actions would lead.

"Buddy, maybe we better stop."

"What? Are you cold?"

"No, it's not that."

"Don't worry. But, if you don't want to, I understand."

"I want to, of course."

"I'll be good to you, Anna. I won't hurt you. I promise. You trust me, don't you?"

Buddy kissed Anna again. She relaxed and allowed him to touch her as he found all the sensitive parts of her body. She felt his need for her grow. He wanted her and she found that she wanted him too.

Anna and Buddy made tender love in his red pickup truck that night. Their passion and need for each other was satisfied. Anna gave of herself without hesitation.

"I truly love you, Anna. You know I would never want to hurt you, don't you?"

"I believe you."

They didn't discuss what they had done. Buddy took Anna home a few minutes after her curfew, but she didn't care that night. As long as she was up in time for church the next morning, maybe she wouldn't get in trouble for it. Buddy gave Anna a long, good night kiss in the darkness of the driveway before she slipped quietly into the house careful not to arouse her parents.

* * *

"Good morning, Anna," the Connolly sisters said in unison.

"Good morning, ladies," Anna responded just as she did every morning. She looked closely at the women on the front seat and wondered what type of man would be interested in them. They were identical in everything, not only in their appearance, but in their thoughts and feelings too. They dressed like their mother, maybe using the same patterns to make their clothes. There were no original ideas or expressions of any kind between them.

"Oh, my God!" Fear suddenly struck Anna in the backseat of their car. *"I don't want to turn out like these women! I don't want to strain over the same monotonous factory work making the same thing day in and day out, listening to the same pitiful life stories for years and years and years..."* She stewed over the possibility during her workday.

Later that evening, she spent time in her bedroom trying to make a list of things she wanted to do with her life. She reminisced about the girls at Bassett House, wondering where they were and if they had been able to move on with their lives. *I have supposedly been given this chance to go on with my life, but I don't know where to go or what to do,* Anna thought. *Are they struggling like me?* she wondered. *"Do they still have nightmares? Long to hold their child? Think about her off and on throughout every single day?"*

Anna wished she could hear from Marilee. They had been so close once. It would be so good to talk about her feelings with her dear friend. She knew she would understand. There was no one in her life she could speak with so openly about her daughter.

Anna looked at what she had on the list so far: Have my own home in a town, a good husband, travel to Atlantic City, see my daughter again. Maybe I'll just save up my money and take a trip to Atlantic City in the summer. I'll bet the Connolly sisters have never been there! Anna chuckled to herself.

* * *

Anna and Buddy continued going out whenever they could. They were usually with Janet and Larry or at a friend's house as Buddy was saving up money to go for his class in January. He was counting down the days until then. It was a life changing event for him and a chance to learn something besides farming. It was imperative that he do well and get his certification.

Anna was aware that he needed to be away and concentrate on his course. She told him how much she would miss him, but then expressed her support for his efforts at improving himself. She wished she could go to a school, too. If she had a high school diploma, she would look into secretarial school or something. She would have options.

Buddy took Anna to their secluded spot on the woods lane a couple more times before Christmas, and even spent a little time there Christmas night as they watched a light snow fall around them.

"I don't think we should stay here too long tonight. It would be pretty embarrassing to have to get this truck towed out of the snowbank, don't you think?" They both laughed as they put their clothes on.

"I hope you liked your Christmas present, Anna."

"Which one?" They laughed again. "Oh, my necklace. I love it! The picture of you inside the heart is wonderful. I'll wear it every day that you are away."

"It's a locket, the jeweler said."

"Yes, I know. Will you leave on Monday for your class? That's January second."

"No, I'll go on Saturday, New Year's Day, after I help my dad with the milking in the morning. My brothers will help him while I'm away. He can do it by himself, but as he gets older, it's just harder on him."

"I understand. Do you think we'll be able to go out Friday night before you leave?"

"How about if I come over to your house and hang out for a while that night? I want to leave out early the next day so I can find my room and move in. I'm staying in a dormitory with a roommate or two. I've never stayed in anything like that," he said, feeling awkward about it. "And look, when I get back, I want you to meet my dad. Would you like that? All this time we've been going out and you haven't met my family yet."

"Absolutely. I'd love to meet them all."

"I know you'll love my sisters. My brothers and sisters are married and a couple of them have kids now. It's always a fun time when we're all together. They'll love you, too. Almost as much as I do."

* * *

As Anna walked in the door that night after Buddy dropped her off, she heard her mother and sisters all laughing and talking at once. Janet was clearly the center of attention and her father stood on the sideline scratching his head.

"What's going on?" Anna asked above the din. "What's happening? Janet?"

"Oh, Anna! You'll never believe it! Larry asked me to marry him tonight! Look at this ring he gave me! It's a single diamond, but isn't it the most beautiful ring ever? I just love it!"

Anna stared at the ring on her left hand, wondering if Buddy knew about the proposal.

"It's very pretty. I'm so happy for you both!" Anna exclaimed.

"You know Larry gave me a necklace last night for my Christmas present. And I thought that was a thoughtful gift, but I didn't expect him to give me a ring on top of it, you know? Did Buddy say anything about Larry proposing tonight?" Janet questioned.

"Not to me," Anna replied.

"Larry kept it all to himself, I guess. I still want him to speak with Daddy. That's only right, don't you think?"

"Not necessary!" Their father yelled out. "I know his father. I'll speak with him one day soon and discuss the matter. Girl, you aren't finished with school yet! I'll not have another child without a school diploma!"

"I'll finish high school, daddy. Don't worry about that. We can wait until I turn eighteen in June. I'll have graduated by then. Besides, Larry wants to be sure he has the Dupont job before we get married."

"I certainly hope so! He needs to be able to support you. Make sure he gets that job, and then we can make wedding plans," Ernie stated with concern before going to bed.

With that message, Anna left and went to her bedroom to sulk. The conversation continued as Janet and her mother made wedding plans not caring that they may not be out of earshot of Ernie. Janet wanted five bridesmaids, all wearing tea length dresses in pink, mint green and white lace. Her mother said they could hold the reception at the community hall, and she would hold back a couple of the country hams from this year's hog killing to have for the meal. The plan making went on into the night getting rather loud and excited at times. Anna closed her bedroom door to block the chatter and covered her head with her pillow. She was happy for Janet, really, she was, she told herself. But she was also honest enough to recognize her jealousy.

* * *

Buddy came by on New Year's Eve and spent a few hours watching the television with her and others in her family. It wasn't what she had expected from him that night. His mind seemed preoccupied, and he was anxious to end their evening. He didn't even stay until midnight. She walked to his truck with him when he decided it was time to go.

"You didn't mention that Larry gave Janet an engagement ring for Christmas. I thought you would be telling all about what she said."

"I'm happy for both of them and it appears that there will be a big, beautiful wedding in June. There's not too much to say about it yet."

"Larry has already asked me to be his best man."

"That's wonderful."

"Should I write you while I'm away? It's not that long."

"You'll probably be busy studying most nights, won't you?"

"I'm not sure what to expect yet. If I'm not, I'll send out a note to you, how about that?"

"That would be great. I'll be right here." Anna paused a bit.

"Anna, you seem like something is bothering you. Is anything wrong? Are we okay?"

"I suppose I'm just going to miss you."

"Well, that's good to hear. Be good for me, you hear? I'll be back before you know it."

Buddy leaned in and kissed her, pressing his body against hers, making her aware of his desire for her. She wanted him to go on but feared that her parents may be watching.

"We'd better stop," she said putting her hands against his chest. "I don't think my parents are asleep yet. I don't need to set them off."

"Well, I'll go then. I love you, Anna! I'll be thinking about you every day."

Anna watched as he drove down the long lane and onto the county road. *Three weeks! What was she going to do until then?* she thought.

* * *

"Oh, dear! Anna!" Dottie called from her desk in the hallway. "I forgot to tell you that a letter arrived for you yesterday. Here it is. Doesn't even have our full address. It's a wonder the mailman delivered it."

"That's part of small-town life, mom. Everybody knows everybody and their business," Anna said, stepping over to the desk to retrieve it.

"Looks like it says Philadelphia on the post mark. Who do you know there?"

Anna ignored the question. She took the letter with her to her bedroom and shut the door. The only person she knew from Philly was Dolores Costello. Had she written her? Anna opened the plain white envelope and removed the single sheet of note paper. She read the words in disbelief.

I know you were friends with my sister, Dolores Costello, at Bassett House so I am writing to see if you have heard from her or know where she is. She was living in New York with our sister and started hanging around with a gang on the lower east side. I tried to get her to leave but she wouldn't go with me. She is drinking too much, and I think she is working the streets too. I haven't been able to find her for a few weeks. I think maybe she left the city. If you have heard from her, can you let me know? If you know anything, please contact me. Mario Costello

Tears came into Anna's eyes as she realized that her friend was mixed up with a terrible crowd and was destroying her life. She wanted to respond to Mario but didn't know what to say. There was nothing she could say, no helpful information to offer. Poor Dolores! Anna felt horrible for her and wished there was something she could do. She couldn't even talk about it. There was no one she could tell. No one knew about her friendship with Dolores or their time together. They all had to move on and pretend that their paths had never crossed. The memories of those days, and the daughter she lost in the mayhem of it all, welled up inside her. She had a good cry that afternoon – a good cleansing cry to start off the year 1956.

CHAPTER TWENTY-ONE

True to his word, Buddy sent a note to Anna just five days after he arrived at the college. He told her about his class and roommate, the amount of homework and the good meals, which really didn't interest Anna that much. However, he ended the letter with a line about how much he missed her and couldn't wait to see her. That's what she wanted him to say!

Anna put the letter in the old black and gold trunk at the end of her bed where she stored her keepsakes and then began a letter to send back now that she had an address. She felt like she didn't have much to say either.

* * *

A heavy snow fell overnight and left over a foot of snow blanketing the ground of the Scott farm. Emmitt was up early clearing areas in front of the barn doors so he and Ernie could get in to milk the cows. They would be busy all day tending to the animals in the bitter cold weather. There was no school for the girls or work for Anna, so they all chipped in to spread straw in the shed to bed down the cows. The snow continued to fall until around noon. By then, Dottie had a nice hot meal prepared for the hungry crew. Vegetable beef soup with hot rolls awaited on the table when they walked in the back porch and kicked off rubber boots, heavy coats, gloves, and the like. They warmed their hands over the oil stove and rubbed their cold feet. The aroma of the soup filled their nostrils with the heavy scent of tomatoes and beef. They couldn't wait to fill their bowls with the hot and tasty, homemade delight.

After cleaning up the dishes, Anna decided to lie down for a nap. She was exhausted from the heavy work that morning and the warmth of the soup made her sleepy. She tossed about for a while not able to feel comfortable and then suddenly, she felt she was going to throw up. The heat grew in her face and her stomach churned until she ran to grab her waste basket. Her entire meal came up. She sat on the floor next to her bed waiting for another round, and another.

After a while, Anna pulled herself up and onto her bed. As she lay thinking about this familiar feeling, she wondered if it could possibly be true. Oh, my God, no! I can't be! But she knew deep down that she was. She had been wiser, but not smarter.

I thought I calculated correctly. That way can't be trusted. Anna thought to herself. A married Catholic woman at the shirt factory had explained how she avoided getting pregnant one day during lunch, much to Anna's interest. She had believed her.

I have to tell Buddy. I can't go through this another time. I will not give up my child again, she declared in her mind.

Anna immediately wrote another letter to Buddy. She had to make sure that he loved her and wanted to marry her. Then, fearing she might sound desperate, she hesitated. She needed to be more in control this time. She tore the letter into little pieces and discarded it.

First, she had to know for certain that she was carrying his child. That meant returning to Dr. Isaac for the test and examination. It was all too embarrassing! She felt stupid for allowing this to happen again. *Don't panic! Think this through,* she told herself.

Anna called Dr. Isaac's office when she returned to work two days later, and he was able to fit her in during lunch break the following day.

"I certainly didn't expect to see you back so soon for a pregnancy test, Anna! Didn't you have a baby in Wilmington not long ago?" Dr. Issacs reviewed her file notes.

"Last March. A little girl."

"Did you get married since then? I see you still go by Scott."

"No, sir. But I'm eighteen now. You don't have to tell my parents, do you? My boyfriend and I want to get married when he gets back from school. I'm sure we'll do it soon."

"He's in school?"

"He's taking a special college course with the Department of Agriculture."

"Well, I hope that works out for you. And, no, I don't have to tell your parents, Anna. You should consider it anyway. I'll have an answer for you on Tuesday. Do you want to stop by during your lunch break again?"

"Yes, I'll do that. Thank you so much, Dr. Issacs."

Awaiting results of the blood test made Anna irritable. There was uncertainty, yet she also had a feeling that she was definitely pregnant. She was nasty to her sisters and went as far as telling Janet that she thought her ring was ugly. She later apologized and the two hugged and cried together. She tried to remain in her room as much as possible, sure that any interaction with her parents was certain to lead her into trouble. There was no way she wanted to lose her freedom and privileges now.

* * *

As expected, the test results were no surprise. Anna wished she could be happy for once in hearing that she had a positive pregnancy test. Instead, she was dispirited, frightened and distressed over not knowing if the lie she told Dr. Issacs would come true. Buddy may not want her now that she was carrying a baby – his baby. He needs to understand that. She hoped he wouldn't think she had been with anyone else but him. So much to think about. Anna felt like her head would explode.

She returned to work at the shirt factory. She didn't have time to eat her sandwich, so her head began to throb.

"You don't happen to have any aspirin, do you?" Anna asked the employee next to her. "My head is killing me."

"Sure, honey. Want a couple? Got the cramps, huh? I know how that is. They double me over sometimes."

She pulled two out of a small tin in her purse and handled them to Anna. "Here you go sweetie. Hope you feel better."

Anna struggled through the rest of that day and through every day until Buddy returned home. She had only sent him one letter while he was away. She received three from him.

The workday ended, and as usual, the Connolly sisters were taking their time preparing to leave. They stopped to hear the latest gossip on one of their colleagues who had been missing from work for a couple of days. Disinterested, Anna walked out the front doors with some other women who had finished work for that day. As they hurried down the steps, they cleared a view of Buddy's red pickup truck parked directly in front of the building. He held up a large white piece of paper and as Anna ran over for a better view, she saw it was a certificate.

"Oh, Buddy, you passed! I'm so happy for you! That's wonderful news!" Anna threw her arms around his neck. He put his arm around her and swung her around to face him again.

"I couldn't wait to get home to you, Anna!"

"I know what you mean! I've been thinking about you all day wondering when you would arrive. This is terrific. I'm so proud of you!"

"Now, will you let me take you out for dinner to celebrate? Nothing fancy, mind you."

"I'd love that," Anna was genuinely pleased to see Buddy and so proud of his accomplishment. In the back of her mind, she pondered how his success with the course and new opportunity for better employment would all affect their ability to be married. She worried that he would find her to be too domineering or conniving to think he would propose this soon after passing. They hadn't been dating for very long, but his best friend had proposed to her sister. The uncertainty of her future distressed her. *My happiness shouldn't depend on whether a man will ask me to marry him or not. I am totally at his mercy. I'll put on my smile and be kind to him; all the while inside I am petrified that he will drop me.*

"I want to change my clothes before I go anywhere. I should also let my mother know that I won't be home for supper," Anna explained.

"Good. We can stop by there first."

"Oh, and I have to let the Connolly sisters know that I have another ride."

Just then Marilyn and Carolyn popped out of each of the double doors, practically pushing each other down the steps of the factory.

"Come on, Anna! It's time to go!"

"Yeah, time to go, Anna! Come on now."

"Hey, girls, I'm going to catch a ride home with Buddy today. I'll see you tomorrow morning, okay?"

"Not a problem for us. I hope you don't get yourself in trouble."

"Yeah, hope you know what you're doing."

"Don't worry. It's alright," she yelled back as the two women crossed the street to find their car. Anna giggled at the sight of their two large behinds swishing back and forth together. Buddy deciphered why she was laughing and broke out in a chuckle too.

"Anna Scott! You are so bad!"

"I couldn't help myself. From this angle… Well, they just look funny!"

"They are a sight!" The pair continued laughing as they watched the two women step into their car, their cherubic bodies causing the car to rock from one side to the other as they plopped onto the bench seat. Marilyn started the engine while Carolyn gave instructions on where she must keep her purse while driving, and with a couple of jerks, the car took off down the street.

"Those two are a little odd, don't you think?" asked Buddy.

"Yes, but I have to tolerate them since I don't have my own car or a license to drive."

"Would you like to drive some day?"

"Of course, but until I can afford a car, what's the point?"

"True for now, I suppose. But, if you ever want to learn, I will teach you."

Buddy held the door open for Anna to enter from the driver's side door. She slid in, stopping in the middle of the bench seat. He jumped in letting his right leg rest against her left. Both were very aware of the heat exuding from their bodies. Buddy drove Anna out of town to one of the less traveled roads on their way to her house. Suddenly he came to an abrupt stop as he pulled his truck to the side of the road. Putting the shift in park, he turned to her with a smile.

"I can't wait any longer. I have to kiss you, Anna! I've missed you so much," he wrapped his arms around her shoulders as he drew in closer to her. She gladly surrendered to his sweetness. They kissed each on the side of the road until Buddy saw a car approaching.

"I think maybe they saw us. I don't care. I've waited long enough. I've been wanting to since I saw you walk down the steps from your job."

"I've wanted you to kiss me, too. Oh, Buddy, it's been so long. I've missed you so much."

"I'm back now. I have a new job to start next week. I'm going to be making better money now."

"It's so wonderful. Kiss me again! I love you, Buddy!"

"You do? You've never said it before."

"Yes, of course, I do. Why certainly I love you. You always say it first, that's all."

"We better get you home or your mom will be calling the Connolly sisters to find out what happened to you."

"No, we don't want that!"

Although the air was nippy, it was a lovely evening out with Buddy. They snuggled in his pickup truck as they drove to a bar and grill called Colby's just outside the town limits of Edentown. The white cinder block building flashed colorful neon signs for Pabst Blue Ribbon and Budweiser beers. A message board hung in another window advertising the daily special, which always included large portions of home cooked meat and potatoes. The single and widowed farmers enjoyed going there for supper, but also to meet up with neighbors to talk about the local news or complain about the government. Anna had never been there since they served beer and other alcoholic drinks. It was rare that her family went out to eat anywhere, but especially not in a beer joint. Their waitress was an older woman with heavy lines in her face and the raspy voice of a smoker. She set clean paper placemats in front of the couple and told them that the special that night was baked chicken with mashed potatoes and green beans and sweet iced tea. It sounded perfectly fine to both of them.

"Too bad we can't have a beer with that, you know," Buddy said.

"No, thanks. I'm not much of a drinker," Anna responded.

"Have you ever had any liquor?"

"Of course, who hasn't? When I was at Rehoboth Beach last year, a gang of us used to go out drinking all the time," she lied, trying to impress him. "Not too many in here tonight."

"Most of the men aren't finished milking yet. It will fill up later on, I'm sure."

"Now, tell me all about your time at the college. Were the classes difficult? Did you have to study a lot?" Anna was genuinely interested, and she was having such a good night out with Buddy that she hated to think about spoiling the night. When was she going to be able to say something to him? Certainly not in Colby's. She feared a blow up from him like the one Jimmy had. Even though it was not crowded, there were a few people and the workers who might see his reaction. She felt she needed to wait for a more secluded place to talk.

As they finished the last of their meal, a few of the young men from Buddy's neighborhood came in. They stopped by their booth on their way to a table further back and closer to the speaker pounding out one country song after another. Buddy introduced Anna to his friends, joked with them a bit, and sent them on their way. Anna wondered if Buddy acted as juvenile as his friends when he was around them. If so, she wondered if he would be good marriage material at all!

"Want to ride into town for a little while? It's too early to take you home yet."

"That's fine with me," Anna said, thinking she might get an opportunity to speak with Buddy then.

They traveled along Main Street but didn't see anyone they knew. "It is Tuesday night. I suppose everyone has other things to do in the middle of the week. Do you mind if we just park and talk for a little while?" Anna asked.

"Not at all. How about in the parking lot behind the Five and Dime?"

"Sure. I just hope the cops don't mind," Anna said with concern.

Buddy parked his truck in one of the spaces and immediately leaned over to kiss Anna.

"Hey! Not so fast," Anna said, surprised that he had acted so quickly.

"Sorry. I just had to have one more."

"We need to take it easy. Don't you think?"

"Why? Did I do something wrong?" Buddy asked as he drew back from Anna.

"No, it's not that. I guess I need to know more about how you feel. About me, I mean."

"I'm crazy about you! Don't you know that? I wouldn't just want to be with any girl, you know, like we have. You're special to me, Anna! I'm in love with you."

"You're sure of that?" Anna asked wanting confirmation.

"Of course, I am. Why, don't you feel the same way?"

"I'm in love with you, too. I wouldn't give myself to you if I didn't love you. I wanted to be sure that you feel strongly about me too."

"What's this about, Anna? Is something wrong? You seem nervous or something."

"Yeah, but I'm afraid to say. I don't want you to get mad at me," she said turning her head to look out the window.

"Did you go out with some other guy while I was away?" he asked, sounding disappointed.

"Absolutely not, believe me! I wouldn't think of doing such a thing!" She snapped back to face him, wondering where he got that idea.

"Then what? What's the matter?"

"I'm going to have your baby," Anna said softly. "I found out the results of my test today."

"And you didn't want to tell me? You're not kidding me, are you? This is for real?"

"Oh, it's for real. Dr. Issac was sure of that."

"I can't believe it. I'm going to be a father. We're going to be parents. This is pretty damn exciting!" Buddy exclaimed slapping his hand against his forehead.

"And you don't feel mad? Aren't you upset with me?"

"Why would I be upset with you? I was there too! Remember?"

Anna nodded her head.

"Maybe this isn't how I thought it would happen or even when, but I think we accept the hand we're dealt and figure out what to do next."

"We'll keep the baby? I want to keep it," she insisted.

"Of course, we'll keep the baby. It's our child. We need to get married though. We have to do that first."

"I can't tell my parents, Buddy! They'll just kill me if they find out."

"Your daddy is not going to be none too happy with me, either. That's for sure! We better elope. Once we are married, they can't say or do anything to us. We're of age. You are eighteen, right?"

"Yes. Where do we go to elope?"

"Let me work that out. I know a couple that eloped last year. Maybe I can find out how they arranged it. How many months are you, anyway?"

"I suppose it happened one of those nights around Thanksgiving or after, so about two months."

"Good. That's still early enough. I'll take care of it. I don't want you to worry about it. You have to take care of yourself now. Alright? Will you do that?"

"Oh, Buddy! Thank you so much for understanding," Anna said as she started to cry with relief. She had been fearful of rejection. This time things were different. This time she had the love of a good and responsible man.

CHAPTER TWENTY-TWO

Buddy Merchant was going to be a father. He was just twenty years old but already knew that he wanted a wife and family of his own. The youngest of seven children, he had grown up having nieces and nephews around and understood the importance of having both parents in a child's life. Even now, he missed his mother and wished he had had her to guide him in life. She was a kind and loving woman who worked hard to provide for her children. She was only forty-eight when she died. Buddy appreciated his two sisters who helped raise him, but they were not always nice to him. They were bossy and preoccupied with their own lives. Sometimes they simply didn't want to be bothered by their little brother. His father had mourned greatly and vowed he would not remarry. She had been his one true love. Buddy also felt that Anna was his true love. He wanted to be loved in return and he was ready to make a life with her and their child.

There was a small two-bedroom cinder block house on Eighth Street, a quiet area in town. It was painted white with black shutters and had a small yard in the front with a single tree. The rent was reasonable, and Buddy could afford it with pay from his new job. He paid the landlord for February's rent even though he wasn't sure that he and Anna would be married that soon. He didn't want to lose this perfect starter home for them.

"Want to take a ride? I have something to show you, Anna," Buddy asked with a grin on his face. He was excited to take Anna by the house to see her reaction. He hadn't seen her for a few days since he started work at his new job. He was up early traveling from farm to farm collecting samples of milk from area farmers, labeling and writing reports for each stop, and submitting it all to a lab. He returned home just in time to help his father with milking. It made a long, exhausting day.

"What is it?" she asked, feeling his excitement.

The red pickup truck stopped in front of the little white house, and Buddy came around to the passenger's side door to open it for Anna.

"Who are we going to see here?"

"We aren't seeing anyone. You are seeing your new home. Do you like it?"

"It's ours?" she asked in disbelief.

"I signed a lease for it. We're renting it. But, isn't it perfect? There are two bedrooms and a bathroom."

"Our own home? I didn't think about possibly having our own place to live. Oh, Buddy, I love it! I'll make it nice for us. I promise!"

"I know you will."

"I thought I would have to live with you and your father."

"No, honey, I want to start our lives here on our own. Don't you think we should have some private time? That would be difficult to do living with others."

"I just can't believe we are going to live in such a cute home. I am so happy!" Anna said giving Buddy a huge kiss right there on the street. "I have money saved up from work that I can spend on plates, glasses, and pans. I can make curtains. What will we do about furniture?"

"I have money saved up too. I'm not rich, mind you, but we can at least get some pieces from that used furniture store on Route 320. How does that sound?"

"Wonderful! It's going to be alright, isn't it? I'm so worried, Buddy."

"Why? We are getting married. We are doing right," he answered.

"I don't want my parents to find out about the baby yet. I want to get married as soon as we can. My father will kill me if he knows I'm expecting. Seriously."

"I didn't know it was as serious as that, Anna. Are you really so afraid of your father? I'm so sorry I got you in this situation, but I will do right by you and our baby. Don't worry so much, please. I will protect you."

"I'll try. Let's get married soon, okay?"

* * *

Anna bought a navy-blue tweed suit and white blouse from Carpenter's that was on sale. Not wanting to spend money on new shoes to match, she chose to wear a pair of black heels she already owned. She also bought a round navy blue cap with a veil and small feather decorating one side. She gave the outfit to Buddy to keep for a couple weeks. He found a minister in Henson who would be able to marry them on Saturday night, February 18, but they needed to find a couple to stand up with them.

* * *

"Oh, my gosh, Anna! It's been forever since I last saw you. Now that we're both working girls with steady boyfriends, it's difficult to find the time to go out with old friends," Betty gushed with excitement as she sat down in a booth across from Anna. They decided to meet at Murph's for lunch the first Saturday afternoon of February.

"Just like old times being in here, isn't it?"

"I hope they were mostly happy memories."

"Yes, mostly."

"Hey, I heard that Janet got engaged at Christmas. Is that, right? Did they say when they are getting married?"

"It looks like big wedding plans are set for the end of June, after she graduates. She and my parents are constantly making arrangements and changing them because of the cost of everything. There are daily discussions about it; some of them get a little loud, if you know what I mean."

"I can imagine. I suppose Janet is giving them a hard time," Betty sniggered.

"I'm just glad they aren't so concerned about my business these days. It's Janet's turn to be picked on."

"Oh, and did you know that Kay made the Dean's list her very first semester at Johns Hopkins? She loves it. Says there are so many more things to do in the city, but she spends a lot of time studying in her room. She's living in a big house with a few other girls, just a couple blocks down the street from the campus."

"I'm really happy for her. She's so smart! It's no surprise that she made the list. I wonder if she will stay in Baltimore when she finishes," Anna said, feeling happy for her friend, but feeling disappointed in herself at the same time. Anna had thought about becoming a nurse or going to a trade school several months back. No chance of that happening now. Anna became serious as she looked across the table at her best friend.

"I need to ask you something, Betty, but you must swear not to tell anyone. No one can know anything. Please," Anna pleaded.

"What is it, Anna? You know I have always been true to my word and would never tell a soul about a secret of yours. You know that, right?"

"Yes, but I must be sure that you understand how important this is to me." Betty was totally intrigued now.

"Buddy and I have decided to elope on February 18. We have the minister lined up already."

"Oh, my gosh, Anna! That's wonderful news! I'm so happy for you!"

"I don't want my parents to get wind of what we are doing. I'm afraid of what they will do to stop us."

"I understand. But you are both of age."

"Yes, but I am still under their roof."

"You have always done your best to please your parents, Anna. At some point in your life, you need to break away and be on your own. It's time you started making your own decisions."

"Thank you. I believe it is, too! That's what I want to ask you. Can you and Doug stand up for us at the ceremony?"

"February 18? I'll ask Doug tonight, but I don't see any reason that we couldn't. Of course, you know I want to be there for you and Buddy. You make a great couple!"

"Do you think Doug can keep the secret, too? I am truly afraid about my father, especially. If he discovered what we are doing…Betty, I really don't know what will happen. He will be furious with me. I don't think any of you know how bad it will be for me," Anna began to show panic in her voice.

"Okay. Okay, Anna! Calm down. I guess I didn't understand. I didn't know your father was like that. He always seems to be easy going around me. Your mom, too."

"Not always," Anna paused as she felt she may have said too much.

"You've never told me that you are afraid of your father, Anna. What's going on?"

"Nothing, really." Anna clammed up. Betty would push her for answers if she didn't come up with a good response. Betty's head was cocked to the side as she awaited further explanation.

"We just don't talk. He avoids being around me. He treats me like a kid. He's too strict on me. I'm over eighteen for gosh sakes! He acts like I'm twelve!" Anna let all the excuses spill out at once hoping one of them would satisfy Betty.

"Yeah, I can see that he is tough on you and Janet. Some farm fathers are like that. Old school ideas are still in their heads. You would think we're living in the 1800's, huh?" Betty paused, trying to read Anna's face. "Look, don't you worry about Doug. I'll contain him and make sure no one finds out about anything. I wouldn't tell anyone else though, if I were you."

"I won't. Thank you, Betty! I really appreciate your help!" she said, giving her friend a hug.

"It's all going to work out, Anna! We'll make sure of it, okay?"

* * *

Doug agreed to be a witness. He was actually pleased to be asked. He and Betty dressed for the evening on the pretense that they were attending a party in town. They had unnecessarily given an excuse for their attire and whereabouts for the night. Unlike the Scotts, their parents did not interrogate them every time they left the house.

Buddy finalized his preparations by picking up a corsage of white carnations, toile, and ribbon to give to Anna. He ordered it two weeks ago because Valentine's Day was so close, he wasn't sure there would be any flowers left for Anna. The girl behind the counter at the flower shop knew him and asked if he was going to a dance or getting married. When he couldn't answer her, she guested that he was eloping. She was used to selling flowers for the quickie weddings.

Larry stopped by to ask Buddy if he could borrow his post hole digger just as he was washing up and shaving. He asked why he hadn't seen much of him lately, hoping maybe they could go on a double date soon.

"Look Larry, I'm sorry but I have somewhere I need to go tonight. I want to tell you all about it, but Anna and I agreed not to say anything. You are welcome to go into the tool shed and take the post hole digger. You know where it is."

"Thanks! I'll bring it back in a couple of days. Wait! Anything about what? What are you two up to? Are you proposing to Anna?"

"Sorta. I guess it's close enough to time to leave that I can tell you. We're getting married tonight!"

"No. No, you can't be. Tonight? Are you guys eloping? Janet hasn't said anything about it."

"Of course not! Anna is petrified of her parents finding out. You have to keep your mouth shut, you hear me? Not a word!"

"Got it! Believe me, I hear all about the way their parents are from Janet. I don't think she will say anything. She is just as afraid of them."

"I don't know about that. Anna is mostly afraid of her father, I think. It's strange to me. My father will probably be happy or indifferent to our news. Maybe he'll just say that he is glad the last kid is married and off on his own!" The boys laughed as they couldn't imagine Mr. Merchant ever getting upset over very much.

"So, you didn't invite me to your wedding? Come on! I'm your best friend!"

"Sorry, Larry!"

"Don't you need someone to stand up with you?"

"Yeah. Anna took care of that."

"Who? Who better than me?"

"Well, Betty is standing up with Anna, so Doug is coming along to stand up with me."

"Doug Wheatman? Are you kidding me? You would rather have Doug there than me?"

"Look, Larry, I just want to get married to Anna as quickly as possible. I'm not concerned about whoever is there. I just want to get it done!"

"Why the urgency? What's going on, Buddy?"

Buddy looked away as he dried his face with a towel.

"What else is going on, Buddy? You're not telling me everything," Larry asked realizing that his friend was hiding something. "Spill it! Buddy, tell me. Is Anna expecting?" Larry urged.

Buddy still couldn't answer him. The silence between them continued until Buddy finally broke it. Facing Larry, he explained.

"Yes. She sure is! Can you believe it? I'm going to be a father!"

"Holy shit! You're sure?"

"Yep. She confirmed with her doctor," Buddy responded. "Now do you understand why we have to keep this a secret?"

"Yeah, of course. I'd still like to be there. If I don't tell Janet where we are going, do you think we could show up?"

"Anna will be furious if you do that. Besides, you don't want to put Janet in the position of keeping this secret from her parents, do you?"

Buddy finished putting his tie on and grabbed his suit jacket as he left Larry to ponder the consequences of including his fiancée. He decided it would not be worth the distress they would cause both girls. Although he would love to see his best friend get married, he preferred to distance himself to insure he would stay in the good graces of Janet's parents.

"Hey, Buddy! I get it. I promise not to say anything to Janet about any of this, okay? I don't want to ruin this night for you two or risk any interference. You two tie the knot! We'll catch up in a few days! Sound good?"

"Thank you, Larry! I appreciate it! We are only spending tonight out. We'll be home tomorrow." Buddy shook Larry's hand as his friend gave him a pat on the back. They both walked to their pickup trucks and headed off in different directions.

* * *

Buddy arrived at the Scott farm around six o'clock, while Ernie and Emmitt were still milking. Anna told her mother that Buddy was taking her out for a nice dinner and slipped her long coat on over her suit before her mother saw the new stylish outfit. Her suitcase was just inside the door of the tool shed. She had placed it there when her parents had gone to town earlier that day. She had already given other clothes and some personal items to Buddy on Valentine's night while most of the family attended a dinner at the community hall and Janet was out with Larry. They were stored at their new home. Buddy grabbed the suitcase from the shed and put it in the back of his pickup. Anna trotted over to him, and they kissed quickly before he opened the door for her to get in. They knew there was no time to waste.

Anna looked towards the barn and saw her father passing in front of an open door. He was carrying a full milker to the dump in one of the milk cans lined up against the wall. She saw his body leaning to the left as he compensated for the weight of the full bucket. How many times had she seen him do this over the years? The exertion of his labors had given him back issues for which he was in constant discomfort and often pain. Anna watched her father take a red handkerchief from his bib overalls and swipe it across his nose. He picked up the milker and walked out of sight of the open door. The barn lights made flickering shadows on the ground from the movement inside the barn. Soon her father and Emmitt would finish up and release the cows back to the field.

"We better go now, Buddy! Looks like they're almost done milking."

"You sure? You seem a little sad, Anna. Are ready to do this?"

"Absolutely. I'm not sad! I'm just thinking how glad I am to never have to deal with those cows ever again!"

Buddy turned the ignition and put his lights on. The high beams were suddenly shinning on Dottie as she ran towards them waving her right hand while carrying a paper bag in the other. She was yelling for them to wait.

"Mom!" Anna cried out as her mother motioned for her to roll down the window on the passenger's side. "Be careful mom! We could have run over you!" Anna exclaimed, as she rolled the window down. "We didn't see you at first!"

"So sorry," Dottie said huffing. "I only wanted to catch you. I just got off the phone with your grandfather and he would like this lima bean soup and cheese biscuits for dinner tonight. I promised them to him. Can you drop this off on your way?" she asked, handing the bag through the window.

"We would be happy to take it, Mrs. Scott," stated Buddy before a reluctant Anna had the chance to respond. He was more worried about Dottie noticing the suitcases in the back of the truck. The light pole by the implement shed gave off just enough light to make out both bags that were standing behind the cab of the truck. Certainly, if Dottie gave a glance back, she would question what they were up to. Buddy waited for her to head back to the house. If he pulled forward while she was standing there, she would surely see them.

Dottie continued to tell Anna what her grandfather had said on the phone. Anna barely heard a word as she grew more anxious to leave. As her mother told Anna that she may want her to take more food tomorrow, Anna saw the milk house light come on. Her father came out wheeling a cart to collect the filled milk cans. Anna knew Emmitt and Ernie were close to finishing up work for the night.

"Okay, mom. I'll help as much as I can," Anna squirmed in the seat and put her hand on the handle to roll up the window.

Buddy saw how restless she was and came to the rescue.

"Well, we better get this dinner delivered, don't you think? We don't want it to get cold."

"Thank you, Buddy! You'll save Ernie a trip tonight. That's a big help."

"Glad to do it, Mrs. Scott," Buddy still waited for her to go towards the house before leaving. She wasn't moving. Only when Buddy nodded to her to go ahead did she finally get the message.

"Oh, my gosh! I thought she would never let us go," said Anna while Buddy laughed nervously at how close they had come to getting caught.

"I thought she had us! From the moment I saw her face in front of the truck, I knew we were dead!" Anna now chuckled realizing that Buddy had been just as distressed.

They continued to laugh all the way to her grandfather's house. He met them in the driveway, so she was sure her mother had called back to let him know they were on their way.

"Thank you so much for delivering this. Your grandmother has not had a good day and I didn't want to leave her even for a few minutes. Want to come in for a bit?"

"Actually, Mr. Daffin, Anna and I are meeting up with friends tonight and we need to catch up with them," Buddy explained so Anna would not need to.

"Sorry, granddaddy, but we can't tonight."

"I understand you young people have better things to do, and you should! Go out and have fun! Enjoy your youth! It's all over sooner than you think."

Wilbur Daffin stepped back from the truck and waved goodbye to the couple as Buddy backed out of the driveway. Anna watched as her grandfather slowly took the steps onto the porch and entered the house.

"He really seemed down tonight; don't you think? I wish I could tell him about us. He is the one person in my family who I can trust. I always have."

"Tomorrow, okay? You can tell him everything when we get back."

"Yeah. Now, can we get ourselves hitched? I want to get to the church before anything else happens tonight!"

Buddy drove to Betty Andrew's house, so Anna could finish getting dressed. She and Betty applied some makeup, teased their hair a little and sprayed it in place. Anna positioned her cap on her head and pulled the veil in front of her face. Betty pinned the corsage on Anna's suit jacket, gave her a quick hug, and handed her a blue handkerchief.

"I know this is a new suit you are wearing. I wasn't sure if you would have the other things needed for a bride, so here is an old, blue handkerchief that was my grandmother's that I will lend to you for tonight." The two young women chuckled and hugged once more.

"You are the best, Betty. Thank you so much for helping me through this."

"It all worked out, you see. My family went over to visit friends and play cards tonight. You made it away from the house without incident. No one knows anything."

"We had a little scare, but all is well now. I have to tell you, I can't stop shaking. I don't think I will stop until we are through the ceremony."

Buddy and Anna drove to the church with Doug and Betty behind them. They pulled up in front of the parsonage, a two-story Victorian-styled home that was built shortly after the completion of the brick church sometime around 1881. The couple walked up the gray painted wooden steps onto a wraparound porch of the same color. A green metal glider and four red wooden rockers were visible in the darkness, as no one had turned on the porch light for them. Buddy knocked on the green front door with a large glass panel covered by a white lace curtain. They heard steps approaching and then the light next to the door came on. The face of an elderly woman appeared in the window as she acknowledged their presence and unlocked the door. The minister's wife offered a pleasant greeting and invited them in from the cold. They walked through the entrance and entered a large parlor, where there were several pieces of Victorian-styled sofas and chairs, along with a piano and a small pulpit.

When Buddy had spoken to the minister over the phone, he had asked why they were eloping or if there was any reason they should not be married in the main sanctuary of the church. Buddy wasn't sure how to answer, so the reverend decided that it was best that they have the ceremony in the parsonage. Buddy felt better about not making that decision; not wanting to lie, but also not wanting to tell Anna why they couldn't be married in the church sanctuary.

"Reverend Todd will be down in a minute. We just finished supper and he is changing for the ceremony," Mrs. Todd said in a soft voice. She lit a few candles in the room before stepping out to check on her husband.

The bride and groom removed their wraps and stood nervously beside their friends in the dimly lit room. The furniture was old, covered in doilies, and there was a smell of vanilla permeating the space, almost as if to cover up another odor. The pictures on the wall were dark prints depicting various biblical scenes. The fireplace appeared to still be utilized since it had three logs placed in a rack ready to burn, and several candles stood along the length of the mantle, flickering against an old gold painted mirror.

"Good evening, young people! Now, who do we have here? Who are the bride and groom tonight?" asked Reverend Todd as he entered through the double doors of the parlor.

"We are," said Anna and Buddy simultaneously stepping forward.

"Good. Good. Let's take care of a couple things before we begin. We'll get this paperwork out of the way first. You are both of age, right?"

Anna thought for a minute that she would need to show him her birth certificate and she began to feel upset. She had a sense of dread overtake her, believing that something was certain to go horribly wrong. The minister had them swear on the Bible that they were over eighteen. No further question on that! Buddy brought the license that they obtained at the courthouse with the help of the clerk who was a distant cousin of Buddy's. She made sure the information wasn't leaked out in advance of their wedding night. She understood how small-town gossip gets around quickly, so she held the copy on her desk until after the weekend.

"Now, Anna, you come stand over here to my right, and Buddy, go on my left, and your witnesses can stand next to each of you, and we'll begin."

Mrs. Todd played part of *Oh Promise Me* on the piano without singing the words. Then, Reverend Todd read from the book he had used for hundreds of wedding ceremonies over his career. There was an exchange of rings. Anna didn't realize that Buddy had handled purchasing those until he presented them for blessing by the minister. They were simple gold bands, but to Anna it meant that she was truly and honestly married. Anna stood admiring the band on her finger as Reverend Todd spoke his last words.

"What God has joined together, let no man put asunder. You may kiss your bride," he then said with a grin on his face. Buddy pulled the veil of Anna's cap up and out of his way and gave her a gentle kiss on her lips. Betty and Doug gave them both a hug as they wished them all the best. Buddy paid for the ceremony after Reverend Todd signed the certificate of marriage and handed it to him. After everything was finished, they all walked out the door and onto the brightly lit porch. They had a few more words before going to their respective vehicles.

"Thank you both so much for being here for us!" Buddy said sincerely.

"Yes, we really appreciate it," Anna said giving Betty another hug. "Oh, and here is your grandmother's handkerchief back, Betty. I suppose it brought me good luck tonight!"

"Do you feel better now that it's over?" Betty asked, noticing that her friend was more relaxed.

"The evening had a bit of a rough start, but we got through it perfectly fine!" interjected Buddy. "Nothing was going to spoil this night. I only needed to convince Anna of that!"

They all laughed. Buddy took Anna's hand and led her to the steps.

"Where are you going on your honeymoon, you two?" Doug asked.

"Oh, no! Who did that?" Anna said, stopping on the top step as she saw the truck covered in toilet paper, 'Just Married' written on the back window with soap, and shaving cream decorated the back and side panels. Fortunately, the only place that was not covered was the windshield.

"This looks like the work of my good friend, Larry! Let's take this toilet paper off before we leave."

"Larry? How did he know we were getting married tonight? I'll bet he has already told Janet!"

"Don't get worked up again, Anna!" Betty chided.

"He just happened to stop by before I drove over to get you," Buddy tried to explain. "He promised not to tell Janet until after we were married. I believe him."

"Larry's a straight up kinda guy, Anna. I don't believe he will say anything to Janet yet," added Doug.

"Anna, do you honestly think that if Larry had told your sister that she would be able to stay away from here tonight? She would have made Larry bring her, too!" Betty tried persuading her.

"You're probably right about that."

"Larry would never break a promise. I know that about my friend! He did this by himself, I'll bet!"

"Don't worry, Anna. You're married now. It's done. Nothing your family says or does can change that," Betty consoled her friend. "Don't let your fears spoil your wedding night! We are of age and can make decisions for ourselves. You are out of your parents' home now."

"It will take some time to get used to that, I suppose," Anna said.

* * *

Buddy took Anna to an inexpensive roadside motel near Dover, Delaware for the night. They spent the first night of their married lives making love in the tiny room of outdated furniture and well-worn sheets and towels. A light snow fell overnight.

Anna and Buddy stood wrapped in each other's arms watching the snow falling in the light of the streetlamp.

"Look how the flakes sparkle in the light! So beautiful, don't you think?" Anna asked.

"I know what's even more beautiful than that," Buddy responded tightening his arms around Anna and pulling her close against his chest.

They felt comfortable together. After all the anxiety and distress of the last few weeks, the pair finally relaxed and enjoyed each other's company.

The following morning, Anna and Buddy moved into their home together. There was still a lot of work to do to set up housekeeping. They hadn't been concentrating their efforts on the house since there was so much to preparing for the wedding, all while working and helping their families. By now, Anna knew that her parents were wondering where she was, but there was no phone in their home yet to give them a call. The newlyweds had hoped for a quiet afternoon cleaning and stocking their kitchen. They had no furniture, not even a bed. Buddy took a stack of blankets from storage at his father's house and placed them on the floor of the bedroom. He bought a couple of pillows from the five and dime and a set of sheets. They planned to search out used furniture later in the month to fill the home.

"Don't you think we better tell our parents that we are married? Maybe let them know where we live?" Anna questioned.

"It depends on how you feel about it. I'll call my dad from the phone booth down the street. I believe he will be happy for us. Do you want to do the same?"

"It's the right thing to do. I don't want them to worry. We might as well get it over with."

There was a phone booth on the corner of the street just two blocks away. Buddy called his dad first so he could catch him before going to the barn. He received a heartfelt congratulations and told Buddy not to worry about helping out around the farm for a while. He felt he was able to handle the work and knew Buddy's job was demanding enough for the young groom.

Anna's call home was different, but not as bad as she had anticipated. Her mother answered the phone.

"Mom? It's Anna."

"Anna! Where are you? We've been worried sick about you!"

"Well, Buddy and I eloped last night. We're married now."

"Married? I should have guessed it was something like that! Are you sure this is what you want? You're not expecting again, are you?"

Anna avoided answering that question. "Of course, this is what I want. We decided to elope so you and daddy wouldn't have more expense of another wedding. I know it's costing you a lot for Janet's, and we didn't want you to spend that much on us."

Dottie felt awful. It was unfair to Anna for she and Ernie to spend so much money on Janet's wedding and give nothing to her. She felt that even though Anna had done wrong in the past, she was still deserving of something. It was a relief to know that she was married. She and Ernie did not need to be concerned about her making any other mistakes. They liked Buddy and felt he was a good match for her.

"I don't want you to feel like we aren't doing for you like we do for Janet. Is there anything we can get you two as a wedding present? I'll speak with your daddy about it. We're happy for both of you, Anna. Let us know where you're living, and we'll come by soon to visit."

"Do you really think daddy will be happy for us?" Anna questioned. Her mother had a tendency to speak for Ernie too, even when she knew his feelings would be just the opposite.

"Of course, he will!"

"We're renting a little place on Eighth Street here in town. It's the cutest little place ever with black shutters and red brick steps. Oh, it's white on the outside. There's a little yard in the front and back where I can grow some flowers this Spring and maybe plant a few vegetables. I can walk to work, so I'll save money by not having to pay the Connelly sisters again. Buddy has a new job. That's why the timing is right for us to marry now. We don't have much furniture yet, but we can get some eventually. We'll be fine."

"That sounds wonderful, Anna! I can't wait to tell your father! He's gone to the mill with Emmitt to pick up hog feed. He was upset that you didn't come home last night, but I'm sure he'll be happy to hear this good news. It's going to be alright now, Anna! I'm sure of it!"

* * *

The newlyweds had an entire week to themselves; working all day and coming home to each other's arms at night. They had little in the kitchen to prepare a full meal, so they ate a lot of tuna fish sandwiches and canned soup before heading into their bedroom to spend time getting to know each other and make love. It felt strange to have such freedom to do whatever they wanted. They had no phone, no television, no radio or record player, no newspapers or magazines to distract them. Their focus was on building a life together and planning for the arrival of their child. They spent time talking until late at night as they discovered new things about their spouse. With each new day, they grew closer and more comfortable around each other. They were amazed and unimaginably overjoyed at this time of life.

Anna's parents came by the following Sunday afternoon. They were pleased to find the little white house with black shutters in a good neighborhood of the town. Since Anna walked the four blocks from work to home in the dusk these days, they were concerned about her safety. As they entered the bungalow, they were struck by the lack of furniture. Anna hadn't exaggerated when she said they didn't have anything yet. There was no place for anyone to sit anywhere in the house. Fortunately, Ernie and Dottie had decided to give the newlyweds a new five-piece kitchen set of chrome legs and a white Formica top with matching red and white chairs. After Buddy and Ernie brought all the pieces in and set it up in the kitchen, they shook hands.

"We really appreciate this gift, Mr. Scott. As you can see, we could use a place to sit down. We are going to buy a few pieces in a week or so. I can only get to the store on a Saturday to take a look." He watched for Ernie's reaction. "I hope you are not upset about us eloping. We were married by a minister, not by the clerk of the court."

"We wish you had gotten married in our family church, of course. But that aside, we are happy that you are our son-in-law." Ernie was also relieved that he didn't have to pay for another wedding so close to Janet's upcoming nuptials. He was not going to complain about the couple choosing to elope.

Anna showed Dottie around and told her about their plans to paint and paper certain rooms before buying too much furniture. As they stepped into the bedroom, Anna realized that they had left the blankets in disarray on the floor. She was embarrassed by the sight and knew her mother felt the same. Both women turned back, and Anna shut the door behind her in an attempt to keep her father from going in or seeing the mess.

"Does your grandfather know you two are married?" Dottie asked. "He has been so busy caring for mother lately that he hasn't stopped by for a visit. Apparently, she has been a handful for him the last couple of weeks. She doesn't want to eat or bathe. It seems she has lost interest in everything."

"No, not yet, but I will. It's upsetting to hear that grandmother is not eating. That was one thing she always seemed to look forward to when I cared for her. That doesn't sound good, mom."

"I agree. What can we do? My mother has been sick for years. I'm surprised that she has lasted this long." Dottie said sounding exasperated. "Please give your granddaddy a call soon. He will want to hear from you."

Anna looked over at Buddy and her father tightening up the screws for the table legs and chairs. They had a conversation going on about his new job and seemed to work well together. She knew Buddy would do his best to prove that he would be a good provider. It was important to him that he stay on his father-in-law's good side as he hoped to mend whatever rift existed between Anna and her father.

"Was dad very upset when he found out Buddy and I had eloped?"

"Honey, he was more worried thinking that you were missing. When you didn't come home that night, we weren't sure what had happened. It was truly a relief for both of us when you called."

"Sorry we didn't tell you sooner."

"Your father even tried calling Mr. Merchant to see if Buddy was home, but no one answered the phone."

"Oh, we didn't tell him either until we returned. He wouldn't have known anything."

Buddy and Ernie looked over the dining set with satisfaction. Anna thanked her parents again for such a lovely gift. It was one item they could cross off their list; and a new set, not used!

Satisfied that their daughter was well and truly married, Dottie gave Anna a hug and Ernie shook Buddy's hand before they walked out the front door to go home.

"She's in your hands now, Buddy. Take good care of her. Anna, you behave yourself, ya hear?" Ernie said as he gave a nod to his daughter and stepped onto the front stoop. She had hoped he would give her a hug before leaving, but he didn't even try. Obviously, becoming a married woman hadn't mended his feelings towards her. *What more can I possibly do to earn his love again?*

Later that day, Anna walked to the pay phone at the end of the street and called her grandfather to tell him of their elopement. She didn't want him to hear it from anyone else but her. She was upset with herself for not calling him sooner, knowing he would be genuinely happy for her. There was no excuse for delay. The news might even raise his spirits.

Wilbur Daffin answered the phone on the first ring as though he had been waiting on a call from someone. Anna thought he must be lonely in a house with a wife who could not be a true partner. She always felt remorseful that he was burdened by her grandmother's illness but admired his steadfastness and commitment to her.

"Hi, granddaddy, it's Anna! I'm calling from a phone booth."

"Anna! It's good to hear from you, sweetheart! Is everything all right?"

"More than all right! I'm calling to let you know that Buddy and I eloped last weekend."

"I was wondering why I haven't seen you the past few days! So, you are a married woman now? I am pleased. Buddy will make a good husband!"

"I'm really happy, Granddaddy!"

"It's time for you to have some enjoyment in your life, darling! I'm glad to hear it. You definitely sound like you are happy!"

"We are renting a little bungalow in town. It's the only white cinder block house on Eighth Street. I would love to have you stop by when you can. We have a table and chair set now so there is a place to sit down and have a cup of coffee with me one day. It was a gift from mom and dad."

"I'd like that, Anna! I know which house you are renting. My little Anna, you have grown up! Suddenly, you are a married woman!"

"Try to come by soon, Granddaddy. Promise? I want to show you our cute little home. I have so many things I want to do to make it pretty."

"I want to see it! I know you will make it a nice home for the two of you. I'll visit as soon as I can. Okay? Thank you for calling me, Anna."

Other gifts began to arrive from friends and relatives as they learned of the elopement. They received several items for their kitchen including a toaster, iron and ironing board, a set of glasses, some pans, a set of dishes and towels for the kitchen and bathroom. Buddy's father bought them a used wringer washing machine and a green plaid chair from an estate sale. Buddy and Anna later went to the used furniture store and purchased a blonde bedroom set with gold-colored handles and knobs. The salesman threw in a mattress because they also bought a dark green sofa. They were ecstatic to start furnishing their home.

Anna continued to work at the shirt factory for as long as she could and was able to walk the four blocks every day. No more rides with the Connolly sisters! They'd barely spoken to her since she married Buddy. Anna felt they were jealous. A collection was taken up at the factory for a wedding gift to present to Anna just as they had done for others. The Connolly sisters didn't contribute to the pretty set of Tupperware storage bowls, nor were they in attendance when Anna received the gift.

On the second Sunday in March, Anna finally met Buddy's family. Pearl, the sister who practically raised Buddy after their mother's death, organized a dinner party for the afternoon at their father's house. The other six siblings, their spouses and children arrived around one o'clock with dishes of food to place on the counters of the large kitchen. There were several makeshift tables set up to accommodate the large family, as well as place settings at the kitchen and dining room tables. Anna was introduced to Pearl first. She thanked the attractive, tall, well-dressed woman for hosting the meal. She was pleasant to Anna, but there was also a sense of scrutiny in her demeanor. Pearl didn't know anything about Anna or her family and felt obligated to pursue more information about this young woman. She hoped Buddy had made a good choice in a bride.

Patsy was next in age to Buddy. She was married to a Navy serviceman and had recently given birth to their first child. She was leaving to join her husband in California in another two weeks. Anna found her very boastful and arrogant. Buddy had told her that he and Patsy didn't get along well as kids, and Anna believed she could see why.

Robert dominated the conversations and knew everything there was to know about everything. Rachel and Abigail kept to themselves and discussed all the problems they were having with their children. Alex was a towering man of six feet four who ducked when passing through the doorways of the farmhouse. He liked to kiss everyone except his wife, a short, petite woman who talked fast and said little. She was not pleasant and was constantly advising Alex of what he could and could not eat. Gertrude was a sweet and gentle woman who stayed busy in the kitchen making sure everyone was served before serving herself. Her husband was a grouch who used a cuss word in every sentence and found the negative in everything around him. The large, boisterous group of new family members made Anna feel uncomfortable. She found solace in sitting next to Willie Merchant, Buddy's father. They hit it off immediately.

Willie was a quiet, undemanding man with a simple lifestyle. Generous to family and neighbors, for although he was not a rich man, he was always willing to lend a hand or give what he had to another – a true shirt-off-his-back kind of man.

"Dad, when are you going to put in a bathroom? My children are afraid to use the outhouse and now one of them has wet herself," yelled Rachel from the other room.

"I don't have a fear of it. I don't wet myself. What's the problem with your daughter?" Willie yelled back. The group laughed at their father's comment.

Willie sat at the head of his dining table doling out advice and telling stories of how things were handled back in his day. He had a dry sense of humor, which his more worldly children found nonsensical. That didn't seem to bother him though; he was content with his life and didn't have unfulfilled expectations of his youth. He had become an old man who lived vicariously through his children and grandchildren.

As the day wound down, Patsy and Pearl sat down next to Buddy and Anna for further interrogation.

"Have you started your new job yet, Buddy?" Questioned Pearl. "It must pay well since you felt the need to marry so soon after completing your course."

"Well enough. I started my job in January."

"And you like it?" Patsy questioned further.

"Yes, of course!"

"And are you still working, Anna? You're a seamstress, right?" Asked Pearl.

"Yes, I am. I'll keep working for now to help provide additional income while we set up housekeeping," Anna explained feeling the women were fishing for information.

"So, you need your income to pay your bills? I've always believed that a woman should never have to work once she is married," Patsy responded in a flippant manner that make Anna uncomfortable.

"We hear you are renting a place in town, Buddy," started Pearl.

"Yeah. On Eighth Street. You should stop by sometime," responded Buddy.

"Of course! Well, Patsy will be leaving this month to go back to San Diego and we thought we might stop by one day before she goes."

"That would be nice. Let us know when and I can prepare lunch for everyone," Anna said, hoping they would give plenty of advanced notice. "We are still setting up our home. It's a little sparse for now, but we have a table set that can seat all of us."

"Now, Anna, don't go to any trouble on our account," Pearl said.

"Anna can make the best tuna fish sandwiches! Maybe she will make some for you," added Buddy jokingly. The sisters looked at each other disdainfully. Buddy had seen that disapproving look before. Although his sisters had the same humble childhood as he, they had married servicemen who became ranking officers. As their wives, they were treated with similar respect and special treatment. Although Pearl's husband was no longer active military, he served on the town council giving him a seat of authority and respect in the community.

"Wonderful! Then, we will look forward to seeing you soon," Patsy said.

* * *

No phone call or letter came about the visit. So, a couple weeks later, Buddy took Anna to a notions store to buy material to make curtains for all the rooms in the house.

"The blinds on the windows are fine for a while, but some pretty curtains will make the rooms look warm and homey," Anna explained to him.

"I just want you to be happy."

"I have the money to get material to start making baby blankets too. I want to look at what they have in baby prints."

"Whatever you think, honey. We have to start thinking about preparing for the baby. Wouldn't you rather buy baby blankets? They shouldn't cost too much. It's not like they are as big as normal blankets."

"You are too funny! We can buy a couple, but I want to make a cover for the crib and a matching pillow. Something special that I can prepare for our child."

Anna found soft flannel with animal nursery prints on sale. It was such a good deal she purchased more than she expected to spend that day. She also found beige material for curtains in the living room and bedroom, and red and white gingham for the kitchen. Since they had no television, Anna decided she could fill her nights with sewing projects. It was going to take a while since she didn't own a sewing machine and it would all have to be done by hand.

"Is that everything you need?" Buddy asked. He was uncomfortable in the store filled with women and items about which he had no clue. Anna searched intensely for the best deals, so Buddy sat near the door to wait for her to finish and make a list of the plants he wanted to buy for his garden.

Once Anna had achieved her mission at the fabric store, they stopped by the Southern States to buy seeds. Although Buddy would be the one to care for a garden, Anna was also excited to grow the fresh vegetables to put on their table this summer. They picked out the packages for their vegetable garden and also a couple of packages of yellow marigolds to plant in front of the house.

When they arrived home, they noticed a car parked in front. Buddy recognized it immediately.

"That's Pearl's car," he said as they pulled into the driveway.

"I wonder where she is. She's not in her car," said Anna curiously.

They left their packages in the pickup and went to the front door. It was unlocked.

"Didn't we lock the door?" asked Buddy.

"I don't remember."

They stepped inside. Pearl wasn't there.

"Pearl?" Buddy called out. There was a slamming sound from the bedroom. Pearl and Patsy stepped out appearing a little flustered.

"We didn't hear you come home, Buddy. We were looking at your bedroom suit. That's a nice set," said Pearl. "We actually just got here."

"You left your front door unlocked. You need to be more careful. Looks like you could use a bedspread, right?" added Patsy. "I want to get you a wedding gift before I leave. Now I know what I can buy."

Anna and Buddy were shocked by their behavior and left totally speechless. They said nothing, hoping the women were as innocent as they proclaimed. But they were certainly acting suspiciously, as if they had been caught red-handed at something. *What could they have been doing?* Anna gave Buddy an inquisitive look. He shook his head indicating that he didn't want her to say anything.

"We thought you were going to let us know that you were coming by," Buddy stated to his sisters as he searched for an explanation for their odd behavior.

"Well, we just found ourselves with some time on our hands today," Pearl responded as she brushed her hand over the seat of their sofa and then sat down.

"And the children are off with the neighbor's kids for a while," added Patsy as she took a seat next to Pearl.

"You know that Patsy is flying home this coming week, right?" Questioned Pearl to divert the conversation.

"It would have been nice to know you were coming," Buddy responded as he walked to the bedroom and shut the door.

"I would have made lunch for you," Anna quickly added as she watched her husband walking toward her. Buddy put his arm around his wife in support. He could tell she was feeling awkward around his sisters, not that they had done or said anything at this point to make Anna feel comfortable or welcome to the family.

"How about some coffee? Or hot tea?" Anna offered the women.

She could see that Buddy was perturbed with his sister's unexpected appearance in their home and wanted to prevent any further escalation of the situation. *I don't want to get off on the wrong foot with these two! I expect them to be in my life for a very long time. They will be like older sisters to me!*

"How nice, Anna! Yes, a cup of hot tea would be just right," Pearl stated.

"Do you have any cream, Annie? I prefer to have mine with a little cream," questioned Patsy, following her into the kitchen.

"I believe so, unless Buddy used it up in his coffee this morning."

"It's Anna, Patsy. Her name is Anna," Buddy admonished his sister certain that she had misspoken her name on purpose.

"Oh, so sorry! I was thinking of someone else, I guess."

"What do you think of our little place?" Buddy asked trying to divert his sisters away from Anna as she prepared the hot tea. He also saw her pull leftover cinnamon muffins from the breadbox to heat up and serve. *Always trying to please. That's my girl!*

"Adorable, just adorable!" said Pasty as she stood up. "I suppose you will be getting some new furniture. Did this sofa come with the rental?"

"No, we bought this a couple of weeks ago at a used furniture store. We really like it."

"Oh, it reminds me of a sofa I once had in a rental we took after the war. It's not in bad shape. I'll bet you got a good deal on it."

"You are just like daddy, Buddy! Always looking for a bargain," said Pearl as she chuckled.

"I need to see if Anna needs a hand," Buddy said thinking it best to step away for a few minutes.

Buddy tried to avoid bringing up the question that he and Anna had on their minds, at least while his sisters were sitting in the other room. Anna couldn't hold her thoughts back. She whispered to her husband as he searched for the creamer, he knew he put back in the refrigerator that morning.

"What were your sisters doing in our bedroom? Are you going to ask them?"

"Let me deal with them. Okay?"

"They were snooping. I know it!"

"I don't know. I don't want to accuse them and then find out we were wrong."

"Here, do you want to carry these cups of tea into them? I'll bring the plate of muffins and napkins. This is all I can put together. If they had called first, I would have more for them."

Buddy brought two chairs from the kitchen into the living room for he and Anna to use as they sat across from one another enjoying the refreshments. Patsy spoke incessantly of her life in California - the wonderful weather, the beautiful ocean, their fantastic home on base. Pearl was chuckling nervously the whole time. Both women seemed uncomfortable spending time with the couple.

Luckily, there was a knock at the door by the time everyone had finished their tea. Anna had started to clean up the dishes, so Buddy went to see who was there. Anna came back into the living room as Buddy swung the door wide open for her to see.

"Granddaddy!" Anna exclaimed with joy. "I am so happy to see you! It's about time you came to see us."

"I'm sorry I couldn't get here sooner. You know how it is with your grandmother. Oh, you have guests. I won't stay."

"No, come on in. I want you to meet Buddy's sisters, Pearl and Patsy. They came by to see our home, too. They have already had a tour. Would you like to look around too?" Anna tugged her grandfather by his arm urging him to come inside.

"This is my grandfather, Wilbur Daffin," Anna said noticing that both women had their purses in hand.

"It's very nice to meet you," Pearl said as she stood up and then suddenly added. "We really need to be on our way."

"True. I need to get back to my baby girl," said Patsy.

"It was a pleasure to meet you ladies, as well. I'm sure we'll meet again," Wilbur said as he watched the pair scoot out the door.

"It was good to see you both, Buddy. Thank you for the tea, Anna!" Pearl said as she motioned for Patsy to get up from the sofa.

"Yes, thank you for the tea. Nice place. Good to see you," Patsy added quickly as she walked with Pearl out the front door.

"What's going on with them? Did I walk in on something?" Wilbur asked.

"No, sir. My sisters are just strange," Buddy said, shooting a look at Anna indicating to let the subject go.

She did for a time. No need to bring it up with Granddaddy there.

"I have a little something to give you as a wedding present. I'm giving the same to all your sisters, Anna. Janet will get hers in June. I know starting out, you need some extra money for things, or maybe you want to put a few dollars away for the future," he handed Anna an envelope with a card inside. When she opened the card, she found a one-hundred-dollar bill inside.

"Oh, thank you, granddaddy!" Anna exclaimed.

"Yes, thank you, sir. This is very generous. We'll put it to good use."

"I figure that you may have some need for it in a few months. Am I right, Anna?"

Anna looked directly into her grandfather's eyes. He knew her so well. She nodded her head and then let it drop. Buddy cleared his throat unsure what to say. Wilbur took his finger and raised his granddaughter's head up to look at him. He gave her a smile.

"You are a married woman now. You stick by this good man you have and make a life together. You make lots of wonderful babies and watch them grow. Enjoy your life together and never give up on each other. You got that?" He said looking at both of them. "This is a good thing. Don't let anyone ruin it for you."

"Thank you, Granddaddy," Anna said as she hugged her grandfather and kissed him on his cheek.

"We appreciate this, sir," Buddy added and shook his hand. Wilbur drew him over and gave and long hug and a pat on the back.

"Take care of my girl, young man. She is precious to me."

"I will, sir. She is pretty special to me, too!"

With that, Wilbur walked to the door and headed back home to handle his obligations.

* * *

Anna and Buddy had their first disagreement. After everyone left, Anna went into the bedroom to see what the sisters-in-law had been into. She opened her dresser drawers, seeing that some of her things were out of place; she was sure they had been snooping.

"Who does that? I would never go through someone else's belongings."

"How do you know that they were touching your things?" Buddy asked.

"You heard the drawer slam when we walked in. And look, my cigar box that has some letters and cards and special things of mine, is not in the same place. It was sitting under this picture and now it's on top."

"I don't think they meant anything by it. I just don't want them walking in and out of our home without knocking first or letting us know that they are coming."

"Are you taking their side? They are a meddlesome pair, Buddy. I don't like it. I'll bet they were trying to find out if I am expecting."

"Maybe so. I don't know. Please don't make a big deal of this. I don't want any trouble with my family, too. It's bad enough that you and your dad barely speak. I am close to my sisters, Anna. Those two practically raised me when my mom died."

"I know. But, I could tell you were upset with them when you shut our bedroom door. I didn't want to have words with them then and now it seems you just want to drop the whole thing."

"I was upset, still am. I just don't think it is worth have an argument and causing upset in the family.

Anna started to cry. She was hurt that he didn't agree that what his sisters had done was wrong and should be addressed. It was frustrating to her. This intrusion was an unbearable violation of trust by women who were now family. If her sisters had done this, she would have set them straight immediately. Buddy wasn't willing to do that for her and it was devastating.

"Come on, Anna. Don't do this."

"Leave me alone. Go away."

Buddy had no idea how to deal with her. He went to the truck and brought in the packages from their shopping trip earlier in the day. He figured it was best to leave Anna alone for a while. Maybe she would feel better later.

He was wrong. Anna opened a can of corned beef and plopped the cold meat with gel covering onto a plate. After boiling some cabbage and potatoes, she drained them in the sink before pouring them into a large bowl to put on the table. Buddy came in from outside and tried to give her a peck on the cheek. She turned her head rejecting him.

"You still mad at me?"

She didn't answer. Buddy was bewildered. *Guys don't act like this when they are bent out of shape. Women can be so moody.*

"Dinner looks good. Do we have any vinegar? I like my cabbage with lots of vinegar."

Still silence. Buddy started opening all the cabinets in the kitchen looking for the vinegar. He found it in the refrigerator door.

"I don't think vinegar has to be refrigerated. You should keep it in the cupboard."

"I can't do anything right, can I?" Anna yelled at him as she started to cry once again.

"What is wrong with you, Anna?"

"What's wrong with me? You. I need you to stick up for me. Why won't you speak to your sisters?"

"Alright! I'll speak with them right now. I'll tell them not to come over ever again!"

"That's ridiculous. Not what I said, at all. The problem is not that they came by without notice, it's the nosey prying they did while in our home. Don't you see the difference?"

Buddy grabbed his keys and slammed the back door as he went to his truck. He drove to Pearl's house which was on the other side of town in a new subdivision.

"Pearl, I've never seen her upset before. For some reason, she is certainly disturbed over you and Patsy coming by today."

"We should have sent a note first since you don't have a phone; it was more difficult to let her know. Poor dear, she was probably embarrassed to serve those dry muffins to us and she didn't have a chance to prepare anything else."

"She didn't say anything about her muffins."

"When you left the door open, we thought you must be close by. Patsy thought we should check inside when we didn't get an answer. I think I see why she is upset, Buddy. You need to know how emotional women can be at certain times. Get used to dealing with it."

Buddy thought he understood what she meant but knew that couldn't be Anna's problem.

"Oh, I noticed that you don't have a television or even a radio yet. We have an old radio that I have been keeping in the attic for no good reason. Would you and Anna like to have it? If you take that home as a peace offering, she will forget all about today. And I will make sure to let her know before coming to visit next time."

"We'd love to have a radio. Thanks!"

Buddy felt calmer after talking with his big sister. Patsy had always been the one he could turn to when he had an issue. His dad wasn't a good listener; Patsy seemed to like resolving his problems. This was the first time the problem was with her. Buddy went home with a better attitude bearing a gift for his wife. He thought he had it all figured out.

"Anna, look what Pearl gave us! It's a little old and dusty, but it works. We can put on a show for a while tonight, okay?"

"What did Pearl say about what happened today? You did speak with her about it, didn't you?"

"Yeah, sure. She said she understood why you were upset, and she won't come by anymore without giving you a note first."

"No apology?

"Of sorts, yeah. I could tell she was sorry for coming into the house. They were worried about the door being open."

"All I wanted was for you to see my side. We need to stick together when there are problems, especially with family."

"I guess I didn't understand how serious this was to you today. I should have listened better. I'm sorry, honey. Can we eat this delicious meal you've prepared now? All this emotional woman stuff has worn me out! I'm starving!"

CHAPTER TWENTY-THREE

Buddy came home from work the following Friday night looking forward to spending some time with his wife. Larry and Janet were supposed to stop by for a visit and he thought it would be fun to play cards with them. When he walked into the kitchen from the back door, he saw Anna sitting at the kitchen table crying. Obviously, she had been crying for quite a while, her face was red and puffy.

"Anna! What's wrong, darlin'?"

She put her head down in her arm on the table. "I can't stop crying."

"There must be a reason. Did I do something wrong? Are you upset with me?"

"No."

He lifted her head. "Then, what? Tell me what's going on."

"I feel really sad. I don't know what's wrong with me."

"There must be a reason for you feel this way. Did something happen today? Somebody say something to upset you? Work? What?"

"No. Nothing like that."

"Have you been thinking about the baby? Are you worried?"

As soon as Buddy said the word *baby*, Anna broke out in large sobs again. She was inconsolable for a while and Buddy took her in his arms to comfort her.

"Tell me what is going on. Please, Anna. Whatever it is, I need to know what's wrong."

"I think I am crying for my baby. I can't stop thinking about her."

"I suppose that is reasonable when you are expecting. The baby is just fine though, honey. No need to be so emotional."

"No. Not our baby. My baby girl. My Suzanne."

"What are you talking about? What other baby?"

Anna covered her face and shook her head. She couldn't say more. She had already said too much.

"Didn't you just tell me that we need to be able to confide in each other when there are problems? Come on, Anna! Tell me what's wrong! Tell me!" Buddy took Anna by the shoulders and held her in front of him. Wearily, she lifted her head and explained.

"I had a baby girl last year. Her birthday is on March 30."

Buddy looked at his wife in disbelief. "You had a baby with another man? Last year? Is that what you are telling me? I don't believe this."

Anna nodded her head sheepishly. She hung her head again unable to look Buddy in the eye.

"Why didn't you tell me?"

"I thought you would hate me. The nuns told me to start over and never say anything about her. They said I would forget all about her and what happened. But I can't! I think about her every day. Every single day!"

"What nuns? You're not Catholic."

"At Bassett House. That is where I went to have my baby girl."

"What's Bassett House?"

"It's a home for unwed mothers. My parents sent me there to have my baby and give her up. It's a Catholic home with nuns who help children get adopted."

"Did they find a family to adopt her? Is that what happened?"

"Yes. I gave her away." Anna labored to say the words. She sat at the table with tears falling down her face as Buddy slid the chair back under the table and walked out the door.

* * *

Buddy walked to the phone booth and called Larry telling him that it was not a good night for him and Janet to come by. Larry could tell that his friend had something serious going on but didn't push for further information. He just let him be.

Buddy walked the streets in town for a bit and then returned to stay in his shed in back of the house thinking over this new revelation about his wife. It was dark outside and, in the kitchen, when he went in to find something to eat. Anna was lying down on the bed still in her clothes. Buddy fixed a couple of peanut butter and jelly sandwiches to take in the bedroom.

"Anna," Buddy said softly. "Won't you have a sandwich with me? You need to eat something."

"Okay," Anna said, sitting up on her pillow. Buddy handed her one of the sandwiches and they each took a bite. Anna couldn't eat more and set the sandwich aside.

"I don't care about what happened in the past. I only care about us and our lives together, our baby. You understand?" Buddy started speaking directly to Anna, making her face him. He had worked everything out in his mind on what he wanted to say.

"As long as that guy, whoever he was, is not a part of your life now..."

"Oh, not at all! He went into the Army when I went away, and I haven't heard from him again. He didn't want me."

"What a low life! Didn't he want to marry you?"

"Never. He ran away."

"Son of a bitch! I would have adopted that little girl as my own to raise with our baby, if I had known about this. A real man doesn't do that to a woman!"

Anna threw arms around her husband, and they kissed. She had feared rejection from him, actually expected it, but instead he confirmed how much he loved her and was committed to their marriage. She loved Buddy so much for his gentle and compassionate nature. How lucky she was to have found a man who would love her unconditionally and never condemn her for an immoral past!

"I understand now. You cry all you want. I'll be right here."

"I feel so ashamed. I can't move past what happened."

"You don't have to today. We'll get over it together. Maybe when our little one arrives."

* * *

Anna started to wear maternity tops to work by the middle of April. She had gotten away with wearing baggy sweaters for a few weeks, but now her boss noticed and asked if she was expecting. When she told him her due date, he told her she could finish out the month. Anna was out of a job by the first of May. On one salary, things would certainly be tighter for the young couple.

The baby was kicking a lot on Mother's Day. It was a day that Anna would normally have spent in church and then at a family dinner to celebrate the occasion. This year, Anna declined the invitation her mother had sent through Janet. Her parents hadn't been to visit since early April while Anna was still wearing baggy clothes. She didn't want to upset her parents, especially on Mother's Day, and she didn't want to put Buddy through the storm of outrage that was sure to come from her father.

Larry and Janet stopped by unexpectedly. Anna had just cleaned up the lunch dishes when the rapid knocking came on their front door. Janet sped inside and explained to Anna that their Grandmother Daffin was dying, and according to her doctor, may not live through the day. Larry went to meet up with Buddy in his work shed and found him repairing an old cradle that his mother had used for her babies. It was in poor shape, but he felt he could stain it and fix the weak spots to use for his own child.

"Mother and daddy said I should tell you to go to grandmother's house now if you expect to see her alive," Janet said.

"Oh, my gosh. I didn't know she was doing so poorly," Anna lamented. "I should have gone sooner. Granddaddy needs us, doesn't he?"

"Anna? Are you wearing a maternity dress?" Janet asked with surprise. "Why didn't you tell me? Do mom and daddy know?"

"Oh, my God, no Janet! And please don't say anything! Promise me you won't tell them!"

"Why not? They will be thrilled! Their first grandchild! When are you due?"

"The end of August."

"How exciting!"

"They will not be happy, believe me! Janet, didn't you hear me, I'm due the end of August? Do you know what that means?"

Janet thought for a moment about what her sister was asking.

"We didn't get married until February 18, Janet! Do you understand?"

"Oh, you and Buddy did it before you got married, didn't you? Is that why you eloped?"

"Now do you see why I don't want mom and daddy to know anything yet?"

"But, Anna, that's ridiculous! Don't you think they will figure it out? It's better to tell them now. You're not trying to wait until the baby arrives, are you?"

"Either way, I will disappoint them. I don't want to put them in a bad mood for your wedding either."

"Oh, my wedding! You are one of my bridesmaids. Will you be able to fit into your gown? It looks like you are getting pretty big. We still have a month to go!"

"The style will allow me to adjust it enough to make it fit. I'll be there!"

"I won't say a word, Anna! I hope you know what you're doing! You better get over to see grandmother soon."

Buddy and Larry walked in the back door just then. It was obvious that Buddy knew about Grandmother Daffin and was ready to take Anna immediately.

"Let me grab a sweater," Anna said.

"A sweater? It's warm outside," Janet advised. "You won't need a sweater."

"Oh, yes, I will!" Anna retorted. She believed she may need it to hide her distinctive dress.

* * *

The two couples drove separately to the Daffin home. Anna explained to Buddy that Janet now knew about the baby. He told her Larry also knew they were expecting but didn't tell her how long he had kept the secret. It was a relief to have someone share their happiness and talk openly about their preparations.

As the four entered the Daffin home, they noticed Dottie sitting in a wooden chair by her mother's side, explaining the dying woman's current condition to all who entered the room. Janet went to her mother and stood rubbing her back in consolation. Anna sat on the other side of the bed and turned her belly toward the window and away from her mother's eyes. She took her dear grandmother's chilled hand and tried to warm it between her own. Her life was clearly slipping away. Margaret Daffin didn't even know her granddaughters were there.

"I love you, grandmother. I will miss you," Anna whispered into her ear. There was an ever so slight movement of her grandmother's hand. Anna believed she may have heard her words. Anna stayed by her side until she started to feel uncomfortable with the skewed manner in which she was sitting. She gently placed her grandmother's hand on her blanket and walked around the bed to her mother.

"I'm so sorry, mom. I know this is difficult for you."

"It's been a long time coming, Anna. You know that. You have been a big help over the years. She is giving up."

The two women had a rare hug. Dottie was not one to display much affection to her children, although she loved them dearly. Anna held her belly back from touching her mother, fearful of getting too close. How ironic that, on this unique occasion when her mother found the need to embrace her child, Anna receded in fear of her mother's discovery of her own child!

Anna stepped back and pulled her sweater up as it had fallen off her shoulders during her hug. She started to walk out of the room and was suddenly aware that her father was standing in the doorway. He came in to see if Dottie needed anything. He gave Anna a dark stare. The pupils of his eyes had turned black, and his jaw had stiffened. Anna waited before trying to pass by him.

"Disgusting whore!" he said. "You lying, filthy whore!"

Dottie looked up in shock not understanding what had happened. Anna tried to squeeze by her father as he grabbed her arm.

"Daddy, please! Let me go!" Anna screamed as she broke free of his grip. She quickly walked towards the kitchen door, not wanting to make a scene in her grandmother's bedroom. There were a few other family members and neighbors in the house who were startled by the commotion and Ernie's language towards his daughter. They watched as she ran out of the house in search of her husband.

Anna found Buddy leaning against his truck having a smoke and talking with Larry. He put the cigarette out as soon as he saw the panic on her face. She wasn't crying but she was clearly distressed.

"What's wrong? Anna tell me what's wrong," asked Buddy.

"Did something happen, Anna?" asked Larry, who was equally concerned by her behavior.

Janet came out behind Anna, hoping to console her. She was appalled by her father's reaction to seeing Anna. *She had been right, but why, she questioned herself.*

"Let's leave now Buddy!" Anna hollered, clearly agitated by something.

"What happened?" Buddy asked.

"Did something happen with your grandmother?" Larry questioned.

"Anna! Don't go!" Janet shouted as she caught up with her.

"I have to leave, Janet! You heard him! He hates me. I can't stay here."

Just then her father came out the kitchen door shouting at Anna and Buddy to wait up. "Is this why you two eloped? Well, at least Buddy, you have decency to marry her!"

"Daddy! That's terrible!" Janet yelled back. "What are you doing?"

Buddy took Anna's hand in his, held it up and said "Mr. Scott, I married your daughter because I love her. She is my wife, and I would never disrespect her like you have done in front of everyone today."

"Respect? You don't know the meaning of respect. You two have only brought shame and embarrassment to the family." Buddy opened the passenger side of their truck and assisted Anna into her seat. As Buddy walked around the front of his pickup, Wilbur Daffin came outside. Standing on the top step, he yelled to Ernie. "Stop it! Ernie, stop it now!"

Ernie turned to see his father-in-law once again reprimanding him for condemning his daughter's behavior.

"Don't you see what she has done?"

"What I see is a fool! Leave them alone. The future will be hard enough for them. They don't need you chastising them."

Noticing that the Scott children were standing behind him wanting to know what was happening, Wilbur turned and scooted them back inside the house.

"Ernie, your wife could use the support of her husband right now. And this nonsense is taking me away from where I need to be at this moment." Wilbur walked back into the house, stepped into his wife's bedroom, arriving by his wife's side just moments before she took her final breath.

Mourning the loss of their sweet Margaret did not last long, for the family knew she had suffered from illness for far too long. They were satisfied that she was at peace and no longer in pain. The void left by her death, however, would go on for many years to come.

Ernie stayed away from Anna and Buddy for the next couple of weeks. He didn't want to see her. He needed time to get over his anger. *Why would Anna get herself into another fix? She should have known better! After all she went through! All she put them through! What was wrong with her? How could she do this again?*

Ernie couldn't find any joy in the news that he would soon be a grandfather. Even though Anna was married now, people would easily figure out that she had gotten pregnant before the wedding. *People, people, people! All the talk! The looks of disgust! I don't think I can take it!*

Ernie found little projects to keep him busy around the barn and away from everyone. Dottie, however, knitted some white booties and a matching sweater that she wanted to drop off to Anna. She asked her father to drive her to town one day so she could deliver them. Buddy was at work and now that Anna was unable to work, she welcomed a visit from family during the day.

"I suppose daddy wouldn't bring you by, right mom?"

"You know how your father is. He and Emmitt are busy in the fields right now. They're out there until sundown these days. I'm not going to bother him."

"I know how he is, for sure."

"I thought you and your father were finished with your feud," her grandfather said.

"Why would you think that, granddaddy?" Anna said feeling a little testy. "He hates me."

"He doesn't hate you, Anna! Your daddy truly loves you. I think he has high expectations for you," Dottie interjected.

"And I am a total disappointment to him, right?"

"I wish you could see his side. He is trying to protect all of us. You still have two other sisters after Janet who are coming up in this family. We want them to have a chance at marrying well. We can't have the scandal, Anna," Dottie tried to explain.

"Anna, your mother is trying to explain your father's actions and words towards you. She is caught in the middle of this nastiness. You need to understand that, however this works out, your mother must always side with your father to keep their peace."

"I understand. I will stay away rather than cause a rift between them. I'm not trying to be difficult. I had hoped that dad would like to know his grandchild. If that's not what he wants, I'll be fine with it."

"Well, we'll leave it at that," her mother lamented.

Dottie left her gifts with a promise to make more as soon as she purchased additional yarn. She hugged Anna and rubbed her little belly. Granddaddy also hugged his granddaughter wishing he could impose some grand wisdom to help her through this dilemma. He came up empty.

* * *

Janet and Larry's big day arrived on June 23, the day after her eighteenth birthday. It had only been three weeks since

Janet graduated high school, an event that was barely recognized. Her parents were spending a substantial amount of money on the food, decorations, flowers, and other trimmings for the wedding festivities of their second daughter. It wasn't that they were disinterested in their second oldest child's graduation; it was simply not that important at that time for a female child who was to become a wife and homemaker in only a few days. Dottie had worked on the wedding dress for weeks. It was the first wedding dress she had made. She didn't realize how difficult some of the materials would handle on her old machine. She was determined to save up enough egg money for a new sewing machine before the next daughter married. Janet's pure white wedding dress was tea length with beautiful floral scalloped lace and a scooped neckline with short sleeves. The dress had a slip with a layer of crinoline giving volume. There was a row of buttons down the back and a soft point that led to the skirt. It was gorgeous, and Janet looked beautiful wearing it.

Anna was thrilled for her sister. She only wished that she could still be one of her bridesmaids. Once her parents found out she was expecting last month, they told Janet to choose another girl to take her place. They would not have their seven-month pregnant daughter on display at the front of the church on Janet's wedding day. It would simply be too embarrassing to think about all eyes on Anna instead of the bride. Besides, people would be smart enough to count the months since the elopement and the gossip would be circulating that day and for weeks after. This was Janet's day, and they weren't going to let Anna ruin it for her. She would help out behind the counter in the community hall kitchen. She could slip out before the end of the ceremony to help the ladies coordinate the meal.

The wedding was beautiful, as several bouquets of large white and pink hydrangeas scattered with leaves of eucalyptus sat at the front of the pulpit, and each girl carried a bouquet of pink dahlia, lily of the valley and baby's breath trimmed with toile, and pink and green ribbon that matched their dresses. Janet carried an assortment of white flowers including roses and lily of the valley, which were her favorites. Her short veil was of the same floral lace attached to an oval cap.

Buddy was asked to be the Best Man and he gladly accepted. He felt guilty for not asking Larry to be his best man at his wedding, too. It was too risky at the time, and mostly out of his hands that night of their elopement. Fortunately, Larry was not one to hold a grudge. He had a ball trimming Buddy's truck; more than he ever would have enjoyed the ceremony.

Anna watched as her father walked Janet down the aisle of their family church. It was just as she had always pictured it would be for her, too. Janet and her dad were beaming. She was happy to finally marry Larry. She waited faithfully for him and had remained chaste just as she promised she would be. What more could a father want from his daughter on her wedding day!

Anna wondered if Buddy wished she had not been so easy giving in to him. *Would he prefer that I had been able to wear white on our wedding day? How did things get so messed up?*

Anna watched with envy as her father gave Janet's hand to Larry and stepped back to his seat with Dottie. She noticed how he looked around for approval from the attendees. *He acts like delivery of a virgin bride has something to do with what an excellent father he is and an upstanding citizen of the county. I will never be able to provide him with a level of satisfaction and stature that he feels today. Janet has achieved this and maybe*

Patricia and Susan can do the same. I will not, however, be able to turn back time in order to give him what he wanted from me. I can only live on giving the best of myself to a family of my own.

Anna scooted out the church doors before the rings were placed on the couple's fingers and went directly to the community hall kitchen to help serve the meal.

At the reception, Anna stayed hidden while Buddy hung out with his guy friends. Long tables of platters containing slices of country ham and rock fish, bowls of potato salad, coleslaw, succotash, candied sweet potatoes, fruit Jello, and crab dip with crackers fed the crowd of family and friends nearing 150 guests. At the far end of the hall was a table covered in a long white tablecloth, and on top sat a lovely three-layer cake topped with a ceramic bride and groom. Little pink roses with green stems decorated the edge of each layer, matching the colors of the maid of honor and bride's maids' dresses. Anna saw Betty in the dress she would have worn posing for the traditional wedding pictures. She agreed to take Anna's place once she was ousted. With a few adjustments, her mother had it ready in plenty of time for the big day. Betty was happy to stand in. She and Anna hoped nothing would ruin Janet's wedding day. Betty watched her best friend enjoying the festivities from behind the kitchen window as everyone ate the food, danced to the music, and interacted jovially with one another throughout the evening. She felt that it was unfair to keep her hidden. *Damn it! Let people talk!*

"Hey, girl! Why aren't you out on the dance floor tonight?" Betty called out as she walked towards Anna.

"Hey! Why do you think?" Anna laughed.

"We certainly don't want that baby to come out this early!" Betty commented. "You doing okay tonight?"

"Oh, you know. It's Janet's day. I'll do what I have to do."

"Are your parents talking to you?"

"Normally my mom does, but today, even she is staying away from the child with the plague. I didn't expect my father to talk to me."

"I feel so bad for you. Want me to hang out with you?"

"Are you sure you want to be seen with me?"

"Stop it! Just stop putting yourself down. I won't have it!" Betty scolded her best friend. She knew Anna was probably feeling blue today of all days, but she also knew what a truly good friend she was, considerate of others and always trying to do the right things in life. She hated seeing her treated as an outcast.

CHAPTER TWENTY-FOUR

Anna and Buddy were glad that they didn't need to hide the fact anymore that they were going to be parents at the end of August. Anna spent most of her days making infant clothes using the skills she learned at Bassett House. She was totally focused on making a home for Buddy and their child.

Willie Merchant was excited to have a new grandbaby on the way. He brought fresh eggs, a few home-canned vegetables and packaged meat from his freezer to help the young couple with the expenses of groceries. Pearl came by for a visit, as soon as she found out, to bring one of her homemade chicken pot pies and some oatmeal cookies that she baked for Buddy when he was a kid. She realized that Anna must have been expecting when they were married by the size of her baby belly. She went straight home and wrote a letter to her sister, Patsy in California, to tell her that it was true what they had suspected all along.

"I don't care what any of them have to say. It's you and me, kid, and whoever else comes along. We are going to stick together, no matter what anyone has to say about it," Buddy said to Anna one night after making love to her.

"You said it right! We are quite a pair!" She agreed.

* * *

Buddy worked longer hours in July as his territory and number of farmers increased. The extra money helped, but he was worried about Anna being alone so much as her due date drew near. He asked Larry and Janet to stop by occasionally to check on her. As the long hot days of July came to a close, Anna and Janet spent some of their days together canning vegetables that had grown in Buddy's garden. Anna was pleased to have the company and help. Janet enjoyed staying with her sister instead of the room she and Larry had taken over the shoe repair shop. It wasn't a real home and she had been disappointed to learn they would need to live there until Larry's employment with DuPont Company was finalized.

"I think Larry is going to start at DuPont's soon, Anna! I can't wait! I want to get out of that dump over the shop."

"I'm sure. There's not even enough room for all your new wedding presents, is there?"

"It's not even that. I can't be out after dark. There are some unsavory characters that hang around that area until late at night. I don't like to be there alone, and I hate it when Larry is out after dark. If he starts working night shift, I might have to come over here to spend the night."

"Come on over! I don't want you to stay there alone either."

One night after work, Buddy bought a fan that he found on sale, the last one on the shelf. Lately, Anna had trouble sleeping at night with all the heat. They opened windows, but that only seemed to worsen the situation as the humidity took over. He also felt uncomfortable, but he knew it must be ten times worse for her as her belly continued to expand. Buddy watched with amazement as his wife waddled her way through each day. She looked so beautiful to him that sometimes he just stared at her in wonder.

Eddie wanted to spend a week with Anna and Buddy before he started school. Anna had promised her little brother he could come for a few days and help her get ready for the baby. He was excited to do that. Surprisingly, her parents said he could stay from Wednesday until Sunday in the middle of

August to entertain Anna and help out while she tried to stay off her feet as much as possible.

They all woke up early on Saturday, August 18, with plans of picking up the crib they had been paying on at the used furniture store and maybe treating Eddie to an ice cream when they finished. Buddy received a nice paycheck on Friday and was ready to make the final payment so he could get the bed set up on his days off. The store opened at 9:00 that morning. Buddy washed up and Anna went into the kitchen to make coffee. As she stood at the sink running water into the percolator, she felt a contraction across her middle. It was familiar to her. She remembered the sensation and knew that they would continue to come.

"Buddy! Can you come here?"

"What's up, sweetie?" Buddy said wiping his arms with a towel as he came into the kitchen. He instantly knew that something was happening. "Is it the baby?"

"I only had a little contraction, but I'm sure there will be more. We better not go to the store yet. I'm early. It's not time yet. I should have a couple more weeks."

"We need that crib, don't we? Where will the baby sleep?"

"Yes, but there will be time for you to get it while I'm in the hospital. I think we should call the doctor and see when I should go. It's probably too soon yet. Can you also call my parents to see if they can pick up Eddie this morning?"

"No, I don't want to go home yet!" Eddie protested. "I'm supposed to go home tomorrow."

"Eddie, Anna is having our baby today. You must go home earlier than we thought. I don't think you can go to the hospital with us."

"Yes, I can. You tell the hospital that I want to go, too!"

Buddy tried to reach the Scotts, but no one was home that morning. It was too hot, and he didn't like leaving Anna to keep running back and forth to the phone booth.

By noon, the doctor told them to head on to the hospital. The heat of the middle of August was unbearable, hitting 97 degrees that day, but Buddy loaded Anna and Eddie into his truck and drove the half hour it took to reach the nearest hospital. With the windows down for air flow and Eddie talking nonsense for the whole drive, Anna tried to breathe and ride out each contraction. Buddy took a quick look over at his wife with every moan she made. He could tell she was holding back so as not to scare either Eddie or him.

Finally, they arrived at the front door of the large red brick building with white trim and large pillars holding up a portico that welcomed new arrivals. An attendant saw Buddy drive up and quickly came out with a wheelchair to take Anna inside. As she was whisked away to the maternity ward, Buddy went in search of a parking space. Luckily, he found one close to the driveway. He and Eddie ran through the front door and up to the receptionist area.

"I just dropped my wife off. She's having a baby today. Where do I go? Oh, this is my brother-in-law. Can he go up with me?"

The receptionist looked up over her glasses and down at the young boy standing next to Buddy.

"Your brother-in-law? Well, unless his wife is also having a baby today, he can't go into the maternity ward. That area is strictly for husbands of the patients only."

"It's too hot for him to stay outside. I couldn't reach his parents before we came here."

"Not my problem. I'm just telling you the rules."

"Come on, Eddie. I wish I could have reached your mom and dad. I need you to stay in the truck for a while. I'll get you a soda and some paper towels soaked with water to keep you cool. I don't know what else I can do. Will you stay in there and be good?" Buddy asked the tyke reluctantly.

"Sure, I have my army men with me too. I want a soda and can I get some licorice too? I'm hungry."

Buddy set Eddie up in the truck with the windows rolled down. The truck was parked under a large old oak tree, and a slight breeze blew through, but no doubt this was the hottest day of the summer, so far. *I hate leaving the kid in my truck, but I need to be with Anna. I really have to be with her now. Poor kid.*

Two hours later, Buddy left the father's waiting area to check on Eddie. He didn't see him as he approached the truck. When he leaned over the window, he found him sound asleep on the bench seat. He felt his head because his face appeared red and thought he was too warm. Eddie stirred. Buddy picked him up and carried him out of the truck. The paper towels he had wet down for him were dry. The soda was gone.

"Let's get you inside for a few minutes. I'm going to try to call your parents again."

Buddy held Eddie's hand as they walked back into the reception area. The woman at the desk pointed to the payphone in the hallway but insisted that no children were allowed to stay in maternity ward or the reception area. Still no answer at the Scott residence. Buddy was torn as to where he should be. He took Eddie into the bathroom and splashed him with cold water, wet his shirt thoroughly and put it back on him. Eddie had seemed too lethargic when he removed him from the truck, but now he had more life. They extended the time in the bathroom as much as possible and then went to buy another soda. Buddy was out of change at that point, or he would have gotten them each a snack. He hadn't eaten at all that day.

Buddy took Eddie back to the truck with surprisingly little protest. He felt bad for the kid.

An hour and a half later, the doctor came into the father's waiting area and announced that Anna had given birth to a baby girl weighing 6 pounds and 2 ounces.

"Is that a lot? When can I see them?"

"The nurses are cleaning up your daughter and she will be in one of the cribs in the nursery very shortly. Your wife is very tired. Let the nurses finish with her and you can see her in a while."

A little girl! Buddy was ecstatic! He still needed to deal with Eddie though, and if he couldn't see either of his girls now, he thought he should check on him again.

Eddie was worse this next time. Buddy was afraid he had passed out. Eddie didn't respond at first and then there was a little bit of movement. He asked for water. Buddy felt his hot little body and became afraid. Quickly, he scooped up the young boy and carried him into the hospital reception area. The woman who had been at the desk earlier was gone and another older woman was sitting in her place. Buddy ran past her and into the bathroom to get cool water on Eddie's body. He removed his shirt and wet it, wiping water all over the child. He started to cry a little.

"My head hurts," Eddie said. "I want to go home now."

When it was obvious that Eddie was feeling better, Buddy took the child by the hand and walked back to the pay phone. He was out of change and needed to ask someone in the waiting area for change for a dollar. A pleasant stranger handed him a nickel and said not to worry about paying it back. Buddy dialed the Scott's number one more time and was elated to hear Janet pick up the phone.

"Hey, Buddy!"

"Oh my God, Janet! I'm so glad you picked up! Anna had a girl!"

"That's wonderful news! I can't wait to tell everyone!" Janet exclaimed. "Larry and I just stopped by to pick up a few more of my things that I left in my bedroom. You're lucky to catch us."

"Look, I have a problem, Janet. Eddie is here at the hospital with me and they won't let him go upstairs or wait in the building. It's too hot for him to be in my truck. Can you and Larry come here and pick him up? We'll wait for you in the front entrance. Can you do that?"

"Oh, my gosh! Of course! We'll keep him with us."

"Thank you so much. I need to be with Anna."

Within a half hour, Buddy was free of his obligation and relieved that the little guy didn't have to suffer further in the heat as it intensified into the afternoon. He was oblivious to how close he was to a tragedy that day while his baby girl was arriving into this world.

* * *

They named her Madeline. Anna didn't want to let her out of her sight. She kept asking the nurses to bring her in the room with her where she sat in a rocker holding her close. She had difficulty sleeping for fear that Madeline would not be there when she woke up. The first night in the hospital was the worst.

"Where is she? I can't find her! Somebody help me!" Anna cried out as she awoke suddenly searching for her baby. She frantically ran her hands over the bed, under the covers and even looked under her pillow. Her roommate woke up and turned her light on wondering what was wrong.

"What's the matter? Are you sick? Do you need help?"

"I can't find my baby. She was just here. I held her. Now she's gone."

"She is only in the nursery, lady."

"No, they took her away. She's gone. Oh, God, somebody help me find her," Anna screamed as she jumped out of the bed and ran around the room. Her roommate had already pressed the call button for a nurse two times. Anna pulled her blanket around her while she sat on the floor at the end of her bed and cried.

A nurse came in the room to an unexpected sight. She thought one of the ladies probably needed some water, but instead, she found a distraught and inconsolable patient huddled and crying on the floor.

"She wants her baby," the roommate advised. "She's been looking for her.

The nurse had heard of this happening to another patient once. Thinking Anna must have had a bad dream, she helped her to her feet.

"Come with me. We can find your baby. Okay? Let's take a walk and you can see her right now," said the nurse as she opened the door, turned out the light, and left the roommate to go back to sleep. They walked slowly down the hall to allow Anna to wake up. Coming to a stop in front of a large glass window, the nurse continued to hold Anna's hand as she showed her all the sleeping babies in their bassinets.

"See how they are all nicely tucked in? Even your little girl. Oh!" explained the nurse until she noticed that the bed that said 'Merchant' was empty. She was startled at first and wasn't sure what else to say for a moment. Then, she saw Baby Merchant being delivered back to her bassinet.

"There she is! She must have needed a change. Since she is awake, why don't we see if you can rock her back to sleep. Would you like that?"

Anna relaxed as soon as she held Maddie in her arms. Still emotional, she shed a few more tears. This time for joy. She stayed in the nursery for most of the night, unable to sleep, and unable to relinquish Maddie to the staff. By 5:00, she was exhausted. They pulled the sleeping baby from her arms and left Anna undisturbed.

"Ma'am, you need to get rest. You'll exhaust yourself before you get home with this baby. Take some time to heal," one of the nurses told her. Anna was too anxious. It was a relief when she and Madeline were released to go home, especially for the nursing staff.

Buddy pulled his pickup truck under the large white portico to retrieve his wife and baby girl. He was ready to take them home. On his way there, he had stopped to make the final payment and pick up the crib they would need tonight. Anna wore one of her maternity dresses home and carried little Madeleine in her arms with a light blanket wrapped around her. She climbed into the truck seat. As the nurse handed the baby over, Buddy took a quick look at her.

"I'm just making sure we have the right one!" he said laughing.

"She's ours alright!"

"Hold onto her. We're heading home!" And with a slight jerk of the truck, they were on their way.

"I think we should nickname her Maddie. What do you think, honey?" Buddy asked as he drove back to the little house on Eighth Street. "Madeline is so formal. Maddie sounds like a kid's name."

"I like it. Maddie, it is. Isn't she too adorable? She has so much wavy, black hair. I suppose that comes from your French ancestry."

"She's perfect! I love you both very much."

* * *

Janet and Larry delivered the news of Madeline's arrival to the rest of the family. Buddy had called his best friend just hours after her birth and asked him to pass the word. Thrilled with the task, the couple immediately drove to the farm to make the announcement.

"She's here! Anna gave birth to a healthy six pound two-ounce baby girl just at six o'clock," Janet exclaimed as she crossed the threshold into the kitchen.

"Oh, my word! A girl! I thought she would have a girl," Dottie said with excitement as she wiped her hands on her apron.

"It's a good thing we picked up Eddie this afternoon. He would have melted in Buddy's truck today," chuckled Larry.

"Yeah, she was in labor a long time, don't you think?" Janet questioned.

"What's her name?" asked Susan and Patricia in unison.

"Oh, do they have a name already?"

"They named her Madeline. Maddie for short," Janet said.

"That's a pretty name. Madeline. Our little Maddie," Dottie pondered which name she would called her.

"I like Maddie better than Mad-De-Lina," Eddie chimed in.

"Oh, stop, Eddie! You know how to say Madeline," Janet chided him.

Eddie started to laugh and everyone joined in with the silly boy. Everyone, except Ernie. He stepped out the back door for a walk outside. Ernie was feeling emotional and couldn't let anyone see the tears in his eyes. There was a strange sensation that had taken hold of him. *Grandfather. He was only thirty-eight years old! He was a grandfather now.*

Ernie had a good cry as he stood along the whitewashed fence behind his barn. He gripped the top plank and hung his head between his arms as he poured out the bitterness he had held in his soul for too long. He was still so very confused as he tried to reconcile all the beliefs he had been taught by his father. The words he had heard repeatedly after he had a family of his own: *"Ernie! These girls are going to give you nothing but trouble!" "Mark my word, girls need to be raised in a strict home. You have to keep a close eye on them, or they will go astray." "Women are just children at any age; you have to use a heavy hand on them sometimes." "Don't you ever let one of your girls bring shame to this family, Ernie! I hold you responsible if they do."*

After Janet and Larry left and Dottie had run the children off to bed, Ernie made his way back to the house. Dottie was washing up the remaining dirty dishes of the day. She didn't even turn around when the screened door slammed behind Ernie. She knew it was her husband and she was so upset with him at that moment that she chose to ignore him.

Ernie took a seat at the kitchen table. Watching Dottie as she scrubbed the coffee pot, he could tell she was mad with him. He had learned to read her body language after all their years together. The silence went on for a few minutes and then Dottie turned to look at her husband.

"If you want some cake, you are too late. We finished eating it while celebrating Madeline's birth."

"I don't want any cake," Ernie said calmly.

"Well, good! There isn't any."

"Dottie?"

"What? I'm really upset with you right now, Ernie!" Dottie shot back a response. "Whatever it is that you want right now, you can get it yourself."

"I don't want anything," Ernie stated a bit pathetically. Dottie heard defeat in his voice and took the opportunity to spill her heart out.

"You know, Ernie, we were young once. We had those same feelings of kids today."

"What do you mean? What are you trying to say?"

"I remember a certain church picnic we went on while we were dating. The one at Wheeler Park. Do you know what I mean?"

"Wheeler Park! Yeah, of course! There was a little train ride, two-seater swings, cages with spider monkeys and the best rope swings ever. My friends and I would climb the ladder to the wooden platform in this one tree that was really tall. Then someone below would bring the rope to us. I remember grabbing that thick rope and taking a leap off. I held on for dear life while flying through the air and across the stream that ran through the middle of the park. Those were great times!"

"That is not what I meant, and you know it. I'm talking about you taking me for a walk on the other side of that stream. Don't you remember that?" Dottie asked.

Ernie didn't respond.

"I know you scoped out that secluded spot in the woods. If the preacher's son and Alice Copper hadn't come along, I don't know what I would have done. You had my blouse unbuttoned and were trying to pull it off when they showed up. I was so glad when they interrupted us. I didn't know how to handle you then."

"I wouldn't have done anything."

"I believe Alice must have gotten with child that day. It was about three months later that the preacher moved his family out west. It was sudden. At the same time Alice and her family stopped coming to church. She was never heard from again, but her parents kept their farm for another five years. One day there was a bank foreclosure sign at the end of the lane. People talked but no one really knew what happened to them."

"Alice was known to be easy. All the boys talked about her. Girls shouldn't be so loose. They bring these things on themselves when they behave like tramps," Ernie explained.

"Is that how you feel about, Anna? How do we know that she was loose, as you say? I wasn't, and you still managed to get my blouse unbuttoned."

"Oh, stop! Just stop it!" Ernie shouted becoming quite annoyed with the conversation.

"Ernie, you have been a good husband and a good father to our children, but you are wrong in what you're doing to this family now. This anger with Anna has got to stop. It's killing me inside and it's harming all of our children. We have a granddaughter now. You keep this up and we may not be able to spend time with her. We might not be allowed to visit or have her visit us. Did you ever think about that?"

"Not really."

"Well, it could happen. You need to come to terms with whatever is causing so much anger in you. Maybe you don't know everything you think you know, Ernie. Make amends with your daughter. Please. Stop this," Dottie said taking Ernie's face in her hands. "Ernie, please."

Ernie looked up at his wife and simply nodded his head. She kissed his forehead and took a step back. "I'm making some food. As soon as Anna comes home with Madeline, I would like to take a couple of meals to them. Will you go? Will you go with me to see our grandchild?"

"Yes, I will. We'll all go. The whole family can welcome little Maddie home."

* * *

For the first couple of days home, Anna and Buddy were bombarded with daily visitors bearing baby gifts, food, cards with money, and some who were just plain nosey.

One surprise visitor was Aunt Victoria who stopped by the first evening they were home as she was driving back to Wilmington from a trip to Virginia Beach.

"Aunt Victoria! How wonderful that you came to see the baby. I'm so happy to see you again!" Exclaimed Anna as she opened the front door.

"It was perfect timing! Wilbur telephoned me at my hotel and told me that little Madeline had arrived, and since you are practically on my route back, I decided to stop by and visit you all," Victoria explained. "Now, where is the pretty little creature? I can't wait to see her!"

"She's here in our room. We just put her crib together today," said Anna leading her aunt into the bedroom.

"Oh, my Lord! She is adorable! What a beautiful baby, Anna! I know you both must be very proud parents."

"The proudest!" said Buddy as he entered the room to meet their first visitor.

"Aunt Victoria, this is my husband, Buddy Merchant."

"Happy to make your acquaintance, Buddy," Aunt Victoria shook Buddy's hand. "You are a very lucky man with a beautiful family."

"I am well aware of that. These are the best days of my life, and I know they can only get better. I man never had a better wife than Anna!" Buddy beamed as he put an arm around Anna's shoulder and gave a squeeze.

"I can't stay long but I didn't want to miss this opportunity. I have to get back to Wilmington. At my age, it's becoming more difficult to drive at night."

"Aunt Victoria, can I get you to sign our baby book as Maddie's first visitor?" Anna directed her to where it sat on her dresser as Buddy let the ladies have some time alone.

As Victoria wrote a quick message and signed her name in the book, Anna asked about her aunt's health.

"Aunt Victoria, how have you been feeling since your operation for the cancer? Are you free of it? Granddaddy told me that the mass was removed."

"For now, I am just fine. It may come back, but until then, I am going on to live my life to the fullest. How about you, Anna? Are you satisfied with the direction of your life now?"

"Do you mean that in spite of everything that has happened, am I living my life to its fullest? I am happy with the life I have with Buddy and Maddie. But, Aunt Victoria, I will always have a hole in my heart for the loss of my Suzanne."

Victoria grabbed Anna and drew her in for a hug. She held her close for a while telling again and again, "I know, darling girl. I know."

Walking to the door to leave, Victoria suddenly remembered the baby gift she brought. The box wrapped in pink paper with white booties and a large white bow, sat on the arm of the sofa. She handed it to Anna as Buddy came into the room to walk Victoria to her car.

Anna carefully peeled the pretty wrapping paper off the box and lifted the lid to find a white lace and satin christening gown and cap. She ran her fingers over the silky material and exclaimed of its beauty. She had never seen anything so lovely.

"Oh, Buddy, look at this gown! It's absolutely gorgeous, don't you think?"

"Wow! Maddie will look adorable in that outfit. Thank you so much!" he said as he shook Victoria's hand in appreciation.

"Yes, thank you, Aunt Victoria! We love it!"

"Now, let me tell you what I would like you to do. Make arrangements with the minister of our family church in Greenville to have Maddie christened. You don't need to do it during a regular service if you prefer not to have your father present. But the announcement will still be in the church bulletin and he will know that you have handled her baptism, with or without him. Will you do that?"

"Yes, Aunt Victoria, we will be certain one way or another to have Maddie baptized," Anna proclaimed as she received a nod from Buddy.

"Good. This little girl, our Maddie, will have a proper start in life! Anna, don't you worry so much. Your father will come to his senses one of these days, or he will suffer from estrangement for the rest of his life. I don't really believe he wants to live that way," said Victoria as she opened the front door and walked into the night.

* * *

Pearl and her husband came by the day after they arrived home. They brought a chicken noodle casserole, chocolate cake, and a cute little pink smocked dress with matching booties for Maddie.

"So sorry we didn't call before stopping by. We won't stay long. I thought you wouldn't have anything made for dinner tonight. This should last for a couple of days. I hope someone in your family will be as generous, Anna."

"Actually, my mom called this morning and said she would be bringing several dishes by tomorrow night when my family visits us. I may have to put your casserole in the freezer for a while. Looks like we may have too much food to eat," Anna retorted.

"Maybe I should have waited then. Oh, well, Buddy might want to eat it now. It was one of his favorites growing up. I used to make it for him all the time," Pearl explained.

As soon as Pearl and her husband were out the door, Buddy turned to Anna with a smile. "And she did, too! She made it all the time! I was sick of it! I think it was the only casserole she knew how to make," Buddy said as he and Anna had a good laugh.

Dottie and Ernie and all the kids stopped by the following evening. Anna and Buddy were quite surprised to see everyone arrive, especially Anna's father. This was only the second time he had been in their home. Each member of the family was carrying a dish. Ernie brought the pot roast in a small covered roasting pan. Susan made her first pie the day before and gave it to Anna.

"Thank you, Susan! Apple pie! My favorite. We will sure enjoy this!" Anna praised her little sister. Then, since she had her arms full holding the baby, she asked her to put the pie on the kitchen table for later.

Ernie handed the pan containing the pot roast to Buddy.

"Wow! That smells delicious! Thank you so much!" Buddy said and motioned for the children to follow him into the kitchen to put the other items in the refrigerator.

"Let me hold that darling girl, won't you Anna?" Dottie asked extending her hands. Anna placed Maddie gently into her arms as she watched a tenderness sweep over her mother's face. Tears came into her eyes as she ran her finger along the baby's hairline and onto her chubby cheeks. Ernie couldn't resist a look at the infant and searched for her feet under her pink blanket to make sure she had all ten toes.

"Oh my, Ernie, we're grandparents!" Dottie stated suddenly. "We have our first grandchild! I'm feeling a little old, how about you?"

"I was feeling old before our grandbaby arrived," he said.

Their first grandchild? Anna wondered how her mother could say such a thing, especially in front of her. It was totally insensitive. She was ignoring Suzanne's existence completely. Anna had thoughts of her every single day. Her mother knew that Maddie was her second child!

Anna was acutely aware of the difference in treatment she received at this hospital and when she stayed at the hospital in Wilmington. She was taken to a shared room, not left in a hallway. Nurses spoke with her respectfully and made sure that she was comfortable with all her needs met. The doctor gave her instructions on how to feed and care for Maddie, and also how to care for herself when she returned home. *Why hadn't she and Suzanne been treated this way? Had she been flagged in some manner, so they didn't waste their time on a mother who wasn't keeping her baby?*

Why couldn't her parents recognize that they have another grandchild in this world? How do you shower one with love and pretend the other does not exist? It hurt her terribly.

Buddy came back into the living room carrying Eddie piggyback. The girls followed behind giggling as Buddy pretended he was going to drop Eddie on the floor. *There is still a lot of kid in my husband,* thought Anna. *And that's not a bad thing!*

Anna saw her father taking an interest in the baby. He seemed different today. The scowl he had on his face the last time she saw him had disappeared.

"Anna, how about a cup of coffee? Do you have any made?" her father asked.

"Not yet, but I can make some," she replied. And with that little exchange, the silence between them was finally broken. No apologies were spoken. For Ernie, it was simply over. As he promised Dottie, he was trying to make amends.

Anna went into her kitchen and started running water into the silver coffee pot, pulled the strainer out of the dish drain, and placed it inside. As she opened the cupboard to reach for the tin of ground coffee, her father stepped in the kitchen behind her.

"She is a beautiful little girl, Anna. I'm so proud," Ernie told his daughter with sincerity.

"Thank you, daddy. Buddy and I are very happy."

"Now, I hope you will forget all that business, you know, what I said when I found out you two were going to have this baby. It all worked out."

"It did? How did it work out, daddy? What is so different now?" Anna was cautious but wanted her father to open up to her. She wished he would talk to her as an adult.

"You know. Now you're married."

"But I still got pregnant with her before we were married. Just like I wasn't married when I got pregnant with Suzanne."

Ernie frowned at the mention of the child's name. He didn't even know that Anna had given her a name.

"Tell me, Daddy, if we had not eloped before you found out, would you have sent me away again? Would you have forced me to give up Maddie, too?"

Ernie stood dumbfounded for a second. "You know your mother and I did what we had to do to protect you and the rest of the family. We made the decision so you could have a better life. And look, you were able to marry a fine, respectable man. Do you think Buddy would have wanted you if he knew you had some other man's baby?"

"He knows, Daddy! He knows everything! And he doesn't care."

"What? Did you tell him? Why would you do that?"

"I didn't want to keep that secret from the man I am spending the rest of my life with. I hope one day that I can find Suzanne. If that happens, I don't want it to be a surprise for Buddy. He needs to know about that part of my life."

"I can't believe he is accepting this. I hope telling him doesn't come back to bite you. You are just newly married. After some years, he may regret it."

"Actually, daddy, he told me that if he had known about Suzanne sooner, he would have adopted her and raised her with Maddie."

Ernie shook his head in disbelief. Anna turned the gas on to perk the coffee and then reached up into another cupboard to grab the plain white cups and saucers they purchased at an auction. She set them on the kitchen table with the only four teaspoons they owned. Staying busy in the silence, she then grabbed a can of evaporated milk from the refrigerator and placed it next to the sugar already on the table. Then she grabbed the back of a kitchen chair with both hands, threw her shoulders back and let her voice be heard. Looking directly at her father, Anna finally poured out her heart.

"Daddy, I know I've disappointed you. Things may never be right between us. I will never be the same sweet, innocent, little daughter you once knew and loved. What happened to me last year almost destroyed me; at the very least, it has changed me forever. I cannot forget any of it and never will. I'm older and wiser now. I have a better understanding. I'll admit that I made some mistakes that night on the beach in Rehoboth, but what I did not do, was to freely or intentionally give myself to Jimmy Baker!"

Ernie Scott's stoic, rigid body went limp, his eyes welled up with tears as he nodded and hung his head. At last, he understood what had happened to his daughter that summer night.

THE END

AUTHOR'S NOTE

Saundra Jo Hayman is a native of Maryland's Eastern Shore where she grew up on a dairy farm. She writes fictional stories based upon true events or facts as they were told to her. Her desire in revealing those truths lies in the hope that lessons from the past may be learned. Saundra and her husband make their home in the "Land of Pleasant Living" enjoying a rural lifestyle.

Made in the USA
Middletown, DE
31 May 2024